THE VEIL OF TAKHSHA

EMARI CHRONICLES
BOOK TWO

AMBER HANSFORD

For Papaw
You hung the moon & showed me how to dream

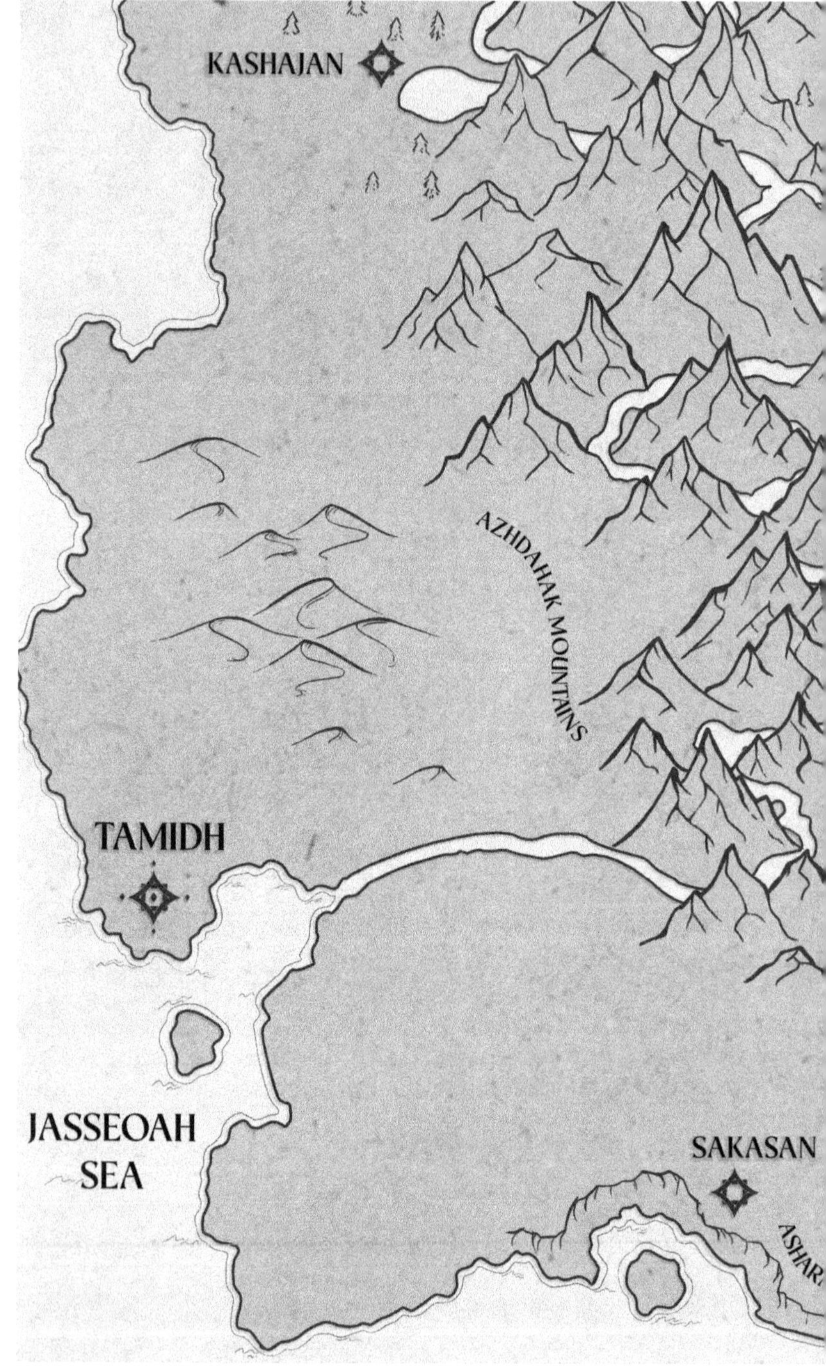

KASHAJAN
AZHDAHAK MOUNTAINS
TAMIDH
JASSEOAH SEA
SAKASAN
ASHAR

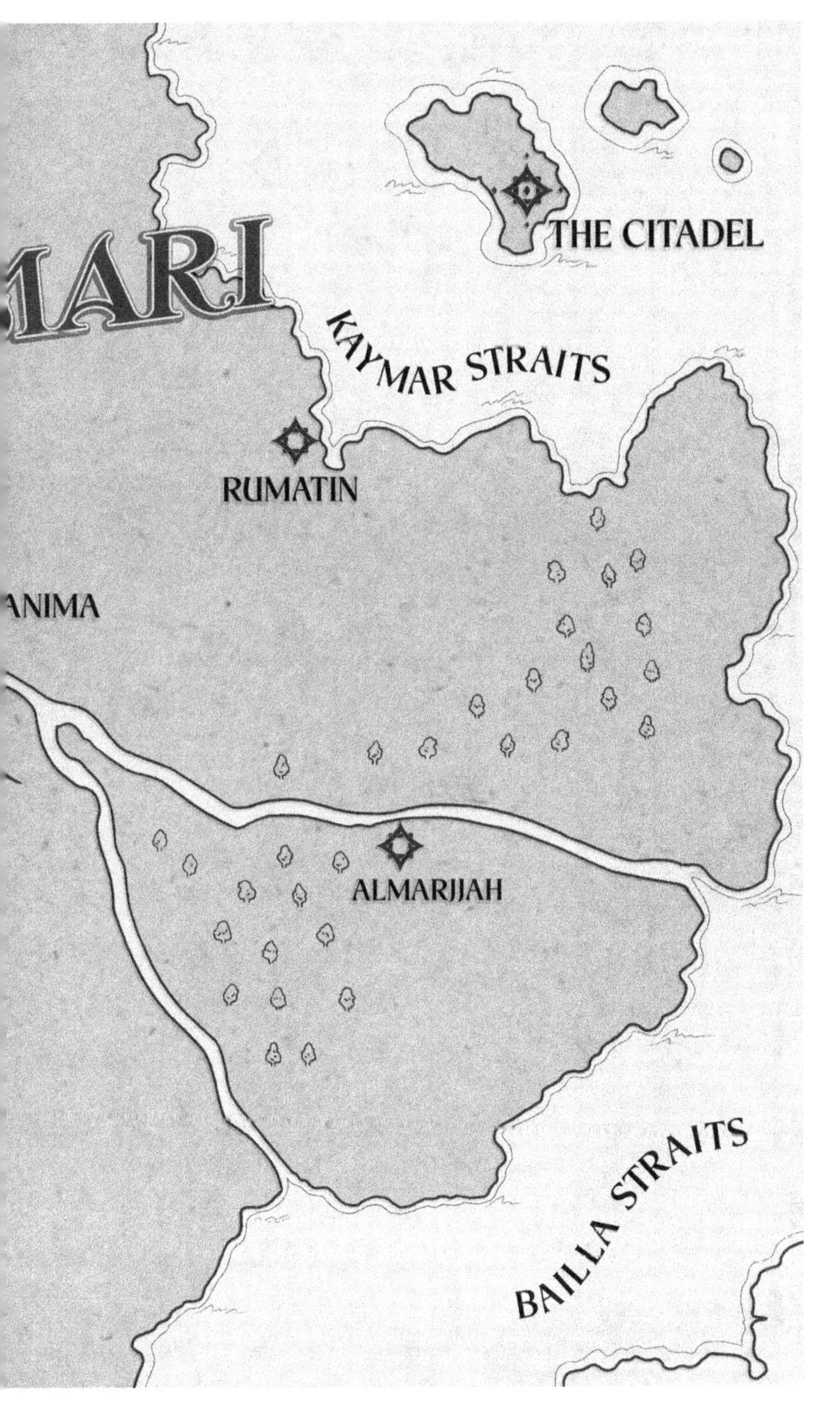
MARI
THE CITADEL
KAYMAR STRAITS
RUMATIN
ANIMA
ALMARIJAH
BAILLA STRAITS

MAR
THE CITADEL

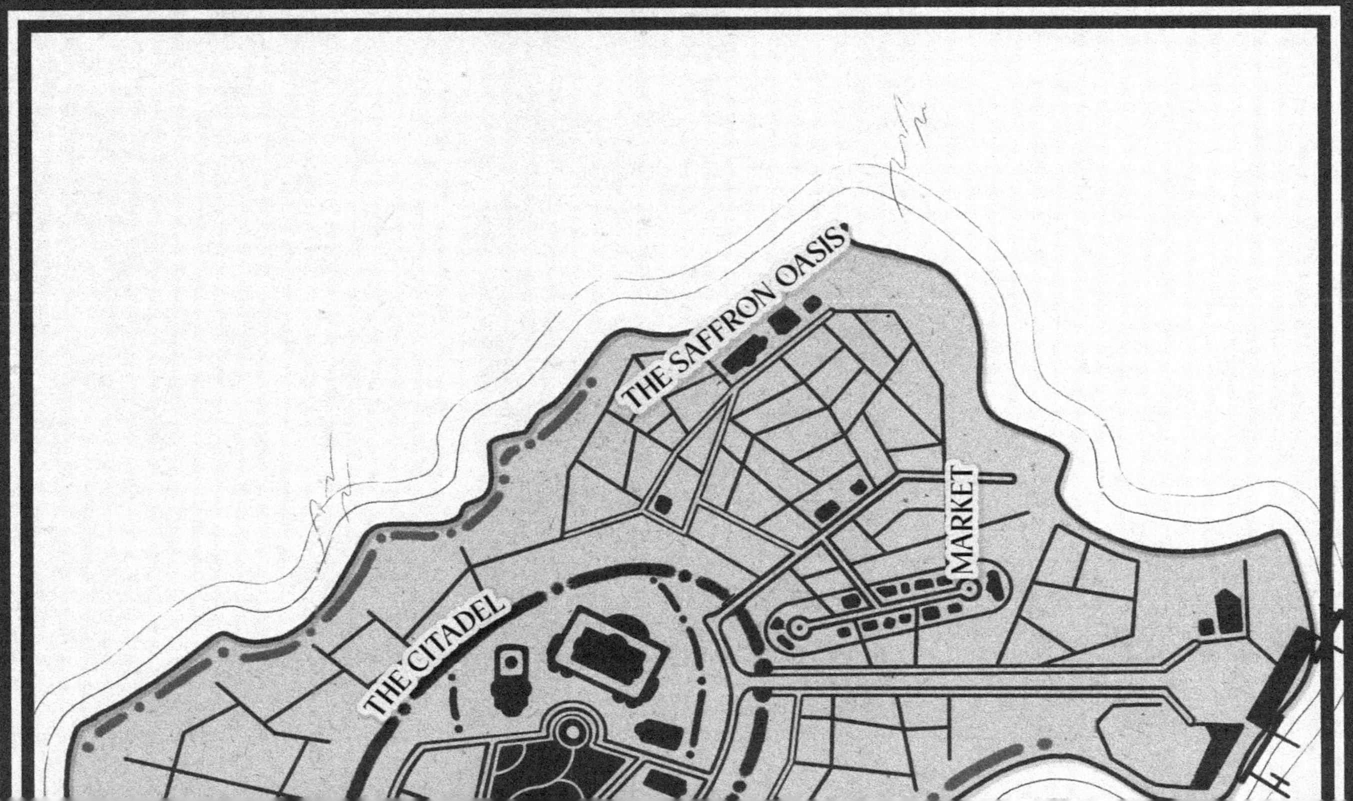

THE CITADEL
THE SAFFRON OASIS
MARKET

CHAPTER I

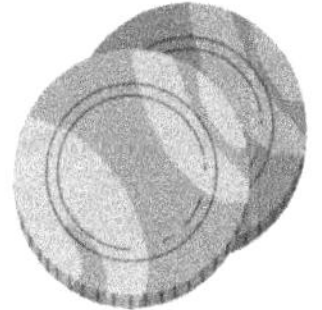

The air in the tavern circled around the players, carrying the low murmur of voices that never quite reached the volume of the real conversations. Even with the windows and doors wide open to the afternoon sun, the light outside never quite made it past the threshold, fading as soon as it hit the wooden beams above. The shadows from the lanterns flickered like ghosts, moving in time with the players' every shift. It reminded Yasher of every tavern he'd ever walked into on his travels, all of them the same in this one detail. No matter the weather outside, no matter how high the sun hung in the sky, the light never truly filled the tavern. It was always muted, always distant to allow for whatever anonymity the player wanted.

The chatter, the clink of coins, the collective breath of the room held together by the game, it was all part of the rhythm of this place. A far cry from the hushed voices of politics and the sterile court practices of the Citadel, where everything felt too loud without a sound, where the silence spoke louder than the words. Here, though? Here, in this room, everything was real. Unfiltered. No masks to hide behind. Just people, cards, and the certainty that things could change with a single hand.

The table was scarred, making it a perfect place for a game like this with nothing new, nothing truly clean. Just the wear of time and the marks of whoever had been here before him. He liked it that way. Clean places, like the Citadel, still made him feel out of place. No matter how long he stayed, he was always the *gharib*, the outsider, the one who didn't belong.

He rested his boots on the table, the worn leather dusted from the island's streets. The scent of the docks still lingered on him, but in here, that did not matter. Here, no one cared where you came from. You were just a player. A gambler. He could slip into the role as easily as he slid the cards between his fingers, savoring the weight of them.

The sailor across from him was tense, his thick neck straining with every move. His fingers drummed on the table, the rhythm of someone who had fought hard in the world and lost often. Yasher felt it worn into the man's skin, the clenched jaw, the muscle that had fought the sea as much as the city. He could see the sailor's frustration already, just in the way he held himself. It wasn't the game Yasher needed to worry about, it would be the sailor's temper when he lost.

Next to the sailor, the merchant was a different story altogether. The sharp, expensive weave to his tunic and the sweat that soaked through it. The look in his eyes said he had stepped onto the wrong side of a page in his comfortable book of life. It didn't take much to see he didn't belong here. The way his hands trembled over the coins, the way he couldn't meet anyone's eyes. This wasn't his world, he was losing too much. Yasher was familiar with that too, the feeling of stepping into somewhere that wasn't quite yours, but trying to make it fit anyway.

His fingers flicked the edges of his cards, the motion smooth, practiced.

"Your play," Yasher said, his voice cutting through the growing tension. It was quiet, a stark contrast to the energy swirling at the table.

The sailor didn't answer right away, eyes narrowing.

The merchant cleared his throat, his voice cracking as he fumbled with the coins. "I'll raise," he said, the words a little too loud in the silence.

Yasher let a smirk dance on his lips. The merchant was still a few moves behind, but that wasn't uncommon. Some men learned faster than others. Some, like the sailor, were already too tangled up in their pride to see the game for what it was. Yasher reached for his coins, his fingers brushing against the metal with an almost lazy confidence.

"Bold move," he said, letting the word hang in the air before he added, "Not very smart, but bold." After a tense moment, the sailor matched the bet.

"Let's make this interesting," Yasher said, stretching the silence just a little longer.

He tossed his coins into the pile, the clink of them music in the otherwise hushed room. He watched the merchant's face pale, watched him glance at his dwindling stack of coins. A sigh escaped the man's lips, the kind of defeat no one had to say aloud.

"Out," the merchant muttered, not meeting anyone's eyes.

"Smart man," Yasher said, his voice low and amused. He turned to the sailor, who was staring at him now, all fire and focus. This was the moment, the final push, and Yasher was happy to oblige.

The man was about to snap. He could feel it. The pressure was there. Yasher let it build.

"Your move," Yasher prompted, his voice light, teasing.

Finally, the sailor growled, his nostrils flaring. His fists slammed onto the table as he pushed the last of his coins into the pile.

"Call," he said, his voice low and rough, the kind of growl that meant he was ready for this to end, one way or another.

The crowd surged forward. He didn't need to see their faces. He could feel their anticipation, their hunger for the outcome. He took his time. A few extra seconds to stretch the moment out. The sailor's eyes bored into him, but Yasher didn't hurry. He was in control now.

When he laid down his cards, the room went silent.

A winning hand.

The sailor's fist hit the table with a force that made the coins jump and scatter across the wood. The crowd recoiled, murmurs rippling through the air like the aftermath of a storm.

"Damned luck," the sailor hissed, his teeth clenched.

"Not luck," Yasher said, as he swept the coins into his pouch, his grin widening."Skill. People always mix them up."

"Luck runs out, friend," the sailor warned, his voice a low growl, muscles coiled like a spring ready to snap.

Yasher tilted his head up, never once breaking the smirk. He let the coin fly from his fingers, spinning through the air.

"Does it?" he said, voice steady. "Tails."

The coin fell, landing neatly in his palm. Tails.

Yasher smirked, flipping the coin once more before closing his hand around it. The sailor's fists tightened, his glare fierce enough to break stone. The room was still, waiting for the explosion that never came.

Before anything could escalate, a voice cut through the tension.

"There you are. I felt there was a fight brewing, and knew it had to be you."

Yasher glanced up, the coin still spinning lazily between his fingers. Kambiz's voice sliced through the crowd. She moved toward him with the effortless grace that only she had, her tray balanced with ease. Her eyes, dark and sharp, weren't full of curiosity like usual. This time, they carried a touch of annoyance. He was very familiar with that look.

He flashed her a grin as she neared, his usual charm slipping into place like an old coat. "Kambiz. Always a vision. To what do I owe the honor?"

She set her tray down on a nearby table, the thud of it more forceful than usual. "Don't start with me, Yasher. You promised the Hand you'd be at the Citadel by now,

By the Shining Halls, she sent a messenger to remind you. What are you still doing here?"

He tilted his chair back, boots propped up on the edge of the table. He caught the coin in his hand, twirling it idly. "Playing cards. Winning, actually. It's practically a public service."

"Winning?" she asked, one eyebrow arched as she crossed her arms. "Is that what you're calling hiding now?"

He caught the coin mid-spin, his grin faltering just slightly, but not enough for her to notice. "Not hiding. Just... delaying."

Her arms stayed crossed, her posture softening with a quiet but pointed frustration. "You're delaying, you're waiting. Meanwhile, the Hand's fighting for you, and people still look at you like you don't belong on this island."

Her words landed like a punch, but he didn't let it show. He still had a reputation to uphold here, in this tavern, in this small world. He could feel the weight of her words, though, and it sat heavy in his chest.

"Farah doesn't need me there," he said, his tone casual, though something inside him tightened. "She's more than capable of handling the room full of nobles with a hand tied behind her back."

"She wants you there," Kambiz countered, softer now. "She trusts you. All you're doing is proving every doubter in that Damned Citadel right by hiding out in this tavern."

He leaned forward, meeting her gaze head-on. "It's staying out of the way."

Her eyes softened, but the frustration remained. "You don't get it, do you? She doesn't need you to be perfect. She just needs you to show up. For her."

Those words, soft but sharp, broke through the shield he'd built around himself. The easy-going mask slipped for just a second. Kambiz noticed, but didn't say anything. She always did, knew him too well to let him hide it.

"I get it," he said, quieter now, his tone still light despite the tightness in his chest. "I'll go."

She shot him a look, an eyebrow arched in that familiar, knowing way. Then, she turned, walking away with that effortless grace of hers, the weight of her words lingering in the air between them.

"Just don't make her regret trusting you," she said, her voice softening but still carrying that undercurrent of warning he couldn't ignore.

He watched her go, her figure weaving through the crowd, and felt a pang of guilt gnawing at him, sharper than he wanted to admit. The coin slipped from his fingers as he stood, the room pressing in around him. Farah was waiting, and gods knew he owed her more than excuses.

But for now, he let the coin spin, catching the flickering light as it tumbled between his fingers. He could delay, just a little longer. Even if he had to face the music eventually.

THE LATE AFTERNOON sun hung low in the sky, casting long golden streaks across the cobblestones of the Citadel, gilding the towering archways and domed rooftops with fading light. The city, built upon layers of history, seemed to hum with quiet expectation, its sandstone walls drinking in the warmth of the day before the evening's chill set in.

The narrow streets twisted through the city like veins, pulsing with the steady rhythm of life—merchants calling out their wares, the murmur of conversation drifting from shaded courtyards, the distant clang of a blacksmith's hammer ringing from deeper within the district. The air was thick with the scent of jasmine and roasting nuts from a nearby vendor, mingling with the faint briny tang of the sea carried in from the Kaymar Straits.

Yasher flipped his coin absently, the rhythmic spin and catch grounding him, though it did little to quiet the restless thoughts. The Citadel was many things—grand, old, relentless... it had never quite felt like home, but it did grow on him.

He paused as the sound of splashing water reached his ears. Ahead, a small courtyard opened between towering buildings, its heart marked by a fountain. It was one of the quieter corners of the bustling city, close to the Saffron Oasis, a bastion of calm. A few children played by the fountain's edge, their laughter rising and falling like birdsong, but his eyes caught on a group a little ways beyond them.

An older woman sat on a low stone bench, watching

over the children with quiet patience. She had a presence that settled rather than demanded, the kind of stillness that suggested she could wait out a storm without flinching. Her hands rested in her lap, her fingers adorned with thin silver rings, and her bronze skin lined with age but not softened by it. Dark hair, streaked with silver, was drawn back into a thick braid, woven with tiny beads and bells that clicked together softly when she moved, while a deep indigo scarf draped over her shoulders, embroidered with silver thread in shifting, intricate patterns—almost like roots tangled in the wind.

Yasher's steps slowed before he could easily stop himself. He knew her.

Jeta Veseli.

Farah had pointed her out to him on a few occasions, even had set up a few meetings that he found ways out of, in that maddeningly practical way of hers. She was one of the old tutors who was still left in the Citadel who still understood Talents as they once were, before the court, before the Mashyana's scheming, before everything had twisted. Farah had insisted Jeta could help him, could make sense of his Luck, especially when it chose to have a mind of its own.

He had agreed. Then promptly ignored that agreement, over and again.

She was speaking in low tones to a boy no older than ten, his thin arms tensed as he concentrated. Yasher watched as the boy raised his hand, his fingers trembling slightly. A thin, wavering thread of light flickered to life between them, unstable but real. The boy sucked in a breath. She nodded once, murmured something Yasher couldn't hear. The thread steadied.

Yasher rolled his coin across his knuckles, slow, deliberate. *Not today.*

And yet, just as he made to shift his focus elsewhere, her gaze flicked up.

She didn't call out to him, didn't change her posture, didn't demand anything. But she had seen him. And she let him know it. A quiet acknowledgment. A single nod.

His fingers tightened around his coin. A chill traced its way down his spine.

He forced himself to keep walking.

Maybe Farah was right about her. Maybe she could teach him something. But the thought of giving himself over to someone else's training, of handing over control to someone who could decide what his Luck should be— it made his chest tighten. It felt like asking a river to decide where it should go before it had even seen the ocean. Whatever she wanted to say, whatever lesson she had waiting—it could wait.

Instead, he turned his attention back to the fountain, putting the old woman to his back to visit with someone who was probably much more appreciative of a good joke.

Pari's head was bent over a piece of parchment, her small hands smudged with charcoal as she sketched with intense focus. The little girl wore a vibrant orange tunic that seemed to glow in the sunlight, its hem embroidered with swirling patterns that danced as she shifted her weight. Her dark braids, adorned with colorful ribbons, fell over her shoulder, the ribbons fluttering faintly in the warm breeze.

Yasher hesitated for a moment, his coin spinning once more in his hand. He hadn't been by Shirin's tea shop where Pari stayed in too long, not for a few weeks at least. Farah had been consumed with managing the repair and rebuilding of the kingdom along side the Mashya, and he had thrown himself into distractions of his own to stay out from underfoot. Pari, though... she also deserved better than his paltry excuses for not being present after the year that they'd all had together.

"Little Divine," he called softly, the nickname slipping from his lips with familiar warmth.

Pari's head snapped up, her wide, dark eyes catching the sunlight, the flicker of a smile barely forming before it faded into her now usual solemnity. She had always been serious for her age, but lately, it felt different, like the brightness in her was dimming a little more each day.

The god Rashnu had spoken to her for as long as she could remember, his voice a constant presence, a guide only she could hear. But ever since Farah had returned Yasher's so-called lucky charm, the Eye of Rashnu, to him, his voice had fallen silent to the little girl. Pari still saw things, still sketched her visions with that same eerie certainty, but she had no voice in her car to explain them, no divine whisper to help her make sense of what she knew.

And Yasher, when he wasn't distracting himself with cards or losing himself in the docks, wasn't sure what was worse. That the God of Death and Justice had left her alone in her visions—or that she had never really been allowed to be just a child in the first place.

"Yasher," she greeted, her voice warm but weighted.

He crouched beside her, careful not to disturb the charcoal sketches strewn across the ground. "What masterpieces have you got today?"

Pari glanced at the scattered pages, her fingers hovering protectively over one in particular. Yasher let his gaze sweep over the others. One captured the fountain in exquisite detail, the water's rippling surface sketched with a precision beyond her years. Another depicted the children playing nearby, their movement and laughter somehow alive in the confident strokes of charcoal.

Her talent was undeniable, almost divine in its execution, and he wondered if Rashnu had granted it to her as a lingering gift, even after falling silent. Yet, he could see the weight of it, the way her frustration surfaced when she struggled to decipher the meaning behind her own creations, the way she sometimes retreated into herself.

"Shirin's been keeping you stocked, I see," he said, gesturing to the thick stack of parchment unbound between two thin lengths of wood which served as her sketchbook and the box of charcoal at her side. He reached out to ruffle her hair, catching the ribbons between his fingers. "Good thing too. I don't know what this city would do without your genius."

She rolled her eyes, but a tiny smile peeked through her mask of solemnity.

"You bought me charcoal last time, remember?" she said, her tone matter-of-fact.

He laughed. "Ah, yes. It's been a little while."

Her smile lingered for a moment longer before fading. She pulled the sketch she'd been hiding into view and handed it to him silently. His breath caught as he took it.

The image was stark and unsettling. A tall, shadowy figure loomed over a familiar silhouette, its jagged edges reaching like claws. The smaller figure below was unmistakably himself, rendered in the loose but telling details of his coat and hair.

He felt a chill crawl up his spine.

"That's a bit dramatic, don't you think?" he said lightly, though his grip on the page tightened.

She didn't answer immediately. She looked down at her smudged fingers, twisting them together before finally meeting his gaze. Her deep brown eyes were steady, holding a seriousness that made Yasher forget, for just a moment, how young she was.

"It's not just a shadow," she said quietly. "It's something trying to reach you."

He forced a grin, tousling her braid again.

"You've been spending too much time at invocations with Shirin, Little Divine," he said, his voice deliberately light. "Next thing you'll tell me it's my destiny to fight a griffin, or what is it that they have in the murals here? Ah, a simurgh." He smirked, picturing the grand, mythical creature woven into the city's art, a vast, majestic bird with the strength of a lion, wings wide enough to blot out the sun.

Pari didn't laugh. She stared at him, unblinking, before grabbing his hand. Her grip grounded him in a way he hadn't expected.

"Go easy on the ominous warnings, yeah, Little Divine?" he said, trying to sound casual. "I've already got enough on my plate without adding your artwork to the list."

She didn't respond. Instead, she reached for another drawing and held it up for him.

"This is for Farah," she said. "And for you. To remember."

He glanced at the drawing of the tea shop and folded it gently with a soft smile. "I'll be sure to give it to her."

Shifting topics, he asked, "How's Shirin? Still making the best tea in the Citadel?" His voice softened with guilt as he added, "Sorry I haven't stopped by lately. Things have been... busy."

Her expression softened. "She's fine. She misses you, though. She said you're always welcome, if you remember where the shop is, that is."

He chuckled, though the sound was strained. "Sounds like her. Tell her I'll come by soon to make up for being scarce."

She nodded, her gaze dropping back to her sketches. The moment hung between them, her earlier words still echoing in his mind.

He flipped his coin, the metallic glint catching the fading sunlight. He watched it tumble through the air, his practiced hand catching it with ease. The motion was comforting and familiar, a reminder of the control he still had, or at least pretended to have.

"Come by tomorrow and we'll sit in the gardens. The flowers are blooming, and I think the Mashya and Rostam miss your smile. I know that Farah does."

As he stood to leave, the coin slipped from his fingers—not with the usual, easy grace of a gambler's trick, but too fast, too sudden. It clinked against the cobblestones, bouncing once, twice, then rolled in a slow, lazy arc.

Yasher expected it to land at his feet. It should have. But instead, the coin veered sharply, curving in a way that defied the natural pull of gravity. It came to a stop at Pari's feet.

She bent to pick it up, turning it between her fingers.

"That wasn't supposed to happen," she mused, head tilting slightly.

He forced a smirk, ignoring the way something hitched in his chest.

"Luck's just getting bored of being predictable," he said, reaching out.

Pari placed the coin in his palm, her gaze flicking up to meet his. "Or maybe it's tired of you pretending you still have control."

His smirk widened, sharp and easy. "Control's a trick, Little Divine. A good one, if you can sell it."

He flipped the coin once more, caught it cleanly, and tapped it against his knuckles before stepping away.

She tilted her head, her dark eyes watching him with an unsettling intensity, one far beyond her years.

"She'll notice when you're late," she called after him.

The streets of the Citadel stretched before him and he walked on, flipping his coin absently, though his thoughts were already elsewhere.

First Kambiz, now Pari… It was Farah, of course, making sure that if she couldn't be there, they'd help make sure he didn't miss the things he'd promised her.

She hadn't sought the weight of rebuilding an empire. But in the wake of Behnaz à Radan's downfall, there had been no one else to bear it. Farah, who had once stood at the Mashyana's side with unwavering loyalty, had been forced to reckon with the truth. The woman she had believed in, had served without question, had built her life around—had been a liar. A thief. A monster who had drained Emari dry in the name of control and power. And when it all came crashing down, it was Farah who had been left standing amid the wreckage, not for vengeance, but for the people Behnaz had broken.

She shouldered that burden now alongside Enayat à Mashayekhi, the rightful Mashya, carving a future from the shattered remains of the past. The nobles distrusted her, the common folk feared her, but they watched her. And Yasher had never known anyone to carry the weight of expectation the way she did. Head held high, shoulders straight, relentless in her resolve.

He had seen it all. The quiet moments of grief when she thought no one was looking, the way she pushed forward anyway.

Before Farah, his life had been one long flight from anything that tied him down. His past, his mistakes, the people he had loved and lost. But she had stopped him in his tracks. She had seen him for what he was and chosen him anyway. She had become his home, and the thought of that settled deep in his chest, terrifying and steadying all at once.

He was late. And she was waiting.

The thought warmed him, chasing away some of the lingering unease from his encounter with Pari. His steps quickened, the guilt of his tardiness fueling his stride. He'd face whatever political posturing or side-eyed judgment awaited him at the Citadel because Farah had asked him to be there. And for her, he would try.

CHAPTER 2

Farahnaz Rahnema, Hand of the Mashya, closed her eyes for the briefest of moments, silently imploring the Unnamed Gods to smite her where she stood. Surely, divine intervention would be kinder than enduring another moment of this endless, circling debate that had already run on too long for the schedule.

When her plea went unanswered as it had every other time, she forced herself to remain still with her fingers gripping the marble lectern as though it were the only thing tethering her to patience. The chamber rang with accusations and counterarguments, voices layered over one another in an unrelenting cacophony, each one vying for dominance.

"The wasting sickness devastated half my fields," bellowed Nadar à Shiravand, his voice already hoarse from a morning of self-righteous tirades. His ruddy complexion deepened as he gestured wildly, his hands cutting through the air as if he could carve out justice with his indignation. "Yet your Parliament expects me to pay reparations to villages outside my jurisdiction? Villages I've never even laid eyes on!"

Farah resisted the urge to pinch the bridge of her nose. Instead, she inhaled slowly, letting the words roll over her, waiting for the inevitable chorus of agreement from the nobles seated beside him. A few of them murmured their support, shifting in their seats as if his anger gave them permission to voice their own grievances.

Fields? The word echoed in her mind, dripping with incredulity. *What do fields have to do with the wasting sickness?*

She cast her gaze upward, away from Shiravand's blustering, allowing it to settle on the murals that adorned the grand chamber's vaulted ceiling. They had been painted in an age of ambition, capturing Emari's golden years in painstaking detail—noble houses standing shoulder to shoulder, banners unfurled beneath an unblemished sky, the entire kingdom depicted as a harmonious whole. It was a fantasy, one she had once believed in, just as she had once believed in Behnaz. Now, the illusion felt almost cruel.

If those long-dead painters could see the chamber now, would they curse their own naïveté? Would they be disappointed to witness the nobles who now stood beneath their work, not as stewards of a unified kingdom, but as scavengers fighting over the remnants of a broken land?

Shiravand was still speaking, still twisting the truth into something that would serve him. She forced herself to focus. His voice carried an air of performative injury, each syllable steeped in self-pity rather than genuine grief. The wasting sickness hadn't touched fields, nor crops, nor livestock. It had not blackened the land or poisoned the wells. It had taken only one thing—people.

The farmhands who had tilled those fields, the smiths who had crafted tools, the children who played in the streets. Anyone who had carried the spark of Talents in their blood, gifted to them from the gods before they abandoned this plane due to their own in-fighting and greed.

And yet, Shiravand, like so many others, was too afraid to speak of that truth. Too afraid to acknowledge that he had profited from the suffering of his own people, turning a blind eye as the Mashyana drained the life from the Talented to fuel her ambition.

Instead, he stood here, weaving a tale of agricultural devastation, as though the death of hundreds of people was just an unfortunate cost of business.

You're not mourning them, she thought bitterly. *You're mourning what they can no longer do for you.*

"Your negligence allowed the sickness to spread! How can you deny responsibility when your tenants suffer under your mismanagement?" A wiry man from the parliamentary council shot back, his voice sharp and unyielding, like the blade of a freshly honed dagger. Farah couldn't even remember this one's name. They all blurred together after a while, the endless cycle of bickering and political maneuvering exhausting in its predictability.

Do they even hear themselves? The thought flared,

unbidden. Her mind wandered, not to these men and their petty grievances, but to the faces of the real victims of the wasting sickness. The ones who had gasped for breath as their strength was siphoned away, who had crumpled in the streets, who had known, in those final moments, that something inside them was being stolen. And yet, instead of addressing that horror, the nobles twisted the truth, turning tragedy into something convenient. A narrative that spared them from guilt.

Farah exhaled, slow and measured, before lifting her chin.

"Enough." Her voice sliced through the rising discord like tempered steel. The chamber stilled at once, resentful murmurs fading into uneasy silence.

She let the quiet stretch for a moment longer than necessary, ensuring she had their full attention before she spoke again.

"This council exists as part of the new Parliament at the service of the Mashya, to heal Emari," she began, her voice steady but carrying the weight of authority she'd spent years cultivating. "Not to deepen its fractures. Aqa à Shiravand, no one questions the toll the sickness has taken on Emari's people. But let me be clear, the wasting sickness did not touch your fields. It did not poison your crops or wither your vines. It only affected those with Talents. The men, women, and children who lived and worked under your protection."

The noble's mouth opened as if to protest, but Farah pressed on, cutting him off before he could shift the narrative again. "Every family lost someone. Every village mourned. The reparations this council discusses are not about your jurisdiction. They are about rebuilding the lives shattered by what happened."

She turned her gaze to the parliamentary council, her eyes narrowing slightly.

"And you," she said, her tone cooling, "accusations of negligence will not mend what has already been broken. If you expect this council to function, I demand solutions from all of you, not recriminations just to stir the pot as the Mashya's representative in this chamber."

She scanned the room, meeting each set of eyes with the kind of steadiness that dared them to look away first. The nobles glared, their resentment like smoldering coals. The parliamentary representatives bristled, caught between their indignation and the realization that they couldn't outmaneuver her here.

Her gaze lingered briefly on Shiravand, whose face had deepened into a mottled red.

"If you wish to discuss the devastation caused by the wasting sickness," she continued, "let us discuss it honestly. Let us remember the lives it claimed, the families it left fractured, and the communities it hollowed. Anything less dishonors their memory."

She leaned back slightly, the tension in her shoulders easing as the room fell into a begrudging silence.

Her authority was tolerated out of necessity, not respect. To the nobles, she was an outsider, an orphan plucked from obscurity and elevated by Behnaz à Radan to be her Beloved, and then her Hand, her weapon in the dark and small spaces. To the rest of parliament, she was a bridge between the past and a future they weren't sure they wanted now that Behnaz had toppled to her own greed.

"She's no better than Behnaz with her need to command," someone muttered from the noble seats, the words deliberately loud enough to carry, their venom thinly masked by feigned nonchalance.

The accusation landed like a dagger, sharp and deliberate, slicing through the thin veneer of detachment she had forced herself to maintain.

She forced herself to remain still, to breathe past the sting of it.

No better than Behnaz. The phrase echoed in her mind, intertwining with her own worst fears, twisting the knife further.

She drew a slow, measured breath, keeping her expression neutral, a mask of unshakable composure. Reacting would only lend their words more power, feed the fire of doubt that already smoldered in too many minds.

She forced herself to focus, her grip on the marble lectern tightening ever so slightly. The noble who had spoken, whoever they were, had no idea how close their words were to her own private fears.

What if they're right? the insidious voice in her mind whispered. *What if, despite everything, you're just following in her footsteps?*

No. Farah shoved the thought aside, drawing on every ounce of resolve she had. She had chosen this path, not for the nobles or the Parliament, not even for the Mashya, but for the people of Emari, the families grieving their Talented loved ones, the children who had been left vulnerable, the laborers struggling to rebuild lives shattered by the Mashyana's greed. She couldn't let the doubts win. She wouldn't.

Her gaze swept over the chamber, taking in the sea of faces, some hostile, some indifferent, a few cautiously supportive. She met their stares without flinching, her mask firmly in place. Let them think what they would. Words were just another battlefield, and Farah had long since learned how to endure their sting.

But the words still echoed in her mind. *No better than Behnaz.*

I am not Behnaz.

But the doubt lingered, clinging like ash in the air after a fire.

THE HALL outside the council chamber was cool and quiet, its stillness a balm after the relentless storm of voices that had battered against Farah's patience. She leaned against a marble pillar, the cold seeping through the fabric of her sleeves, grounding her.

The vaulted ceilings arched high above her, gilded in the soft glow of the late afternoon sun, but the weight of the space felt heavy, as if even the palace itself bore witness to the fractures in Emari's foundation.

She exhaled slowly, pressing her palms against the polished stone. The Mashya and Rostam seemed convinced she could corral the nobles and parliamentarians, could navigate their egos and grievances with measured precision, but doubt gnawed at her.

Do they not see what I see? That they are still fighting for themselves, not for Emari? That they will not let go of the past, no matter how many times I try to pry it from their fingers?

"Phoenix?"

Her eyes snapped open at the sound of his voice. Yasher stood at the far end of the hall, his long strides eating the distance between them. His coat hung open, the fabric catching faint drafts of air as he moved, and his brown hair that he refused to cut in the court style fell haphazardly into his pale blue eyes. To others, his disheveled charm often masked his sharp wit, but to her, it was just Yasher—familiar, grounding. The sight of him sent a soft ache through her chest.

When he reached her, his steps slowed, and he tilted his head as if trying to read her mood. His grin flickered into place, soft and crooked. "You look like you could use a rescue. Long day?"

She straightened, unwilling to show the vulnerability she had allowed to surface here. He would only worry.

"You're late," she said, arching a brow, though she didn't put any heart into it.

He lifted his hands in mock surrender, his grin widening just slightly. "Caught me. I was perfecting my dramatic timing. You have to admit, it's impeccable."

Her lips twitched, the barest hint of a smile escaping before she smoothed her expression again. He didn't wait for permission to step closer to pull her in an embrace, ignoring their presence in a public hallway to pull her towards him and place a kiss on her neck.

"Forgiven?" He whispered before pulling away.

She couldn't help but smile at him then. "You're safe. The chattering fools in the chambers are also running long. It's like they're in love with the sound of their own voices."

From his coat pocket, he pulled a folded slip of paper and offered it to her with a small flourish. His eyes softened, his voice dropping to something lower, quieter. "A gift from the Little Divine may make you feel better."

Farah took the paper, carefully unfolding it.

Pari's sketch was unmistakable in its detail. The drawing depicted a quiet moment at Shirin's tea shop in the Saffron Oasis. The two of them sat across from each other at one of the carved wooden tables beneath the woven awning, cups of steaming tea between them. Yasher was mid-laugh, his head tilted back. She was watching him, her posture relaxed in a way it rarely was, one hand resting lightly against her cheek, her other fingers curled around the rim of her cup.

It was a moment she recognized—not from a single day, but from the countless times they had sat there together, letting the world outside the Saffron Oasis fade away. The details were intimate, deliberate. The curve of Yasher's ever-spinning coin, half-caught between his fingers. The faint embroidery on Farah's sleeves. The tea set, carefully rendered in shadow and light, as though Pari had traced the memory itself.

Her fingers hovered over the charcoal lines, the familiar tension uncoiling in her throat.

"She's gotten better," she murmured.

His hand moved to her cheek, his fingers brushing lightly against her skin. The gesture was gentle, his touch lingering just long enough to make her feel like she was the only thing in the world that mattered.

"She has." he agreed softly, his eyes holding hers.

She looked at him, catching the faintest flicker of something behind his pale blue gaze—concern, maybe even regret. He stepped back, leaning casually against the pillar beside her.

"How much longer do you have sitting with the mewling children?" He smirked. His coin appeared in his hand as if by magic, flipping idly between his fingers.

"One more meeting, then I have to prepare for the gala." She ran her hand down her face. "Your clothes for tonight are already on the bed, delivered along with the new boots."

"Remember, Phoenix. You're not here to change their minds," he said, his tone light but steady. "You're here to remind them that they don't get to decide what Emari becomes without listening to the people."

The words struck something deep within her. He always seemed to know when she was unraveling, always found the right thing to say to knit her edges back together. But even as his charm worked on her, she couldn't shake the feeling that something was weighing on him.

"You think I'm capable of that?" she asked, unable to keep the vulnerability from her voice.

He glanced at her, his smile fading into something softer, more earnest. "Phoenix, if I didn't believe in you, I'd be halfway across the continent by now."

The words should have reassured her, but the way he looked at her, like she was the sun and he was just a shadow drawn to her light, made her heart ache. She knew he struggled with himself, with the parts of him that he thought were so different, especially with his unruly Talent.

She stepped closer, catching his hand as he flipped the coin again. His fingers stilled under hers, his eyes widening just slightly.

"You're wrong," she said softly, holding his gaze. "If you weren't here, I'd—" She stopped herself, not sure how to finish the thought without laying herself bare.

He chuckled, low and warm, breaking the tension. He turned his hand over, letting her fingers rest against his palm.

"You'd be fine," he said with a wink, his grin creeping back. "Better, probably."

She tightened her grip, her brow furrowing.

"You're wrong," she said again, her voice firmer this time. She let her hand fall away, but the weight of her words lingered between them.

His smile softened. He reached out again, his hand brushing her cheek.

"You're stronger than you think," he said quietly. "And far stronger than I deserve."

Before she could respond, he stepped back, flipping the coin once more. He caught it effortlessly, the metallic clink echoing in the empty hall.

"You've got this, Phoenix," he said, his usual charm returning as if to lighten the moment. He set the coin down on the railing gently, then touched the bangle that she placed on his wrist ages ago that he refused to let her take off.

With that, he turned and started down the hall, leaving her with the sketch and the coin resting on the marble railing. She stared at them for a long moment, her fingers brushing over the rough paper and cool metal. His footsteps faded, but his presence lingered, grounding her as she squared her shoulders.

She tucked the coin into her pocket, her thoughts straying to him even as she steeled herself for the battles ahead. Whatever he thought of himself, he was wrong. He was the reason she hadn't given up on herself or Emari. And he doesn't even know it.

There was the matter of his Talent, though. She knew he had avoided the tutoring she'd kept on arranging for him, sessions that could have helped him gain control over the Luck that seemed as much a curse as a gift. It wasn't just frustration she felt when he sidestepped her attempts to address it—it was exhaustion. His avoidance became one more thing for her to fix, one more broken piece to try and mend, like the restoration of the kingdom and the fragile faith of its people. Her heart belonged to him, but that didn't mean that he didn't frustrate her to no ends at times.

"Insufferable." She mumbled with a small smile as she put Pari's drawing in the pocket with the coin.

A movement in her periphery pulled her attention back to the present and she slid back on the courtly mask she built up over years in these halls, turning to the newest member of the nobles to enter Parliament.

Siavash à Ardashir stood just far enough away to make himself appear to not to be waiting for her to notice him. He'd made a splash when he came to the

Citadel with the courtiers with his looks before he'd even spoken. His face, sharp and sculpted, all high cheekbones and an angular jaw, framed by neatly trimmed dark hair, his complexion a rich, sun-warmed olive. He moved with deliberate ease, his posture effortless, his hands still clasped behind his back in a way that suggested both restraint and confidence as he took her acknowledgement as permission to move closer. His court tunic was dark, embroidered with subtle silver detailing, the fabric finely tailored but without the ostentation so many nobles favored.

She had no doubt he turned heads wherever he went. He was exactly the type that noblewomen sighed over behind their painted fans, the type whose striking features and poised demeanor made people assume he was as charming as he was clever.

She had spent too much of her life surrounded by men who thought their beauty meant something. Pretty faces were common in court, competence was not.

But Siavash was competent. He did not speak just to be heard. He spoke when it mattered.

That, more than anything, was what made her wary.

"Hand," he said smoothly with a short bow, "It seems that you could use another ally in the chamber today."

She exhaled slowly. Siavash had kept his distance in the debates, speaking only when necessary, but when he did, people listened. Unlike the other nobles, who scrambled to reclaim whatever scraps of power they could from the wreckage of Behnaz's reign, he had not played their game.

Not openly, at least.

She studied him now, reassessing. He had not been raised in the Citadel, had not grown up at court like the rest of the noble sons who vied for power in these halls. He was a younger son, unremarkable in the eyes of his family, sent away to his family's holdings near Kashajan while his elder brothers stood at their father's side. She had not expected much from him when he arrived for the Mashya's Parliament. Just another name among many, another noble sent by his house as a peace offering without backing to Enayat.

But he had surprised her.

Siavash had not spoken in defense of his own house, had not fought for the remnants of the old ways. He had spoken for alliances, for shared survival, for a future shaped by something other than the debts of the past.

And now, here he was. Watching her. As if gauging whether she had the strength to carry that vision forward.

Farah crossed her arms, keeping her tone neutral. "And what is it you want from me, Aqa à Ardashir, in return for allying yourself to me?"

A flicker of amusement crossed his face, though it was gone just as quickly. "A fair question," he said. "But not the right one."

She arched a brow.

He stepped closer, his voice lowering. "You assume I am here for something transactional. That my interests align with those men in there, grasping at what power they can still reach." His lips curved slightly, though it was not quite a smile. "You're wrong."

She didn't answer.

"The real question, Hand," he continued, his tone calm but pointed, "is whether you are willing to let them define you. To let them shape what Emari will become while you spend all your energy simply trying to hold it together."

"You fight," he went on, "but you fight to maintain. To repair. That is not the same as shaping what comes next."

She bristled, instinct telling her to push back—but against what? The truth in his words?

"I don't have the luxury of shaping things," she said, voice edged. "I am cleaning up the mess left behind by —" She stopped herself. By Behnaz. By herself. By the choices she made when she still believed in the Mashyana's vision.

He inclined his head slightly, as if acknowledging the weight of what she wasn't saying. "And will you spend the rest of your life undoing the past, or will you decide what the future should be?"

The words landed sharper than she expected. She looked at him, really looked at him.

His expression remained unreadable, composed. But his gaze held something weighty. Conviction.

"I said nothing in that chamber that I did not mean," he said, his voice quieter now. "Change is coming, whether those nobles accept it or not. I intend to shape it, not claw after what is already lost." His head tilted slightly. "Do you?"

Her hands curled into fists at her sides. "You assume I have a choice."

He did not hesitate. "Everyone has a choice. Even you."

"You are no one's shadow, Hand," he said, quieter now, but his words cut deep. "Not anymore. But if you let them, they will keep you tethered to one. They will let you shoulder the burden of the past while they shape the future. Do you want that?"

The weight of his words settled in her chest, unwanted but impossible to ignore. She hated that he was right.

Finally, she squared her shoulders, her voice steady once more. "You're very sure of yourself."

He exhaled, something like a quiet laugh. "No. But I am sure of you."

Farah stared at him. The certainty in his words, in his belief that she had a choice, even when she wasn't sure she did, was unsettling.

But she had spent her whole life being shaped by others. By Behnaz. By the court. By the expectations placed upon her. Maybe it was time to decide for herself.

She exhaled deeply. "Let's see if you're as persuasive as you seem to think you are. We have a little time before we break for the gala's preparations to try and change some of their minds."

Siavash's lips quirked, but his expression remained composed. "Let's."

THE GRAND BALLROOM of the Citadel gleamed with the weight of its own history, a monument to Emari's golden age, built by a past Mashya who had believed wealth was proof of power. Gilded columns stretched toward the domed ceiling, their engravings telling tales of gods, Yazatas, and victories long past, a testament to an empire that had once been sure of itself. Above, lanterns flickered in polished metal casings, casting a warm golden glow that made the silk tapestries shimmer like molten rivers.

And yet, beneath all that splendor, the scent of saffron, rosewater, and spiced wine hung thick in the air, unable to mask the sharper edge of unease rippling through the crowd.

At the entrance, Farah's fingers grazed the edge of her coat, grounding herself. The deep crimson fabric fastened at her waist before sweeping open, the delicate folds beneath tailored for movement as much as presentation. The gold embroidery at its edges caught the light with each step, sunbursts of captured fire, but it was the split in the coat's front that mattered most, with her court boots and matching trousers. It reminded those watching her that she was a weapon first, a diplomat second.

Her dark hair was braided into a crown, golden pins shaped like hawk wings gleaming amid the woven strands. Kohl lined her mahogany eyes, sharp as flint beneath the softened glow of the chandeliers. Her lips, painted with the barest hint of rose, were set in a way that brooked neither hesitation nor invitation. A different type of armor, but armor nonetheless.

At her side, Yasher was an effortless counterpoint to the tension she carried.

His indigo tunic fit him like a glove, the embroidered cuffs catching the lamplight just enough to suggest quiet extravagance beneath his usual roguish ease. His wavy brown hair fell messily across his forehead, the blue in his eyes flashing. Were it not for the pale skin, he would fit in perfectly with the nobility, if not a little eccentric.

He adjusted his sleeve over his bangle and smirked as if he was about to make trouble.

She shot him a sidelong glance, irritation and affection warring beneath her ribs.

"It's insufferable at how at ease you are," she murmured.

He tilted his head, a smirk creeping onto his lips. "You stop my heart as well."

A small laugh escaped her, and he offered his arm with a dramatic flourish.

"Shall we dazzle them, my Phoenix?"

Farah placed her hand on his arm, her grip firmer than it needed to be, and together, they stepped into the heart of the ballroom.

Silence followed them.

The lull of conversation was subtle, but there as they entered. The barely perceptible shift as heads turned, gazes tracking their every move. She felt their weight, sharp and assessing, curiosity twined with judgment. Every movement she made, every measured step, was a performance in itself.

She didn't know if she'd ever understand this kind of battlefield, but she would make sure that she could at least walk away from it by the end of the night.

Her gaze moved across the room, cataloging the

combatants and their chosen arenas. The nobles clustered in their gilded corners, laughing too brightly, their voices dripping with practiced civility. Members of the Parliament, mainly merchants and laborists, stood stiffly along the edges, their expressions sharp with calculation, watching everything while revealing nothing.

And at the heart of it all stood the Mashya, Enayat à Mashayekhi, his regal presence illuminated under the grand arches of the dais.

Enayat had the look of a man carved from ivory and firelight. Tall, stately, with the kind of presence that turned heads without the need for raised voices or sweeping gestures. His skin was the warm, golden-brown of old parchment, smooth despite the years of strain that had settled into his bones. His sharp cheekbones, strong, dignified jawline, and the deep-set eyes of a man who had seen too much, were framed by a neatly trimmed beard and dark, curling hair streaked deeply with silver at his temples. He carried the weight of the kingdom on his shoulders with a quiet grace, his long robes of indigo and gold silk draping over his frame like the night sky dusted with stars. A single ring, the seal of his rule, gleamed on his right hand.

Her attention moved to Commander Rostam Etemad, standing close at his side. Not too close, not enough for scandal, but close enough that anyone watching could see the truth between them. They spoke in low voices, heads inclined toward one another, a conversation that existed in the space between duty and something far more personal.

Where Enayat was refinement and diplomacy,

Rostam was iron and war. Broad-shouldered, with a frame built for battle, the kind of presence that spoke of strength without the need for embellishment. His skin, tanned and weathered from years under the sun, bore the faint marks of old wounds, each scar a testament to a war fought and survived. His face was hardened by time, marked by a long, jagged scar that ran from temple to jawline—evidence of a near-fatal battle long before Farah had ever known him.

His once-black hair, now more gray, was tied back in a no-nonsense queue, and his beard was short but rugged, more practical than styled. Unlike the Mashya's flowing silks, Rostam wore the crisp, deep blue of the Royal Guard with the polish of a man who respected his station but had little patience for vanity. The sword at his hip was old, its hilt worn from use in countless battles.

The court had always whispered about Enayat and Rostam.

As young men, their closeness had been ignored as a passing indulgence, something the nobility could politely overlook until Enayat married Behnaz, the queen they had chosen for him from the long line of Talented noble family. After that, whatever had been between them was meant to be buried, a relic of youth traded for duty.

Farah caught the flicker of disapproval from the nobles nearby. The tightening of jaws, the faint narrowing of eyes.

To them, Rostam was dangerous not because he had joined the rebels to overthrow Behnaz, but because he had Enayat's complete and unwavering trust. He was not a courtier, not a nobleman schooled in their manipulations, but a man who spoke plainly and had the Mashya's ear. And worse still to them, it was an open secret that their relationship had been rekindled, that the bond they had tried to sever for the sake of politics had never truly broken. That was what the nobles despised most of all.

Enayat might be the rightful Mashya, but what kind of ruler chose love over obligation?

Farah resisted the urge to roll her shoulders, to shake off the tension pressing against her like a storm brewing in the marble-lined halls.

She knew these people too well. They were waiting for the moment to strike.

Beside her, Yasher shifted slightly, and the movement pulled her focus like the tug of a thread. His presence was an anchor, a quiet certainty in a world where nothing else ever seemed still.

Yasher studied her for a beat. "We both need a drink."

Before she could react, he leaned in, pressing a light kiss to her cheek. Then he was gone, vanishing into the throng of silk and gold.

A voice, smooth as oiled steel, cut through her thoughts like the glint of a dagger.

"Hand."

Farah turned, already bracing herself for the gauntlet of thinly veiled insults and disapprovals that this night would be.

Vahid à Daryush emerged from the crowd, his wine goblet balanced delicately in his hand. His long, richly dyed robes of forest green were tailored to perfection, his thin smile practiced but sharp.

She met his gaze with calculated indifference. His voice was always one of the louder in the chambers she moderated.

"Aqa à Daryush," she said evenly. "Your family honors this evening with its presence."

Daryush chuckled, swirling his wine as if he found the scene terribly amusing. "An honor, indeed. Though the times grow ever more… interesting."

Farah did not, would not take the bait.

"The Mashya is ensuring Emari's unity," she replied. "Your support is, of course, appreciated."

Daryush's smile widened, as if she'd walked straight into his trap.

"Unity." He let the word hang between them, deliberate. "A noble cause. But fragile, don't you think? Particularly when the crown is so… distracted."

She stilled. There it was. The first parry.

Daryush's gaze flicked toward the dais, to Enayat and Rostam. He swirled his wine again, the motion slow, deliberate. "Trust is such a delicate thing in these times. And trust in a leader even more so."

She kept her voice measured. "The Mashya's decisions are his own, and his judgment is beyond question."

Daryush tilted his head, feigning consideration. "Oh, of course. But leadership is not just about judgment, is it? It is about stability. And stability…" He took a slow sip, savoring the pause. "Stability requires an heir."

Her fingers curled at her sides. The court had danced around this for months, but now they were bringing it into the open. Behnaz had been dead for almost a year. At least they let it go for that long.

Daryush smiled, as if sensing the shift in the air. "The Mashya is still in his prime, yes. And while Emari heals, its people must look to the future, especially since his marriage was cut... short."

She met his gaze, steady and unwavering. "The future is being built with every decision the Mashya makes. It is not dictated by the expectations of the past."

Daryush let out a soft laugh, shaking his head. "Hand, you mistake me. I do not speak of the past. I speak of Emari's survival. Its strength. A ruler must be more than just beloved. He must be secure. Rooted. A crown without an heir is like a house built on sand. It will not hold. Especially with so many... changes to our systems."

She forced herself to relax her posture as she forced her thoughts away from slipping a blade between this man's ribs.

"The Mashya's focus is on rebuilding Emari," she said coolly. "As it should be."

Daryush's gaze lingered for a beat too long before he inclined his head. "Of course, Hand. Forgive me if I overstep. Emari's future is in capable hands, I'm sure."

He turned smoothly, retreating into the crowd. Farah exhaled slowly, her jaw aching from how tightly she had clenched it during the conversation.

Before she could cool her thoughts away from a bloody death at her hands, Yasher appeared at her side. He carried a glass of wine in one hand, his grin firmly in place.

"You look like you're considering a murder," he said lightly, his pale blue eyes glinting with something softer beneath the humor.

"Only if you offer to help me dispose of the body," Farah muttered, her voice low.

"Always for you, Phoenix," he replied, passing her the wine. His fingers brushed hers briefly, grounding her in a way that words never could. "Although, I'd recommend against starting here. Too many witnesses. One of the balconies would provide the amount of discretion required."

Farah took a sip, the bitter liquid cooling her rising anger. "Daryush is an absolute snake."

"Most of them are," he said, his gaze sweeping the room. "But you handle them better than they deserve."

"Thank you," she murmured, her gaze holding his.

"For what?" His tone was casual, but his eyes searched hers, as if he didn't quite believe her gratitude was real.

"For being here," she said simply.

He met her gaze, his eyes gleaming with mischief that barely masked the affection beneath. Instead of a quip, he leaned closer, his voice dropping to a conspiratorial murmur. "You know, if I didn't drive you mad, you'd have to admit how much you like having me around. We can't have that, can we?"

His fingers brushed against her waist in a fleeting, gentle touch, his grin softening into something quieter, something meant only for her. "But between you and me, I'm the lucky one, Phoenix."

Before she could respond, a commotion across the

room drew their attention. A group of nobles had gathered, their voices rising in a heated discussion that bordered on an argument. At the center stood Amir à Behrouz, his tall frame towering over the others as he gestured toward Rostam. The disdain in his expression was unmistakable.

Farah set her glass down at a nearby table, her jaw tightening.

"Stay here," she told Yasher, already moving toward the dais.

"Not a chance," he said, falling into step beside her. "If there's blood, I need to lay my bets on you with the books."

She cast him a sideways glance but didn't argue. Together, they crossed the ballroom, stepping into the storm waiting ahead.

She kept her stride steady, though her pulse thrummed in her ears like a drumbeat. The gilded columns and glowing lanterns of the ballroom blurred into indistinct shapes as her focus narrowed on the figure ahead. Behrouz stood with his usual commanding presence, a man in his late fifties, his broad shoulders encased in layers of opulent silks. The intricate embroidery on his deep green robe shimmered with threads of gold, proudly displaying the crest of his family. His graying beard was meticulously groomed and oiled, framing a face etched with the hard lines of a man who had spent decades wielding power.

But those days of easy authority were long gone. Behrouz's once-unassailable position had crumbled alongside Behnaz's fall. His vocal support of the late

Mashyana, even as her schemes unraveled, had tarnished his reputation in the eyes of everyone. Where once he had stood as a pillar of tradition, now his influence teetered on the edge of irrelevance, propped up only by the fading memory of his connection to the old ways.

Still, the man did not relinquish his position without a fight. His booming voice carried over the murmur of the crowd, rich with bluster and righteous indignation.

"The glory of Emari will not be restored through the whims of these unproven policies," he declared. "We must remember the strength of the Mashya's father, of the golden age when discipline reigned, and Emari's borders were impenetrable."

Her steps faltered for just a moment as his tone sharpened.

"And what of the company the Mashya keeps now?" Behrouz's voice dropped into a conspiratorial growl, the kind meant to dig into the softest parts of a listener's resolve. "A man who was once a Commander, now a shadow of his former self. Rostam, who faked his own death and slunk into the rebels' ranks like a thief in the night. Now he stands at the Mashya's side, less a trusted advisor and more… a pet." The word dripped with venom, drawing a ripple of murmurs and uneasy glances.

Her nails pressed into her palms, as she stopped just short of them, forcing her face into a neutral mask. Rostam had sacrificed everything for Emari. His position, his safety, and his name. He had been her strongest ally to stay and help correct the damage done, and more importantly, he had been right. When the court had dismissed the Mashyana's darkness as mere rumor, he had seen it for what it was and had acted.

Behrouz turned, and his dark eyes landed on her. He inclined his head in a mockery of respect, his smile thin and sharp as a blade.

"Ah, the Hand herself. Perhaps you can explain how this... experiment," His hand swept dramatically toward the raised dais where Rostam stood near the Mashya. "Is meant to inspire confidence in the people of Emari? After all, what kind of leader trusts a traitor?"

Her breath was steady, though each word from Behrouz felt like it clawed at the fragile fabric she was trying to weave. She met his gaze unflinchingly, her tone even and deliberate as she replied, "The kind of leader who values loyalty to Emari above loyalty to a broken past."

The murmurs grew louder, some nodding in agreement, others shaking their heads. Behrouz chuckled, the sound low and bitter. "You speak of loyalty as though it's currency, Hand. But loyalty is earned, not bought with empty promises of unity. Perhaps it is not the past that is broken, but your vision for Emari's future."

Farah stepped closer, her presence commanding. "It is easy to demand loyalty from a pedestal, Aqa à Behrouz, when you have no intention of earning it yourself. Rostam's actions have always been for Emari, not for himself. Can you say the same?"

The crowd stilled, the tension between them palpable. Behrouz's jaw tightened, but he didn't respond. Farah didn't wait for him to find his footing again. She inclined her head, as if dismissing him, and turned to address the rest of the nobles, her voice carrying across the ballroom.

"We are here to move forward, not to linger in the shadow of old regimes. The Mashya's vision is one of strength through unity, not fear. And I, as his Hand, will help to see that vision realized." Her words were met with silence, save for the faint clink of glasses and shuffling of feet.

Her voice dropped—softer now, almost thoughtful, but no less cutting.

"And if you long for the old days, Behrouz..." Her dark eyes found his, unyielding as tempered steel. "Perhaps you should ask the late Mashyana how well that served her—if she could still answer. I was there when she fell, if you remember."

There were a few gasps, the shifting of silk and polished boots against marble, but no one dared to speak.

Behrouz's smirk faltered. His fingers curled slightly at his sides.

Farah squared her shoulders, her heart hammering in her chest as she met his cutting gaze. Let them pretend all they wished. She had been the one to strike Behnaz down. And she would do it again.

She let the weight of her words settle, let them sink into the cracks of a court that had spent too long pretending not to see what was right in front of them.

"Aqa à Behrouz, I wasn't aware your interest in my personal life had grown so... enthusiastic."

The Mashya's voice was steady but carried a razor's edge, the kind that silenced a room with its subtle force.

Enayat stepped forward, making a point to ignore the last part of Farah's defense. His dark eyes turned just to Behrouz instead, unreadable but heavy with judgment.

Beside him stood Rostam, his posture as solid as the mountains. His striking features were composed, though his dark brows arched just slightly, a silent warning that paired well with the sword resting at his hip. The murmurs in the crowd died down to a tense silence as the two men approached.

Behrouz, ever the opportunist, offered a low bow, his expression carefully arranged in feigned humility.

"Your Majesty," he began, his tone oozing false respect. "I meant only to point out the... concerns some of us share about the company you keep. Emari's people deserve clarity, after all."

"Clarity?" Rostam's deep, steady voice cut through the tension. His words were calm, almost casual, but there was no mistaking the challenge in them. "And I suppose twisting the truth is your way of providing it?"

Behrouz stiffened, his eyes narrowing slightly. "I merely voiced what many are already thinking. Should the commander of Emari's armies not be above reproach, especially one who," His pause was deliberate, calculated. "chose to walk away when the Crown needed him most?"

Farah's fists clenched at her sides, but the Mashya stepped in before she could speak.

"You seem to misunderstand the difference between loyalty to a person and loyalty to Emari," Enayat said, his voice smooth yet heavy with authority. "Rostam saw corruption and chose to act. Not for himself, but for the people this court claims to represent."

The crowd's unease rippled as eyes flickered between the Mashya, Rostam, and Behrouz. The older noble's face tightened, but he recovered quickly, bowing again.

"Of course, Your Majesty. I would never question your wisdom, or that of your Hand." His gaze briefly darted to Farah, and she caught the faint sneer lurking at the corners of his lips. "Though I do hope this new era will not forget the strength of the old ways."

Rostam's mouth quirked into a dry smile, a rare show of amusement.

"The strength of the old ways?" he repeated. "Or the strength of fear and subjugation?"

Behrouz bristled, but before he could retort, the Mashya lifted a hand. "Aqa à Behrouz, Emari needs leaders who can look forward, not wallow in nostalgia for a time that fractured us. Let that be your clarity."

Behrouz dipped another shallow bow, his lips pressed into a thin line.

"Of course, Your Majesty." With that, he turned and melted into the crowd, the tension lingering in his wake.

Farah released the breath she hadn't realized she'd been holding. The Mashya turned to her, his stern expression softening.

"You handled yourself well," he said, his voice low enough that only she and Rostam could hear.

Rostam's eyes flicked to her, the faintest hint of approval in his usually stoic gaze. "Behrouz is loud, but he's losing ground. His bark is louder than his bite."

She nodded, though the weight of the nobles'

watchful eyes lingered like a cloak she couldn't shed. As Rostam and the Mashya ascended the dais, their heads inclined in close conversation again, she felt Yasher step closer beside her, his presence a quiet but steadying force.

Yasher leaned in, his voice pitched low, his tone a mix of wry humor and sincerity. "For a room full of nobles who spend so much time posturing, you'd think they'd learn to shut up and let you work."

Her lips twitched, a faint smile breaking through the tension that coiled in her chest. "And here I thought you preferred them this way. It gives you plenty of material to work with."

"Oh, it does," he said, his grin unmistakable in his voice. "But even I'm not clever enough to salvage Daryush's opinions on heirs or Behrouz's attempts at nostalgia. I'd rather focus on more interesting things."

She turned her head slightly, catching the glint of mischief in his eyes. "Such as?"

His grin widened, though his voice dipped lower, softer, as if the entire ballroom had disappeared around them.

"Like how stunning you looked while dismantling Behrouz. Or how much I'd rather get you out of this ball-room, and that outfit, than let the rest of these jackals waste another minute of your time."

The warmth that bloomed in her cheeks betrayed her, though she kept her composure intact.

"Insufferable," she murmured, the word carrying no real bite.

"As you prefer me to be," he replied, his tone both playful and quietly reverent.

Farah shook her head, turning her focus back to the dais where the Mashya and Rostam stood close, drawing whispers that prickled at the edges of her awareness. Her fingers tightened briefly at her sides.

She took a deep breath and straightened her posture. "Let's hope I don't have to regret that display against Behrouz."

"Regret? Never," Yasher said, a cheeky smile on his face. "You'll handle them all."

A measured voice cut through the quiet moment.

"Aqa à Behrouz does enjoy making a show of the past. But I suspect even he knows nostalgia is a weak foundation for power." Siavash à Ardashir stood just beside them, hands clasped loosely behind his back. He hadn't been there a moment ago, or at least, he hadn't made himself known.

He inclined his head slightly, a ghost of a smile playing at his lips. "Hand. You are learning to handle courtly warfare as precisely as you do steel. It is admirable."

Farah studied him. The words were carefully chosen, the compliment neither empty nor overly flattering. She felt like a bumbling child next to that capable phrasing without thought.

She narrowed her eyes slightly. Although he'd had shown himself to be a true supporter of the Mashya's reforms in the chambers in that last meeting, she wasn't sure about him yet. He not only provided insights to sway the room but to actively stand up for her words, which was a relief after days of her being ignored and dismissed by the Parliament, more specifically, the nobles.

Yasher, still holding his glass of wine, took in Siavash with a flicker of curiosity. His grin remained intact, but there was something sharper beneath it.

"And you are?" Yasher's voice was casual, but she knew him too well to miss the underlying challenge.

Siavash turned his gaze toward him smoothly, as though he had anticipated the question.

"Siavash à Ardashir." He extended a hand, his posture open, not deferential, not demanding. "The Khānum and I have been working together to help Emari move forward."

Yasher, still lounging in the posture of someone who had long mastered the art of appearing unimpressed, let the moment stretch. Then, with a flick of his wrist, he set down his drink and accepted the handshake.

"Yasher Gavrilov," he said easily. "Itinerant gambler. Frequent problem solver. Occasional nuisance. "

Siavash's smile curved slightly, as though entertained but not surprised. "Your reputation precedes you, Aqa."

Yasher tilted his head. "Good. Saves me the trouble of extended introductions." He flicked a glance toward her before his gaze returned to Siavash, still light, still easy. "And what kind of support are you offering?"

Siavash turned back to Farah, meeting her gaze directly.

"The kind that doesn't need to be spoken aloud in a ballroom full of people with lesser intentions."

She studied Siavash for a moment longer. He had aligned himself beside her, not in front of her, not as if he were guiding her steps, but as though he was making it clear to anyone watching that he stood with her. A useful ally. Or a dangerous one. She hadn't decided yet.

Siavash inclined his head, as if reading the thought and accepting the scrutiny without offense.

"For now, Hand, I'll leave you to your evening. But should you find yourself needing another voice to cut through the noise, I hope you'll consider mine."

Her lips pressed into a thin line, neither acceptance nor dismissal. "You're certainly persistent, Ardashir."

Siavash's smile didn't falter. "A trait we seem to share."

Without another word, he stepped back into the current of the ballroom, disappearing into the clusters of nobility as seamlessly as he had arrived.

Farah sighed, aware that Yasher had remained quiet at her side, watching the exchange with the sharp-eyed amusement of someone cataloging a new player at the table. She didn't have to look at him to know what was coming.

"So," Yasher drawled, finally breaking the silence. He slid his hands into his coat pockets, his voice as casual as the roll of his coin over his knuckles. "Should I be worried?"

She sighed again. "About?"

He shot her a grin. "Oh, I don't know. The polished, well-spoken nobleman who just called you Hand like he's already carved out a place at your side."

She gave him a sideways glance.

He hummed, clearly waiting for more. When she didn't immediately offer it, he took it upon himself to fill the gap.

"Siavash à Ardashir," he mused. "I've heard the name tossed around the court, mostly by people who can't decide whether he's here to help or to make things worse. Though they were all right on his looks. He's from one of the old noble families, right?"

She nodded. "His family was loyal to the Mashya's father, but he wasn't in court during Behnaz. He was away, serving in one of Emari's outer provinces. He seems to want to help build Parliament."

He let out a low whistle.

"So he's clever, ambitious, and just happened to arrive at a time when Emari is restructuring itself from the ground up?" His grin widened. "You do attract the most interesting people, Phoenix."

She gave him a sidelong look. "You're assuming he's interested in *me*."

His grin didn't fade, but something in his posture shifted, his natural ease retreating.

"Oh, I think he is," he said, too easily. "The question is whether he wants to be your ally, your problem, or something else entirely."

She scoffed, and held out her arm. "I think you've had too much wine. Let us walk."

She looked ahead, where the Mashya and Rostam were still in conversation, the shifting tides of the gala moving around them like a river around a stone.

They walked in step, weaving through the crowd, the warmth of lanterns casting long shadows across the marble floor. She felt the weight of Siavash's words still lingering in the back of her mind, a carefully placed stone in an already unsteady foundation.

Yasher, ever perceptive, closed the space between them, his hand sliding to the small of her back as he pulled her in towards him. Not roughly, but deliberately. His grin was easy, but his gaze was sharper than before, something keen and unreadable flickering beneath the pale blue.

"Just let me know if I have to start actually worrying about him."

She arched a brow, ignoring the way his fingers curled against the fabric of her coat, the touch unmistakably possessive. "And if you do?"

He shrugged, the motion deceptively casual, but his hold on her didn't loosen. "Then I might just have to be very, very charming." His voice dipped lower, just for her, his breath warm against her ear.

She huffed a quiet laugh, but he didn't let go right away. Instead, his hand lingered, a silent claim, before he finally released her just enough to let her take his arm.

CHAPTER 3

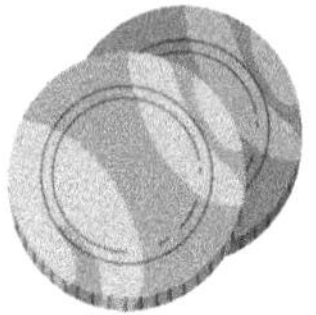

THE SUNLIGHT SPILLING through the latticework burned brighter now that the morning was fully here, its shifting patterns creeping across Yasher's bare chest as he lay sprawled on the bed. He stared up at the intricately carved ceiling, letting the morning's warmth pull him from his memories and into the quiet of the present. Farah's absence was a palpable thing, her side of the bed cool to the touch.

Her scent still lingered faintly, rose oil and the tang of metal that never quite left her skin. It was as if she had left some intangible part of herself behind, even as she moved on to wrangle the responsibilities that consumed her days.

He exhaled slowly, draping an arm over his eyes with a groan.

"Gone before dawn again," he muttered. Not that it surprised him. Farah never lingered.

Not when there was a kingdom to hold together with sheer force of will. He could picture her already, her courtly clothes from last night exchanged for something practical, her dark hair pulled back in sharp, efficient lines of a simple braid, her gaze scanning documents or locking onto some unfortunate noble who dared to oppose her.

The thought made him grin despite himself.

But there was a tug beneath the amusement, a gnawing something that never quite let go. Not guilt, not exactly. Just... the awareness that she gave so much of herself away, piece by piece, until there was barely anything left for herself. Last night had been no different.

She had carried the weight of Emari's fractured court on her shoulders, endured the veiled barbs, the cutting remarks, the whispers behind painted fans after Behrouz's performance. He had watched it all, had stood beside her as nobles tested her, as Parliament measured her, as men like Behrouz and Daryush tried to undermine her authority with nothing but pointed questions and sharper smiles.

She'd weathered it as she always did with unflinching poise, the steel of her will concealed beneath the velvet of diplomacy. But it had cost her.

He'd seen it in the careful way she had unclasped her coat last night, in the way her fingers had hovered for just a breath before removing the thin steel and silver bangles she always wore to have metal at the ready.

She slipped off her boots without a word, her fingers already reaching for the clasps in her hair as she walked toward the mirror. He had leaned against the wall, arms crossed, watching her with a mixture of admiration and frustration as their eyes met in the mirror. The tension in her spine had yet to release.

"You survived," he had said, his voice light as he tried to pull her from the fog of duty.

She had glanced at him through the mirror's reflection, one brow arching in a way that was both weary and amused. "Barely. Though your commentary almost made me spit wine over Khānum Khosrow a few times."

He had crossed the space between them in two strides, his hands finding her waist as he leaned in close. "I do have a talent for keeping things interesting."

She sighed, but her lips curved faintly. "Insufferable."

"You adore me," he murmured, brushing his lips against the side of her neck. Her scent filled his senses, grounding him.

"Some days I wonder why," she retorted, though her tone lacked any real bite. She turned in his arms, her hands resting lightly on his chest as she met his gaze. "Yasher, I—"

"You're going to say something noble about how you'll endure it all," he interrupted, his grin softening into something warmer. "But you don't have to tonight."

Her expression faltered, her composure slipping just enough for him to see the cracks beneath. She trusted him with that vulnerability, a trust that wrapped around his heart and tightened like a fist. He brought his hand to her cheek, his thumb brushing against her skin as he tilted her face toward his.

"Let me," he whispered. And she had.

Now, in the morning light, the ache of it settled deep.

Yasher ran a hand through his hair, exhaling.

It wasn't just the weight of Emari pressing down on her. It was him, too. He knew it.

Because for all his silver tongue and easy charm, for all the ways he deflected and danced around the edges of his own problems, Farah was the one person who saw through it all. She knew the truths he tried to keep buried. That his Talent was slipping further from his grasp, that every day without confronting it felt like one step closer to disaster. He'd kept a tight rein on his Luck during the gala to make sure that nothing slipped, no random happenstance of drinks spilling on spoiled nobles or plates tipping onto their expensive garb, but it was a struggle.

Then there was that pretty noble, Siavash à Ardashir.

The polished nobleman had made his presence known last night, standing at Farah's side with that careful, deliberate ease. Not a challenge, but something close enough to make him grind his teeth.

He hadn't missed the way Siavash had spoken to her, the way he had played the game with subtlety and precision.

But he had spent his life reading people for tells, and Siavash wasn't just another politician sniffing for influence.

No, he had positioned himself carefully. Not as someone vying for power over her, but as someone offering to share the burden.

And Farah, despite everything, had listened, though she was still holding back, sizing him up.

He shifted his gaze to the ceiling. He wasn't jealous. Not exactly.

But there was something about the way Siavash had looked at her, the way he had stepped into her space with calculated ease, that left him with an unfamiliar edge of unease.

Because maybe, just maybe, she deserved someone who didn't make things harder for her.

Yasher wasn't blind. He knew what he was. Trouble, wrapped in charm and unpredictability, a man who had spent his life drifting until Farah had given him a reason to stay. And as much as he joked, as much as he played at confidence, there was a part of him that whispered, in the quiet of the morning, that maybe Farah would be better off with someone who could help her carry the weight of Emari without adding to it.

Someone like Siavash.

The thought burned, sharp and unwelcome. He closed his eyes, shaking it off. Because whatever Siavash might be offering, whatever future he thought he could build beside Farah, she was still here, sharing a bed and a life, with him.

He shoved aside the lingering thoughts and sat up, rubbing the back of his neck before swinging his legs over the side of the bed. The marble floor was cool beneath his bare feet, the city already alive beyond the open balcony doors.

Farah had gone to work.

And Yasher was done waiting.

If Siavash wanted to play at alliances and diplomacy, fine. Yasher would play the game in his own way.

And it started with finally meeting the old woman who could fix his Luck.

Yasher jogged down the marble steps of the Citadel, his shirt only half-buttoned, his old boots scuffing against polished stone. The air was warm already, the scent of sea salt mingling with the lingering perfumes of last night's revelry, but his thoughts churned elsewhere.

Sitting in that room alone, letting his thoughts circle back to Farah and Siavash, to his own damn insecurities, wasn't an option. So he focused on the one thing he could actually control—finally finding this cursed tutor Farah kept pushing him toward. Jeta Veseli. Some old scholar who, if Farah was to be believed, could teach him how to control his Talent before it unraveled completely.

He raked a hand through his hair to pull it from his face as he descended the last step, already weaving through the morning bustle of the courtyard. He had no idea what to expect. Whether Jeta would be some dry academic full of theories or another mystic spouting riddles would be something he'd find out. He wasn't in the habit of doing things just because someone told him to.

Then again...

He also wasn't blind to the way his Luck had been slipping through his fingers lately.

If he could get a grip on it, if he could stop it from twisting on him, turning reckless when he needed control, maybe then he could stop feeling like—

A small figure stepped into his path, arms crossed. Waiting.

Pari.

She stood in the center of the walkway, her dark braids catching in the morning light, the ribbons woven through it shifting in the breeze. Her expression was unreadable. Not annoyed, not sulking, just watching.

It took exactly two heartbeats for Yasher to remember.

The gardens.

Shit.

The realization hit him like a slap to the back of the head. *Yesterday? Or was it two days ago?* He'd promised her they'd sit together in the Citadel gardens. That she could bring her sketchbook, and she could tell him all about whatever new recipe Shirin had that they needed to try. And, naturally, he'd let it slip through the cracks, buried beneath politics, the gala, Farah, and the uneasy feeling that still hadn't let go since last night.

Twelve hells.

Still, she wasn't glaring at him. Just tilting her head slightly, assessing.

Yasher ran a hand through his hair again, offering a slow, sheepish grin. "Little Divine."

She blinked once. "Yasher."

No anger. No sharp remarks. Just patience. And somehow, that was worse.

He hesitated, waiting for the scolding that would let him brush it off, the dry quip that would give him an excuse to deflect.

It didn't come.

Instead, she tilted her head again. "You forgot."

He rubbed the back of his neck. "I wouldn't say *forgot* exactly…"

Pari gave him a steady, unimpressed look.

He sighed. "Alright, fine. I forgot."

She nodded, as if she had already accepted that answer before he'd even spoken. No accusation. No disappointment. Just quiet understanding that made the guilt settle deeper.

"I got caught up in things," he added, glancing toward the city gates. "But listen, how about we just delay our plans instead of scrapping them?"

She didn't answer immediately, but something in her posture shifted. Listening.

"I was on my way to meet someone," he continued, crouching slightly to be more at eye level with her. "Farah's been on me about it for weeks. Some old tutor named Jeta. Supposed to help me get a handle on my Luck."

Something flickered in Pari's deep brown eyes. Interest. Understanding.

He grinned, letting the offer settle between them before nudging it forward. "Want to come? I figure you're probably better at making sure I don't run off than anyone else. You can be my official supervisor, and report back to Farah how good of a student I was."

She hummed softly, considering. He could practically see the wheels turning in her head, weighing the importance of their original plan against the necessity of this one.

Then, after a few long seconds, she gave a single, decisive nod.

"Good choice," he said, straightening with a chuckle. He reached out, ruffling her hair lightly. "You can make sure she doesn't try to lecture me to sleep. Pinch me if I start to nod off, even kick me if it gets bad."

Pari smoothed out her ribbons with practiced ease, lifting her chin slightly.

"You should listen," she said simply. "Your Luck is funny, and Shirin said she can't afford to replace cups if it keeps breaking them."

He blinked, caught off guard by the seriousness in her tone. "Yeah?"

She nodded, like it was the most obvious thing in the world. "You won't stop it from slipping if you don't learn how to hold on."

It wasn't the first time Pari had cut straight through his bullshit, and he knew it wouldn't be the last.

Instead of answering, he nudged her forward lightly with a hand on her shoulder. "Alright, Little Divine. Let's go find this tutor before I change my mind and teach you a new card game that Shirin will hate instead."

She perked up beside him. "Can we do both?"

He blinked down at her. "Both?"

She nodded. "Find the tutor and then you teach me the card game. I like learning. And I want to beat you next time."

He gave a quiet snort. "Ambitious, aren't you?"

Pari shrugged like it was the most obvious thing in the world. "You said I was clever."

Yasher chuckled, shaking his head. She still hadn't smiled, but her eyes were brighter now. And she walked a little taller.

He exhaled, his own steps falling into rhythm beside hers.

That was good enough for now.

***

THE MORNING CROWD had thickened by the time Yasher and Pari slipped past the Citadel gates and into the winding streets beyond. Vendors yelled out their calls, the scent of baking bread and roasting spiced nuts threading through the crisp air. The hum of the city felt alive, restless. The same energy that always buzzed through the Citadel.

Yasher adjusted the cuffs of his coat as he glanced down at Pari. She had tucked her hands into the folds of her tunic like a woman far older than just nine years, her ribbons swaying with each step.

"You're sure you know where she is?" Pari asked, not breaking stride.

He smirked, nudging her lightly with his elbow. "You doubt me?"

Pari shot him a look that was entirely too familiar. *Farah's unimpressed stare condensed into a much smaller frame.* The learned behavior to gang up on him. "Yes."

He chuckled, stuffing his hands into his pockets. "Fair enough."

In truth, he wasn't sure. He knew Jeta Veseli taught somewhere near the Saffron Oasis since they'd dismantled what little was left of the Beloveds, had seen her once by the fountains, and had spent the better part of four months pretending she didn't exist. It wasn't that he didn't believe in what she could do, Farah did, and that should have been enough. It was that looking too closely at what he was, at what his Talent actually meant, would mean acknowledging the things he tried to outrun.

Still, he had promised Farah. And now, he had Pari watching him, waiting to see if he would keep his word. He really loved backing himself into corners, didn't he?

The streets narrowed as they neared the heart of the Oasis, the buildings pressing in close, their sandstone walls streaked with the morning sun. The scent of cardamom and honey wafted from the tea shops, mingling with the sharper bite of freshly worked metal from the artisans' stalls.

Jeta Veseli stood at the edge of a shaded courtyard, her long coat trailing behind her as she bent slightly, speaking to a cluster of children. They were gathered on the worn stone floor, some cross-legged, others perched on the fountain's edge, their small hands clutched in concentration.

Jeta nodded, murmuring something too low to hear. Her posture remained steady, patient, though her bright green eyes carried an intensity that set her apart from the usual stuffy tutors that still ranged around the Citadel.

She was older than he'd thought before, her face lined with the kind of wisdom that came from knowing too much rather than simply living long. Her dark, curling hair was streaked liberally with silver, pulled back into an intricate knot that left a few strands loose around her temples.

Yasher's breath hitched, the sight of her stirring something deep in the quiet places of his memory. The cut of her deep emerald coat, the way her rich blue scarf draped over her shoulder, the subtle, poised way she carried herself, it was familiar in a way that had nothing to do with the Citadel. She wasn't just Emarian. No, there was something else in the lines of her face, in the richness of her voice, in the way her brilliant green eyes missed nothing but revealed little in return.

She was a Lom, from the Travelers in his country. Or at least, part one, as he was. Farah had mentioned once that the Emari called them Koulan, a name wrapped in history, distant from the way they were known in Rohkaz. As good as any other name for people without a home, people he came from.

The realization settled over him like a ghost from another life. A memory flickered, unbidden. The scent of sun-warmed earth, the weight of a coarse-woven blanket wrapped around his shoulders, the murmur of a low, steady voice telling him that he would survive this, even if he didn't believe it yet.

She reminded him of a woman long dead, one of the many that he'd had to bury, both in the ground and away in his memories.

He forced the thought away before it could take shape, but the sensation remained, a whisper at the edges of his mind.

Jeta Veseli was not just another tutor, and if she was anything like the woman who had once pulled him back from the brink of starvation and loss, then he wasn't sure if that made her more dangerous to him, or exactly what he needed.

She had, of course, already noticed him.

The old woman's gaze flicked up, sharp and assessing, locking onto him as if she had been expecting him. She said nothing at first, only tilting her head slightly, the weight of her attention pressing against him like an unseen force.

He tipped his chin up in what he hoped passed for casual confidence.

"Guess she saw us," he muttered to Pari.

Pari, unbothered, simply nodded. "She was waiting for you."

He caught the ghost of a smirk as Pari stepped forward, tugging lightly on the sleeve of his coat to pull him with her.

They closed the distance slowly, Jeta saying a few final words to the children before they scattered into the marketplace, their excited chatter trailing behind them.

By the time they reached her, she was waiting patiently.

"Yasher... Gavrilov," Jeta said, his name rolling easily off her tongue. "The Hand has spoken to me about you. I was beginning to wonder how long you would run before you finally arrived."

He let out a slow breath, rocking back on his heels. "I like to make an entrance."

Jeta studied him for a beat, then glanced down at Pari, her expression softening just slightly. "And you've brought company. Greetings, little herald."

Pari folded her arms, tilting her chin up. "He needs supervision. Otherwise he'll find a card game and forget to take me to the gardens, and teach me a new card game, as he promised."

Her lips twitched in amusement. "That much is clear."

He sighed dramatically. "I see where Farah gets her wit from. Must be in the water here."

Jeta ignored him, her gaze lingering on him just a moment too long, as if weighing something unseen. Then, she turned slightly, motioning toward the empty bench beside the fountain.

"Come," she said, voice even. "If we are to begin, we might as well do so properly."

He hesitated, every instinct in him screaming to bolt in the other direction, to turn away from this woman who was both his present and his past. But Pari was watching. Farah was waiting.

And, for the first time in a long while, he had nowhere left to run.

With a resigned sigh, he followed Jeta to the bench.

"First, and most important. Your Talent isn't a separate thing from you, *saqalu*," she began. "It is as much a part of you as your skin, your breath, or your soul. Stop treating it like it's a trinket to gamble away, or a damned Divine gift from that pompous bird."

And just like that, the lesson began, not letting him ask all of the questions that he had for this woman and the things she already seemed to know.

CHAPTER 4

THE SMALLER COUNCIL chamber smelled of parchment, ink, and the faint tang of oil from the brass lanterns burning overhead. Late morning light filtered through the stained glass, casting fractured shapes across the mahogany table where Emari's most influential voices gathered for a smaller meeting than the day before, and yet still as draining as the larger group.

Farah sat at the head of the table, listening to yet another debate that felt more like a battlefield, she wondered if anything meaningful would ever be accomplished here.

"The Mashya's proposal is not without merit," she said, keeping her voice measured, controlled. "Banima is one of Emari's strongest agricultural centers. If we let their farmlands fall to ruin after this year's drought, we'll be paying the price for years to come."

A scoff came from the other side of the table.

Behrouz leaned back in his chair, fingers steepled over the curve of his stomach. "And what price will we pay now, Hand? The treasury is stretched thin enough as it is. Unless you plan to conjure grain from the sea, I fail to see how we can afford to redirect resources for a single province."

Her rings on her fingers spun as she hummed softly, giving in to the need to burn off some of her Talent as it boiled with her anger. Not a single province.

"Banima is one of Emari's most vital suppliers of grain, fruit, and livestock," she said coolly. "The taxes from their exports have filled your coffers more than once, Aqa. Surely you haven't forgotten that."

Daryush, swathed in another set of rich green robes, waved a lazy hand. "Tax revenue is only useful when it exists. If Banima's harvest is already lost, what incentive do we have to throw gold at a sinking ship?"

She inhaled through her nose slowly, steadying herself. "We do not let our people starve. That is the incentive."

A hush fell over the chamber. A single crack in the noise—before the grumbling resumed.

Narjis à Shiraz adjusted the golden rings stacked neatly along her fingers. "No one is suggesting we do nothing, Hand," she said smoothly, voice rich with the polished diplomacy of an aristocrat who had never starved a day in her life. "But how we act is just as important. If we allocate grain from the reserves to Banima, other provinces will demand the same leniency. The first crack in the wall invites the flood."

Farah kept her expression neutral, though the metaphor was a ridiculous one. These people thought in advantages and leverage, not in empty hands and hollowed-out bellies.

"The difference," she said, "is that other provinces have had successful harvests this year. Banima is the one at risk of famine."

Behrouz sighed theatrically, shaking his head. "And yet, the citizens of Emari already struggle under the weight of instability. You ask us to subsidize Banima when we should be securing our own future. Our military still requires reinforcements to finish the rebels in Tamidh that will not disband despite the envoys for parlay, our borders need strengthening to the North, those barbaric Rokhani are making noises again in the mountains—"

Her patience snapped, and she let her thoughts out of their cage. Though she clenched her hands for a moment before shaking them out, stopping the shaking of metal chalice on the head of the table.

"The only way to secure our future is to ensure our people can feed themselves," she said, voice sharp as a drawn blade. "If we let Banima collapse, it will not only be them who suffer. Trade routes will falter. The price of grain will skyrocket. The merchant class will hoard what little remains, and famine will reach beyond Banima's borders before you even have time to tighten your purse strings."

She let the weight of her words settle over them, sinking into the air like iron.

And then, predictably, Behrouz scoffed.

"A dramatic interpretation, Hand."

Narjis shook her head, polite but dismissive. "We

appreciate your concern, Khānum Farahnaz, but these matters are more nuanced than simple cause and effect. You have a warrior's mind. You see a problem, and you want to strike it down before it festers. But the court does not function like the battlefield."

A warrior's mind.

The words grated more than they should have. She had spent years proving herself—had carried Emari's survival on her back, had bled for this kingdom. Yet in moments like this, they still treated her like a child, pressing their hands over a game map and claiming she could not understand the pieces at play.

Then, Siavash spoke.

"It is not simply a matter of charity," he said, his voice smooth and unhurried. "It is an investment. We invest, rather than squander."

Farah stilled. That was eerily close to what she had said not moments before. She turned her head slightly, eyes narrowing as she watched him.

Behrouz frowned, but it was Narjis who tilted her head, appraising Siavash like he was a particularly interesting opponent in a game of chess.

"And I suppose," she said, "you have a suggestion, Aqa à Ardashir?"

Siavash leaned forward, his expression calm but unrelenting. "I do. We do not need to drain the treasury or the reserves. Not simply to survive this season, but to recover next year's harvest. Tools, seed stock, labor assistance."

Farah clenched her jaw.

She watched the room's reaction carefully, a slow burn kindling inside her.

Daryush still waved a dismissive hand, but this time, he actually engaged. "That would require cooperation from the merchant class. You are assuming they will part with their wares at cost rather than profit."

Siavash smiled, though it did not reach his eyes.

"Emari's merchants have benefited from Banima's trade for years. I suspect they will recognize that a temporary delay in profit is preferable to an economic collapse. However," he added, voice lighter now, "if they need convincing, I am sure that we can gather a contingent more than capable of speaking to them to sway their concerns."

A faint ripple of amusement crossed a few faces. Narjis gave a considering hum. Behrouz's frown deepened, but he seemed less eager to outright dismiss Siavash as he had Farah.

That—*that*—was what stung the most.

They had scoffed at her, disregarded her argument as *too simple, too rash*, but the *same* words spoken from Siavash's mouth were now suddenly worthy of consideration. It was a special kind of infuriating.

Before she could voice her irritation, another voice entered the room, low and edged with authority.

"You seem to misunderstand the difference between governing with foresight and governing with fear," said the Mashya.

The room fell silent as Enayat strode into the chamber, his dark robes trimmed with gold, his presence an undeniable force. He moved to the head of the table, standing next to Farah, his gaze sweeping the council, assessing each face with quiet judgment.

"My Hand and Aqa à Ardashir speak with my voice," he said, "and they are correct. We do not rule a nation by punishing its misfortunes. We will aid Banima. Not with blind charity, but with the means to rebuild. This is not a request, though you may have thought that, given that I do not tend to speak as forcefully as you would like."

Behrouz's mouth pressed into a thin line, but he bowed his head in shallow acknowledgment. Narjis sighed, but there was an amused glint in her eye. Daryush only raised his goblet, as if he had not been invested in the outcome at all.

Farah exhaled, her irritation simmering beneath the surface. She could disregard Enayat's stepping in as the Mashya as was his right, but her ire was directed at Siavash. He had done what was necessary to at least get them to listen, but that did not mean she had to like it.

When Siavash met her gaze, something flickered in his eyes. Not smugness. Not victory, but an acknowledgment.

She inhaled deeply, smoothing her expression into neutrality.

She would let this play out.

For now.

THE COUNCIL ADJOURNED NOT long after the Mashya spoke, leaving Farah standing at the head of the table as the nobles and parliamentarians filtered out. Some murmured amongst themselves, their hushed voices dripping with recalculations now that Enayat had made his stance clear. Others exited in stiff silence, their reluctance barely concealed beneath layers of courtly decorum. Even those who had seemed inclined to agree only hours ago now measured their next words more carefully, adjusting their positions like merchants weighing coin.

Siavash remained seated, his hands folded neatly on the table in front of him, watching her with a gaze that was too calm, too knowing.

Farah inhaled slowly, steadying herself before turning toward him.

"I said the same thing," she said, voice measured, though the edge was unmistakable. "Minutes before you did. And yet, it only mattered when it came from you."

He tilted his head slightly, considering her. "I noticed."

A flicker of something hot and sharp twisted in her chest.

"Is that amusing to you?" she asked, crossing her arms.

"No," he said simply. "But it was predictable."

She scoffed, shaking her head. "You think I expected to be ignored?"

He studied her for a long moment before answering. "I think you should have."

She clenched her teeth. "Of course. Because no matter what I do, I'll always be—"

"The Hand," Siavash interrupted, voice quiet but firm. "The warrior. The weapon. The blade in the dark.

That is how they see you, and they will not unmake that perception easily. You could give the most eloquent speech of your life, craft the most flawless strategy, and they would still dismiss you. But me?"

He offered a dry smile. "I am harmless. A noble without a Talent, a youngest son who will never be heir. An idealist with no army behind him. I am not a threat. And so, they listen."

The words settled into her like sand sinking into water. She knew this. Of course she did. Hadn't she been fighting this same battle since the moment Behnaz fell? It was one thing to be the Hand—it was another to be something separate from Behnaz à Radan, something of her own making.

They didn't see her as just the Hand. They still saw her as *Behnaz's* Hand.

Farah let out a slow breath, gripping the edge of the table.

"They don't see me as a courtier," she said, keeping her voice carefully neutral. "Not truly. Not the way they see you. They still see me as an arm of Behnaz, someone molded by her, meant to enforce her will. Even after everything, that shadow hasn't left me."

He exhaled, his dark eyes assessing. "No. It hasn't."

"And it won't, not easily," he added, voice quieter now. "Behnaz ruled for decades. Yes, with Enayat at her side, but no one thought that he would be as effective on his own. You can't expect them to rewrite their perception of you in a handful of months. They don't trust change that fast and they don't trust you yet, because the woman they served for years made sure they never had the opportunity to question her authority. That isn't a failing of yours. It's conditioning."

A bitter chuckle escaped her. "Is that supposed to make me feel better?"

"No," Siavash admitted, shrugging slightly. "But it should remind you that their hesitation isn't because of you, not truly. It's because they fear they were wrong about her."

They had been wrong. About Behnaz. They never saw the cracks beneath it until it was too late.

Farah had been wrong, too. She had seen Behnaz as her savior, her guide, the woman who had plucked her from obscurity and made her into something valuable. But that belief had shattered. It had ruined her.

The others—the nobles, the parliamentarians—they had built their entire lives around the certainty of Behnaz's rule, letting Enayat's piety be what he would always be known for. And now they had to live with the knowledge that they had upheld something rotten. That they had been blind.

Of course, they wouldn't trust the woman who had been her right hand. Of course, they wouldn't take her at her word. Because if they did, they would have to admit they had been complicit in everything that the Mashyana put this country through.

She swallowed, forcing the tightness from her throat. "And in the meantime?"

Siavash leaned back in his chair, regarding her carefully. "In the meantime, we let them believe I'm the reasonable one in the room."

She huffed a sharp breath. "That's what you think of yourself?"

"No," he said, lips twitching at the corners. "But it's what they think of me. And that's useful."

Farah studied him, searching for some trace of arrogance or amusement. There was none. Siavash was simply stating a fact, the way a scholar might recite an old text. It made her hate him just a little bit less.

She exhaled. "You're enjoying this, aren't you?"

A smirk ghosted across his lips. "Would it help if I said no?"

"No."

"Then I won't bother lying."

Before she could summon a sharp retort, the chamber door creaked open again.

Farah straightened instinctively, pushing her frustration down into something more palatable as Enayat stepped inside.

The Mashya's gaze swept across the now-empty room before settling on the two of them.

"I take it you've already spoken with Aqa à Behrouz and the others to get their agreement," he said, walking toward them.

Farah nodded, her spine still stiff with the weight of the conversation she had just had.

"They won't oppose you openly," she said. "But they won't support you without finding ways to make it cost you."

Enayat's mouth pressed into a thin line. "As expected."

Siavash, still lounging in his seat as if they weren't

discussing political maneuvering that could determine the future of Emari, nodded. "You made a stronger statement than they anticipated. They'll have to spend time reshuffling their positions now."

Enayat exhaled.

"Good." He glanced at Farah then, something softer in his gaze. "And you?"

Farah hesitated. "It would have been better if they had listened when I said it."

Enayat's expression darkened slightly. "Yes. It would have been."

Something about the way he said it. Without hesitation, without trying to soften the truth, unraveled the last threads of irritation still tangled in her chest.

At least he saw it. At least he didn't pretend it wasn't happening.

"I'll handle it," Farah said, voice steady.

The room fell into silence, thick with things unspoken.

Not for the first time, she wondered what might have happened if Enayat had truly ruled from the beginning. If he had been the one they had all shaped themselves around, instead of Behnaz.

He turned his gaze to Siavash now, something unreadable shifting in the depths of his expression.

"You've done well," he admitted, though the words carried a weight beyond simple praise. "But I need you to do more than just soften the edges for them. Farah needs more than that to support what needs to be repaired with my kingdom."

Siavash studied him for a moment before giving a slow nod. "You need them to trust her."

Enayat inclined his head. "She shouldn't have to fight this battle alone. And I need people in this court who will put Emari first. Not their own power, not their own ambitions."

Siavash's expression did not shift, but Farah caught the flicker of something in his gaze.

Then, Siavash stood, brushing off his coat with practiced ease. "Well, now that the kingdom is saved for another day, I believe I'll go find some tea before I'm dragged into another round of noble dramatics."

Farah shot him a dry look. "You make it sound as though you don't enjoy it."

Siavash smirked. "Oh, I do. But I find it's best to let them wonder exactly how much."

"Your Majesty." He bowed to the Mashya before taking his leave, the chamber door swinging closed behind him.

She pressed a hand to her temple until she felt Enayat's gaze lingering.

"You know you've placed me in an impossible position," she said, her voice quiet but steady. It was something she'd never have dreamed of saying to Behnaz.

His expression didn't shift, but there was a flicker of understanding behind his dark gaze. He inclined his head slightly. "I do."

She exhaled sharply, shaking her head. "You've given me a battle without a blade. You ask me to protect you, to hold this court together, to navigate a world I was never trained for. I know how to fight. I know how to break a man. Damned Divine, I could take all of Narjis's largesse before she even noticed. But this—" She gestured at the empty chamber, at the long table where she had spent the morning defending his vision against men who still saw her as Behnaz's shadow. "This is a war I was never meant to lead."

Enayat leaned against the edge of the table, his expression thoughtful. "You do it well."

She huffed a humorless laugh. "Not well enough."

"You think so?" he asked, tilting his head slightly. "Because I just watched you take a room of nobility who would rather see you fail and force them to listen."

"Listen," she repeated, voice thick with frustration. "Not act."

He sighed, rubbing a hand over his face.

"I know." His voice was quieter now, like that of a man who carried too much on his shoulders. "I know it's not fair to you, Farah. That I've asked you to do this. To be something you were never trained for, never given the chance to choose. I told you once that the choice was in your hands, and yet I've not fulfilled on that promise. And I still can't, at least not yet."

Farah's throat tightened. Enayat had spent his life preparing for a throne he was never meant to take, living in the shadow of a brother whose legacy had been written before he'd drawn breath. And yet, when that brother fell, it had been him, the second son, the quiet one, the scholar, who had been required to step into the role. Finding companionship and a strong ruler in Behnaz, before she chose a darker, more sinister path.

And now, here they were.

Two people who had been forced into their positions by the choices of others.

He looked down at the polished wood of the council table, his fingers drumming absently against its surface.

"You were always meant to protect the throne, Farah. That part hasn't changed." His gaze lifted to hers, steady and certain. "But Behnaz made sure you only ever saw one way to do it."

"She taught you to be a dagger," he continued, his voice carefully measured. "Because a dagger is something she could control. But a leader? A ruler? That's something else entirely."

She let out a slow breath. "I was never meant to rule."

"No, and be thankful for that," he admitted with a small laugh. "But you were always meant to serve Emari. The difference is now, you get to decide what that looks like. What Emari looks like."

She turned away slightly, staring at the tapestries that lined the chamber walls, their intricate patterns woven with scenes of Emari's history. The weight of its past sat heavy in the air, in the very stones beneath her feet.

"I don't want to fail you," she said finally.

"You won't," Enayat said, with a certainty that made her chest tighten.

A muscle in her jaw twitched. "You're sure of that?"

He pushed off the table, stepping closer. "I am."

Farah met his gaze, searching for any trace of doubt. There was none.

"Because you're stronger than Behnaz ever allowed

you to be," he said. "You see what she never did. And because you want to fix what she has broken, not just hold power over it."

She swallowed hard, forcing herself to hold steady beneath the weight of his words.

Enayat exhaled, his certainty tempered with something softer. "But I know this isn't just about politics, it never is in this world."

She had fought battles for the Crown. Killed for the kingdom in darkened alleyways. Stolen for the betterment of the country. And now, she fought a different war. One waged in glances and veiled barbs, the suffocating demand for heirs and tradition, the questioning of Rostam, a man who should be beyond reproach for what he'd done for the kingdom, for Enayat.

"I won't let them turn Rostam into a weakness," she said, her voice sharp with conviction.

He nodded once, his eyes softening. "I know you won't."

She clenched her fists at her sides. "They won't stop, though. Daryush, Behrouz, all the others. They'll keep circling, waiting for the moment to strike. If you don't give them an heir, they'll use him against you."

His jaw tightened. "And if I did produce an heir, do you think they would suddenly accept the world we're building? Let us be to create a new kingdom because of a child?"

Farah didn't answer. Because they both knew the truth. It wasn't about an heir. It wasn't even about Rostam.

They wanted a ruler who looked like the past. Who

carried the same iron grip as Enayat's father, as even Behnaz did. They wanted a leader who bent to their expectations and put them above the rest of the kingdom. But Enayat had never been that man. She had never been the kind of Hand they expected, either.

A long silence stretched between them, heavy but not uncomfortable.

Finally, Enayat let out a breath, shaking his head. "You shouldn't have to bear this alone. They would not speak as they do to you if I were able to be here."

She arched a brow. "Isn't that why you've paired me with Ardashir as my guardian?"

A short laugh escaped him, but there was no humor in it. "I'll do what I can to shift the weight, Farah. Lean on Siavash, though, don't push him away. He sees the vision of what Emari can and will be. He is a strong ally for what we are building."

She sighed, the last of her irritation settling into something closer to resignation. "I'll... try."

Enayat studied her for a moment longer, then nodded. "Then I'll leave you to it."

As the door shut behind him, Farah let out a slow, measured breath.

The chamber was empty now, but the echoes of their voices lingered. The weight of the morning pressed heavy on her shoulders.

CHAPTER 5

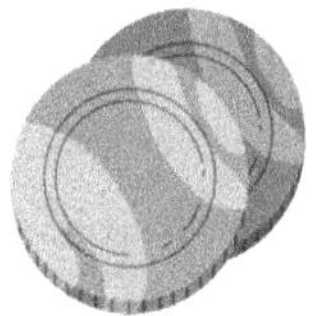

YASHER CLENCHED HIS JAW, fingers drumming against his knee as he fought the frustration that was hell-bent on escaping him.

Jeta hadn't asked him to use his Talent. Not once. No exercises, no structured lessons, not even a parlor trick. Instead, she had sat across from him with an infuriating calm, drinking tea and weaving circles around every direct question he asked. She talked in vague riddles about intent, about understanding the *currents* beneath fate, about the nature of luck as if it were some mysterious force he was supposed to *feel* instead of *control*.

He had tolerated it for a while, assuming she was building up to something useful. That there would be a moment where she would shift from philosophy to something practical. But after what felt like an eternity of verbal sparring with no real answers, his patience snapped.

"This is a waste of time," he muttered, pushing up from his seat. His boots scraped against the courtyard stones, the sound sharp in the quiet space. "If I wanted riddles, I'd listen to the nobles prattle on about land-holdings, crops, and family trees."

Jeta didn't react immediately. She set her cup down with the same unshakable patience she'd shown all day. The late afternoon sun caught in her silver-streaked curls, warming the deep blue of her headscarf where it draped over her shoulders.

"Luck is not something you control, *saqalu*," she said evenly. "Not in the way you think."

"So what, I'm just supposed to accept that it happens and let it *happen*?" He shook his head. "That's not how this works. I need to be able to guide it, to..." He exhaled sharply, searching for the right words. "To stop it from throwing me and the people around me into chaos."

Jeta's dark eyes flickered with something unreadable. "Tell me, *saqalu*. When a river carves through stone, reshaping the land over centuries, do you think it's because the river willed it? Or because the land simply did not know how to yield?"

His fingers curled into fists.

"I don't have centuries," he said, voice tight. "I don't have the luxury of waiting for fate to carve me into something useful. I need to control this before it hurts someone."

Jeta studied him for a long moment, then exhaled and turned away.

"You're not ready."

"That's it?" he said, disbelief barely masking the anger simmering beneath it. "That's all you've got? I tell you this isn't working, and you just... what? Decide I'm a lost cause?"

Jeta didn't answer him. Instead, she turned her gaze to the other side of the courtyard, where Pari sat cross-legged on the ground, charcoal moving steadily over the parchment in her lap.

Yasher had almost forgotten she was there. She had been silent the entire time, sketching with the kind of focus that made the rest of the world seem like background noise. Now, though, Jeta's gaze lingered on her drawings, and after a moment, she spoke to the little girl.

"It's a difficult thing," Jeta murmured, her voice carrying the weight of something older than time, "when gods don't live up to the stories we tell of them. When they forget that they need to remember us, to help us when we're in need."

Pari didn't look up from her drawing, but her hand stilled, fingers hovering over the parchment.

She finally set her charcoal aside, her small fingers smudged with dark streaks. She tilted her head slightly, eyes scanning her work before nodding in quiet satisfaction.

"I think that's why they fail," she said softly. "Because they don't know what we need from them. We aren't them, we're us, and that confuses them. But they don't ever just ask us."

Jeta hummed in agreement, as if this was a conversation they had both had before, as if they were speaking a language he wasn't meant to understand.

He swallowed, rubbing a hand over the back of his neck and shifted uncomfortably. Pari carefully picked up her drawing and tucked it into the stack of others. She still hadn't looked at him. Neither had Jeta.

"You're both talking in riddles," he muttered, breaking the silence. "What does any of this have to do with my Talent?"

Jeta finally turned her gaze back to him, slow and deliberate. "Everything," she said simply. "And nothing."

Yasher let out a sharp breath, frustration bubbling over. "That's not an answer."

"It's the only one that matters."

He clenched his jaw, muscles tightening. He didn't like this. The feeling of being outmaneuvered without even knowing the game. He was used to people underestimating him, used to letting them. This just felt like he was being discarded.

Pari pushed herself to her feet, brushing the charcoal dust from her fingers and looked at him.

"It's not about learning tricks," she said, as if she had already known what he was thinking. "Not the way you want it to be. It's not something you can steer like a ship on water, it's not something that you own."

He didn't answer, because she wasn't wrong.

Jeta made a quiet sound, something like amusement and understanding tangled together as she finished the little girl's words. "And Luck isn't a ship," she said. "It's the sea."

He forced out a rough exhale, shaking his head. "That doesn't mean anything."

Jeta lifted a brow, unbothered by his frustration. "Then you're not listening."

He wanted to argue, wanted to tell her that she was

the one not listening. That he wasn't some fresh-faced pupil eager to sit at teacher's feet and nod along to whatever wisdom they decided to hand down in scraps. He was here because Farah had asked him to be. Because he knew that if he didn't do something, his Luck would keep unraveling in ways he couldn't predict or control.

But saying that wouldn't change anything.

Not with Jeta. Not with Pari watching him like she already knew exactly how this would end.

A sharp breeze stirred through the courtyard, rustling the ivy clinging to the stone walls. The scent of damp earth and sun-warmed fabric filled the air, the weight of an oncoming storm lingering at the edges of the wind.

Jeta stood, adjusting the drape of her coat. "That's enough for today."

Yasher's head snapped up. "Are you kidding me?"

She gave him a look, one that was as patient as it was final. "You're not ready to listen. So I won't waste any more of either of our time."

"I didn't ask for riddles. I asked for help."

"And you'll get it," Jeta said, brushing invisible dust from her sleeve. "When you're willing to understand what that means."

He stared at her, irritation boiling beneath his skin. "And when will that be?"

She met his gaze with something far too knowing. "When you stop trying to bargain or cheat with the sea."

Yasher shoved a hand into his coat pocket before remembering he hadn't brought a damn coin with him, needing to work off some of this anger.

Pari stepped beside him, tucking her rolled drawing beneath her arm.

"That wasn't a waste of time," she said simply.

He let out a dry, humorless laugh. "Could've fooled me."

She just shook her head. "You'll see it later. I have a good feeling about that."

He didn't know what irritated him more. The fact that she sounded so sure, or the fact that somehow, he believed her, as he always did with her pronouncements.

The old woman turned, making her way toward the far end of the courtyard, where a narrow stone arch led back into the winding paths of the Citadel. She didn't look back.

Yasher let out a long breath, shaking his head. "Well. That was about as fun as pulling my own teeth."

Pari hummed, tilting her head. "You're just mad because she didn't give you an answer you wanted."

He gave her a flat look. "I'm mad because she didn't give me anything."

Pari's lips twitched in something that was not quite a smile. "Are you sure about that?"

Twelve Hells, I don't need two of you.

She laughed, already stepping toward the archway, her braids swaying behind her. "Come along. Shirin will have tea and cakes. That always makes you feel better. It always makes me feel better. And you promised to teach me a new card game. We can go to the gardens later."

Yasher lingered for a second longer, eyes trailing after Jeta's disappearing form.

He hated feeling like he was missing something. Like

he had walked into the middle of a conversation that had started long before he ever arrived.

But more than that, he hated the nagging feeling that Jeta was right.

That whatever he thought he knew about his Talent, about his Luck, wasn't the whole picture.

And that, whether he liked it or not, he was going to have to learn how to swim before the sea decided to drown him.

***

THE SCENT OF SAFFRON, cardamom, and honey filled the air, thick with the hum of conversation that always made the Saffron Oasis feel more alive than the rest of the Citadel. Yasher sat at a small table near the back of Shirin's tea shop, the cushions beneath him worn and comfortable, the kind of comfort only years of use could create. Pari sat across from him, balancing a small clay cup of sweetened tea between her hands, her latest sketch beside her plate of half-eaten rice and spiced lamb.

It had been a long day. Longer than he'd expected.

Jeta's words still clung to the edges of his thoughts like burrs on fabric, but he wasn't ready to unravel them. Not yet.

Instead, he picked at the food in front of him, the warmth of the meal easing something in his chest. He hadn't realized how much he missed this. The simple, familiar pleasure of sitting in Shirin's shop, away from court, away from expectations. Here, he wasn't the

Hand's Companion. He wasn't a man with an unruly Talent he couldn't control. He was just himself, and that was enough. Well, almost enough.

The bell above the door chimed softly, and he glanced up, wondering if these damned gods were going to fulfill the rest of his thought. He couldn't help but whisper her name when he saw her.

Farah stood in the doorway, still in the embroidered coat from the council chamber, her hair braided down her back, curls slipping out to frame her face. She looked tired, though she carried it well, her shoulders squared, gaze sharp, every movement measured. But he knew her well enough to see the tension that settled in after a day spent fighting battles no one else would acknowledge as wars.

Shirin noticed her a half-second later, her face lighting up with something like relief before shifting into concern.

"Ah, there you are, my Little Phoenix."

She barely had time to respond before Shirin was ushering her further inside, clucking her tongue. "You've been running yourself ragged again, haven't you? Come, sit. You'll eat before I hear a word of protest."

Farah let herself be led toward their table, exhaling a long-suffering sigh but not resisting. That was the way with Shirin. There was no fighting her care, no dodging her insistence.

Pari scooted to the side to make room, though she didn't seem surprised to see Farah there.

Yasher leaned back against the cushions, watching as Farah sank beside him.

"Didn't think I'd see you before midnight," he said, voice light, though he studied her carefully.

She glanced at him, something flickering in her expression before she reached for the cup of tea Shirin had already set in front of her.

"I'd hoped to find you here," she admitted. "It's been a long day, and I'm sick of listening to others speak around me instead of to me."

"Tell me about it."

Farah arched a brow. "I'd rather hear about yours first. You don't have a black eye, so you didn't decide to show off down at the tavern. What have you been up to?"

He smirked, resting his elbow on the low table. "Nothing much to tell. I spent the afternoon being lectured in riddles by an old woman who thinks Luck is an ocean and that I'm too stupid to understand how to swim."

Farah went completely still.

He had expected some reaction—maybe a knowing look, maybe a half-hearted jab at his stubbornness—but not that. Her fingers tightened slightly around the cup, her gaze locking onto him with sharp focus.

"You went to Jeta?"

He frowned, confused by the edge in her tone. "Yeah. Figured it was about time, with the way you keep badgering me about it."

Farah leaned back slightly, exhaling through her nose. "I thought I was going to have to drag you there myself," she said finally. "Or at least find some clever way to make you cross paths and lock you in a room together."

He let out a short laugh, but it didn't quite reach his eyes. "You seriously thought I wouldn't go at all?"

She gave him a look, one that said everything without needing words. "You've been avoiding it for weeks, no... months. Many months."

"Not avoiding," he corrected smoothly, though even to his own ears, the excuse sounded thin. "Just... postponing."

She hummed, unimpressed. "And now? What changed?"

He hesitated. Because how was he supposed to explain that he had spent the entire night at the gala shoving his Luck into a cage, forcing it to behave, to stay inside the boundaries he set, but it had seemed to anger it, leaving it wild and wanting? That for all the years he had relied on it, coaxed it, let it dance at his fingertips, something was shifting? And worse, he had no idea if it was slipping away without the constraint that the Eye had put on it or waking up to the fact that it had never belonged to him at all.

Then there was Jeta herself. She had gotten under his skin faster than he expected, peeling him apart with nothing but patience and knowing looks. She saw through him in a way that reminded him of another woman, one who had once told him, long ago, that he could not outrun the things written in his bones. He hadn't believed it then. He wasn't sure he believed it now.

And last but not least, the pretty nobleman, Siavash à Ardashir. Yasher had spent years pretending he didn't care how the world saw him, how it measured his worth, but seeing how easily Siavash worked standing next to Farah... it had grated, sharp and bitter. Because Siavash was steady. Composed. A man with clean hands and the ability to make people listen. And as much as Yasher hated the thought, he couldn't shake the feeling that if Farah wanted peace, wanted a partner who wouldn't pull her into chaos because he couldn't control himself, Siavash would be the better choice.

But Farah was still looking at him, waiting.

He exhaled, dragging a hand through his hair. "I don't know," he admitted finally. "Thought I might as well see what she had to say."

Her gaze lingered on him, searching. She wasn't satisfied with that answer, not really, but she didn't push.

Shirin reappeared with a fresh plate of food, setting it in front of Farah with a decisive nod. "Eat."

Farah didn't argue. He watched as she flexed her fingers slightly before breaking off a piece of bread.

After a few bites, she finally spoke again. "Siavash has been... helpful."

His fingers stilled against the rim of his cup. He didn't let the reaction show in his face, just kept his tone easy, even. "That so?"

She nodded, reaching for another piece of bread. "He's been defending the Mashya's plans, countering the nobles who are trying to keep things exactly as they were. Today was particularly grating, but he held his ground."

He didn't miss the way her jaw tightened slightly, the frustration threading through her words.

"Sounds like he's making things easier for you," he said casually, though the words settled oddly in his chest.

She gave a short, dry laugh. "Not exactly. No one listens when I say the same things he does. I'm still..." She hesitated, but only for a breath. "I'm still an arm of Behnaz to them. Not one of them. But Siavash?" Her mouth pressed into a thin line. "They may not like him, but they'll listen."

He leaned back, tilting his head as he studied her. "That bother you?"

Farah scoffed softly, shaking her head. "Wouldn't it bother you?"

A smirk tugged at his lips. "I don't know. I rather like it when people underestimate me."

She huffed, shaking her head. "You would."

But something about this whole conversation itched at him. Not jealousy, not exactly, but something close. Something restless.

Siavash was too damn good at this. Too smooth. Too careful. Yasher wasn't blind—he could see the way the court bent, ever so slightly, when Siavash spoke. How they let their guard down just enough to be led. His face began the conversation, but his words finished it.

Farah was still fighting to be heard. Siavash was already in their ears.

He took a sip of tea, masking the sharp edge of that thought before it could turn into something else. "He plays the game well, I'll give him that."

Farah didn't look at him right away. "He does."

Yasher studied the way she said it. The way she didn't defend him, didn't dismiss him either.

The nobles might not trust her yet, but she was still the Hand. Still the force holding the Mashya's plans together. Siavash was playing the game differently.

And he wasn't sure he liked what would be a logical next move for him.

Before he could say anything else, Pari cleared her throat. "If you two are just going to keep dancing around it, I'm going to go get more tea."

Farah glanced at her, one brow lifting slightly. "And what exactly are we dancing around?"

Pari gave them both a look that was far too knowing for a child. "Oh, nothing. Just a conversation neither of you wants to have about the Aqa that Yasher is jealous of."

He let out a bark of laughter. "Twelve Hells, Little Divine. You're worse than Jeta."

The little girl just grinned, slipping off her cushion and heading toward the counter, her braids swaying behind her.

Farah sighed, rubbing a hand over her face before glancing at Yasher. "I don't know why I let you two spend so much time together. She's picking up on your smart mouth."

"Because you love us," he said easily, grinning as he took a sip of tea.

Farah just shook her head, though the corner of her mouth twitched slightly.

Shirin returned then, setting down another dish

between them. "Eat, both of you. You look like two people planning a war without rations."

Farah picked up her cup again, staring down into the dark liquid. "Maybe we are. Just not with weapons, but words."

He met her gaze over the rim of his own cup, something unspoken settling between them.

The soft clatter of teacups and the low murmur of conversation filled the Saffron Oasis as the evening deepened. The scent of spiced tea and fresh bread wrapped around them like a comfort, grounding Yasher even as his thoughts remained tangled in the conversation.

Pari returned with a small, satisfied smile, setting a fresh pot of tea on the table. Yasher expected her usual quiet amusement at their bickering, but she sat down without a word. Her fingers lingered against the porcelain of her cup as if she was bracing herself for a question she didn't want to answer.

"What have you been working on?" Farah asked, gesturing toward the bound stack of parchment Pari always carried with her.

Her fingers curled slightly around the stack, and for just a second, just long enough for him to notice, she hesitated.

It was small. A pause. A breath. But it was there.

"Just sketches," she said, thumbing through them, her fingers stained faintly with charcoal. "Places I've been, people I've seen."

Yasher watched as she flipped through them, his own curiosity piqued despite himself. The first few drawings were what he expected. Scenes of the Citadel's streets, the bustling markets, the winding alleys where children played. There was one of Shirin, caught mid-motion pouring tea, the lines of her face softened by the warmth Pari had captured in her strokes. Another of the Mashya's chambers, rendered with meticulous detail, right down to the folds in the heavy banners draped behind the council table.

Then there was one that made Farah pause. He leaned in to see what it was.

Pari had hesitated as she shuffled through her work, but a single sheet slipped from the bottom of the pile, tumbling onto the table's surface.

He reached for it, not wanting it to be stained by the food or the tea, but Farah was faster, plucking it from the table before he could. The moment her gaze settled on the image, her body stiffened.

The drawing showed the two of them, Farah and Yasher, standing together. But they weren't alone. Shadows twisted around them, reaching with claw-like tendrils, their forms unnatural, writhing as if alive. The landscape in the background was unmistakable, with jagged cliffs rising from a storm-churned sea, waves crashing against dark rock. Similar to the landscape from the piece that Pari had shown him the other day, the difference being that it was both of them instead of him standing alone. That was a small favor, at least. Ominous still, but the two of them nonetheless.

"Pari," he said, his voice slow, careful. "What is this?"

Pari pressed her lips together, her fingers tightening around the stack of drawings still in her lap. "I wasn't going to show you that one."

Farah glanced up, her brows drawing together. "Why?"

Pari exhaled, as if trying to decide how much she wanted to say. Her grip on the parchment stack relaxed slightly, her fingers brushing over the edges of the remaining pages. "Because it keeps coming back. Because I can't make it go away."

Farah placed the sketch down on the table, smoothing out its curled edge. "You mean you keep seeing this?"

Pari nodded.

"Usually, when I draw something I've seen, it stops lingering in my head. Like... like spilling water from a cup. The image is on the parchment, not in my head." She tapped the image lightly. "But this one won't go away."

He frowned, his gaze flicking from the drawing to Pari's somber face. "Since when?"

Pari hesitated. "Weeks. Maybe longer."

Farah inhaled sharply. "And Rashnu?"

Pari's fingers curled into her sleeves.

"He still doesn't speak to me," she said softly. "Not like he used to. He used to show me things but he would explain them...choices, paths people could take. Now... now it's just this." She gestured at the image, her voice barely above a whisper. "I don't know what it means, but it feels... wrong. Heavy. Thick. And I think it's coming soon."

He resisted the urge to glance over his shoulder at her tone, like these shadows were right behind him. He knew better than to ignore her visions. Pari might be a child, but she had seen more than most grown men. The God of Death had given her glimpses of fate itself, though what she chose to do with those glimpses was always her own burden.

Pari's hands trembled slightly as she pulled the sketch toward her, her gaze darting between Yasher and Farah as if expecting them to confirm her fears. He exhaled, lowering his voice to something softer, steadier.

"Hey, Little Divine," he said, leaning in just slightly, the warmth in his tone meant to anchor her. "It's just a drawing. It doesn't mean it's happening right this moment."

She didn't look convinced.

"But it won't go away," she murmured. "No matter how many times I draw it, I still see it. Over and over again. Different people. You, or you, people I don't know…"

Farah reached out, brushing Pari's dark hair back from her face, her touch light but grounding.

"Then we'll be ready for whatever comes when it comes," she said simply. No fear, no hesitation, just certainty. "As we always do, together."

Pari hesitated, then nodded slowly, though the tension in her small shoulders remained.

The quiet creak of a door opening drew their attention. Shirin stepped into the room, her sharp gaze sweeping over them before settling on Pari, her lined face softening.

"It's late, Pari *joon*," she said, her voice gentle but firm. "You need rest."

She hesitated for a moment longer before sliding

from the cushion, clutching her sketchbook to her chest, and gave him one last look. "You won't ignore it?"

He felt the weight of the question settle over him, heavier than he liked. He forced a lopsided grin, though it didn't quite reach his eyes. "Since when have I ever ignored your advice?"

Pari narrowed her eyes. "You always do. Remember—"

Farah made a noise that was suspiciously close to a laugh, and he shot her an exaggerated look of betrayal as he cut her off. "I listen sometimes."

Pari only hummed skeptically before allowing Shirin to guide her toward the back rooms. Shirin cast them both a knowing glance before disappearing with the girl, leaving Yasher and Farah alone in the lantern-lit quiet of the shop.

The silence stretched between them for a moment before Farah stood, gathering the edges of her long coat. "We should head back."

He rose as well, stretching before falling into step beside her as they stepped out into the cooling night air. The streets of the Saffron Oasis had quieted, the usual hum of voices and distant music reduced to the occasional sound of footsteps on stone and the rustling of wind through hanging banners.

They walked without speaking at first, their strides naturally aligning as they made their way toward the Citadel. Her expression was unreadable, though he had spent enough time with her to recognize the tension in her posture, the way her fingers twitched slightly at her sides as if resisting the urge to curl into fists.

After a while, he broke the silence, his voice lighter than he felt. "You know, if I'd known you were going to drop in tonight, I would've asked Shirin for something fancier. Maybe a whole roasted lamb. Something suitably extravagant."

Farah gave him a look, unimpressed. "You barely finished the bread on your plate."

"Saving room for hypothetical roasted lamb," he quipped.

She shook her head but didn't pull away when he brushed his arm against hers in an easy, familiar motion.

The cool night breeze carried the scent of salt and spice through the air, the Citadel's distant lanterns glowing like scattered stars. He glanced at her out of the corner of his eye. "You had a long day."

She huffed softly. "You have no idea."

"Ardashir helped you," he noted, testing the words, watching for a reaction.

Farah glanced at him sideways. "He did."

He waited for her to elaborate, but she didn't. Just kept walking, her gaze focused ahead.

He made a face. "That's it? No grand retelling? No recounting of your glorious triumph over the bureaucratic horde? You didn't finally stab one of them, did you?"

She exhaled sharply, and it took him a second to realize it was meant to be a laugh. "Not every battle is worth recounting."

He placed a hand over his heart, feigning disappointment. "And here I thought you were about to admit I'm your favorite person to complain to."

She arched a brow. "You're the only one who doesn't run when I start."

He grinned. "See? That counts for something."

Farah rolled her eyes, but the tension in her shoulders had eased slightly. He let the silence settle between them again, this time more comfortable, less weighted. He pulled her hand toward him, grazing her knuckles with a kiss.

Still sharing a life together.

CHAPTER 6

THEIR DOOR CLICKED SHUT behind them, muffling the world beyond. The nobles, the Parliament, the echos of the past holding on were all far away in this room. The weight of the day still clung to Farah's shoulders, layered like armor she couldn't take off. Arguments, veiled threats, too many eyes watching her every move. She had held her ground through it all, found a surprising ally in Siavash, even managed to walk that fragile line between deference and defiance to the Mashya.

But none of it mattered now. Not here.

The brazier's glow threw soft, golden light across the chamber walls, and the air was warm, touched with the scent of fire-smoothed cedar and iron. She tugged loose the fastenings of her cross coat and let it fall in a heap on the nearest chair, not caring where it landed. Her boots followed with dull thuds against the floor. She'd put them away. Later.

The Saffron Oasis still clung to her skin, the scent of rose tea and sweet smoke, the memory of laughter and conversation not meant for courtly ears. Her pulse was still threaded with it, with the heat of his gaze when she'd met him there, and the way her name had left his lips like it was something precious.

Yasher stood near the foot of the bed, arms crossed, a lazy grin tugging at the corner of his mouth. His hair was tousled from the wind, his collar loose, sleeves pushed up like he'd just wandered out of a tavern instead of walking into the Citadel.

"I expected you to be exhausted," he said, voice light but edged with something more careful. "Usually you dive headfirst into sleep and leave me to fight off your boots."

She crossed the space between them, slow and deliberate, until the air was too thin to breathe.

"I am exhausted," she said, reaching for the collar of his shirt. Her fingers curled in the fabric. "But I don't want to sleep."

She pushed at his shirt, fingers impatient, needing the feel of his skin more than the softness of words. He let her strip it away, the fabric whispering to the floor. Her palms found the warmth of his back—sun-touched skin stretched over lean muscle, the familiar curve of his spine beneath her fingers, scars that held stories from his life. He tensed, not in surprise, but as if her touch had ignited something he'd been holding all day.

He leaned in, his mouth brushing the sensitive spot just beneath her jaw, breath warm as it ghosted across her throat. When his teeth grazed her there, she shivered. Her grip at his waist tightened instinctively, grounding herself in the press of him.

His hands slipped beneath her tunic, gathering the fabric slowly, reverently. She lifted her arms, letting him peel it away. Cool air kissed her skin, followed by the heavier heat of his gaze. He didn't speak right away, just looked at her like she was something sacred.

"Say what you're thinking," she whispered.

He exhaled a laugh, breathless. "If I ever take this for granted, I need to be put in the ground."

Then his hands were on her again, slow and certain, trailing up her sides. His mouth followed, brushing over her collarbone with aching patience. She tilted her head, letting him find his path. Her fingers slid into his hair, pulling him closer, anchoring him to her.

He guided her back until her knees touched the bed. She sank into it, reached for him as he followed, his body warm and solid over hers. She pulled him down, wanting the weight of him, the steadiness of him, the way he made her forget the rest of the world.

"Just this," she whispered. "Just now."

"I wasn't planning to do anything else," he said, then he kissed her.

Slow. Deep. The kind of kiss that unraveled her. That left no space for anything but him.

His hands moved like he was memorizing her again, like her skin held the only truth that mattered.

She arched into him, breath catching as he kissed down the column of her throat, over her collarbone, lower still. Each pass of his lips stirred something in her, something coiled tight. The rasp of his stubble scraped lightly over her ribs, the contrast sharp and exquisite.

"You're impatient," he murmured against her skin.

"And you talk too much," she breathed, though her fingers curled in his hair, keeping him close.

He laughed, the sound rough, intimate and then he was kissing her again. The kiss pulled something deeper from her, something raw and full. She wrapped her legs around his waist, anchoring him to her. Their bodies aligned with practiced ease, as natural as breathing.

His breath stuttered against her lips, and still he moved slowly, like he wanted to feel everything.

"Phoenix," he whispered.

She kissed him again, silencing the word before it could carry too much weight. Her nails scraped lightly down his back and he groaned, low and helpless, all control finally slipping away.

There was nothing careful after that—only movement and sound, the press of mouths and the clutch of hands. Her world narrowed to the feel of him, the way he moved with her, the breathless rhythm that built between them until her name broke on his lips and she shattered beneath him. He followed with a sound she felt in her chest, his body sinking into hers, both of them trembling in the aftermath.

He curled beside her, one arm slung around her waist, his breath still ragged. Farah stared at the ceiling for a long moment, her chest rising and falling with his.

She had stopped thinking about anything but the two of them, here, in the moment. Just for a while. It was wonderful. She reached out, brushing a stray lock of his hair from his face. He caught her wrist before she could pull away and pressed a kiss to her palm. A welcomed warmth curled in her chest.

She breathed in slowly, grounding herself against the slow rise and fall of his chest, and let her fingers trace a lazy pattern along his shoulder.

But even now, her curiosity stirred. And her mind, traitorous and tireless, wasn't ready to let go of earlier words.

She wanted to know. Needed to understand what had unsettled him earlier, what Jeta Veseli had said to get beneath his skin in ways few ever did. She could feel it still in the way his muscles had held tension through the walk home. In the way his kiss had felt just a little more searching, like he needed something from her he hadn't said out loud.

"So…" she murmured, her voice soft, "how was the meeting with Jeta, really?"

He groaned, throwing his arm over his face in theatrical defeat. "Twelve Hells, Phoenix, is this really the moment to talk about the old woman?"

He gestured vaguely between them. "We're lying in bed, basking in the afterglow of my undeniable charm, and you want to discuss my afternoon being emotionally filleted by a woman who looks like she could kill me with the damned bells in her hair if not just by her words?"

She smirked, utterly unbothered. "You did meet with her, then."

He exhaled like a man being asked to recount a particularly traumatic encounter. Rubbed a hand over his face, as if trying to physically wipe the memory away.

"Met is a strong word," he muttered.

"Oh?" she prompted, settling more fully against him, her cheek brushing his shoulder.

He paused. "I don't know what to make of her."

She had all the patience in the world to wait him out. She smirked lazily, but beneath it, she was watching. The way he deflected, the way his fingers toyed with the stray curl of her hair like he needed something to anchor him. Yasher avoided things in the same way he gambled. Carefully, with charm first, truth last. But charm wouldn't work on the old woman, and that was what unsettled him most, wasn't it?

He groaned again, this time muffling the sound in her hair that had fully escaped the braid. "More like she poked at me until I got irritated, dismissed everything I thought I knew about my Talent, and then decided I wasn't ready to learn."

His fingers twitched against her. "Does that sound like a meeting to you?"

She hummed, shifting onto her side to see his face more clearly. The dim brazier cast flickering gold over his features, sharpening the line of his jaw, the bridge of his nose.

She had known Jeta Vesili to be many things. Calculating, discerning, impossibly patient, but never careless. She would not have agreed to teach him unless she saw something worth the effort.

"Yes, it sounds exactly like Jeta," she said stifling a chuckle at his frustration. What was it that she saw in him to have pushed him this far into frustration in a single day?

She had trained the Beloveds in combat and survival using their Talents, yes, but she had never been interested in just skill. She didn't waste time on people who wouldn't amount to something, sending them off to any of the other tutors when they disappointed her.

He blinked. "You know her that well?"

"She's always been at the Citadel," she murmured. "I worked with a different tutor growing up, but everyone knew Jeta. Feared her, a little."

His frown deepened. "And?"

She chose her words carefully, knowing it would either irritate him or intrigue him, more than likely the latter. "The Mashyana hated her."

That made him pause.

"Hated?" he echoed.

A wry smile flickered at the corner of her lips. "She never let it show in court of course, but yes, in private she would rail about her methods, her dress, everything to do with the old woman. Jeta was one of the few Behnaz tolerated only out of necessity because she got results. She trained the Beloveds, but she was never one of us."

His brows furrowed. "Why?"

She traced absent patterns against his shoulder again, thinking. "Beyond being half foreign which Behnaz always blamed for her manners, Jeta never played by the court's rules, never played especially to Behnaz. She wasn't impressed by power, didn't bend or flatter the way others did. That made her useful, but it also made her dangerous."

He snorted softly. "Sounds familiar."

She arched a brow. "If you're comparing her to yourself, I promise, you are far more annoying and insufferable."

He laughed, warm and easy—but it didn't last.

"She never had me use my Talent once, to see what it does. Just kept asking questions, poking at things I didn't want poked at, or, even worse, in flowery verse of incomprehensible philosophy." His fingers twitched against the sheet. "It felt like a waste of time."

But there was something about the way he said it, something too sharp beneath the words. Yasher could complain about anything, Damned Divine, he enjoyed it to no end. But this wasn't just frustration. It was defense. A barrier thrown up between himself and whatever Jeta had seen in him.

She thought about the gala, the way he had kept his Luck buried so deep it might as well have not existed. A man used to wielding chance itself should have felt at ease in a game of power and influence. Yasher had been too careful, too contained, nothing out of place. She could feel it with every breath he took in the ballroom last night.

She exhaled, keeping her voice neutral. "She doesn't waste her time. If she's prodding, she's looking for something."

His jaw tightened. "Well, she's not going to find much as long as all she does is talk at me."

She wasn't so sure. Jeta had seen something. The woman had been training Talented individuals her entire life. She didn't make mistakes.

She tilted her head, considering. "She wouldn't have agreed to train you if she thought that. She would have walked away without an acknowledgment of your existence. I saw it happen even with Beloveds who'd not had whatever it was she wanted out of them. They were sent to other tutors, but for the rest of their time, they were like blank spots in her vision."

She traced her fingers along his arm, grounding him as much as herself. Yasher wasn't an easy man to shake, but she could feel it, the undercurrent of tension running through him like a wire pulled too tight.

His expression flickered, something guarded settling behind his eyes. He turned onto his side, mirroring her, their faces only inches apart. "You trust her?"

Farah exhaled slowly. "I trust that she knows more about Talents than almost anyone at the Citadel."

"Not an answer, Phoenix."

Did she trust Jeta? No. Not in the way she trusted Yasher, or even Siavash, despite their differences. The old woman had always been an outsider, existing in the spaces between power rather than standing in it. The Mashyana had tolerated her, not valued her, and Farah had learned long ago to be wary of those who survived in that court without ever pledging allegiance.

She shook her head slightly. "No. I don't trust her. I don't know her. But I don't think she's your enemy."

His lips pressed into a thin line. He didn't like that answer, but he didn't argue.

She reached out, brushing a thumb along his cheekbone. "She doesn't do things without purpose. If she's taking you on, she sees something in you."

His gaze flickered. "Or she just enjoys watching me squirm."

She laughed. "That's also possible. It is enjoyable to watch you squirm."

He groaned again, covering his face with one hand. "Remind me why I agreed to this?"

She shifted closer, her bare leg sliding over his beneath the sheets. "Because you know you need it."

He sighed but didn't argue.

Farah let the silence settle between them, her fingers continuing their slow patterns against his skin. She could feel the tension still coiled in him, the frustration that hadn't faded with release, the way his mind was still turning over whatever the old tutor had said to him.

She wouldn't push more, at least not tonight.

Instead, she pressed a kiss to his shoulder, the warmth of him steady beneath her lips.

"Sleep," she murmured. "Tomorrow will come soon enough."

He huffed a quiet laugh, letting his arm drape over her waist, pulling her in. "It always does."

But his grip tightened slightly, and Farah knew despite the irritation, despite his frustration, he wasn't going to walk away from Jeta. Because she asked him.

THE *RAP-RAP-RAP* of knuckles against wood jolted Farah from sleep. Urgent. Insistent. Not a measured summons, but a demand. The sound cut through the warmth of the room like a blade, slicing away sleep in an instant.

She was upright before she was fully conscious, instinct shoving her into motion. The sheets pooled at her waist, her skin still flushed with the residual heat of Yasher beside her.

The knocking came again—harder this time, frantic.

"Twelve fucking hells..." Yasher groaned into the pillow, his voice slurred with sleep. "It's the middle of the bloody night."

She kicked off the sheets, rising into the cool air, her bare skin prickling as the temperature shift stole away what was left of warmth. The contrast was jarring, going from soft silk, body heat, the press of Yasher's limbs against hers, now replaced by cold air, sharp urgency, and the tightening edge of reality snapping back into place.

She barely registered that she was naked as she reached for her cross-coat, shrugging it on in a practiced motion to cover herself. The linen lining dragged against her still-warm skin.

The door. Focus.

The cold stone met her bare feet as she crossed the room in a few quick strides. Behind her, Yasher pushed himself onto one elbow, squinting against the dim glow of the low light. His hair was a tousled mess, his bare shoulders still marked with the ghost of her nails.

Another knock.

"There better be fire," Yasher stretched, his voice half-distracted. "Or at least a little blood to justify this rude..."

Farah wrenched the door open before he could finish.

The corridor beyond was dimly lit, the flickering sconces barely illuminating the figure in the doorway. A royal guard, clad in the Mashya's colors of deep blue and gold, his breath fast and shallow, the sheen of sweat at his collar catching in the light.

"The Mashya requires you both. Immediately," the guard said, his voice clipped, controlled—but the urgency in his eyes gave him away.

"What's happened?"

The guard hesitated, his mouth tightening into a firm line. "I was ordered to retrieve you. The Mashya is waiting in his private chambers," he said instead.

Behind her, Yasher let out a muffled groan as he sat up, rubbing a hand through his disheveled hair. He squinted against the dim light, his bare chest rising and falling with slow, steady breaths as he worked through his sleep-hazed thoughts. The bed creaked as Yasher shifted fully upright, the sheets slipping to his waist.

"Great," he muttered, voice still thick from sleep. "Am I at least allowed breeches for this, or is this a more casual affair?"

The guard blinked. His shoulders locked into something too stiff, his mouth tightening.

She turned away from the door long enough to yank on her trousers under the coat, lacing them tight, and grabbing her boots from the floor. Yasher, still looking gloriously unbothered, scratched his chest absently before finally getting up. He stretched his arms above his head, utterly naked, shameless as ever.

The guard averted his eyes.

Yasher smirked as he bent to grab his discarded shirt. "Twelve Hells, you'd think you'd never seen a naked man before."

She shot him a look, grabbing his trousers and tossing them at him—hard.

"Get dressed."

He caught them with a laugh but obeyed.

She turned back to the guard. "We're coming."

The man nodded sharply, stepping back.

She pulled up her boots in quick, precise motions, tightening the lacings with more force than necessary. Her mind was a battlefield of worst-case scenarios. A breach in the Citadel's defenses? An assassination attempt? Something happened to Rostam? The thought struck like a blade, quick and cold. Her chest tightened, but she shoved the fear aside. *No use jumping to conclusions. Not yet.*

Yasher sighed, pulling his shirt over his head as he muttered, "Do I at least have time to grab tea?"

Farah shot him another look, one that would have ruined any other man.

"Right, not the time." He pulled on his boots and straightened, rolling out his shoulders as though shaking off the last remnants of sleep. "At least tell me we're getting something before the Mashya asks us to solve his problems again."

She didn't have an answer for that. Instead, she turned back to the guard. "Let's go."

The man nodded sharply and stepped back, falling into step beside them as they strode into the corridor.

The air was thick with the scent of old stone and lingering lamp oil, and the usual night sounds of the Citadel felt distant, muffled. The palace was never truly silent. There were always murmurs of passing guards, the faint hum of the sea in the distance, the occasional flicker of torchlight catching on movement.

Yasher's voice was quiet, but edged with curiosity as he fell in step with her. "This feels like bad news."

Her hands clenched at her sides. "It usually is at this hour."

They moved swiftly through the darkened halls, their footsteps quiet against the polished marble. The grand arches loomed above them, the intricate designs carved into the stone barely visible in the low light.

Her mind churned through every possibility as they neared the Mashya's chambers. She could only hope that Enayat's call in the middle of the night was something she could stab and not someone she'd need to convince to do something.

Beside her, Yasher walked with easy, unhurried steps, as if this were any other stroll through the Citadel. But Farah wasn't fooled.

He wasn't looking at her. He was looking at everything else.

The sconces lining the halls. The number of passing guards, or the lack of them. The stiffness in the men they did see, the subtle way they avoided looking at them. Cataloguing everything, checking out the probabilities surrounding them. He got a certain look in his eyes when he was waiting on his Luck to tell him something.

"Feels like everyone's holding their breath," he murmured, barely above a whisper. He hummed, but it wasn't a real sound. It was a confirmation.

Farah knew the moment he came to the same conclusion she had.

Whatever awaited them beyond the Mashya's doors, it was not good.

CHAPTER 7

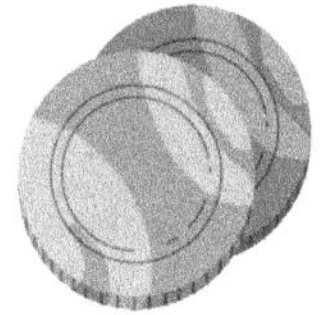

THE MASHYA'S chambers loomed ahead, the golden doors catching in the candlelight, reflecting something too warm for how cold Yasher suddenly felt. He should've expected this. His Luck let him know that the knock at the door was something important, just not exactly what.

He took a slow, measured breath and rolled his shoulders, trying to shake the unease clinging to his skin like damp silk. Beside him, Farah's stride was unwavering, her posture unreadable. Her hands weren't fists yet, but they would be soon enough, he was sure.

Harun, the royal guardsman who had pounded on their door, led them ahead with quick, clipped steps. Yasher recognized him from their late-night card games, the kind of soldier who had seen enough trouble to know when something was *worse* than it sounded. And the tightness in his shoulders? The way he didn't look back?

He already knew this was bad.

Harun rapped twice against the gilded surface before pushing the doors open.

The Mashya's chambers were warm, filled with the low flicker of candlelight and the lingering scent of old parchment and ink. The air held a faint trace of sandalwood and something richer beneath it, wine, perhaps, or exhaustion. Enayat stood near the long table in the center of the room, his silk robe hanging loosely over his shoulders as if he had thrown it on in haste. His dark hair, shot through with more silver every day, was slightly tousled, and his usually composed features were set in tight lines.

But it wasn't just Enayat. Rostam stood by the hearth, arms crossed, his battle-worn features cast in sharp relief against the firelight. His shirt was untucked, the collar loose, his belt hanging undone from where it had been hastily strapped on. He looked like he had been dragged from sleep just as abruptly as they had, his longer hair loose and not in its normal tail.

"Good, you're here," the Mashya said. His voice was steady, but there was an edge to it, a thread of urgency woven beneath his usual poise. His dark eyes flicked between them, assessing. "Close the doors."

Yasher did as he was told, the dull thud settling into his bones. Farah took three steps forward, straight to the heart of the room, her presence commanding even before she spoke.

"What's happened?"

Enayat exhaled, pressing his fingers to the bridge of his nose. "There's been an incident in Sakasan."

He frowned. Sakasan. If he remembered the Emari

map that Farah had, it was a coastal town near the Asharan Cliffs down to the south of the kingdom. He'd not been that way before, but from what little he'd picked up, it felt like the very place Pari had drawn in her vision, surrounded by shadows. His Luck pitched as if in agreement to his thoughts. *Twelve Hells.*

"A local patrol along the roads went missing earlier," Rostam picked up, his voice rough but measured. "At first, we thought it was an accident, either bad weather or something else innocuous. But now the entire town has gone silent. No messages. No travelers. The last report we received came from a merchant caravan trying to pass through who made the barges bring them over as soon as they reach Rumatin. The town's gate was locked tight, and no one visible."

"They said the cliffs were crawling with shadows," Enayat added grimly.

Yasher's pulse thrummed against his ribs. He glanced at Farah, and from the way her brow furrowed, he knew she was thinking the same thing.

Mazdavir. The Darkness that terrified even the Unnamed Gods.

The shadows in Pari's drawings. The pull of something dark against the edges of their awareness.

Farah's voice was even, but there was steel beneath it. "You think it's the corruption."

The Mashya didn't hesitate. "I think it's something we can't ignore."

His pulse slowed. A thick, deliberate beat.

Shadows were crawling along the cliffs.

The words shouldn't have made his stomach turn, but they did.

It was just a merchant's story, just a persistent vision from a little girl.

Except it wasn't, of course.

He forced a grin, shifting his weight onto one foot. "You woke us up because a few patrolmen got lost in the dark?"

Rostam shot him a look. Not irritation. Not amusement. Just flat, solid distaste.

"This isn't just lost men," Enayat said. "This is a dead town."

Enayat's gaze flicked to Farah first, then to him.

"I need you to go to Sakasan. See what's happening. If the corruption has taken hold, if Mazdavir's influence is spreading…" He shook his head, his expression dark. "We need to know. So far rumors of shadows coming in and taking over have been just the stuff of legend, but I'm afraid we've been lulled into a sense of false security since… since Behnaz's death."

"We'll leave at first light," Farah said.

He exhaled slowly, rubbing a hand over his jaw.

Of course we will.

His Luck had been good lately, playing along mostly. That was the problem.

Jeta had tried to tell him—Luck wasn't something he could trap in a box and pull out when needed. He'd done it at the gala, shoved it into a cage, forced it into a shape it didn't want to take. He had pushed and pulled it until it became something unnatural, something too still. It was as if these Emari gods laughed at him.

Rostam shifted. His dark eyes fixed on Farah, his expression unreadable, but his voice was firm. "You're not going in alone."

Farah bristled. He felt it before she said a word.

"Yasher will be with me," she said, her tone cool and absolute.

Rostam didn't flinch. "Not enough."

He wasn't wrong. Yasher knew that, even if it sat like gravel in his gut.

Luck wouldn't do shit against shadows.

Still, he couldn't help himself when it came to poking the old bear that was Rostam.

He shifted, just slightly, and offered Rostam a lopsided smile. "What's the plan then? Full procession? Trumpets? Maybe a dramatic horse or two?"

Rostam's glare could've peeled paint.

"Just a small, competent team," he said flatly. "But it will take a few days to pull together."

Yasher let out a soft hum, glancing at Farah. "Did you hear that? He thinks we're incompetent."

That earned him a twitch of her lips. Barely there, but he saw it.

Too bad it also earned him the tightening of Rostam's jaw. That look, the one that promised Yasher might find himself having a holiday in a cell downstairs if he kept talking, settled into place.

Probably best to stop while he was ahead. Or at least, *not* behind bars.

After a breath, the moment passed. Rostam exhaled, slow and deliberate, his attention shifting back to Farah, as if he no longer warranted acknowledgment.

Fine by him. He had stopped trying to win the man over a long time ago.

If not for one shared truth, their love for Farah, their need to keep her safe, Rostam probably would've had him tossed off the island the moment he opened his mouth. As it was, tolerance was the closest thing they had to understanding.

She loved them both. That was the only reason he was still in the room.

He let the silence stretch, kept his mouth shut for once, watching as she worked through her frustration. Her jaw was tight, eyes narrowed slightly as she weighed the inevitability of taking a detachment.

Then Enayat spoke, voice quieter, steadier. "Rostam's right. This isn't a simple investigation. If the reports are accurate, you'll need more than just the two of you."

Rostam didn't look at Yasher when he replied. "I'm not sending an army. Just a small, competent team, of my choosing, to make sure you have hands if you need them."

She sighed, folding her arms over her chest. "Fine. But before we leave, I want to speak with whoever the merchants brought with them."

Enayat tilted his head. "Who?"

"The ones the caravan found." Her gaze sharpened. "You wouldn't have woken us for a patrol gone missing and a frantic merchant, even with the shadows being spoken of. But someone managed to escape Sakasan, didn't they? They told you something."

A flicker of something passed across Enayat's face. Approval, perhaps. He inclined his head. "Yes. The caravan brought a family in with them a few hours ago. They're resting in the lower guest wing of the Citadel. They are... still very shaken from what they experienced. Haven't spoken about anything yet."

"I want to hear what they saw, what they experienced," Farah said. "Before we ride into whatever's waiting for us."

Rostam nodded. "I'll have them brought to you in the morning."

Yasher shook his head as he leaned against the closed doors. "Should've known you'd drag me into something cursed. Again."

Farah arched a brow at him, her lips twitching in the faintest hint of a smirk. "Wouldn't be the first time, won't be the last, I'm sure."

Enayat stepped forward, his tone firm but quiet.

"This isn't a mission I send you on lightly. I know what I'm asking." His gaze lingered on Farah before flicking to Yasher. "And I know how much I have already asked of both of you."

For the first time, he heard the exhaustion beneath Enayat's words. The Mashya wasn't blind. He knew the burdens they carried. Knew the weight of what they had been through. And yet, he still needed them to go and do it again.

Finally, he sighed and pushed off the door.

"Well," he said, grinning just enough to keep the edge from cutting too deep. "Guess we'd better start packing. What do you wear to confront shadows again?"

Farah shook her head at him, but there was warmth in her eyes. And that was enough.

Enayat dipped his chin. "Rostam will have provisions prepared for you. You leave in no more than three days."

With that, the Mashya turned back to the maps spread across the table, already lost in the next problem demanding his attention.

Farah moved toward the door, her posture shifting back into something composed, unreadable. He followed, casting one last glance at the flickering candlelight behind them before stepping into the corridor.

As the doors shut behind them, Yasher exhaled and ran a hand through his hair.

"Well, Phoenix," he murmured. "Looks like we're heading for the Cliffs after all. Little Divine's drawing has come round."

Farah's gaze was unreadable in the dim torchlight, but she didn't argue.

And that, more than anything, told him exactly how serious this was.

MORNING LIGHT STRETCHED LONG over the Citadel, burning away the last clinging traces of night. The air still carried the crispness of dawn, but the city was already stirring, carts rattling over stone streets, voices rising as merchants set up for the day.

Yasher made his way toward the docks. Farah was already with the family that had fled Sakasan, and as much as he wanted to be there, he knew better than to add more eyes to the conversation. Fewer people meant more honesty, and no one knew how to pry truth from the wary better than Farah.

That left him with time to kill before finalizing their plans and supplies.

He figured Kambiz would already be busy at the tavern, maybe setting up an early dice game or skimming coins off unsuspecting sailors. A good round of cards might do him some good, keep his mind from turning circles over what Pari had drawn, what she had seen. The Cliffs, the shadows reaching for him and Farah—

"Saqalu, you're out early."

He turned, already knowing who he'd see.

Jeta Veseli stood a few steps away, her presence as intentional as ever. Her headscarf was tucked neatly around her dark, graying curls, her deep green coat embroidered with gold glinting in the early light. Her hand rested loosely on the head of a cane she didn't seem to actually need, the wood covered in carved vines sprouting roses.

Running into her irritated him more than it should have.

Her expression was unreadable, as he was coming to expect. Assessing without being outright confrontational, a woman who had spent her life watching and weighing what was worth speaking aloud.

He tensed, though he kept his stance easy, shifting his weight as if this was a casual run-in rather than something inevitable. Jeta had a way of finding people when they least wanted to be found he was also coming to find.

"Veseli," he greeted, lifting a brow to see if she reacted to his dropping her honorific of Khānum. The Emari seemed to be very particular about using the proper ones, and he took advantage of that whenever possible. "Didn't expect to see you here. You out for a morning stroll, or did the gods send you to test my patience for another day?"

She hummed a little. "You're not the first man to ask me that, you know. Though usually, they ask after I've had a proper conversation with them, not before."

A quiet laugh escaped. "I'm getting ahead of myself, then."

"You usually do."

She let that sit between them for a beat, gaze sharp, as if she were peeling back layers of him just by standing there.

He exhaled, tilting his head. "You're here for me." It wasn't a question.

"Not everything is about you, *saqalu*," she said mildly. "Though, in this case, yes. I wanted to see if you were ready yet, so I thought I'd take the choice out of your hands of avoiding me after your... demonstration yesterday."

He rolled his shoulders. "Not my fault you insist on cryptic lessons of philosophy instead of actual training."

Jeta smirked, but there was something knowing in the way she looked at him. "You think what I did isn't training?"

"Feels more like a waste of time. Many words of nothing in particular."

"Mm. And yet, here you are, still thinking about it. Tell me, did you feel anything last night? A shift? A pull?"

He had felt something—before his mind had made sense of it, before he could call it anything other than wrong, but then Harun had banged on their chamber door. His breath had hitched, his pulse had skipped like a misdealt hand.

It had been nothing, just a figment his mind conjured of the timing. Hadn't it?

Jeta watched him closely, like a gambler waiting for a tell.

"You're still resisting," she murmured, shaking her head. "Still running from what's already in your hands."

"Running is a strong word," he muttered.

Jeta chuckled, low and amused. "You Koulan have always had a knack for avoiding what you don't want to face."

Something in the way she said it made his spine stiffen.

"Ah, I'd almost forgotten you aren't from Emari, the way you carry on, but from the north in Rokhaz. You are part of the Lom, aren't you?" she mused, tilting her head in a way that made him feel pinned beneath her gaze. "I can see it in the way you move, and a little in your features. You remind me of someone I knew long ago."

He kept his tone light, casual, trying not to swallow. "You knew a lot of people long ago, I imagine. Lots of years to meet and annoy people."

Her lips curved, but there was something knowing in her expression. "That I did. And yet, some leave more of a mark than others."

She brushed nonexistent dust from her coat. "You're heading to the docks, yes? To waste time with cards while your mind churns over what you'd rather ignore?"

He narrowed his eyes. "You've got a real talent for making people regret running into you."

Jeta laughed. "*Oh, saqalu,* if you regretted it, you wouldn't still be standing here."

She wasn't wrong. And that irritated him more.

He exhaled sharply. "I'm not making promises, Veseli. But when I return from this... task they have for us in a few weeks, we will talk again."

"I wouldn't ask you to promise me anything. I only ask that you stop lying to yourself about what's already happening."

She turned, adjusting her scarf, the conversation apparently finished in her mind.

He ran a hand through his hair, cursing under his breath.

Damned old woman.

"Enjoy your day," he muttered.

Jeta didn't look back. "Enjoy your losing streak, *saqalu.*"

He watched her go, his pulse steady but his mind restless. He didn't like how easily she got under his skin.

Shaking his head, he shoved his hands in his pockets and continued toward the docks, hoping Kambiz had a game going to give him something to shake off the twitch that had appeared running down his cheek.

THE DOCKS of the Citadel were already humming with life, the air thick with salt, fish, and the sharp scent of burning oil from lanterns still guttering in the early light. Yasher stepped onto the worn wooden planks, moving past crates of imported spices and cloth from the mainland, past dockhands rolling barrels toward waiting carts. The rhythm of the place was constant and predictable, a steady beat against the chaos swirling in his head.

Jeta's words sunk into his skin like burrs he couldn't shake.

Then there was the way his Luck had lurched last night that he'd buried behind being woken by a knock at the door in the middle of the night. Not a roll of the dice, not a gambler's instinct, but something deeper. A pull. A shift. Like a tide changing course, dragging him somewhere whether he wanted it or not. Had that old woman not pointed it out, he could have ignored it. But it had happened a moment before the first knock.

He rubbed a hand over his jaw. He'd barely gotten a handful of hours of sleep, and it was starting to catch up to him. The weight behind his eyes, the low, buzzing fatigue that made everything feel half a step out of sync. *Thinking too much.*

He stepped through the open doorway to the dockside tavern, stepping into the dim warmth of the place. The scent of spiced rum and old wood filled the air, mingling with the low murmur of conversation and the occasional burst of laughter. Dockworkers crowded the back corner, already deep into a round of cards, their faces drawn with the kind of focus that only came from putting too much coin on the table.

And Kambiz was exactly where he expected her to be. Balancing a tray on her hip, her dark curls pinned back in a loose twist, her expression already sliding into a knowing smirk."You look like trouble waiting to happen," she said, "Or at least a drink to drown it in."

"Maybe both," he admitted, leaning against the bar.

Kambiz snorted. "That bad?"

He shrugged, reaching for a stool. "Depends. You ever heard the word *saqalu*?"

Kambiz stilled for half a second before bursting into laughter. A genuine, full-bodied laugh that had a few of the nearby dockhands glancing over.

"*Saqalu*?" she repeated with a raised eyebrow, chuckling. "You've been hanging around with grandfathers' fathers, have you? Your Emarian has gotten good, but I'm not surprised you didn't understand it. That's old Emarian. Where did you hear it?"

He smirked. "Just someone talking. Thought I misheard at first."

Kambiz grinned, setting the tray down. "That's an old one. My grandmother used to call the chronic gamblers that."

"What's it mean?"

She leaned her elbow on the bar, eyes glinting with amusement. "Roughly? *Lucky bastard*."

He let out a short laugh, shaking his head. "That supposed to be an insult or a compliment?"

Kambiz shrugged. "Depends on how much trouble your Luck's gotten you into."

He huffed. "Enough."

Kambiz smirked. "Then it fits." She jerked her chin toward the back. "Cards are running, if you're looking to find some coin if you're here to… delay again."

For a moment, he considered it. The easy pull of the game, the weight of the cards between his fingers, the rush of a well-played hand. But the thought sat wrong today.

Jeta's words echoed in his mind. *Enjoy your losing streak.* Best not test that coming to pass from that old witch.

He shook his head. "Not today."

She studied him for a beat, her gaze sharp, calculating. Yasher had met plenty of gamblers who thought they understood people, who thought they could read a twitch of a hand or a flicker of hesitation.

But Kambiz? She didn't just read tells at a table. She read people the way someone who's spent their whole life surviving learns to, not needing a Talent to do it. Which was exactly why he trusted her.

She poured him a drink instead, the clink of glass filling the quiet space between them. "Then you'd better drink."

He took the cup with a half-smile, letting the burn settle warm in his chest before exhaling slowly.

"Now that is good advice."

She clinked her own glass against his before leaning an elbow on the bar. "So." Her voice had that knowing lilt, the one that usually preceded her dragging something out of him. "You gonna tell me what's got you looking like you just walked through a storm, or are we pretending you're here just for the atmosphere? Get into a fight with your Khānum?"

He rolled the cup between his fingers, studying the amber liquid. "Maybe I just wanted to be somewhere that didn't feel like the Citadel was closing in on me."

She snorted. "Fair enough. That place doesn't seem to be suited for you, honestly. All that gold and marble? So sterile, so clean."

He smirked. "What, you saying I don't fit in with the nobles?"

She arched a brow. "I'm saying you'd rather be anywhere else if it weren't for you being in so deeply with the Hand. That's why you disappear from here for a while, then come back like you want to let the room upstairs again."

He huffed a short laugh. "You've known me, what, a year? That really enough time to read me like a book?"

She tilted her head. "A year's plenty if you know what to look for. You walked off that barge last winter like a man who didn't plan on staying. And yet, here you are, wearing expensive weave in the cheapest way."

He tapped a finger against the rim of his cup. "Lucky me."

She smirked. "More like unlucky. Anyone with half a brain could see you were just passing through. But now? You're tangled up in the Mashya's business. And worse, you're tangled up with *her*, but I don't think that bothers you at all."

Kambiz leaned in slightly, lowering her voice just enough to keep the conversation private. "You ever stop to wonder if the island's keeping you here, pulling you to stay?"

He exhaled sharply through his nose, staring down at his drink. "You think I'm cursed?"

Kambiz gave him a slow, knowing smile. "Not cursed. Just caught. And while you never struck me as someone to allow themselves to get caught, you seem to be comfortable, nay, happy."

He rolled his shoulders, letting the words settle. She wasn't wrong. He hadn't expected to stay. Hell, he hadn't planned to. But then Farah had happened, and everything shifted, the way the tides change without warning.

Kambiz tilted her head, watching him like she was waiting for him to say something more. When he didn't, she sighed and pushed the bottle toward him. "Another?"

He hesitated. It would be easy to keep drinking, to sink into the familiar warmth of it, let the worries of the day slip away for a little while. But he shook his head. "Better not. Got things to do. Journeys to prepare for."

Kambiz gave him a knowing smirk. "Things, huh? Sounds serious."

He rubbed the back of his neck. "Let's just say I've got a long road ahead."

Kambiz chuckled, picking up her tray again. "Then don't trip over your own Luck on the way."

He tossed a few coins onto the counter, pushing away from the bar with an easy grin. "No promises."

She chuckled, already shifting her focus back to her waiting customers. But her words stayed with him, curling around his thoughts like smoke.

You ever stop to wonder if the island's keeping you here?

The street outside was bright, the sky an endless stretch of blue, but Yasher still felt the weight of the conversation pressing against him. He hadn't meant to stay. That had never been the plan.

He'd always been good at slipping away, at leaving without a trace, at moving through places without letting them get under his skin. Home was always a strange concept to him, after all he'd been through. The war, the soldiers, all the death, had made sure of that. Everywhere else had been temporary, caravans, villages, towns, whole countries passed through with barely a trace left behind.

Emari had always been just another stop on the map. But now, it wasn't. Now, it was something else. And the reason for that? Farah.

His hands slid into his pockets, and for a moment, he felt the weight of the city against his chest. It wasn't just Farah, but she was the tether, the thing that held him here. The thing that had pulled him in, that had made him hesitate long enough for the world around her to take hold, staying here for of all things his heart when that would have been laughable to the man who showed up at that tavern.

He stepped into the morning light, rolling his shoulders, still trying to shake off the lingering weight of the conversation. His boots hit the cobblestones with familiar ease, his pace unhurried—until he felt it.

A flicker, a shift in the air.

Not much. Just a whisper of something moving

beneath the surface, like the roll of dice before they settled.

His steps slowed. He glanced to his left, then his right, scanning the street as instinct kicked in.

There.

Two dockhands, arms laden with crates, moving toward each other from opposite directions. One misstep, and they'd collide—the kind of moment that happened every day, mundane and forgettable. Except he *felt* it before it happened, before either of them even knew they were on a collision course.

He adjusted his pace, stepping sideways without thinking. A heartbeat later, the men crashed together, one of them swearing as he fumbled the crate, the scent of crushed fruit spilling into the air.

He exhaled slowly. He didn't know if he'd avoided bad luck or simply sidestepped into a better hand.

That was the problem, wasn't it?

Luck moved, whether he willed it or not. Whether he understood it or not.

Jeta would have something poetic and useless to say about that.

He shook his head, rolling his shoulders again as he pushed forward.

The city stretched before him, golden light spilling over the rooftops, casting long shadows between the winding alleys. The scent of salt and spice filled the air, the slow churn of the tide echoing against the docks. The morning crowd was already in full motion.

His hands flexed at his sides, itching for motion, for distraction. He knew himself, knew that when the walls of a place started pressing in, when his name became too familiar in the mouths of others, when the stakes grew too high, he left. Before his Luck pushed too far, when people got hurt. Also, before he could be caught, before he could be expected to stay.

His Luck had made that decision for him to stay. But more than that, she had too. Farah's pull was something he couldn't escape, didn't want to escape from, whether his Luck pulled them together or just allowed it to happen.

She was the weight in his chest when he thought of leaving. The pull that kept him here, in this city of stone and shadow, of politics and expectations, of war and whispers and things he had never wanted to be a part of.

She had become a part of him, in ways he had never let anyone else be.

If he left, he wouldn't just be leaving the Citadel. He'd be leaving her, and that was the one thing he knew he could never do.

Not now. Not ever.

His jaw tightened, exhaling slow and measured. *Twelve Hells.*

The last time he'd felt a pull like this, he'd ended up in Emari, grinning over a hand of cards that changed everything, having Farah come into the tavern like one of their Emarian gods to swoop in and take him on an adventure.

And now? Now the pull was stronger, stronger than it had ever been.

And it wasn't just leading him toward a city this time.

It was leading him toward the Cliffs. The Darkness. The thing Pari had seen waiting for them.

And he would meet it. Because if his Luck was tied to Farah, then he wasn't walking into this alone.

He turned on his heel, heading toward the Citadel, his path set with no room for second guesses.

No more running. Not this time.

CHAPTER 8

THE CHAMBER ASSIGNED to the refugees was small, tucked away in one of the quieter wings of the Citadel where they wouldn't draw attention. Farah didn't want to distress them even more, so she said she'd meet them where they were more comfortable.

She stepped inside, closing the door softly, and had the scent of stale sweat and damp cloth filling her lungs. The family huddled together on the low cushions—mother, father, and their daughter, who couldn't have been more than seven. The girl's arms were wrapped around her mother's waist, her face buried in the folds of her tunic, while the father sat stiff-backed, his eyes darting toward Farah the moment she entered.

She softened her stance, keeping her movements slow as she approached. "You are safe here," she said, careful to keep the steel from her tone. "The Mashya himself ordered that you be given protection."

The mother's fingers twitched against the girl's shoulder, but she said nothing. The father looked away.

Farah fought against the tightening in her chest. *They don't trust you.*

She dropped into a crouch before the little girl, keeping herself at eye level. "What's your name?"

The child did not answer.

Silence stretched, thick and uncomfortable. The girl curled tighter into her mother's side, the mother's grip on her only tightening.

The father finally spoke, his voice hoarse. "She won't talk."

The exhaustion in his tone struck a chord in her chest. "Has she spoken since you left Sakasan?"

He shook his head.

She glanced at the mother, but she only clutched her child closer, her face tight with wariness. They were cornered animals, too afraid to trust the hand reaching for them.

She fought the instinct to push, to demand. She knew how to pull truth out of people through force, through manipulation, through fear. But here? That wouldn't work.

This is why Yasher would have been better.

He would have known what to say. Would have leaned back against the wall, easy and disarming, made a comment about how nothing was ever as bad as people feared. A lie, but one they would believe coming from him. He had a way of making people feel safe, even when they shouldn't. Even when he was dangling the idea they had a chance in a game of cards or lying through his teeth. Farah had no such skill.

She could kill a man unarmed, she could slide a blade

in just the right place to have the victim never make a sound, she could strike fear into the hearts of nobles twice her age. But this? Convincing frightened people to trust her, to let her in?

This, she had never been taught, and it was infuriating.

She tried again.

"You don't have to tell me everything now," she said, her voice measured. "But I need to know what happened. If there is danger in Sakasan, I must understand it so I can stop it."

The father's jaw tightened. He looked to his wife, who only shook her head in a sharp, desperate motion.

"Please," she pressed. "I need to help."

The mother's grip on her daughter trembled. Finally, she spoke, her voice barely more than a whisper. "You cannot help. You cannot stop it."

The woman's voice was the voice of someone who had already accepted that survival had been an accident, not a victory, and it was just a matter of time for it to catch up and finish the job.

What happened to you?

The father swallowed thickly, his fingers twisting into the folds of his tunic. "We shouldn't have left."

Farah stared at him. *Shouldn't have left?* They had fled Sakasan in the dead of night, traveled days on the road, desperate enough to seek sanctuary in the very heart of Emari's power. And now, faced with safety, he regretted it?

"Why?" she asked.

Neither of them answered.

If she pressed too hard, they would only close off further. She knew what it was like to carry fear like a blade at the throat, knew the way silence could become a shield, even when words were the only thing that might save you. She needed to rethink her approach.

She shifted her gaze back to the girl. She reminded her of Pari, and that may be a way in, a way to break through the shell of fear. Words weren't going to work. Not with this girl. Not with what she had seen. Maybe this girl didn't have words for what happened in Sakasan. But that didn't mean she couldn't show her.

"Do you like to draw?" she asked softly. "You remind me of a friend who loves to draw."

The girl hesitated. Her tiny fingers twitched, barely perceptible.

Farah reached into her belt, fingers closing around the familiar feel of charcoal. A folded scrap of parchment, stuffed into her pouch from some random meeting. She set them down carefully, slowly. The girl's dark eyes flickered toward them.

Farah straightened up and took a step back.

"You don't have to speak," she said carefully. "But if there is something you want me to know, you can show me."

Her mother, still wary, remained stiff as stone beside her, but didn't stop her when, after a long pause, the little girl hesitantly reached out.

She took the charcoal.

Farah watched, waiting, as the girl hesitated for a breath before pressing the blackened tip to the parchment. She began to draw.

The girl's fingers moved slowly, hesitantly, at first. Each stroke of the charcoal left smudged trails across the parchment, dark shapes forming with the uncertain tremor of a child's hand. But as the minutes passed, her movements became more deliberate.

Farah knelt, silent, as she watched the image unfold.

First, the town.

Jagged rooftops, pressed together in rough strokes. The cliffs, curling like blackened fingers behind them. The waves, too dark, too thick, rose against the shore, swallowing the coastline and filling in caverns and cutouts in the cliffs.

Then, the figures.

The girl's hand wavered, just slightly, but she didn't stop. The charcoal dragged heavy shadows across the town, the shapes long-limbed, wrong. Curling tendrils stretched outward, creeping over the rooftops, twisting into claws.

Farah's pulse skipped.

She had seen these shapes before. In Pari's drawing.

A slightly different scene, different figures at the center, a little more mature drawing style. But the shadows? They had been the same.

Pari's drawing had been a warning. A vision of what was to come. Now, she was looking at what had already happened.

The Darkness was no longer creeping at the edges of the world. It was already here.

Farah frowned. "Who is this?" She pointed at the woman in the center.

The girl hesitated.

"She leads them," the mother murmured, her voice barely above a whisper.

Farah's gaze snapped to the woman. "Who?"

The mother's grip on her daughter's shoulder tightened. Her husband spoke instead, his edged with grief.

"A woman came. Not long before the shadows." His hands clenched into fists, the muscles in his jaw twitching. "She didn't speak, but people started… listening to her. They trusted her." His throat bobbed as he swallowed. "Then they changed."

Farah's skin prickled. "Changed how?"

The woman shifted, pressing a hand to her lips as if to steady herself. "They stopped fearing the Darkness," she said, the words trembling. "Even when it came for them."

The hair at the nape of Farah's neck lifted. "Are you saying she brought it with her?"

The father's gaze flicked toward the drawing. "I don't know. But she was there. And the ones who followed her… they… belonged to it, by the end."

Belonged to it.

She stared at the black, clawed figures on the parchment.

The Mashya had suspected Mazdavir's influence was spreading, corrupting the land beyond Behnaz's siphoning, but this was something else. This wasn't just corruption, it was control. Dominion gathering followers.

She exhaled slowly, pressing her fingers into her palms. "Why did you leave?"

The mother shuddered. "Because we didn't want to *belong* to her."

The girl hesitated, then lowered the charcoal. She slid the parchment toward Farah without a word.

Farah picked it up carefully, examining the shapes again. The pull of something deep and old stirred in her blood.

"We grabbed this before we left," the mother said suddenly.

Farah glanced up as the woman pulled something from the folds of her tunic. A small lacquered wooden box, unremarkable in appearance, its edges worn from years of handling.

The moment it touched Farah's hands, she felt it.

The faint but unmistakable pull of something *alive*.

She inhaled sharply.

"What is it?" she asked.

The woman shook her head. "I don't know. But it wasn't theirs to have."

Farah turned the small wooden box over in her hands, feeling the worn edges beneath her fingertips. It was no larger than her palm, its lacquered surface dulled by time, but it bore the faint etchings of something a once intricate pattern. It looked similar to the boxes that Behnaz had made for keeping relics, but it was just a little rougher, a little different.

She let her senses stretch toward it, the way she had been trained to detect metal, to feel its song beneath her skin. Fainter, subtler, the whisper of something buried deep, forgotten. A relic.

The pull of it coiled around her body, humming low, like the soft vibration of a string plucked in the dark.

Her grip tightened slightly. *It's a relic, has to be.*

She inhaled slowly to steady the sharp pull in her chest. It was faint, weaker than the relics she had encountered before. It did not hum with the same power as the Shard of Ameretat or the Eye of Rashnu. But it was there. Hidden. It felt somehow wrong.

"We didn't take it because we wanted it."

Farah's eyes flicked up, locking onto the woman's.

"We took it because they shouldn't have it."

The words sent a prickle down her spine. She turned the box over in her hands, the soft pull of its presence curling in her ribs.

The ones who had already become.

The girl, however, let out a small exhale, barely a sound. Her eyes, too large for her thin face, drifted toward the drawing.

"She was... beautiful," she said at last.

It wasn't the word she had expected.

The girl's fingers found the edge of the parchment, smoothing it absently. "Not like the other women in town. She had... something *else*. Something inside her."

Her heart gave a slow, uneasy beat.

"What did she do?"

The girl hesitated.

The father turned his face away.

"She spoke," the mother whispered at last, her hands trembling in her lap. "And they listened."

Farah felt a prickle crawl up her spine. That wasn't how persuasion worked. Words alone didn't strip a town of its fear.

"What did she say?"

The woman shook her head. "It wasn't about what she said. It was what she made them feel."

A silence settled over the room, thick and pressing. Farah could hear the dull hum of the corridors outside, the murmur of palace guards exchanging shifts, but inside this chamber, it felt distant, like something happening in another world.

She exhaled slowly, pushing her thoughts into order. The who was still unknown. But the what? That, at least, she could begin to piece together.

Some woman had arrived in Sakasan, speaking to the people in ways that made them ready for the Darkness. Not just open to it, but welcoming it. And she had followers, ones who had changed.

The Darkness was not merely spreading. It was being embraced.

And the relic, however weak, had been kept by them.

The father exhaled sharply, pressing the heels of his hands against his eyes. "We should have left sooner."

The mother shuddered. "We should not have left at all."

The words twisted something deep in Farah's gut. Not regret. Not guilt. Dread.

She turned the box over again, her grip firm. The hum of it still curled at the edges of her awareness, a quiet echo of something waiting.

She looked at the mother again, her voice low but steady. "You said you took this. Was she looking for it?"

The woman shook her head immediately. "Not her."

Farah stilled. "Then who?"

The mother's gaze flickered toward the girl's drawing, the smudged black figures reaching toward the cliffs.

The father swallowed hard. "The ones who had already changed."

Farah's breath pressed tight in her ribs. Changed. Not corrupted. Not touched by the Darkness.

"What did they become?" she asked, her voice barely above a whisper.

The mother pressed her lips together. The father didn't answer. But the little girl—

The little girl turned over the parchment.

Farah's pulse skipped.

There, hastily drawn on the back, was a single figure. Not dark like the others. Not shrouded in twisting ink.

But wrong.

The body was thin, stretched. The arms were too long, the hands too sharp, the eyes—

Farah's blood ran cold.

The little girl hesitated, then tapped the figure once, lightly, with the tip of her finger.

Her voice was barely a breath.

"They were still smiling."

She turned the box over in her hands once more. A weak relic. A town swallowed by darkness. A woman who did not fear the shadows. And now... a new kind of creature.

She tucked the box into the inner pocket of her coat. The puzzle was growing.

She had her next step.

Farah moved quickly through the halls, the weight of the relic pressing against her side with every step. The morning sun had crept higher, filtering through the stained-glass windows in fractured bands of color, but the warmth did nothing to ease the cold coil in her stomach. She had answers, or at least fragments of them, but each one only made the questions worse.

The guards outside the Mashya's chambers stepped aside at her approach, their polished armor catching the light. One of them gave a stiff nod, rapping once on the heavy wooden door before pushing it open for her.

She stepped inside, her eyes immediately scanning the room.

Enayat was seated near the large window, his expression unreadable as he listened to someone speaking across from him.

She slowed.

Siavash stood near the polished table in the center of the chamber, his hands folded neatly behind his back. His dark tunic was immaculate, not a single thread out of place, and he wore the same effortless poise that made it seem as though he belonged in every room he entered.

"—does not seem inclined to push further, but his influence among the old guard remains an issue," Siavash was saying. His tone was measured, each word precise. "He will not stand against you directly, not yet, but he will undermine wherever and whenever he can. If given an opportunity, though, I'd recommend keeping someone close by."

The Mashya exhaled, rubbing a hand over his temple. "Disappointing, but I expected as much."

She lingered just inside the doorway, unwilling to step fully into the space.

Enayat noticed immediately. His gaze flicked toward her, his dark brows drawing together slightly before he straightened.

"Farah," he said, his voice carrying the weight of authority even in casual address. "You're earlier than I expected."

Siavash turned at the sound of her name, his expression polite, unreadable, but there was curiosity in the tilt of his head, the way his eyes lingered a moment too long.

She kept her face composed, touching the box within the interior pocket to make sure it wasn't visible.

He didn't know. About what they had seen, about what they had barely survived. Very few knew the real story of what happened with Behnaz and the Darkness. For now, he couldn't. Whatever Siavash suspected, however close he stood to the throne, he was not part of that circle, and she would not bring him into it.

The fewer voices in the room when they spoke of it, the better.

She gave him nothing. Not the shadow of a thought, not the shape of what pressed against her ribs each time she remembered.

"I have news from the folk who arrived last night," she said instead, her tone clipped and steady.

Enayat's attention sharpened at that. "Go on."

She hesitated, her gaze flicking briefly toward Siavash.

Enayat caught the glance. He leaned back slightly in

his chair, tapping a single finger against the armrest. Then he sighed.

"Siavash," he said, his tone even. "Give us the room."

Siavash hesitated only a fraction of a second, and in that hesitation, Farah saw the shift, the quiet calculation behind his eyes. He didn't argue, but he didn't need to. He had already learned something. That there were conversations he was not yet meant to be a part of. And in court, all knowledge was power, and he was just as hungry for it as many others.

He inclined his head, all smooth grace. "Of course, Your Majesty."

As he passed Farah, he slowed just slightly, his voice dropping low enough that only she could hear.

"Don't keep all your secrets to yourself, Hand," he murmured.

She didn't so much as glance at him. But her teeth pressed together.

The door closed softly behind him before she let herself exhale.

Enayat rubbed his jaw, watching her carefully. "You don't trust him."

"I trust that he has his own interests." She met his gaze evenly.

The Mashya let out a quiet chuckle. "As does everyone in court. But he's more useful with us than against us."

Farah said nothing. Enayat trusted easily, while she and Rostam trusted none. It was the balance they'd come to an unspoken agreement on.

Enayat sighed again, shifting in his seat. "What did you learn?"

She reached into her coat. "The family that escaped Sakasan, they didn't just leave because they were afraid. They left because the town was already gone."

Enayat's expression darkened.

She continued, her voice steady. "Not destroyed. Not abandoned. They said it was taken by shadows who changed the people there."

That word settled between them like a stone dropped into deep water.

"They spoke of a woman," she went on. "Someone who arrived before things changed. She didn't force anyone to accept what was coming, she only had to speak."

The Mashya's fingers curled subtly against the armrest of his chair.

She exhaled. "And when the shadows came, the town was ready."

Enayat studied her, his expression carefully controlled.

She tapped the box lightly with her fingertips. "They took this from them before they fled. I haven't opened it, but I can feel it."

The Mashya's gaze drifted back to the box. He sat forward, reaching for it with careful hands. His fingers brushed the lacquered surface, tracing the carved edges, intricate and unmistakable. His shoulders tensed, just slightly, but it was enough.

"You recognize it," she said. It wasn't a question.

Enayat didn't look at her. His hand lingered on the lid a moment longer before he withdrew, resting it in his lap.

He exhaled, slow and deliberate, before finally speaking.

"It's one of Behnaz's," he said quietly. "The craftsmanship, the lacquer, the design of the inlay... it matches the relic containers she had commissioned when she first began collecting them."

"She never let them out of the Citadel," he continued, voice low. "She kept them in a hidden vault, one even Rostam didn't know about for years. If this came from outside..."

He didn't finish the thought. He didn't have to.

Whatever was within was still humming softly in her blood, in her bones. She could feel it, even if Enayat couldn't.

Enayat studied her. "This woman," he said carefully. "Did they give you a name?"

She shook her head.

"Then we need to find one."

He turned the box over in his hands, his fingertips lingering on the edges, as if he was remembering something that he didn't want to share. The weight of what lay inside pressed against the air itself, heavy with something unseen but undeniable.

Enayat exhaled through his nose, his gaze sharpening. "You said you could feel it?" he asked.

She nodded. "It's faint, but it's there. The pull is different from the relics Behnaz hoarded. Less direct, less overwhelming. But it's tainted. Whatever it's supposed to be, it's been touched by something else." She hesitated before adding, "It feels corrupted."

The Mashya's jaw tightened. "Mazdavir."

It wasn't a question, but she inclined her head in confirmation.

A long silence stretched between them, the air thick with unspoken thoughts. Enayat had seen what the corruption of relics could do. They both had. Behnaz had taken what was once sacred and turned it into something monstrous. If there were other collected relics that had begun to fall to that same darkness...

She suppressed the thought, a shiver running through her.

Enayat set the box down carefully on the low table between them, his fingers lingering on the lid before pulling away.

"You said the family that brought this to us took it from people before they left," he mused. "That means there are others who wanted it, others who knew what it was."

"I need to know what it does now. What relic is here, and why it would be in a small town in the Cliffs." She flexed her fingers absently, feeling the weight of her own Talent stir beneath her skin. Metallurgy, the forging of strength, of structure. But even she couldn't fix something like this.

She glanced at Enayat. "What do the scholars know about fractured or corrupted relics?"

The Mashya shook his head.

"There hasn't been much to study on corruption,

only the few that you have found since… ," he sighed, shaking the memories away. "A few of them have begun cataloging what she left behind. I'll have them look this over and see if it was something that was either lost in the chaos… after. Or if it was never in the Citadel at all."

She looked back at the relic and a thought struck her. "I want to test it."

Enayat's brows lifted.

"On yourself?" His voice carried the unmistakable warning of a king who could order her not to.

She shook her head. "No. Not until we understand it better. But someone else already has tested it. The people of Sakasan. And that means they left traces, something tangible. I need to speak with the scholars, but I also need this examined by someone who understands how relics, and people, are changed by the Darkness."

He considered her for a long moment before nodding. "Agreed. I'll have it studied discreetly. We can't afford to let word spread that there are relics out in the kingdom that may be corrupted and corrupting as she did, not until we know the full extent of the damage."

She glanced at the door. "Siavash will want to know. What do we do about that?"

Enayat hummed. "Siavash will eventually know. But for now, he doesn't need to." He looked at her, his gaze unreadable. "He's useful, but he doesn't have the history to be able to help us decide how we handle this."

She sighed, rolling the tension from her shoulders. It was always like this. Always politics, always maneuvering. Always playing a game she hated.

"I should go."

He nodded, though his eyes lingered on her with something more than simple authority. He studied her a moment longer, then, satisfied, he leaned back. "Find out what you can. And be careful, Farah. Please."

She gave him a look. "Always."

She picked up the relic, tucking it carefully into the folds of her coat. Without another word, she turned and left.

She stepped out of the Mashya's chambers, the door closing behind her with a muted thud. The weight of the relic in her coat felt heavier than it should, pressing against her side like a secret itching to be revealed. She adjusted her cuffs, schooling her expression into something neutral, unreadable.

Siavash was waiting, of course.

He stood hands clasped loosely before him, his courtly attire impeccable despite the long hours of debate that he had taken over for her while she was on this task. His dark eyes flickered with something unreadable as he took in her arrival, the faintest smile curving his lips.

"Hand," he greeted smoothly, inclining his head. "The Mashya seems quite occupied these days."

She didn't break stride, moving past him without pause. "He has a country to run."

Siavash fell into step beside her effortlessly. "And yet, he sends you away on a task, not just for a day, but a journey."

Her jaw tightened. *Enayat, you could have at least warned me of what he did know.* She gave nothing away in her face, her pace unchanging. "The Mashya sends many people on tasks."

"Of course," Siavash said, his tone as light as a feather. "But this one seems particularly pressing, given that he declined to elaborate when I asked."

Farah didn't slow. "Then perhaps you should take that as an answer."

Siavash chuckled, the sound low and knowing. "You're a difficult woman to understand fully, Farah."

She shot him a sidelong glance. "Mayhap you should stop trying too hard."

"Wouldn't you if you were in my shoes?" He spread his hands, his voice effortlessly diplomatic. "I am, after all, a man of politics. And politics, as you must know, is about trust."

"You and I are working toward the same goal. Building a stable future for Emari," Siavash pressed, his voice smooth but persistent. "Wouldn't it be easier if we didn't keep things from each other?"

She gave him a bland smile. "You assume I have anything worth keeping from you."

"Don't insult us both," he murmured. "The Mashya has given you a task, something significant enough to keep it from me. And while I have the utmost respect for the chain of command, it would be helpful to know where exactly the Hand of the Mashya is being sent." His tone remained polite, but there was steel beneath it. A test.

She did not rise to it. "Then I suppose you'll have to live with the mystery."

He sighed, shaking his head slightly, but his expression betrayed no irritation. If anything, he looked amused. "You really are the hardest person in this court to win over."

"Good," she said, tilting her chin up. "I'd be concerned if I wasn't."

The corner of Siavash's mouth twitched upward, but before he could reply, a familiar voice cut through the air behind them.

"Ah, my two favorite people, lurking in the halls like conspiring lovers."

She nearly groaned, knowing how this looked to Yasher.

She turned just as he strode toward them, his gait loose, casual—too casual. His white shirt hung open at the collar, the sleeves pushed up to his forearms, and his dark coat swung easily with each step. His hair was slightly mussed, as though he'd run his hands through it one too many times, but the sharp, knowing glint in his pale blue eyes told her that he was in the mood to play a game.

He stopped between them, his gaze flicking between her and Siavash like he was walking into a private joke. "Siavash, what a surprise. I'd have thought you'd be too busy charming half the court to be lingering outside Enayat's chambers."

Siavash remained unimpressed. "Some of us work to build alliances, Aqa," he replied evenly.

Yasher pressed a hand to his chest. "And *some* of us find that alliances work best when there's actual trust involved. A rare thing, these days."

Siavash tilted his head, his dark eyes assessing. "Indeed."

She sighed. "Must you? There is —"

Yasher turned his grin on her, all warm mischief. Too warm. Too easy. He was most definitely in one of those moods. "Must I what, Phoenix? Exist? Breathe? Support my companion in her noble endeavors?"

Siavash sighed, his expression as measured as always, but something flickered in his dark eyes.

"I do hope that you don't take this the wrong way, Aqa," Siavash stood just a little taller. "I have had many encounters and conversations with Rokhazi in my time on my father's estates, and you are so much... more than most."

"It really is part of my charm," Yasher mused, letting the words roll slow, deliberate, "I am a bit... more... reckless than most."

Something in his tone made Farah glance at him. His posture was loose, but there was an edge beneath it. A tension too subtle for most to catch. Not anger. Not quite. But something protective, something sharp.

He was posturing. Not for sport. Not for amusement. For her.

Siavash's gaze flickered just slightly before settling into its usual mask of patience. If he noticed the shift in Yasher's tone, he didn't acknowledge it.

Farah did.

She had spent too many years being claimed by others—by titles, by power, by the weight of someone else's expectations. Yasher had never been like that. He had never tried to possess her, never made her feel like anything less than her own person.

But this? This felt close. Too close.

He's not doing it to control you, she told herself. *He's doing it because he thinks he has to.*

Because Siavash is playing a game, and Yasher always refuses to sit out when he was around one.

She did groan this time, rubbing the bridge of her nose. "For the love of—"

Yasher reached for her, resting a hand against the small of her back in an unmistakable claim. He leaned in slightly, not quite whispering but lowering his voice enough that it felt intimate. "Don't tell me you were out here entertaining other men while I was off being a dutiful citizen."

Farah flicked a glance at him. "I was working, and you smell of a tavern."

"So was I," Yasher said, affecting wounded pride. "And yet, you don't see me standing in shadowed corridors with, oh, I don't know, a pretty face."

Siavash scoffed. "Please."

But his eyes flicked to Yasher's hand at her back. A small movement—barely noticeable. But Farah caught it.

A flicker of understanding. Of quiet calculation. Siavash wasn't just tolerating Yasher's presence. He was studying it, measuring it like a scholar.

And unlike Yasher, he had no interest in playing the part of the jealous rival. That would be too obvious, too blunt. Siavash wasn't that kind of man. He fought wars with words, not daggers. And right now, Yasher was practically handing him a map of all his weak spots. She'd have thought he was throwing the game if she didn't feel the tension all over him.

"You mistake me, Aqa." Siavash's voice was smooth, deliberate. "I am not vying for anyone's affection. Unlike you, I do not need to stake a claim to feel secure in my position."

Yasher's grin didn't waver, but she felt the subtle shift in his stance. A slow breath, a tension barely there.

"That's a nice way of saying you know you'd lose," Yasher mused.

She folded her arms and turned to him, staring him down to just be quiet. "You are ridiculous."

"I am," Yasher agreed cheerfully. "As always, Phoenix." His fingers brushed along the small of her back before he stepped fully beside her.

She let out a breath and turned back to Siavash. "Are we done here?"

Siavash glanced between them. "For now."

With a nod, he inclined his head toward the door behind them. "Give the Mashya my regards."

She said nothing as Siavash turned on his heel and strode off down the corridor, his posture as measured and controlled as ever.

As soon as he was out of earshot, Yasher hummed. "I don't think he likes me."

"And that surprises you?" She arched a brow.

He grinned, pulling her into his side just enough to feel the warmth of him. "No. But it does entertain me."

She sighed, shaking her head. "You're lucky I love you."

"See?" He beamed. "Now that's what I was fishing for."

She rolled her eyes and started walking away, with him falling into step beside her.

"So," he mused as they strolled down the corridor, "what did you talk about with Enayat?"

She shot him a look. "We are not having this conversation in the open."

"Which means something interesting happened." He grinned. "You know you're just making me more curious."

She was torn between exasperation and something quieter, something that settled in her chest in a way she wasn't ready to name. Yasher had always been this way—charming, quick-witted, frustrating in all the ways that made her life more complicated. And yet... she knew he wasn't just provoking Siavash for amusement.

He was claiming space. Here, in a court that would never fully accept him, that would always see him as foreign, as reckless, as her shadow.

He knew they would never listen to him the way they listened to men like Siavash. But he could make them notice him. He could remind them that he was here, at her side, whether they liked it or not.

That was the difference. Siavash thrived in the world of politics, manipulating its pieces with a diplomat's grace. Yasher? Yasher burned through it like a wildfire, disrupting the careful lines people had drawn around her. He made them see her differently, even if that wasn't his intent.

And maybe that was why, for all his nonsense, she never stopped him.

She rolled her eyes and started walking. Yasher fell into step beside her, his presence familiar, grounding.

He watched her for a moment, then, with the ease of a man with nothing to prove, he pulled her to him to stop her, wrapped his arms around her, and kissed the top of her head.

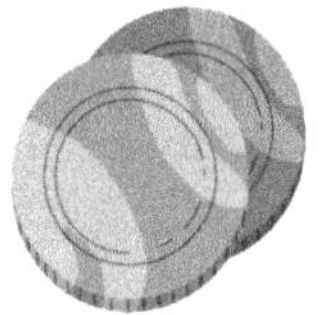

Yasher tossed his coat over the back of a chair, rolling his shoulders as he turned to face Farah after they made it back to their chambers. He wasn't sure if it was the exhaustion or the way she held herself, too contained, too measured, but something about this felt different.

"So, what's the verdict?" he asked, forcing lightness into his tone. "Are we about to ride into another mess we'll barely crawl out of, or is this one of those 'just a minor crisis, nothing to worry about' situations?"

She shot him a look as she unfastened the belt of her cross-coat, shrugging out of it. Always so precise, as if control could keep everything from unraveling. He recognized that need. The way she folded her movements into something methodical, structured. A habit born of necessity, of survival in the old court. And yet, she had the same sharp gaze when she looked at him, as if she could see straight through the space he filled with easy words and lighter tones.

She didn't press to berate him for losing his temper

with Siavash. Not yet, but he knew she was waiting to catch him off-guard.

"Depends on how you define 'minor.'" She folded the coat neatly over her arm. "The family was terrified. Whatever happened in Sakasan, it left them shaken to their core. I couldn't get a clear answer on what they saw, only that they were desperate enough to flee in the middle of the night with barely more than the clothes on their backs."

He frowned, crossing his arms as he leaned against the edge of the table.

"Did they say anything about the shadows?" His mind drifted to Pari's drawing, the way the darkness had curled around their figures, reaching like grasping hands. That sketch had settled in his thoughts like an itch he couldn't quite reach. "Anything that sounds like what she sketched?"

She rubbed at her temple, like she could smooth away the tension coiled there.

"There was a woman," she said, voice measured, thoughtful. "The little girl drew her first, then the mother said she was watching them, standing at the edges of their town. The way she described her, it was unsettling. Something about the way she moved, the way the shadows seemed to follow her, the way she spoke."

She hesitated, then met his gaze. "It looked and sounded far too much like Pari's drawing."

His fingers tapped a restless rhythm against the table, his mind racing over the image that had fallen onto the tea shop's table just the night before. The jagged black tendrils curling around them, the stark contrast between them and the looming figures hidden in the darkness of the cliffs. He hadn't liked that drawing then, and he liked it even less now.

"You think it's the same thing." he asked. "Whatever Pari saw is what happened to this family?"

She didn't answer immediately. Instead, she pulled the small box from her belt and placed it between them.

"I don't know," she admitted. "But they were too afraid to say much of anything at all. It wasn't just fear of what they left behind. It was fear of being heard speaking about it."

Her fingers traced the edge of the lid, not quite opening it.

"And then they gave me this. Said they took it before they ran."

His gaze flicked to the box. A prickle ran down his spine, sharp and sudden, like stepping onto unsteady ground. The air between them felt heavier, thick with something unspoken. A gut-level wrongness that curled at the edges of his awareness, telling him not to reach for it.

He could feel it. Whatever was in that box didn't want to be touched. No, it wanted to be touched the same way something that wanted to kill you painfully wanted to be touched.

Relics. He'd had enough of them.

He exhaled sharply, forcing his shoulders to stay loose. He'd already given up one relic for Farah—his so-called Luck, sealed in a filagree ball. He wasn't sure if he'd been a fool for thinking it gave him is Luck, or if the real mistake had been assuming he'd ever needed it at all. Either way, he wasn't eager to get tangled up in another.

He dragged a hand through his hair. He wasn't afraid of much, but this?

This, he didn't trust.

She tapped the lid of the box with a finger. "They said they took it from the people who had already... changed. Whatever's inside, it has a pull to it. Faint, but familiar."

A muscle tensed in his jaw. Familiar how? Like the Eye, whispering in the back of his mind? Like the moment before a fall, before the air turned against you and sent you spiraling?

"You're sure it's a relic?" he asked, keeping his voice even.

"A fragment of something," she corrected. "It doesn't hum the way the Eye did, but I can feel it. It's been broken, or touched, corrupted."

His mouth quirked, but the humor felt thin. "And I assume cracking it open right now is a bad idea?"

"Unless you'd like to find out if it reacts to uncontrolled Luck," she said dryly.

He held up his hands. "I'm reckless, Phoenix, not an idiot."

Her brow arched.

He exhaled, shaking his head. "Most of the time."

She laughed softly, shifting her attention back to the box. "I'll examine it before we leave with the scholars, but I want to keep this quiet. If it's connected to what's happening in Sakasan, we need to be careful."

"Let's hope whatever's inside stays quiet," he

muttered, casting the relic a final wary glance. But Yasher had never been good at hope.

"So, let me get this straight. We're riding into a town where people are too afraid to talk, with something that might be causing the whole mess, and we have no idea who or what we're actually up against?" He let out a sharp breath, rubbing a hand over his face. "Twelve Hells, Emari really doesn't get a break, does it?"

Farah didn't hesitate. "Sounds about right."

He let out a slow, sharp breath, running a hand through his hair. *Twelve Holy Hells.* He wasn't sure what he'd expected her to say. Some reassurance, some promise that it wasn't as bad as it sounded. But this was Farah. She didn't deal in false comforts.

Her fingers brushed his. Light, at first—then firmer.

She didn't say anything right away. Just let her touch settle against his skin, anchoring him. No rush, no demand. It was a steady, deliberate weight, something real in the middle of everything that wasn't.

He tilted his head slightly to look at her.

She was watching him, her dark eyes sharp—not with judgment, not even with caution, but with knowing. She had seen the tension winding through him, the shift in his stance, the way his fingers curled when he was trying too hard not to react.

She knew him too well.

Her thumb brushed over the inside of his wrist—once, twice. A wordless promise.

Yasher's shoulders relaxed just enough for her to notice.

"Then I guess we'd better be ready," he murmured. Less biting now. Less distant.

She tilted her head slightly, searching his face. "We will be."

He swallowed. It was ridiculous, how much weight those three words carried coming from her.

She gave his wrist a final squeeze before letting go, but the ghost of it lingered.

She watched him with that sharp, assessing look she always wore when she was about to call him on something. *Ah, there it is.*

She stood, pulling him with her and towards her, her fingers still loosely curled from where she'd steadied him.

"Ready for the Cliffs," she said, voice even, "or ready for you to posture like an angry peacock at every conversation I have with Siavash?"

He groaned, dragging a hand down his face. "Twelve Hells, Phoenix. I wasn't posturing."

She lifted a brow, unimpressed.

"I was merely ensuring that His Noble Smugness knew his place in the grand scheme of things." He pressed a hand to his chest in mock sincerity.

"Which is?"

He grinned, sharp and easy. "Below me."

She scoffed, but there was the faintest twitch of amusement at the corner of her mouth.

"Come on, you know I had to." He leaned in slightly, nudging her shoulder with his.

She sighed, shaking her head. "You are insufferable."

"And yet," he mused, "here you are, suffering me."

Her lips parted—maybe to argue, maybe to call him a fool—but he saw it, the flicker of warmth beneath her exasperation. She wasn't annoyed, not really.

And he would rather die than let her see how much he had needed that.

She made a quiet, amused sound, shaking her head. "I can handle Siavash."

"Oh, I know you can," he said, tugging her just slightly toward him, enough that their bodies brushed. His free hand settled against her waist. "But that doesn't mean I have to like him acting like he belongs at your side."

She let out a breath of laughter, soft and disbelieving. "Didn't expect you to be jealous."

"Jealous? No." His voice dropped lower, quieter, the teasing edge smoothing into something more certain. "But I've lost too much by not standing my ground before. I won't make that mistake again."

She exhaled sharply, something flickering in her gaze. "I'm not a thing to be claimed, Yasher."

His thumb brushed just beneath her bottom lip.

"I know." His lips quirked, but there was no sharpness in it now, only honesty. "But I also know what's worth fighting for."

She let out a quiet breath, shaking her head. "You really are impossible at times."

He grinned, but there was something else beneath it, something not quite so careless. His fingers flexed at her waist, as if grounding himself before he could say the wrong thing.

"Maybe. But I'm also right."

The skeptical look she gave him. "About?"

He tilted his head, his voice lowering into something quieter, rougher. "That he doesn't know you."

Her fingers pressed more firmly against his chest. "And you do?"

He could have answered lightly, made some jest, turned it into something easy. But he didn't.

"Yeah," he said, quiet but sure. "I do." And for once, he didn't follow it with a smirk.

Farah tilted her chin slightly, eyes flicking over his face, searching. "Then I suppose you have nothing to worry about, do you?"

Yasher opened his mouth with a ready quip, but stopped. No. This was different.

Maybe once, he could have pretended he wasn't afraid of losing her. Could have leaned on charm, on that easy, slippery Luck that had gotten him through a thousand close calls. But this, this thing between them, wasn't something he would gamble on. It was already his, settled deep into the marrow of him.

And he wasn't about to lose something that had already become a part of him.

He let out a breath, almost a laugh, but it softened into something else. Something truer. His fingers skimmed up her back, pulling her flush against him, his lips ghosting just over hers.

"No," he admitted. "No, I don't."

For the first time, he didn't say it like he was trying to convince himself.

He kissed her, because there was no reason not to— because it had nothing to do with luck at all.

Farah fit against him like something inevitable, like the turning of the tide, like steel drawn to a forge's heat. He had spent so much of his life moving from place to place, never letting himself believe in permanence, never letting himself want. But here, with her, there was no question of wanting. He already had her.

Her fingers curled into his shirt, holding him there, and he felt something settle deep in his chest. Not the reckless thrill of a gamble, not the fleeting heat of victory —but something weightier. Steady. A choice.

She sighed against his mouth, soft and familiar, and he drank in the sound like it was something sacred.

When they finally broke apart, she rested her forehead against his, her breath warm against his lips.

He exhaled, a slow, easy breath, letting his fingers brush the curve of her waist.

"You know," he murmured, voice rough with something he wasn't quite ready to name, "I think I like it when you tease me."

She hummed, amusement flickering in her eyes as she tangled her fingers in his shirt. "Then you're in luck."

His lips quirked, but this time, the grin felt different —softer.

"I always am, Phoenix."

YASHER SPRAWLED IN HIS CHAIR, bare feet resting on the edge of the low table as he idly twirled a piece of dried fruit between his fingers. The morning light filtered through the lattice screens, casting golden patterns across his skin, highlighting the lines of his torso. A cooling cup of tea sat untouched beside him, the scent of cardamom and honey curling in the air.

Farah had already finished eating. She stood near the wardrobe, fastening the clasps of her coat with efficient, practiced movements.

He smirked, watching as she adjusted the belt at her waist. "You know, I don't think the world will end if you sit back down for five minutes."

She shot him a look through the mirror's reflection. "You'll forgive me if I don't take time management advice from the man still half-naked at breakfast."

He stretched, unabashed, the muscles in his abdomen shifting as he rolled his shoulders.

"I'd argue this is the best way to have breakfast. Comfortable. Leisurely." He popped the piece of fruit into his mouth. "And with excellent company."

She shook her head, her lips twitching despite herself. "Well, your excellent company is about to be put to use. You're coming with me."

He groaned dramatically, tilting his head back against the chair. "Phoenix, it's too early for whatever you're planning."

"You've been awake for at least an hour," she countered, tugging on her boots. "And we're taking the box to the Mashya and the scholars."

That made him sit up a little straighter. His eyes flicked to the small wooden box still resting on the table. He had almost convinced himself it wasn't there, had ignored the nagging weight of it pressing at the edge of his thoughts.

"I'm sure you can handle that on your own," he said lightly, watching her from beneath heavy-lidded eyes. "You know, like you do everything else."

She turned, crossing the room until she stood over him, her gaze steady. "You should be there."

He huffed a breath, raking a hand through his hair. "You're not dragging me into another scholarly discussion just to watch them sneer at me when I don't phrase things 'intellectually' enough because I don't know enough of the language."

"This isn't a debate," she said. "You handled a relic for years, along with helping me to find another. You'll recognize if this thing feels like the Eye. If it's dangerous, or if it's something we can use." She leaned down, bracing her hands on the arms of his chair, effectively caging him in. "And, if I recall, you said you wanted to help."

She brushed a kiss to his forehead and then looked him right in the eyes. He met her gaze, knowing that look. She wasn't asking. She was expecting.

He sighed dramatically. "I was hoping you'd just say, 'I want you there,' and we could skip all the convincing."

Her lips quirked. "Would that have worked?"

"Absolutely."

She rolled her eyes, stepping back. He grabbed her wrist before she could retreat entirely, tugging her back just enough to brush a kiss against her knuckles. "You're lucky I'm completely yours."

She arched a brow. "Is that so?"

"Mm." He grinned against her skin before releasing

her. "And because I know you'll make my life infinitely difficult if I don't go."

"Then get dressed," she said, already moving toward the door.

He groaned again, dragging himself upright, but there was no real complaint behind it. He watched her for a moment longer before shaking his head and reaching for his shirt.

"Remind me again why relics always seem to lead to terrible decisions?"

He pulled his shirt over his head with a resigned sigh, running a hand through his hair to shake out the lingering sleep. The weight of her request settled over him as he reached for his boots. He'd been hoping to pretend, at least for the morning, that the box wasn't sitting on their table, whispering at the edge of his awareness.

Farah, of course, had no interest in pretending.

As he tugged on his boots, he glanced at her. She was fastening the last jeweled dagger to her belt, her brow slightly furrowed in thought, already leagues ahead of him in whatever plan she was constructing.

"So," he drawled, standing and stretching, "what are the odds that the scholars will take one look at this thing, declare it an insignificant trinket, and send us on our way?"

Farah shot him a dry look. "Not high."

"Right," he muttered. "Didn't think so."

She grabbed the box and tucked it into the belt at her waist, securing it as though it were any other piece of equipment. It wasn't. Even without opening it, he could feel that much. It wasn't like the Eye of Rashnu, humming with something alive beneath its surface, but it carried a weight that made the back of his neck itch.

"You sure you want to let them poke at it?" he asked, keeping his tone light. "If this thing is connected to the shadows—"

"That's why we need to know what it is," she said firmly. "Before we walk into something worse."

He couldn't argue with that. But he didn't like the way the box sat against her side, as if it were already a part of her kit. As if it already knew more than they did.

Still, he wasn't particularly keen on putting this thing in a room full of people who would probably argue over its significance for an hour before actually doing anything useful with it.

They left their quarters, walking in step down the stone corridor. The Citadel hummed with its usual morning activity. Servants moving briskly with trays and baskets, armored guards stationed at key junctures, and the faint, distant murmur of councilors in their own debates. But he barely noticed the movement around them.

Farah was too quiet. Not just her usual brand of quiet, the focused, assessing silence of a woman already thinking five steps ahead, already measuring every possibility before they even reached the Mashya's chamber. She wasn't tense, not exactly. She never showed her edges that way. But he could see it in the way her hands stayed still at her sides, rather than resting on the hilt of her blade or flexing as if she was readying a punch. In the way she walked just a little too straight, shoulders drawn back as though bracing for another burden.

"You didn't answer me last night," he said, stuffing his hands into his pockets as they turned a corner.

She glanced at him. "About what?"

"The odds," he clarified. "Come on, Phoenix. Give me something. How bad do you think this is?"

She hesitated for a fraction too long.

He narrowed his eyes. "That bad, huh?"

"I don't know," she admitted. "But if it was nothing, those people wouldn't have risked everything to run."

That sobered him. He thought of the woman, the way Farah had described her standing in the middle of town, the way the shadows clung to her. The image bled into Pari's drawing in his mind, the cliffs in the background, the dark tendrils reaching. It was all pieces of something, but none of it was fitting together yet completely. That was the part that worried him.

They reached the double doors leading to the chamber where the Mashya had called for the scholars to meet. Two guards stationed outside straightened as Farah approached, offering quick bows before pulling the doors open.

"Well," he muttered, stepping inside beside her, "let's see what kind of mess we're dealing with."

The chamber was dimly lit, the morning sun filtering in through high windows, casting long, slanted beams across the polished stone floor. The room itself wasn't large, more suited for private discussions than grand councils, and at its center stood a wide table, already cluttered with scrolls, ink pots, and various instruments used for examining artifacts. Several scholars had gathered, their muted robes marking them as experts in historical and mystical study. The Mashya stood at the head of the table, his hands clasped behind his back, his expression carefully neutral.

Farah strode forward, removing the box from her belt and setting it onto the table with deliberate care. He followed, less eager but no less curious, eyes flicking between the gathered scholars and the unassuming container that had already stirred too many questions.

"This is what was taken from Sakasan?" One of the scholars asked, staring at the box.

Farah nodded. "They stole it from the ones who had already fallen under the corruption. They were afraid to bring it, but more afraid to leave it behind."

He saw the way Enayat's fingers curled subtly at his sides before he stepped forward and reached for the box. He didn't open it.

"You felt it," the Mashya said, not looking at Yasher, but directing the words at him all the same.

He tensed. He didn't want to answer that.

"I felt something," he admitted. "It's not like the Eye, not like something whole, but it's—" he exhaled sharply, rubbing his jaw. "Wrong."

A sharp glance from Enayat. "And you know what right feels like?"

He met the Mashya's gaze, but this time, there was no smirk, no easy deflection. No quip to hide behind. His skin still prickled with the weight of the fragment's presence, like the air had shifted just slightly out of sync with the world around them. He rolled his shoulders, trying to shake the sensation, but it clung to him, just at the edges of his awareness.

"I carried a relic for years," he said, voice lower than usual, like speaking it too loudly might make it real. "I know what they feel like when they want to work with you, or want something from you."

His fingers flexed, resisting the urge to touch his coat pocket, where the Eye of Rashnu had once sat. That relic had hummed with purpose, with certainty. This one—it was different.

He nodded toward the box.

"This isn't like the Eye. That one had a direction. A will. This?" He shook his head. "It's broken. Like it's trying to pull at something, but there's nothing for it to hold on to. And if it ever finds what it's looking for…"

A muscle in his jaw twitched. "I don't think we want to be anywhere near it when it does."

Silence settled in the room, heavy as iron.

He flicked a glance at Farah. She was watching him, her brows drawn just slightly, her dark eyes unreadable. She felt it too.

The Mashya's gaze remained steady, but Yasher didn't miss the way his fingers flexed at his sides like he was weighing something, calculating. He had seen enough rulers to know when a man was debating whether to acknowledge a problem or bury it.

Finally, Enayat exhaled, slow and measured.

"Then we have to find out what it wants."

He let loose a quiet breath, shaking his head, taking everything in his power not to say what he was thinking out loud. *Right. Because that always ends well.*

The Mashya nodded once, turning to Farah. "Open it."

She undid the latch, her hands steady. The moment the lid lifted, the air in the room seemed to shift—shudder.

A whisper, too faint to be sound, too present to be ignored, crawled along Yasher's spine. The light from the windows dimmed. Not entirely, but enough that the room felt smaller, the air heavier.

The box contained only a small scrap of fabric, no larger than his palm. It was dark, a deep indigo threaded with silver and gold embroidery that shimmered in the low light, but looked as though it was deeply tarnished.

And it pulsed. Breathed.

No one else reacted.

Or, at least, the scholars didn't. They were too busy muttering about the stitching, the faded embroidery, while Yasher clenched his fists, forcing himself to stand still. Something about this thing was twisting around the edges of his Luck, catching on threads he hadn't meant to pull.

And when he flicked a glance at Farah—She felt it too.

She stiffened beside him, her hands gripping the edge of the table. Her face was pale, her dark eyes locked onto the fragment like it had whispered something meant only for her.

A tremor passed through him, something cold slithering beneath his skin. He didn't just feel the fragment, he saw it. Or maybe it saw him.

The edges of the room blurred. Shadows stretched

unnaturally, curling toward them, wavering like figures barely out of reach. And then—

A soundless voice.

A pull.

Not from the fabric fragment itself, but from something beyond it.

He staggered back, cursing under his breath, wrenching his gaze away from the fabric as if severing an invisible tether. His breath came quicker, heart hammering, the residual weight of the moment still pressing down on his chest.

The scholars, oblivious to whatever had just looked at them through that scrap of fabric, exchanged cautious whispers.

One of them, a woman with sharp features and a severe braid, leaned forward, studying the fragment. "This... this is a piece of the Veil of Takhsha. We have notes that the Mashyana had found a piece of it, but it was never catalogued within the collection."

The words rang out like a hammer striking metal.

Enayat's head snapped toward the scholar. "You're certain?"

"There is no mistaking it." The woman gestured to the embroidery, tracing the delicate silver thread. "The design is unmistakable. The Veil was woven with celestial imagery, stitched with starlight itself, according to the legends." She hesitated, before adding, "This fragment is... corrupted with some other essence. Its energy is wrong."

He let out a humorless laugh, shaking out his hands

as if he could rid himself of the sensation still lingering under his skin. "Yeah, no kidding."

Farah exhaled slowly, her grip loosening from the table at last.

"If it's corrupted," she said carefully, "then it could explain what's happening in Sakasan."

"The Veil of Takhsha was meant to guide and protect, from the Yazata it is named for," the scholar murmured. "If it has been tainted, twisted... it could be doing the opposite."

A slow, creeping realization settled over them.

He frowned, rubbing the back of his neck. "So what happens when we take this thing back to the Cliffs?"

Farah met his gaze. "We find out what's waiting for us. They'll want it back."

"Great," he couldn't help himself. "I love bringing the bait to something that would love to kill us."

His thoughts flickered back to Pari's drawing, to the dark figures curling around them, the Cliffs looming at their backs. They'd thought the sketch was a warning of something coming. But what if it wasn't a warning?

What if it was a promise?

The weight of the air in the chamber pressed down like the moment before a storm, thick and waiting. The Veil fragment rested in its box, unmoving. Harmless in appearance.

Yasher had seen enough illusions in his life to know better.

He could still feel the ghost of that pull in his chest, the lingering awareness of something reaching, something watching. The Veil's fragment sat there innocuously, a strip of fabric that shouldn't have been able to press down on him like a storm about to break.

The Mashya's voice cut through the thick air, his hand reaching out to close the lid of the box but hovering over it instead.

"We cannot risk leaving this unchecked." His expression was grim, his usually composed features betraying a flicker of unease. He turned to Farah. "If this fragment is what warped Sakasan, if more of the Veil is there, we need to contain it before it spreads."

Farah nodded, her gaze unreadable, but he knew her well enough to catch the tension in her stance.

One of the scholars hesitated, looking between them.

"We should study it first," she suggested. "If we move without understanding what we're dealing with—"

"Understanding won't change the fact that people are already suffering," Farah cut in, her voice sharp. "We don't have time to debate theory while families are fleeing in the night from ten times more of the corruption that we all just felt."

He watched the way the scholar ducked her head, conceding to Farah's certainty. He had seen it a hundred times before. Farah's presence in a room could be as cutting as a blade. She didn't wield her authority through intimidation, not like Behnaz had. But she had the weight of experience behind her, and that left little room for argument.

Still, he didn't like this. The fragment wanted something. He had felt it. Farah had felt it. The way it reached… he rubbed his chest absently, trying to shake off the sensation.

"If this thing has a hold on Sakasan," he said, watching the flickering shadows from the torches along the walls, "what makes us think it won't have a hold on us too?"

The scholars murmured amongst themselves, but the Mashya's gaze stayed steady.

The Mashya's gaze stayed steady. "Farah, you can sense these relics for what they are. And Yasher—" His dark eyes flicked to him, assessing, weighing. "You seem to have an affinity for things others don't see."

He didn't like the way Enayat said that.

That was the problem with people who sat on thrones. They saw value in people as things. Saw usefulness. And Yasher had been useful before. He knew how that game worked, and he knew what happened when you let someone in power start expecting things from you.

The Mashya thought Yasher's Luck, the same thing that had carried him through every near-miss and disastrous choice, could be turned toward a purpose. But his Luck didn't work that way. Not predictably. Not safely. Especially not lately.

He forced a smirk, the kind meant to push back just enough without getting himself kicked out of the room. "I prefer to call it bad luck."

The Mashya didn't return his humor. "Then let's hope your bad luck serves Emari well again."

Yasher didn't argue. He didn't need to. The moment

Enayat had turned that sharp gaze on him, the decision had already been made.

Farah reached for the box again, but this time when she closed the lid, something shifted. Not the relic, but the air itself.

A flicker. A ripple that he felt before he saw.

It was like standing on a deck when the current suddenly changed beneath the hull. Like the split-second before a dice roll that you knew was going to land wrong. His pulse stuttered in his throat, his chest tightening with the kind of instinct that had kept him alive more times than he cared to count.

Luck bent in moments like this. Twisted.

He wasn't sure what the fragment had reached for, or who it reached for.

Farah barely reacted, her expression controlled, but he knew better. She'd felt it too.

Still, she pressed the lid down, locking whatever hum of power it carried back into silence.

He rolled his shoulders, but the tension didn't fade.

The Mashya turned to Farah, his expression solemn. "Gather your team. Leave as soon as preparations are ready."

She inclined her head, but his focus stayed on her hands, on the way her fingers pressed against the lid of the box, as if feeling for something unseen.

She wasn't entirely sure what they had just walked into.

Neither was he.

Her fingers stilled, just for a fraction of a second. A pause so brief no one else in the room would have caught it. But he did. He knew the way she moved, the way she held herself. And right now, she wasn't just holding onto the box, she was bracing for something.

Her dark eyes flicked to him, only for a moment. Not questioning. Not uncertain. Just aware.

The others could argue over relics and corruption. They could theorize. Debate.

But whatever had just reached for them through the fragment, whatever had *seen* them—

They were already part of it.

And they both knew it.

CHAPTER 10

THE ARMORY SMELLED of oiled leather and steel, a grounding scent that wrapped around Farah like a second skin. Outside, the Citadel was stirring, the hush of dawn giving way to the measured rhythm of the day's first movements—guards switching shifts, servants changing out the braziers, the distant murmur of voices beyond the stone corridors. The sky was the soft blue-gray of early morning, the air thick with salt from the Kaymar Straits.

The barge was waiting.

Of course, she was picking the weapons she usually used, but this time, she let her talent take over. The slight humming that came from each piece of metal in the space forced a small on her face. It wasn't long before she'd chosen her weapons for each situation they might find themselves in. She cinched the ties of her traveling coat, adjusting the drape of the fabric so it wouldn't hinder her movement. Beneath it, she wore only the essentials, reinforced bracers strapped over her forearms, the light leather harness that secured her weapons.

She tugged the belt at her waist tighter, checking the weight of the twin blades at her back. The small throwing knives at her wrists. The daggers hidden beneath the folds of her coat. It was enough for most anything she'd need on the road, though she wondered still how to fight shadows with her weapons.

A familiar presence filled the space behind her before she heard him move. Steady steps, measured and deliberate, each one carrying the quiet authority of a man who had spent his life walking into battle and surviving it. She didn't need to turn around to know who it was.

"You're early," Rostam said, his voice carrying the dry rasp of someone who had been awake long before dawn.

She smirked faintly. "So are you."

He huffed, a sound that on another man, might have passed for amusement. But Rostam had never been a man prone to laughter.

She heard the muted rustle of cloth as he set something down beside her. A weapon belt, heavier than her own, the familiar creak of leather-wrapped steel filling the space between them. Even after all these years, Rostam handled each piece of his armor with the reverence of a man who understood its weight. Not just in battle, but in what it meant to carry.

"Your team is ready," he said, fastening the straps of his bracers. "Hand-picked, as promised. They know how to move unseen. They know how to fight. And they will protect you."

She nodded, adjusting the blade at her hip. "I trust your judgment."

He grunted, which in his language was an acknowledgment.

"I don't like this," he admitted after a long moment.

She straightened, turning to face him fully. "You don't trust Sakasan."

"No," he said plainly. "And I don't trust what's waiting for you there."

She let out a slow breath, already expecting the argument but unwilling to bend. "We've been over this."

"And we'll go over it again," he said, his dark gaze sharp as flint. "I don't want you walking into this alone."

She squared her shoulders. "And again, I won't be alone. I have Yasher, along with your team. I won't say it will be fine, but we are as prepared as we can be."

Rostam's jaw tightened. He exhaled through his nose, slow and heavy, his eyes narrowing just slightly as he looked at her.

She arched a brow, knowing she was in for another lecture. "You don't approve."

"It's not about approval." He adjusted his belt, the motion sharp, as if it helped rein in whatever response he wanted to give. "I don't like him. I never have. He talks too much, he acts before he thinks, and he plays every situation like it's a card game he can win, more often than not because he's cheating."

"But," he said, voice lower now, steadier, "you trust him. And more than that—he's good for you. He sees you." His gaze met hers, unflinching. "And if he's the one at your side when it all goes to hell, I'd rather it be him than anyone else."

The words settled like stone between them, heavy, unsaid for too long.

"However, this isn't a game. Don't forget that."

She swallowed, throat tight. "I haven't, and I won't."

"Have you?" Rostam studied her, not with doubt, but something deeper. Concern. "Because I know how you throw yourself into a fight. I've seen you take risks no one else would because you thought it was your responsibility to set things to rights that can't be."

She held his gaze, something tight winding in her chest. "It is my responsibility."

Rostam sighed, rubbing a hand over his face, the weariness in his eyes deeper than just a lack of sleep. "You remind me of him far too often."

Her hands stilled on the buckle of her belt. "Who?"

Rostam didn't answer immediately. Instead, he adjusted the bracers on his forearms, his fingers tightening on the leather straps, as if grounding himself.

"Enayat," he said at last.

She exhaled slowly. "I'm not him."

"No," he said, his voice quieter now. "But you're standing where he stood. Carrying what he carried, which is always more than you need to." He hesitated, then added, "And I saw what it did to him, long before that Crown sat on his head."

She wanted to argue, to say it wasn't the same, but she saw his point. She had been made for this, trained for it since she was old enough to hold a sword. Not just to fight, but to serve. To bear the weight of decisions others couldn't. To stand in the spaces no one else dared. Which really was just a different space but the end was the same for the Mashya.

She lifted her chin. "Then I'll carry it well."

Rostam watched her for a long moment, then nodded. "See that you do."

But the way his fingers tapped against the edge of his belt, the slight shift in his stance, betrayed him. Rostam wasn't just uneasy. He was ready.

Farah knew the way he measured the space between them, the unspoken calculation of whether he could change her course. But they both knew he couldn't. She tightened the strap of her vambrace, glancing at him from the corner of her eye. "You're standing like a man ready to draw steel."

Rostam exhaled through his nose, low and sharp. "I don't like sending you into this. Everything around this feels wrong."

She tilted her head, studying him. "You're not coming."

A flicker of something crossed his face. Regret, frustration, something quieter beneath the surface, something heavier.

He adjusted the strap of his vambrace, but the movement was too sharp. "If the Mashya would allow it, I would. My place is here."

She understood what he wasn't saying. It was killing him to stay behind. She would love to have him at her side in so many ways, but she knew it wouldn't happen.

Enayat needed him. The Citadel needed him. His

absence, after everything, would be noticed. It would be felt, and taken advantage of by certain factions.

He stepped closer, placing a firm hand on her shoulder.

"You were my best student," he said, voice quieter now, rough around the edges. "You still are."

She held his gaze, feeling the weight of the moment settle between them.

"Come on," he said, his voice shifting back to something gruff and familiar. "Let's get you on that barge before your gharib starts causing trouble. Again."

She chuckled, shaking her head as she turned back to her weapons, checking the blade at her hip.

The sky had shifted from the blue-gray hush of dawn to something sharper, something brighter. The sun crested over the horizon, casting long streaks of gold across the stone walls of the Citadel. The tide was coming in. The barge would be waiting.

***

THE BRINY AIR of the Kaymar Straits filled Farah's lungs, sharp and clean, a contrast to the quiet tension pressing at the back of her mind. The early morning breeze lifted the edges of her coat as she walked, familiar in its weight, routine in the way it settled around her. This wasn't new. She had crossed to the mainland countless times, overseeing repairs, negotiating uneasy settlements, tracking the remnants of Behnaz's damage across Emari.

They descended the worn stone steps leading down

to the docks. A barge waited at the end of the pier, its hull bobbing slightly with the gentle pull of the tide. The oarsmen were already loading supplies, their movements efficient and practiced.

"This is your last chance to pretend you've come to your senses," Rostam said, voice pitched low enough that only she could hear. "We can tell Enayat..."

She didn't slow, didn't entertain the question, because it wasn't one. "This is what I've signed up for."

He sighed. "I know."

She flicked a glance at him, catching the way his jaw tensed, the muscle feathering like he was biting down words he wanted to say but knew she wouldn't listen to. Rostam didn't waste breath on unnecessary warnings, didn't try to shield her from the truths she already carried. But his concern was woven into every action, each time he checked the equipment again, asked yet another question, and even started pulling on the ropes as though he knew what it took to make a ship safe.

And now, the way his fingers twitched at his side. Restless, unspent energy in a man who was always prepared for a fight. Rostam didn't like many things, but when he voiced it, it usually meant his instincts had already measured the risk.

Yasher stretched his arms over his head, casting a glance over his shoulder. "Rostam, I think this might be the first time I've seen you this tense. It's almost like you don't trust us."

Rostam didn't break stride. "Trust has nothing to do with it."

Yasher smirked. "Ah. So, you're just leaning into being naturally brooding?"

Rostam shot him a look. Dry, unimpressed, but missing the usual edge of irritation when he looked at him. "No. I'm naturally wary of reckless idiots found on the roadside."

She chuckled, adjusting the strap of her pack before he would go on another rant about Yasher. "You're letting us go anyway."

"Not by choice," Rostam muttered, staring him down.

Yasher's grin widened, but he didn't press further, thankfully.

They reached the edge of the pier, the barge swaying gently as the oarsmen secured the last of the provisions. The soldiers behind them adjusted their packs, shifting their weight as they prepared to board.

Rostam turned fully to her, his dark gaze steady, unreadable. "You know your priorities."

She nodded. "Find out what's happening in Sakasan. Handle it."

"Without getting yourself killed," he amended.

Farah tilted her head. "That part's implied."

Rostam exhaled sharply, something close to a scoff, but the tension in his shoulders didn't ease. His dark eyes lingered on her, searching. She didn't know what he expected to find. Reassurance? Certainty? She couldn't give him that. She was going, and they both knew there was no stopping her.

After a long moment, Rostam turned his attention to Yasher.

"Watch her back, gharib," he said, voice quieter, weighted. "Don't let her do everything alone. And bring her back."

The humor in Yasher's expression faltered, just slightly. He only nodded.

"I will."

He held Yasher's gaze a beat longer, then gave a short nod.

Rostam clasped her shoulder, the weight of his grip solid and grounding. "We'll be ready if you need us."

She nodded, her throat tightening against the response she wanted to give.

The wooden planks of the dock groaned beneath their boots as they made their way toward the waiting barge, the early morning mist curling in lazy tendrils around the ropes and moorings. The water lapped gently against the hull, the tide pulling steady beneath them.

Farah grounded herself in the movement around her. The creak of rigging in the wind, the low murmur of oarsmen preparing to shove off, the rhythmic sound of boots against damp wood.

One step. Then another. Then—

"Farah."

She turned before the voice had fully registered, recognizing it the same way she recognized the scent of saffron in the air.

Shirin stood at the edge of the dock, arms crossed, her dark eyes steady and knowing. Beside her, gripping the straps of a rucksack too large for her small frame, was Pari.

Farah exhaled. "You shouldn't be here."

Pari, undeterred, lifted her chin. "But I am."

Yasher groaned under his breath. "Oh, for the love of—"

Pari ignored him.

Shirin, ever patient, inclined her head slightly. "She's been packed since last night," she said, voice light, but threaded with something that made Farah's stomach twist. "She drew the three of you on a barge and decided it was happening, whether I liked it or not."

She had learned, over time, that when the little girl drew something, they were not guesses. They were certainties waiting to unfold.

"She's right," Pari said, her voice softer now. "You need me."

"Pari." Her voice carried the weight of command, but Pari didn't waver. She already felt the argument slipping through her fingers before she could even shape it.

"I know it's dangerous," Pari cut in before Farah could continue. "But I keep drawing it. I keep *seeing* it. And Rashnu—" She hesitated, her small hands gripping the straps of her pack. "He won't show me anything else. The Cliffs."

Farah's jaw tightened. "That's not enough of a reason to—"

"You won't change her mind," Shirin interrupted gently. "If I try to keep her here, she'll just find another way to follow you."

"*I* would," Pari confirmed with an unapologetic nod.

Yasher let out a breath. "She's got us there. Not like she hasn't before."

Farah shot him a look.

"I'm just saying," he continued, lifting his hands in surrender, "she's annoyingly persistent. And first time we took a barge to Rumatin, she just appeared and never told us how she got there to stop you from throttling me. You, of all people, should appreciate that."

Farah's glare softened just a fraction.

Pari, sensing the shift, turned her wide, earnest eyes on her. "Please," she said, voice quieter now. "I have to be there."

Farah glanced at Shirin again, but the older woman just gave her a small, knowing look. It was the same one she'd given Farah every time she walked into Shirin's tea shop looking like she'd been wrung dry by duty. The kind of look that said *You already know what you need to do. You just don't want to admit it yet.*

Pari's words hung in the air, wrapping around Farah with an inevitability she didn't want to acknowledge.

You need me.

Her gut reaction was to refuse, to send Pari back, to remind her that this wasn't a game, that visions, no matter how certain or how persistent, weren't reason enough to drag a child into danger. That wasn't how this would work.

Pari had already seen it. And Rashnu did not give warnings for things that could be undone.

Farah felt the weight of Shirin's gaze, knowing what she would see reflected there. Sadness, a little bit of fear, but also an acceptance that this had already been decided. Not by Shirin. Not even by Pari. Her fists clenched at her sides. She hated this, she hated that she couldn't stop it.

"Damned Divine," she muttered under her breath.

Pari didn't smirk, didn't celebrate. She only waited, her expression as serious as Farah had ever seen it.

Farah inhaled and exhaled deeply before setting down the rules. "If you're coming, you stay near Yasher or me at all times. If anything feels wrong, if I say we need to leave, you don't argue, you don't say a word. You do everything exactly how I say to do it. Do you understand?"

Pari nodded, her small hands tightening around the straps of her pack.

She closed her eyes briefly before reaching out to adjust Pari's rucksack to sit more comfortably on her shoulders.

Shirin said nothing, but when Farah looked at her, there was something quiet in her expression. Something that understood how painful it was to agree to the little girl's demand.

Yasher sighed dramatically, ruffling her hair. "Now I have two of you to keep out of trouble."

Pari grinned. "I'll keep you out of trouble."

"With you, Little Divine, I never doubt that."

Shirin huffed a quiet laugh, shaking her head before turning to Rostam, who had been watching with the patience of a man who had long since given up trying to steer fate.

Shirin stepped closer, reaching up to cup Farah's cheek with the ease of someone who had done it a hundred times before. The warmth of her palm was steady, grounding, a touch that had soothed Farah in childhood, had reminded her of softness in the years when all she had known was steel.

She should have pulled away. Should have been used to this by now.

But the weight of it nearly undid her.

"You always act like you have to bear it all yourself," Shirin murmured, her voice quiet, firm. "But you don't, Little Phoenix. You take care of that child, but take care of yourself too."

Farah closed her eyes for the briefest moment. When she opened them again, Shirin was still watching her, still waiting for a promise.

"You come back, all of you," Shirin said, her voice softer now, edged with something that felt dangerously close to hope. "No matter what."

Farah nodded, sharp and quick, before she could do something foolish like break.

Shirin exhaled, then, because she knew Farah, because she understood what she could and could not say, she let her go.

Rostam's hand found her shoulder, a heavy, steady weight. "The barge is waiting," he said, voice unreadable.

Farah knew what he wasn't saying. *I should be going with you.*

Rostam didn't look convinced.

Yasher clapped him on the shoulder as he passed. "I'll bring her back in one piece."

Rostam didn't dignify that with a response.

"You don't come by the shop anymore, Rostam," Shirin said, her tone stern, but putting her arm in his.

"You need to change that soon. I keep your favorite blend at the ready."

Pari, beaming, took Yasher's hand as they stepped onto the barge.

Yasher sighed, looking to Farah. "This is going to be a disaster, isn't it?"

She arched a brow. "Hasn't it always been?"

The barge rocked gently, pulling away from the dock with quiet inevitability. Farah stood near the bow, the briny wind tugging at the edges of her coat, carrying the scent of salt and damp wood. She didn't turn back. There was nothing behind her she hadn't already memorized, no faces she hadn't already committed to memory.

A familiar warmth pressed against her side. Yasher, standing just close enough that their shoulders brushed, his presence grounding, steady.

"You're thinking too much again," he murmured, his voice a low thread of sound meant only for her.

She sighed, the tension in her ribs refusing to loosen. "Not thinking enough is how people end up dead."

He hummed, then, with quiet deliberation, reached down and laced his fingers through hers. His grip was loose but certain, a touch meant to remind her that she wasn't carrying this alone.

"Still," he murmured, tilting his head toward her, his breath warm against her temple, "don't let the ghosts get to you before we even reach them."

Farah didn't answer right away. The mist thickened around them, swallowing the horizon in a pale shroud, erasing the line between where they had been and where they were going. She stared into it, the weight of Pari's drawings, of the relic, of whatever waited for them at the Cliffs pressing heavier against her ribs.

She turned her head just enough to meet Yasher's gaze, his blue eyes sharp even in the dim light. His thumb brushed absently over the back of her hand.

"Then let's hope we don't meet any ghosts," she murmured.

Yasher's fingers curled tighter around hers.

The mist swallowed them whole.

CHAPTER II

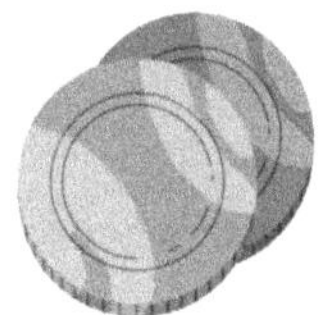

The barge rocked gently as it pulled away from the docks, the lanterns of the Citadel shrinking into the mist curling over the water. The morning air carried the scent of salt and damp wood, thick with the lingering smoke of the torches lining the harbor. Yasher leaned against the railing, watching the dark waves shift beneath them, their surface broken only by the occasional crest of white foam.

The straits were calm this morning. Too calm. He had learned not to trust quiet, especially when it came wrapped in the illusion of smooth sailing. Luck had a way of tipping the scales just when you started thinking they might stay balanced. He rolled his shoulders, the tension in his spine refusing to unknot, like a gambler holding a bad hand and waiting for the final card to turn.

He turned his head, letting his gaze drift over the deck.

Farah stood near the center, speaking with one of Rostam's soldiers, her voice low and measured. The wind tugged at the loose strands of her hair, but she barely seemed to notice. Even here, with no court watching, no nobles scheming, she carried herself as if she were still in the Citadel, still bearing the weight of Emari's future on her shoulders. She never let it go, not fully. He knew better than to tell her to relax, it wasn't in her nature and at best he'd get an eye roll out of her.

Pari had settled herself near the coiled ropes by the mast, knees drawn up, sketchbook resting on her lap. She hadn't spoken much since they'd boarded, only humming softly to herself as she moved her charcoal across the page.

And then, at the bow, settled in as if she'd been there from the start, was Jeta Veseli.

He froze mid-step.

The old woman sat with her legs folded neatly beneath her, the long sleeves of her emerald coat framing the slow, steady movements of her hands as she knitted with a patience that felt unnerving in its certainty. The golden embroidery, worn as it was, still catching the pale morning light like glinting thread spun from secrets. He hadn't noticed her when they boarded—no one had. But that was the problem with Jeta Veseli.

She was never where you expected her to be, she was where she chose to be.

Yasher pushed off the railing and crossed the deck, stopping a few feet from her.

"Did you get lost?"

Jeta didn't even look up. Her hands kept working, needles clicking softly against each other.

"I don't get lost," she said simply.

He tilted his head, crossing his arms. "That so? Funny, I didn't realize Sakasan had become such a popular destination." He arched a brow. "Or did I miss the part where people are lining up to visit a town that's barely on the maps?"

Her hands never stilled, the steady rhythm of her knitting never faltering. "My plans do not include stopping in Sakasan." She tilted her head slightly, as if considering something unseen.

A soft click of her needles, a pause just long enough to be intentional as she gave him a sidelong glance, her lips twitching slightly. "But then, the gods have a way of turning the best-laid plans into their own private joke. Fickle bastards."

Her needles clicked, deliberate, final.

He narrowed his eyes. "Then why are you here?"

She lifted her gaze just slightly, her expression as unreadable as ever. "This barge runs between the Citadel and Rumatin, does it not?"

He exhaled sharply. "Don't dance around it, old woman. Where are you going?"

Jeta's lips twitched in something that wasn't quite amusement. "Tamidh."

That gave him pause. His eyes flicked to the bundle at her feet. A travel pack, modest and neatly tied. Not much for a journey across the entire country, but Jeta didn't seem the type to need much.

"You're going all the way across the kingdom?" he asked, skeptical. "And you're taking a barge to Rumatin first?"

Jeta finally glanced up, her sharp gaze unreadable. "You say that as if there's another way off the island."

While he'd pose that was a fair point if he wasn't so irritated at her existence, he didn't trust the old woman. Tamidh was an exhausting journey across Emari, either by caravan or, if she was particularly unlucky, on foot. And even if she got there in one piece, the rebels surrounding the second largest city in Emari would hear one smart thing out of her mouth and possibly burn her at the stake.

"You plan on taking the roads alone?" he asked. "Because if so, I've got to say, that's a terrible plan. You've heard that there are riots in Banima because of the harvest shortages."

Jeta's lips quirked slightly, though it barely qualified as amusement. "Your concern is noted."

"You're being cryptic."

"I prefer to think of it as practical." She resumed her knitting, as if that settled the matter.

He felt the sigh escape. He knew better than to try dragging answers out of someone who had no interest in giving them. He'd dealt with enough smug bastards in his life to recognize a professional when he saw one. Still, something about it gnawed at him.

"What's in Tamidh?"

Jeta's hands didn't pause. "Would you believe me if I said old friends?"

"No."

Her lips twitched again. "Then let's just say I'm needed there. My time in the Citadel has drawn to a close for now."

He didn't like the sound of that. There were a thousand reasons someone might be needed in Tamidh, and few of them were good. The city had been the heart of the rebellion, and even now, with Enayat trying to stitch the country back together, it was far from stable, with anyone sent to speak with them turned away as they built up their defenses. If Jeta was heading into that storm, it wasn't just for a social visit.

He folded his arms, glancing toward where Farah stood just a little ways away, deep in conversation with one of Rostam's soldiers. "And you just happened to pick the same barge as us?"

Jeta didn't look up. "Oh, *saqalu*, your ego is healthy. You think I'm following you."

"I think you have a knack for showing up exactly where you shouldn't be."

She let out a quiet chuckle. "Then we have that in common, don't we?"

He scowled, but before he could respond Farah called his name, waving him over. Jeta's attention flicked briefly to her before she returned to her work, her dismissal as clear as if she'd said it outright.

Whatever she was up to, she wasn't going to explain it here. But he couldn't shake the feeling that, whatever it was, it wasn't something he was going to like.

Farah glanced up as he approached, her gaze flicking past him toward the bow. "Did I just see Jeta Veseli sitting on this barge, knitting?"

He huffed a dry laugh. "You did."

Her brows furrowed. "Why is she here?"

"She says she's going to Tamidh."

"Tamidh," she echoed, her tone carefully even.

He leaned against the railing beside her, keeping his voice low. "Apparently, she's taking 'the long way round.' Didn't say much beyond that."

Farah frowned, her gaze flicking back toward the bow where Jeta still sat, her hands working methodically over her knitting.

"That doesn't make sense," she murmured. "She's been in the Citadel for as long as I can remember. No interest in leaving after the chaos, just kept teaching."

He grunted. "Maybe she finally got tired of being useful."

Farah's expression remained unreadable, but he knew her well enough to see the gears turning behind her eyes.

"Tamidh is not exactly friendly territory," she said at last. "While the rebels have calmed down since the Mashya retook the throne, they have been a thorn in the sides of the nobles down that way still."

"You think she's heading into trouble?"

"I don't know," Farah admitted. "But if she's going there now, it means she thinks something is worth the risk. Or you've run her off with not listening to her."

He tapped his fingers against the railing, casting a glance back toward the bow, ignoring Farah's jab. Jeta hadn't so much as looked their way since he'd walked off. "She doesn't seem the type to take a trip for sentimental reasons."

"No," she agreed. "She's not. I'd say she's the exact opposite of sentimental."

They fell silent for a moment, the only sound the

rhythmic creak of the barge and the gentle lap of waves against the hull.

Finally, he sighed. "Should we be worried about the old woman on her own?"

She hesitated, then shook her head. "Not yet."

That wasn't exactly reassuring. But he'd learned that with Farah, "not yet" was usually the best he was going to get.

"Well," he said, pushing off the railing, "if she is heading into trouble, at least we don't have to be the ones dealing with it for once. Whatever caravan she travels with can put up with her cryptic words and random irritations."

She shot him a look, unimpressed.

He grinned. "What? I can't be happy that for once, we're not the ones making questionable life choices? At least, not the same questionable life choices. The difference in having a royal mandate for our poor choices makes it better, right?"

Farah didn't respond right away. Instead, she exhaled sharply, her jaw tightening in that way that meant she was biting back whatever she actually wanted to say. Not unusual. Farah kept things locked down tighter than a noble's vault, but this was different. More brittle. Like something had already worn her thin before he even opened his mouth.

"Fine," she muttered, shifting her weight, adjusting the strap across her torso with a movement that felt too deliberate.

He arched a brow. "Easy, Phoenix."

She glanced at him, the barest flicker of something

unreadable passing through her expression before she looked away again. Whatever was under her skin, she wasn't ready to talk about it. Not yet.

He let it go for now. But he clocked the way she stood a little too rigid, the way her fingers flexed at her side like she wanted to shake something off. He'd seen her tense before a fight, before a kill. This wasn't that. This was something else. Something crawling under her skin.

Instead of pushing, he sighed, rubbing the back of his neck. "There's a lot we don't like, but that doesn't mean we can fix it before we dock."

That, at least, got a response. She huffed, shaking her head, some of the tension in her shoulders loosening, even if it didn't vanish completely. She still wasn't looking at him, though. Instead, her gaze flicked toward Jeta, then past her, toward the mist curling over the water. Watching. Thinking.

He frowned, a nagging itch settling between his ribs. It wasn't like her to get stuck in her own head like this, not unless something was clawing at her from the inside.

He didn't like that she wasn't telling him something.

Jeta hadn't moved. Pari was still where they left her. The soldiers were keeping to themselves.

Nothing had changed.

And yet, Yasher had the distinct feeling that, somehow, too many things had.

YASHER ADJUSTED the strap of his pack, keeping pace with Farah as they threaded through Rumatin's tangled streets. The city was loud even in the early hours, alive with the scent of salt, spice, and sweat, the kind of layered filth that never really washed out of the stones. Dockworkers hauled crates from freshly arrived ships, traders barked their offers, and sailors—too well-paid or too desperate—lingered near tavern doors, already seeking trouble.

Familiar. Predictable in its chaos the only way a port town could be.

He felt his shoulders loosen, just a fraction. Whatever waited for them in Sakasan, at least Rumatin was exactly as he remembered—loud, crowded, and thoroughly unconcerned with anyone else's problems as long as there was coin to get you from one point to another.

Jeta walked a few steps ahead of them, her pace steady, her presence unhurried, as if she had nowhere to be and all the time in the world to get there, using her cane as an accessory instead of a needed implement. He wasn't sure if that was an affectation or just how she was. The old woman had a way of making him feel like he was the one who wasn't moving fast enough, no matter how quick his steps.

They had to cross the city to reach the stables where Rostam's soldiers had prepared their horses and supplies. The staging grounds were near the caravan quarters, where traders stopped before setting out across the mainland.

He kept his stride easy, his voice casual. "Didn't take you for someone heading to Tamidh. Thought you'd be bound for somewhere... quieter. Somewhere to be the most aggravating with your fruits and vines."

Jeta didn't slow. "Didn't take you for someone who paid attention."

He smirked. "I pay attention when things don't add up."

She adjusted the strap of her satchel. "Tamidh isn't welcoming these days. Not to outsiders. Not to insiders, either." She cast him a sidelong glance. "A wise man may steer clear."

He hummed. "And yet, here you are, old woman, running straight into it."

Jeta smiled, but there was no warmth to it. "I never claimed wisdom."

He couldn't help but laugh, shaking his head. "Fair."

Farah, who had been walking in silence, finally spoke.

"You could have left at any time," she said, her voice careful. "But you waited until now."

Jeta's lips twitched slightly, though she didn't quite smile. "You think I was waiting for something?"

"I think you were waiting for an opportunity," Farah said.

"Isn't that what we all do?" Jeta countered.

Farah didn't answer immediately. He recognized the look on her face, trying to unravel something. The old woman wasn't giving her much to work with, though. She never did.

"You could have stayed," Farah finally said. "You had a comfortable life, finally."

Jeta gave her a look that was equal parts amused and exasperated. "You already said that once, girl. And who needs comfort all the time?"

Farah's lips pressed into a thin line.

Jeta sighed through her nose. "I told you, I go where I'm needed."

"And you're needed in Tamidh," Farah repeated.

Jeta shrugged. "Seems that way."

He glanced between them. He'd spent enough time around Farah to recognize her emotion. She wanted to know why Jeta was leaving now, why she was choosing Tamidh, but she wouldn't pry if the woman didn't want to share.

Jeta must have seen it too because she let out a quiet chuckle, shaking her head.

"Don't look at me like that," she said. "I'm not abandoning your precious Citadel for all time. I never belonged there in the first place, as That Woman would remind me when I annoyed her too often. The winds may change, and the vines of time may weave me back that way again."

Farah's expression didn't change, but he caught the faintest flicker of something in her eyes. He wasn't sure if it was understanding or something sharper.

As they neared the caravan staging grounds, Jeta finally spoke again. "The road ahead of you isn't a kind one."

He laughed. "Is it ever?"

Jeta chuckled softly. "No," she admitted. "But this one? It's worse."

Farah didn't react, but he saw the way her fingers flexed at her sides.

Jeta came to a stop at the edge of the staging grounds, where traders loaded up wagons and prepared for the long trek inland. She turned toward them, her gaze steady. "Watch your backs," she said simply.

Farah nodded. "You as well."

Jeta paused before stepping fully into the flow of travelers, her gaze shifting past Yasher and Farah to where Pari stood, clutching the straps of her rucksack. The little girl had been quiet during the exchange, watching Jeta with wide, knowing eyes.

Jeta lowered herself with slow, deliberate ease, the movement practiced. She reached out, adjusting the edge of Pari's scarf where it had slipped from her shoulder. A quiet gesture. A grounding one.

"You've always seen too much, little herald," Jeta murmured, voice softer than he had ever heard it. "And you know how dangerous that can be."

Pari's fingers curled into the fabric of her pack. A beat. A hesitation. Then, barely above a whisper—

"I know."

Jeta sighed, her expression unreadable. "Good. That will keep you alive."

She slipped a hand into the folds of her coat and pulled out something small—a single wooden bead, dark with age, its edges smoothed from years of wear. The faded thread where it had once been strung into a necklace was still visible, frayed at one end. Jeta turned it between her fingers for a breath before pressing it into Pari's palm, closing the little girl's fingers over it.

"This was given to me when I was your age," Jeta said, quiet but firm. "It was once part of something whole. A necklace. A protection. A promise. But this—"

she tapped Pari's closed fist lightly, "this is all that remains."

Pari studied the bead in her hand, her thumb tracing the worn edges. "It's not magic," she murmured.

Jeta's lips quirked. Not quite a smile, not quite sorrow. "Most things that matter aren't, little herald."

She held Pari's gaze for a moment, then tilted her head. "Keep it safe for me."

Pari blinked up at her. "Until when?"

Jeta's brows lifted faintly, as if she were amused by the question.

"Until we cross paths again," she said simply. "And I will be very disappointed if you've lost it, or let that one," she pointed at him. "Gamble it away."

Pari straightened slightly, nodding as she tucked the bead into the small pouch at her waist, securing the drawstring carefully, as if protecting something far heavier than wood.

She lifted her chin, her dark eyes clear, steady. "I'll remember."

Her fingers brushed over Pari's braid, a fleeting touch.

"Good girl."

She reached up, brushing a hand over the little girl's head, smoothing down flyaway hair before straightening. Her eyes flicked to Farah, then Yasher, something unreadable settling in her gaze.

Then, without another word, she turned and slipped into the crowd.

Yasher watched her go, a strange tightness settling in

his ribs. Not quite worry, not quite regret. Just… something he couldn't shake.

He let out a breath, rocking back on his heels. "Well," he muttered, "that wasn't ominous at all."

Farah didn't respond immediately. Her gaze lingered on Pari, watching as the girl patted the pouch where the bead sat. Not just tucking it away, but holding onto it. Protecting it.

He dragged a hand through his hair, exhaling sharply. "You think she'll be all right?"

Farah didn't answer at first. Then, slowly, she turned toward the waiting soldiers, her shoulders squared, repeating what she'd said about the old woman a few days before. "Jeta Veseli doesn't do things without a reason."

That wasn't an answer.

He sighed, adjusting the strap of his pack. "Great. That's reassuring."

Pari, who had been silent throughout the exchange, turned her head just slightly, as if listening to something only she could hear.

Farah reached out, resting a steadying hand on Pari's shoulder. "Come," she said. "We have a long road ahead."

Pari nodded, and followed as Farah stepped toward the waiting caravan.

Yasher hesitated for just a second longer, casting one last glance toward the shifting crowd, where Jeta had vanished.

He had a feeling that whatever road she was walking, it wasn't any kinder than theirs.

THE ROAD STRETCHED LONG and dusty ahead of them, the last traces of Rumatin fading into the hazy horizon behind them. The sun had reached its zenith a few miles back, its light washing over the dry fields and low shrubs that lined the worn path, casting rippling shadows across the uneven ground. The scent of sun-warmed earth mixed with the distant brine of the coast, the salt lingering in the dry air like a ghost of the waters they had left behind.

Farah adjusted her grip on the reins, her mare moving at an easy, steady pace beneath her, but her mind was anything but still. A slow, creeping unease had taken root in her chest since they had left the harbor, settling just beneath her ribs, whispering at the edges of her thoughts. It was a weight, not unlike the pressure of a storm before it broke, thick and cloying in the back of her mind. She told herself it was nothing—just nerves, the accumulation of too many unknowns pressing down on her at once. Pari's drawing, the cryptic warnings, the uncertainty of what waited for them in Sakasan. It was enough to leave anyone on edge.

But she had spent years learning how to separate instinct from paranoia. And this... this was something else.

Her fingers curled, brushing the inside lining of her coat, where the small wooden box lay pressed against her side. She had decided this morning, just before they left, to carry the relic with her rather than leaving it secured in the strongbox at the back of the wagon. The soldiers had reinforced it well, Rostam had ensured that much, but something about locking the fragment away, separating it from herself, had felt wrong. It had felt better to keep it close, within reach. Just in case.

Now, as the weight of it sat against her, the faint pulse of something beneath the surface of her skin, she wondered if that had been a mistake.

She exhaled sharply, shaking the thought away. It was nothing. The relic was dormant. Just a fragment of something lost, something broken. And she had spent too long allowing herself to be shaped by things beyond her control. She would not let a forgotten remnant of the past dictate her now. The chain she kept in her pocket twisted and twirled with her Talent, bleeding the thread of tension she was carrying.

Behind her, the wagon creaked as its wheels jostled over uneven ground. Pari sat cross-legged on a bundle of supplies, her sketchbook propped against her knees, utterly absorbed in whatever she was drawing. The three soldiers—Taj, Mehran, and Younis—rode a short distance behind, quiet and watchful. They were good men, ones

Rostam trusted, and their silence was a comfort while she worked through what was bothering her. Unfortunately, Yasher was not one of those men who handled silence well.

He nudged his horse closer, the shift of his weight effortless, his presence pressing against the edges of her thoughts with all the patience of someone who had decided, without hesitation, that she needed his interruption.

"You know, if you keep brooding like that, you're going to give the shadows something to aspire to."

She shot him a dry look. "If you're trying to be poetic, you should stop."

"Oh, absolutely not," he said, shaking his head. "I'm only just getting started. What if I compared you to a storm cloud? Ominous, brooding, full of potential destruction—"

"If you're waiting for me to strike you with lightning, I can arrange it."

He grinned. "See? That's what I like about you, Phoenix. Always so proactive."

She sighed, rubbing at the back of her neck. The humor was welcome, familiar, but it didn't change the tension sitting at the base of her spine.

His smile lingered, but his eyes flickered over her, sharp beneath the charm. "You feel off."

The words came too direct, lacking his usual teasing edge, and for a moment, she hated how easily he saw through her.

"I'm fine," she said, nudging her horse forward.

He didn't argue. He just watched her for a beat longer

before tilting his head, pretending to consider. "Mm. I think I preferred the lightning threat." His voice was softer this time.

She almost smiled. Almost. Instead, she let out a breath, letting the words settle between them.

She glanced at him out of the corner of her eye. "I can still arrange it."

His grin returned, easier this time. "That's my girl."

"I don't like this," she admitted finally.

"Which part?" Yasher asked, his voice losing its usual glibness. "The going in blind? Or the fact that Pari's drawing is starting to feel like more than just a bad dream?"

Her fingers curled around the reins, gripping them a little too tightly. "Both."

He nodded. "You know, there's a third option."

She glanced at him warily. "Which is?"

"That we make it out of this unscathed, solve the mystery of the ominous shadows, and return heroes," he said, flashing her a crooked grin. "I mean, technically, we'd have to do something heroic first, but we're good at that part. Usually by accident for me, but still."

She let out a slow breath, some of the tension in her shoulders easing just slightly. "I don't think the last is going to be how it goes," she muttered, feeling the handle of her dagger vibrate against her leg.

"Why not?" He countered. "You never know. Maybe this time, we get a straightforward win. No elaborate betrayals, no hidden costs. Just a simple problem, easily solved."

She gave him a flat look. "You don't even believe that."

"Not in the slightest," he admitted cheerfully. "But I thought I'd try optimism for once."

She huffed, somewhere between amusement and exasperation. "It doesn't suit you."

"That's because you like me the way I am," he said, winking. "Charming, roguish, a little bit infuriating—"

"A lot infuriating."

"Ah, see, I knew you'd exaggerate."

She shook her head, but before she could reply, a small voice interrupted them.

"You two talk a lot," Pari observed from the cart, her eyes still on her sketchbook as her fingers moved deftly over the page.

Yasher turned, raising a brow. "And yet, you listen to every word, Little Divine."

Pari gave a tiny shrug, as if to say she couldn't help it. "You're loud."

He gasped dramatically, clutching his chest. "Loud? Me? I'll have you know, I have the voice of a man trained in subtlety and discretion."

Pari finally looked up, meeting his gaze with the kind of unimpressed expression that only a nine-year-old could master. "You yelled at a goat in Rumatin."

"The goat started it," Yasher said, affronted. "And that was a private matter between me and them."

Pari wrinkled her nose. "Goats don't talk."

"That one did," he muttered darkly. "With its eyes."

Farah sighed, pinching the bridge of her nose. "Yasher."

"Phoenix," he mimicked, though his tone was warm. He turned back to Pari. "Alright, Little Divine. What are you drawing?"

Pari hesitated, her small fingers pressing against the edge of the paper before she turned the sketchbook around. The page was only half-finished, a rough landscape emerging in careful, deliberate strokes. The road stretched ahead, the horizon sketched in bold lines, but something about it looked... unsettled. Off-balance.

"The road," she said simply.

Yasher studied the drawing, his usual glibness absent. Farah, too, lingered on the details. Pari was precise in her work, too precise for the smudges along the edges to be anything but intentional. A hesitation captured in charcoal.

She pressed her palm against the corner of the page, as if deciding whether or not to turn it. "I draw what I see," she murmured at last.

Yasher glanced at the page again, his voice light but his gaze sharp. "And what do you see now?"

Pari looked at him for a long moment before flipping the page, starting a new sketch without answering.

Yasher and Farah exchanged a glance. Neither of them liked the silence this time.

Pari's concentration was complete, her small brow furrowed in focus. Farah knew what it was to carry too much at too young an age. And she hated seeing it in the little girl.

Farah exhaled and turned her attention forward, toward the winding road ahead. *Keep moving. Keep your focus.*

She'd had enough of being trapped in her own thoughts.

"You didn't answer me, Little Divine," Yasher said suddenly, his voice light, but careful. "What do you see?"

Pari hesitated, her charcoal stilling mid-stroke, pressing just slightly too hard against the page before she lifted it. A slow breath, barely audible. Then, finally, she looked up, her dark eyes flicking between them before dropping back to the unfinished sketch.

"Nothing bad," she said at last. Too careful. Too precise.

Yasher's gaze flicked to Farah's, and she knew he caught it too. That pause. That measured, deliberate answer, like someone stepping around words they didn't want to say out loud.

Farah kept her voice even. "You'd tell us if it was?"

Pari's fingers tightened on the edge of her sketchbook. Then, slowly, she nodded.

Yasher hummed, tilting his head. "Not exactly reassuring."

"It's just the road," Pari murmured. She rubbed at the paper with the side of her hand, smudging the charcoal further. "I don't always see things."

Farah caught the way Pari's shoulders tensed. A small movement, but telling.

Pari had always been direct before. When she saw something, she spoke of it. She had no fear of prophecy, no hesitation about sharing the things when Rashnu whispered to her. But this was different. There was something else here, something unspoken, and it made Farah's stomach knot.

Farah wasn't the only one haunted on this journey.

She shifted in the saddle, choosing her words carefully.

"If something changes," she said, keeping her voice even, "you'll tell us?"

Pari hesitated. Then, slowly, she nodded.

That would have to be enough.

Yasher sighed dramatically, shifting his weight in the saddle. "Well, since we're all pretending this isn't the most ominous conversation imaginable, I suppose I'll change the subject."

Farah cast him a dry look. "You? Changing the subject? Shocking."

"I know. I have many talents," he said easily. "So, rations are dull conversation, we've already talked about the weather, you roundly scared off those bandits at the last crossroads by your sheer presence, and the road ahead is obviously cursed. What should we discuss next?" He looked between them with a grin. "Philosophy? The meaning of life? The best way to cheat at dice?"

Pari glanced at him, expression carefully neutral. "You don't cheat at dice. Cards, yes, but not dice."

He gasped in mock offense. "Little Divine, I am appalled at your lack of faith."

"You use your Luck on dice," Pari said simply. "That's not the same as regular cheating."

Farah smothered a laugh at the genuine indignation that flickered across Yasher's face.

Pari turned back to her sketchbook, seemingly satisfied that the matter was settled.

Yasher muttered under his breath, shaking his head.

"Well. That's me put in my place." He shot Farah a look. "Are you enjoying this?"

"Immensely."

He groaned, running a hand through his hair. "I am terribly outnumbered on this journey. I should have fought harder to leave Pari in the Citadel."

Farah shook her head, nudging her horse forward. Yasher matched her pace without hesitation, his usual ease returning. Pari, for her part, kept drawing, her small form curled against the bundle of supplies, charcoal smudging her fingertips.

The moment passed, but the weight in her chest didn't.

She rolled her shoulders, adjusting the reins, as if that would shake the feeling. The relic sat against her ribs, quiet but present, its weight more than just physical. She should have left it in the strongbox. Should have let it sit untouched, unseen.

But she hadn't.

And Yasher, without knowing why, stayed close. He always did.

***

THE SUN HAD NEARLY VANISHED behind the distant hills, leaving behind a wash of deep amber and violet streaks across the sky. The road beneath their horses had begun to harden with the chill of the coming night, the distant tree line of the cedar forest now a looming presence not far away. Even from here, Farah could see the dark shapes of the massive trees, their branches swaying gently in the evening breeze. The scent of resin and dry earth drifted toward them, a whisper of the deeper woods ahead.

She dismounted, boots hitting the packed dirt with a dull thud. The ache in her legs barely registered but there was a heaviness in her bones that wasn't all from the road. It sat in her chest like a swallowed stone, dragging her down.

The soldiers moved with the steady rhythm of men who had done this a hundred times before. Efficient, practiced, and silent when there was nothing worth saying. Taj unbuckled the last of the saddlebags with the ease of someone used to packing light, while Younis muttered about the state of the way their rations were packed as he crouched to check their supplies. Mehran moved to grab the cook pots out of the wagon.

Pari hopped down from the cart, sketchbook tucked under her arm, eyes flicking over their camp.

Then, simply, she said, "There's no tent for me."

She should have checked. She should have asked. But Pari had been so certain she was coming with them that no one had thought to question whether she had what she needed.

Before she could say anything, Mehran spoke.

"She can take mine," he said, already moving to unroll his bedroll near the fire. "I've slept in worse places."

Pari tilted her head at him, considering. "What's the worst place?"

Mehran didn't hesitate. "A riverbank during a flood."

Taj snorted as he tossed down his pack. "You *chose* that. We did try to warn you."

"Not my brightest moment," Mehran admitted, but there was a glint of dry humor in his eyes.

Pari nodded solemnly, as if this was the most natural solution in the world. "Thank you."

He only inclined his head before returning to his work.

Farah adjusted the strap of her pack. She should have thought of it.

She knelt, undoing the ties of her pack with more force than necessary, her fingers stiff with an irritation she couldn't name. The whisper of unease had followed her since morning, coiled beneath her ribs, sinking deeper with each passing hour. It wasn't a voice. Not quite. Not yet. But it pressed against her, like something reaching through fog, brushing just close enough to be felt—then retreating before she could grasp it.

It's nothing. Just exhaustion.

Behind her, Yasher shifted, his boots crunching softly against the dirt.

"Alright, Phoenix," he said, voice lighter than the look she could feel him giving her. "You going to tell me what's gnawing at you, or should I start taking bets?"

She exhaled sharply through her nose. "I'm fine."

"That so?" His footsteps crunched on the dry grass as he moved closer, his tone easy but not careless. "Because from where I'm standing, you look like you're about three deep breaths away from gutting someone."

She let out a sharp sigh, pulling out her whetstones

with a little more force than necessary. "It's been a long day."

He crouched beside her, resting his elbows on his knees, his usual smirk softened just a little. "And yet you're still wound tighter than a sailor counting his last coins in a rigged game."

She shot him a glare. "You could try not talking."

He grinned, entirely unrepentant. "I could. But where would the fun be in that?"

She huffed, shaking her head. "I just want to get some rest outside of the saddle."

"Uh-huh." He leaned his weight onto his elbows, watching her too closely. "That why you've been on edge since we left Rumatin? Or is it because something's sitting wrong with you, and you don't want to name it?"

Her jaw tensed. He always did this. Got too close, too perceptive, digging his way under her defenses without even trying.

"It's nothing," she muttered as she stood, but the words felt hollow.

He didn't look convinced. He tilted his head slightly, gaze flicking over her face like he was searching for something she wouldn't say.

"Well," he said, easy as anything, "I suppose I should let you get all the rest you can before I inevitably get us into trouble tomorrow."

Farah gave him a flat look. "For once in your life, try not to."

His grin widened, a glint of mischief in his eyes. "Where's the challenge in that?"

She shook her head, but when he reached for her

hand, brushing his fingers against hers, she didn't pull away. He pulled her up and wrapped his arms around her.

"Maybe some food will improve your mood," he said, kissing the top of her head before releasing her and setting up their tent.

THE MEAL that the soldiers made was simple but hearty with flatbread, dried fruit, and a thick stew that had been simmering over the fire. It was filling, but Farah barely tasted it. She ate mechanically, her mind still tangled in the weight pressing against her ribs. Next to her, Yasher chewed lazily, his usual chatter absent.

For once, he let the silence sit between them. He had read her well enough to know she didn't want conversation, and he was, at times, smart enough to know when to leave something be.

The fire crackled softly, sending occasional sparks into the night air. She leaned back on her hands, stretching her legs out in front of her, listening to the slow murmur of conversation around the camp. The soldiers had settled into a quiet routine, Mehran sharpening his blade, Taj finishing off the last of his stew, and Younis muttering about how his knees didn't tolerate long rides the way they used to.

Pari sat cross-legged by the fire, her small fingers tracing absent shapes in the dirt beside her. She had eaten little, too focused on her sketchbook earlier, and now she watched Yasher with a look that meant she was thinking about something far too big.

Then, without preamble, she said, "Tell me a story."

Yasher, who had been absently tearing apart a piece of flatbread, blinked. "A story?"

Pari nodded, tucking her feet beneath her. "A good one."

He leaned back on his elbows, exhaling through his nose in mock exasperation. "All right, Little Divine. I've got tales about a clever thief who tricked a dozen noblemen, or a sailor who played dice with the gods and won—"

"No." She shook her head, gaze steady. "Something true."

That made him pause. His fingers stilled where they had been absently toying with the torn bread. He tilted his head, considering her in that way he did when someone had caught him off guard, when he was weighing whether to sidestep or meet something head-on.

"Truth is dangerous," he murmured, almost to himself. Then, flicking a glance at Farah, he added, "People don't always like it."

Pari didn't blink. "Tell it anyway. I'll like it, I promise."

He let out a quiet breath, shaking his head with a small, rueful smile. "You're worse than she is, you know that?" He leaned over and nudged Farah.

She let out a small laugh. "I wouldn't promise that. There are plenty of your stories that aren't interesting."

Pari ignored their banter, watching Yasher with quiet patience. She didn't need to press further.

Finally, he sighed, brushing crumbs off his fingers. "All right. You want a truth? Here's a truth."

The firelight flickered, casting shifting shadows across his face as he spoke.

"Once, there was a boy who never lost a bet."

She stilled. His voice was easy, his usual storyteller's cadence slipping into place, but something was different this time. Even the soldiers paused what they were doing and came to sit around the fire as he began.

"Didn't matter if it was cards, dice, or guessing how many steps it took to cross a room. Luck followed him like a stray dog that had decided he was worth sticking around for whatever scraps were thrown its way."

Pari shifted slightly, pulling her knees up. "Did he know why?"

He hummed, tilting his head. "No. Not at first, not for a very long time. He just thought he was clever, that he was faster than the people trying to cheat him. He never stopped to wonder why his hands always drew the right card, why he could slip through the world untouched when others weren't so lucky."

She watched his face, the way his expression barely flickered, but his voice—his voice had softened at the edges, remembering versus telling.

"The boy had a family once," he continued. "A mother, a father, two older brothers. They were kind, really too kind and good for the world they lived in. They took in those who needed shelter, gave food to those who had none, medicines for those that were sick. The boy always tried to be as good, but there was always another trick, another game calling to him. One day, their kindness cost them everything."

Pari's small hands curled slightly in the fabric of her tunic. "Because of bad people?"

He flicked a glance at her, something unreadable in his gaze. "Because the world is not usually good." He let the words settle.

"The soldiers came in the night. Not for any reason that mattered. A mistake, a misunderstanding, maybe just bad luck. But the boy survived. Not because he was stronger, not because he was smarter. Because chance tipped in his favor. Just like it always did."

The fire popped, sending a stray ember spiraling into the air.

"So, the boy ran," Yasher said simply. "Because what else was there to do? He wandered, stole when he had to, gambled when he could. He was good at it. Too good. Luck still clung to him, kept him fed, kept him moving."

Pari was utterly still, her dark eyes fixed on him.

"And then, one day, he got careless." Yasher exhaled slowly, his voice quieter now. "Bet on the wrong thing. Stole from the wrong person. Got caught. Got beaten. Got left on the side of the road to die."

Pari tilted her head. "What happened?"

His mouth quirked slightly, but it wasn't amusement. "A woman found him, one that reminded him of his mother through his swollen eyes. Someone who saw a boy too young to be alone and too proud to ask for help, so she was very special out in the cold world. She gave him a place. Not much, but enough. And for a while, he thought maybe, just maybe, he could stop running."

She felt something tight in her chest. He had never told her this. Not like this. No matter how much she shared in the dark about her youth, he kept this locked away.

"But Luck doesn't let go so easily," Yasher murmured. "And when it turned again, when the woman died because she didn't have the boy's luck, and ended up in the wrong place at the wrong time, he ran once more, over and over again, keeping his distance from anyone and everything that he couldn't trick or charm for so many years. Because it was easier to keep moving than to risk losing everything all over again. If he never cared about anything but himself, no one else would get hurt because of him."

The firelight flickered, and he sat very still. He wasn't looking at anyone, just past them, to something only he could see.

Pari, in the small, solemn way of a child who understood far too much, whispered, "And then?"

He hesitated for only a breath before meeting her gaze. His voice was steady, but softer now. "And then he found a firebird, a phoenix, who stole his luck and his heart."

Farah felt his hand find hers and she squeezed.

Pari studied him carefully, then turned to Farah, as if she was trying to piece something together. After a moment, she simply said, "Did she give it back?"

Farah's lips parted slightly.

Yasher, however, chuckled low, shaking his head. "Oh, Little Divine. That's the real question, isn't it?"

Pari tilted her head, considering, then nodded to herself as if filing the answer away for later.

The fire crackled between them, the night stretching long and quiet.

Yasher reached for his water skin, taking a slow sip before standing and stretching with exaggerated laziness. "All right, enough storytelling. Time for you to get some sleep, Little Divine."

"You'll dream of something better tonight," he murmured to her, tucking the edges of the blanket around her shoulders. "Not shadows. Something soft. Something good."

Pari made a soft sound of protest but didn't resist when he helped her up, guiding her toward the tent Mehran had given up for her. She leaned against him, already half-drowsy, her small fingers clutching his hand.

She sat motionless, watching the fire, listening to his quiet murmur as he settled Pari into her borrowed tent.

The story still lingered in the air, in the spaces between what had been spoken and what had not.

She watched him in the quiet that followed as he returned to the fire, the way the firelight flickered against the lines of his face, how the easy charm he carried like armor had softened into something real. He caught her watching and tilted his head slightly, that ever-present glint of amusement lingering at the edges of his gaze.

"Turning in?" he asked, voice low.

She nodded, pushing herself up and dusting off the

back of her tunic. "I should. We'll reach the forest soon, and then onto Almarijah the day after, if the weather holds."

Yasher gave a small hum of agreement but didn't press. He watched as she turned toward their tent, slipping inside and pulling the flap closed behind her. The space was small, only just enough for the two of them and their supplies, the scent of canvas and damp earth thick in the cool air. She settled onto the bedrolls, stretching out on her side and trying to will away the restlessness still humming through her.

She had nearly convinced herself that he had chosen to stay by the fire for the night when the canvas rustled. He ducked inside, the last traces of warmth from the flames still clinging to his skin, the scent of smoke and dry cedar curling in the air between them.

She didn't move as he settled beside her, stretching out with the ease of someone who had spent his life finding comfort wherever he could, wrapping his arms around her. Since they'd set out, the creeping unease in her chest loosened slightly.

For a while, neither of them spoke. The night hummed outside, wind shifting through the dry grass, the distant crackle of embers breaking the quiet. Then, Yasher exhaled, voice soft in the dark.

"You've been carrying something all day, Phoenix." He didn't phrase it like a question. Just a quiet truth. "And it's not just the ride."

She swallowed, staring at the canvas overhead. She wanted to tell him it was nothing. That it would pass.

But she had spent the whole day trying to push the feeling away, and it hadn't left her. Hadn't even faded.

She rolled onto her side, her fingers finding comfort on his chest. "It's... just everything. The road. Sakasan. Whatever's waiting for us there. It feels... bigger than any of the other journeys we've made."

His gaze flicked downward, following the motion of her hand. His voice was lighter when he spoke again, but she knew better. "Ah. So, not me, then? That's a relief. I was worried you were regretting letting me in your tent."

She smiled softly. "Not yet."

"Good. I'd hate to start keeping you up for the wrong reasons."

She scoffed, but the warmth of his voice pulled some of the tension from her spine.

A beat passed. Then, quietly, she said, "I was short with you earlier."

His lips twitched, amused. "I noticed."

She exhaled, tilting her head slightly so she could see him better in the dim light. "I wasn't—it isn't you."

"I know," he said easily. He reached out, his fingers brushing over her cheek.

And just like that, the pressure that had been sitting against her ribs—silent and suffocating—eased. It didn't vanish completely, but it was as if the warmth of his touch forced it back, pushing it to the edges of her mind where it couldn't settle as deeply.

"But I'll take the apology anyway," he added, moving to lace his fingers through hers, pulling it away from his chest.

She laughed softly, rolling her eyes, but didn't pull

away. The warmth of his palm was steady, his presence a quiet tether to something real. Something that held her here, rather than letting her spiral deeper into whatever had been pulling at her all day.

A moment stretched between them, softer than the ones before. The kind that made it harder to hold her distance.

She shifted slightly, their bedding rustling between them. "Your story tonight." Her voice was quieter now, as if speaking too loudly might disturb something fragile between them. "That wasn't just a tale."

He didn't flinch, didn't deflect the way he so often did when the past came too close. Instead, he hummed softly, considering. "It wasn't, though there were a few bits I skimmed over. I didn't think Pari would appreciate some of the finer details of a decade on the road, nor would you."

She searched his face, finding only open honesty there, the ease of someone who had already chosen to lay himself bare. He had told her pieces before, wrapped in teasing or slipped between words meant to distract, but tonight had been different. He was raw and honest, no affections or deflections.

She shifted closer, resting her forehead lightly against his.

And the last remnants of that gnawing wrongness, the thing she had been unable to name, faded into nothing.

"You are a wonder sometimes," she murmured, meaning it in ways she couldn't quite put to words.

His hand slid up her arm, trailing warmth as he

curled his fingers over her shoulder before pulling her close.

They lay like that for a while, curled into each other, his presence steadying her in a way nothing else had that day. His breath evened out, slow and steady, and Farah let herself be pulled into its rhythm.

CHAPTER 13

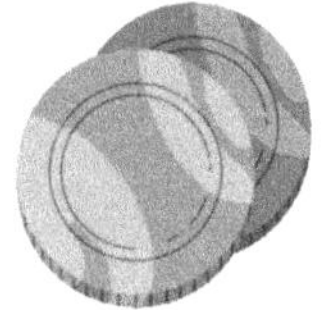

YASHER HADN'T REALIZED how much he missed being in a forest until they'd spent the morning traveling through the cedars. It wasn't the same as the forests of his childhood—those had been wild, tangled things, thick with damp earth and the scent of rotting leaves. Here, the cedars stood tall and deliberate, their trunks stretching skyward in even rows, the undergrowth sparse. The air smelled different, too. Sharper, full of resin and a little citrus rather than loamy decay.

But it wasn't just the scent or the way the light slanted through the high branches. It was the quiet. Not the kind of silence that sat heavy and waiting, but something deeper. The way sound softened beneath the canopy, the world hushed beneath layers of fallen needles. He'd spent most of his life knowing how to disappear in places like this, slipping between trees and tracing old game trails until the world beyond the forest no longer mattered.

As the horses moved steadily along the muted path, he let himself breathe easier. Even if this wasn't his forest, it was still something familiar he'd not felt in years. Something steady beneath the shifting road ahead.

He stretched out his shoulders and back against the stiffness that had settled there from hours in the saddle. The gelding beneath him was steady, its movements familiar, but his body ached in ways it hadn't when he was younger. He'd become accustomed to the soft beds in the Citadel against his better judgement, and was paying for that comfort.

Ahead, Pari sat in the cart, her legs swinging lazily over the edge, her fingers tracing invisible patterns into the worn wood as she hummed under her breath. She had been quiet most of the morning, content to listen to the rhythm of the forest, occasionally glancing at Farah as if waiting for something. He hadn't pressed too much, no matter how much he wanted to. Farah had been distant this whole trip, her usual sharp presence dulled by something heavier. He didn't know what it was no matter how much she'd said it was nothing yesterday, but he felt it like a stone in his gut.

The soldiers rode in a loose formation, their presence steady without being stifling. He'd spent enough time around fighters to read them without much effort Mehran, led with a steady hand, his posture straight, his gaze sharp. He had the air of a man who followed orders without fuss but thought through every step before taking it. Younis, older and heavier in the saddle, looked the least rigid but was likely the most experienced. There was a patience in the way he rode, the kind that came from surviving too many fights and knowing when to expect the next one. Taj, the youngest, still had the habits of someone who hadn't learned how to sit still on a long journey, shifting in his saddle every so often, adjusting his gear even when it didn't need adjusting.

A solid group. Capable. Rostam hadn't picked them just for their swords.

Mehran's hand lifted in a sharp signal—Slow.

Yasher reined in his gelding as the others followed suit, the sudden change in pace sending a ripple of awareness through the group. Horses shifted. Hands hovered closer to weapons. Even Pari, still perched in the cart, straightened slightly, her gaze flicking toward the road ahead.

A caravan.

It sat just ahead, half-blocking the road, a wagon tilted at an awkward angle where a wheel had split clean through. The others stood clustered near the trees, painted bright with once-bold reds and golds, though the sun had long since faded the colors to something more lived-in. The travelers moved around the damaged wheel, their gestures edged with frustration.

He scanned the scene, narrowing his eyes. "Merchants?"

Mehran gave a slight nod, but his hand didn't leave his reins. "Looks like it."

Younis made a low, unimpressed sound. "It could be a trap."

Taj's lips twitched. "Everything looks like a trap to you."

"That's why I'm still alive."

That was the question, wasn't it? He'd seen enough in his life to know that appearances meant little, especially out on the road. A broken wagon might be exactly what it looked like—bad luck, a rough patch of travel— or it could be bait. A clever way to slow down passersby, make them drop their guard.

His fingers tapped idly against the saddle horn. "Think they need help?"

Younis exhaled, rubbing a hand over his graying beard. "Maybe. Maybe not. Hard to say from here."

Yasher's gaze flicked to Farah, watching the way her eyes moved—not just looking, but tracking. Measuring. She wasn't tense, exactly, but she was thinking too much, and that never boded well. He knew that look. Knew the sharp precision in it, the way she weighed risk like a set of finely tuned scales, trying to decide if this was duty or danger.

He nudged his horse closer, his voice pitched low. "What's the call, Phoenix?"

She didn't answer right away. The trees loomed around them, quiet but watchful, as if waiting to see what she would do. The caravan ahead didn't move. No one waved them down. No shouts of greeting. Just stillness.

Farah's grip on her reins tightened, her knuckles faintly pale against the worn leather. Then, finally, she exhaled.

"We keep moving forward. Slowly." A pause. Then, quieter, "If they ask for help, we see what we can do."

"Fair warning," he murmured, his lips barely curving into something like a grin. "If this turns into a shitstorm, I'm going to say I told you so."

She shot him a look, dry as desert air. "Try not to gloat before anything even happens."

He had a quiet laugh but followed as she nudged her horse forward.

The wagons weren't far now. Whatever they were about to walk into, it wouldn't be long before they found out exactly what kind of trouble awaited them on the road to Almarijah.

The wagon creaked under its own weight, tilted awkwardly where the broken wheel had split along one of the spokes. A group of travelers moved around it, some standing watch while others gestured in frustration at the damage. Yasher's sharp gaze skimmed over them, cataloging details.

The woman at their head radiated confidence. Brassy in voice, sharper in wit as she yelled out to her companions, utterly unbothered by the fact that a group of armed travelers had just appeared on her road. Her dark curls were pulled back with a vibrant scarf, but a smudge of grease streaked her cheek. She leaned against the wagon with an easy swagger, her hands on her hips, her expression equal parts assessing and amused.

Beside her stood the contrast—a tall man, broad-shouldered but quieter, his stance more measured. He had the same sharp features as the woman, the same deep brown eyes, but where she burned bright, he held his energy close, exuding the kind of watchfulness that spoke of a man who didn't trust easily. His tunic and vest, though travel-worn, were well-kept, the fabrics layered in practical folds that suggested long weeks on the road.

As their group slowed, the woman turned toward them with a practiced, sweeping glance, the kind that took in everything, assessed it, and dismissed whatever wasn't useful in a single heartbeat. Then, her lips curled into an easy, knowing grin.

"Well, well," she drawled, her voice full of warmth and amusement. "Vohun must be smiling on me today with fortune. I was about to start pleading with the Unnamed Gods, and instead, they send me a man with sharp eyes and a sharper jawline."

He barely had time to let his smirk settle before Farah let out a slow, measured exhale beside him.

"We're not divine intervention," she said dryly, already sliding off her horse. "But we might be able to help."

The woman lifted a brow, entirely unbothered. "Help, divine intervention… when your wagon's stuck in the dirt and wheel's split, does it really matter which?"

Then her attention slid back to him, her expression full of the kind of deliberate interest that made it clear she enjoyed seeing people squirm.

"Tell me, gharib," she said, voice lilting, "are you any good with your hands?"

He let out a low, appreciative chuckle, meeting her gaze with easy mischief. "I like to think so."

Farah, to his endless amusement, made a sound that

was just shy of exasperation and swung down from her saddle without another word.

The woman's grin widened. "I knew I liked you. I'm Laleh, and this eternally miserable creature beside me is my brother, Samir. The rest of the crew ain't important."

Samir rolled his eyes skyward. "You can ignore most of what she says."

Laleh ignored him entirely, stepping closer to Yasher and sweeping an appraising glance over him. "So, are you here to rescue us, or just to stand around looking devastatingly attractive?"

Farah let out a short breath that he was certain was meant to be a laugh, but she schooled it quickly.

"We can't stay long," she said, already pulling off her gloves. "But if it's just the wheel, I can fix it."

Laleh turned, brow raised. "You?"

Farah ignored the implied doubt, stepping past Yasher toward the broken wagon.

He grinned, swinging off his horse and offering Laleh an easy shrug. "I'd put my money on her, if I were you."

She hummed, watching Farah with open curiosity as she crouched near the broken wheel, brushing her fingers along the splintered wood. Farah was already listening to the metal around the wood, reading the breaks, the cracks, the wear of the road.

"You two must be important," she said after a moment. "Not that I mind important people stopping to help, but it's not often I see such nice weaves on clothes on the road, or honest soldiers without there being importance surrounding them."

He shrugged. "We get around."

Laleh smirked. "Oh, I bet you do."

Farah, to his endless delight, pointedly ignored them.

Samir, more cautious than his sister, gestured toward the road. "You've come from Rumatin, then?"

Mehran, still mounted, nodded. "Yes."

Samir exhaled, his gaze shifting toward the distant stretch of road ahead. "We'd planned to stop for a few days in Almarijah, then straight to Sakasan. At least we were until we'd heard that Sakasan had closed up their gates to work through a rather ugly illness. After the wasting disease hit the Talented so badly, I don't want to think that it's jumped to the rest of us."

Samir looked down to Farah, frowning slightly. "Didn't peg you for a smith."

Farah didn't look up. "Something like that."

She pressed her palm against the iron rim, fingers skimming over the splintered break, her breath slow and measured as she pulled off one of her steel bangles. The metal whispered back, a song only she could hear, fractures humming as they remembered how to be whole in tune with her low hum.

The wood groaned, metal heating under her touch, reshaping itself thread by thread. The repair was small, easy. A break this simple didn't demand much of her, just a reinforcement with metal around the split wood.

The wagon creaked as it settled into place, whole once more.

Yasher, lounging nearby with the ease of a man watching a favorite trick, caught the flicker of surprise in both Samir and Laleh's expressions.

Laleh let out a low whistle, arms folded. "Huh." She

looked Farah up and down. "Not every day you see someone bend metal like it's butter."

Farah arched a brow. "You don't fix your own wheels?"

Samir's lips pressed into a thin line. "Not like that." He tilted his head. "You Talented don't usually wander around patching up merchant wagons. You keep close to power. To nobles. Not to people like us."

Laleh hummed, eyeing Farah like she was a puzzle with missing pieces. "So, tell me, what's a Talented woman doing this far out from a city, playing at being useful?"

Yasher, ever the opportunist, grinned. "Maybe we're just feeling generous."

Laleh shot him a dry look. "Or maybe you're important enough that I should be asking what the hell you're doing out here."

Farah ignored the bait, adjusting the cuff of her sleeve. "You're not wrong that Talented have been scarce on the roads. I imagine the last year has made it difficult."

Samir exhaled sharply, crossing his arms. "Difficult is one word for it. After the wasting sickness, most of the Talented left in the cities were holed up, protected. Those that weren't…" He shook his head. "Well. It's not exactly been safe for anyone."

Laleh looked over the group again.

"I mean, no offense, but it's not every day I see a Talented traveling with a small band of soldiers and a—" She glanced at Yasher, eyes narrowing in consideration. "Charming gharib."

Samir ignored their banter, his gaze sharp as it lingered on Farah.

"It's unusual," he said, his voice even. "Talented don't travel roads like this—not without a patron, a title, or a damned good reason."

Farah's expression remained impassive. "We have reason."

Samir hummed, not satisfied. "And this reason—it wouldn't happen to involve Sakasan, would it?"

Laleh's head tilted slightly, her amusement fading. "You're not seriously heading there, are you?"

Before Farah could answer, Yasher spoke up. "Why does it matter?" His tone was casual, but his posture wasn't. "You were planning to go there yourselves."

Samir let out a slow breath, rubbing a hand over his jaw. "Were. Past tense." He flicked his fingers toward the road. "Word from passing traders is that the city's shut its gates. They're not letting anyone in or out."

That got Farah's attention. "Why?"

Samir's mouth pressed into a thin line. "Illness. Or at least, that's the safest guess."

Laleh clicked her tongue, her fingers drumming against her belt as she considered them. "Thing is, rumors move faster than truth out here. Plenty of stories about Sakasan, but none of them match. Some say there's sickness. Others say people have been vanishing. Then there's the fun ones." She smirked, but it didn't quite reach her eyes. "Shadows moving in the cliffs. Voices in the dark. Things watching from places they shouldn't be."

He kept his face blank, but he felt the weight of

Farah's silence beside him. Rumors always started somewhere.

Samir exhaled sharply, shaking his head. "Doesn't matter which one's true." He glanced at their horses, at the weapons strapped to their saddles. "Whatever's happening in Sakasan, it's nothing good."

Farah's expression didn't change. "We can handle trouble."

Laleh studied her for a moment longer, then let out a slow breath. "Well, whatever your business is, I won't pry. Just be careful."

He smirked. "Always."

Laleh smirked back. "You, I doubt."

Farah mounted her horse without another word, clearly done with the conversation. He swung up onto his own, tossing Laleh a lazy salute as they turned back toward the road.

"If you ever decide court life is too stifling, gharib," Laleh called after them, "I'm always looking for pretty men with quick hands."

He laughed, nudging his horse forward. "I'll keep it in mind."

Farah clicked her tongue, urging her horse into a brisk pace.

He caught the look she shot him, all exasperation and faint amusement. He grinned. "What?"

She shook her head, not answering, though he could see her trying to keep a smile from crossing her face.

They rode on, leaving the merchants and their repaired cart behind, the trees swallowing them in shadow once more.

THE FOREST HAD DEEPENED into true dusk by the time they finally stopped for the night. Yasher swung down from his horse, rolling his shoulders, wincing at the dull ache that had settled between them. The clearing Mehran had chosen was a good one—flat, shielded from the worst of the wind, and not too close to the road. The trees stood tall around them, a protective wall of dark cedar and dense underbrush, their scent thick in the cooling air.

Younis dismounted with practiced efficiency, moving toward the supply cart where Pari sat perched on the edge, swinging her legs.

"We should be in Almarijah soon," the older soldier said, checking the cart's axles with a habitual glance before nodding in satisfaction.

"Good," Mehran muttered, scanning the tree line with sharp eyes. "Better roads past there. The horses will thank us for it."

Yasher let out a low hum, unfastening his saddlebags and tossing them near a tree. He'd never been one to mind rough roads, but even he was looking forward to something flatter, less winding, maybe even a real bed. Something about this road itched at the back of his neck, an unease without a name. He wasn't sure if it was the trees, the silence, or the way the air felt heavy, thick with something unseen.

Farah was quiet as she dismounted, barely acknowledging him as she tied her horse's reins to a low-hanging branch. Her movements were efficient, methodical, but there was something clipped about them, too precise.

One of the steel bracelets on her wrist was spinning smoothly as she moved through her tasks. Her mind was heavy, and she still wasn't letting him in.

Mehran and Younis built the fire, coaxing the flames into a steady glow. Taj pulled the food from their rations, tossing a cloth-wrapped bundle toward him with a smirk. "Hope you're not picky."

He caught it easily, settling onto a fallen log. "After some of the things I've eaten on the road, this is fit for royalty."

Taj huffed a laugh, tearing into his own meal. Pari, cross-legged near the cart, accepted her share with a quiet "thank you," already picking apart the figs with small, deliberate fingers.

Farah ate without comment, her gaze on the fire.

Yasher didn't try to start a conversation this time. He'd spent enough nights with her to know when to wait her out. Instead, he let the forest sounds settle in. The rustling of leaves, the low murmur of wind through the trees. Something was off in the air, but no one else seemed to notice. Well, Pari probably noticed, but it wasn't enough for her to comment on, at least not yet.

Each time Taj tried to start a conversation, the quiet swallowed the words too fast, left them hanging awkwardly in the air before fading into nothing. Even Pari, usually so keen to fill the space, only picked at her food, her small hands idly arranging the bits of dried fruit into patterns on the cloth.

The weight of the day settled deep in his bones. Maybe it was the forest. Maybe it was Farah's silence, thick like unshed words pressed against the inside of his skull. He stole a glance at her as she stared into the fire, the flickering light carving shadows beneath her eyes.

Eventually, she pushed up to her feet, brushing the crumbs from her hands. "I'm going to bed."

His gaze followed her as she crossed the clearing, disappearing into their shared tent without another word.

He let out a slow breath and leaned back against the log, tilting his head up toward the dark canopy of cedar branches overhead. His unease hadn't faded. It still sat heavy in his ribs, an itch just beneath the skin.

Taj exhaled, stretching his arms over his head. "Well. That was a lively meal."

Mehran shot him a look, but Yasher only smirked. "Could've used more wine."

Taj barked a short laugh, but the edge of tension in it didn't go unnoticed. The silence that had settled over the camp was the wrong kind—not the easy quiet of companions who had run out of things to say, but the kind that hummed beneath the surface, as if something unseen had set its teeth into the edges of the night.

Pari yawned, rubbing at her eyes. He nudged her toward the tent. "Time for bed, Little Divine."

She didn't argue. He helped her up, tucking her blanket around her small frame before stepping back.

As she settled in, his gaze drifted once more to their tent. Farah's outline was barely visible through the canvas, unmoving. He considered following her. He could press, needle her until she finally snapped, until she gave him something—frustration, a glare, anything to prove she wasn't sinking too deep into herself. But her shoulders were already drawn too tight, the weight of whatever she carried pressing into her spine.

No, he'd wait.

"Cards?" Taj asked, pulling Yasher from his thoughts with a grin.

He arched a brow. "Depends. Am I playing a skilled opponent or just a desperate one?"

Taj smirked, flicking a card between his fingers. "Only one way to find out. The soldiers love talking about the games you drop into at the Citadel. Bit of a legend."

He chuckled, leaning forward as Taj dealt the first hand between them on the flat bit of ground between them. The game was a simple one, fast-paced and ruthless. Taj played aggressively, taking risks with the confidence of someone who'd spent too many late nights gambling away his rations. Yasher, by contrast, played as he always did—with a mix of instinct and just a pinch of Luck.

After the third round, Taj let out an exasperated groan. "You should not have won that."

He grinned, flipping his final card over with a flourish. "Tell that to the cards."

Taj muttered something under his breath and gathered the deck again, dealing the next round with a little more force than necessary. "One more."

They played until the fire dwindled into glowing embers, until the wind picked up and carried the scent of cedar and earth through the clearing. Eventually, Taj let out a long sigh, rubbing a hand over his face.

"We'll see how smug you are when you have to wake up at dawn," he muttered, pushing himself up.

Yasher smirked. "I'll manage."

Taj shook his head, already heading toward his tent. "Try not to be so damn lucky in your sleep, will you?"

He let out a quiet chuckle, shuffling the deck absentmindedly before handing it back to Taj. The night had settled into that deep, still silence, broken only by the faint rustling of leaves and the distant call of some unseen bird.

With a final glance around camp, he pushed himself up and made his way to his tent.

The embers outside cast a faint orange glow through the thin canvas of the tent, barely enough to make out Farah'sshape. He didn't need to see her face to know she was still awake. He could feel it in the quiet stiffness of her body, in the way her breaths came too evenly, too measured, like she was holding herself together even here, even now.

He sighed softly, dragging a hand through his hair before shucking off his coat and boots. The air inside the tent was warmer than outside, but not by much. He settled in behind her, the fabric rustling as he moved, but still, she didn't stir.

He moved closer, the warmth of his body pressing against hers, steady and sure. His arm slid around her waist, his fingers tracing slow circles against the fabric of her tunic. The tension in her shoulders hadn't eased all day, wound tight from whatever haunted her thoughts.

He pressed a slow, deliberate kiss to the nape of her

neck, just beneath the loose strands of hair that had slipped free from her braid. She smelled like the forest now, like smoke and the faintest trace of metal. His lips lingered there, warm against her skin, and he felt the smallest shift—her body recognizing him, even if she didn't answer.

"You don't have to pretend everything is fine," he murmured against her skin.

She didn't flinch, didn't stiffen, but she also didn't reply. He knew the difference between exhaustion and avoidance, between silence that begged to be left alone and silence that just didn't know how to ask for help.

His fingers splayed against her stomach. He kept his voice quiet, a low murmur meant only for her. "Tell me how I can help, Phoenix."

A breath, slow and shallow. Then another.

He felt her shoulders relax just slightly, her body pressing back into his warmth. That was answer enough.

He adjusted, his arm tightening around her as he pulled her even closer. His nose brushed against the side of her neck, his lips pressing another kiss there, softer this time. He felt the small, involuntary shudder she gave, the way her fingers twitched slightly where they clutched the blanket.

"You're holding something in, something you don't want to share the burden of," he whispered, his lips grazing her ear. "I can feel it."

She let out a breath—just a breath—but it sounded like something unraveling.

Still, she didn't speak.

He pressed his forehead lightly against the back of her head. He knew better than to push her, better than to force words she wasn't ready to say. But he also wasn't going to let her drift further into that quiet isolation she wrapped herself in like armor.

Then, finally, she moved.

Not hesitantly, not uncertainly—just a decisive shift, a space closed, her breath warm against his jaw as she pressed into him. Her eyes, dark in the dim firelight, held something raw, something aching. He barely had time to register the shift before her hands slid up his chest, fingers curling against his bare skin.

Then she kissed him.

It wasn't soft. It wasn't a question. It was a claim—a press of lips that stole the air from his lungs, a kiss that tasted of unspoken words and too-heavy silences. Her fingers twisted in his hair, pulling him deeper, and he let her take what she needed, meeting her with equal fire.

He inhaled sharply, a sound swallowed by her mouth, by the way she clutched at him like she was trying to ground herself. His body reacted before his mind caught up, his grip tightening around her waist, pulling her closer. He met her intensity, matching the heat of it, tilting his head to deepen the kiss, to drink in everything she was finally giving.

Her fingers traced down his spine, nails dragging lightly, sending a shiver through him. He groaned into her mouth, the sound low and rough, and he felt her lips curve slightly against his. A challenge, maybe. A dare.

She was always the one in control, always the one who held herself back until he broke through. But now, here, she was claiming this moment, taking what she wanted. And he would give it to her.

He rolled, shifting his weight until he had her beneath him, her body molding against his as he braced himself above her. Their breathing was unsteady, their skin fever-warm where it pressed together. His lips traced down the line of her jaw, over the curve of her throat, lingering at the pulse fluttering beneath her skin.

Her hands slid up his back, gripping his shoulders, urging him closer. "Just this," she murmured.

He kissed her again, slow but deep, his hands moving over her body, pulling the last layers of clothing from her skin. He felt her tremble beneath him, whether from the chill of the night air or from something else entirely, he didn't know. But he would chase that shiver down, drown her in sensation until there was nothing left but them, this, the heat that burned between them.

They moved together, slow at first, then faster, more desperate, their breaths mingling, gasping, lost in the dark. Every touch, every kiss, every stolen sound between them was an unspoken promise, a reminder that this was real.

She clung to him as she came apart, a soft moan against his lips, her nails digging into his skin. He followed, his body tensing, the pleasure cresting sharp and overwhelming. He buried his face in the crook of her neck, his breath ragged, his heart pounding.

For a long moment, neither of them spoke. Their bodies were tangled, their skin damp with sweat, their breathing slowly evening out.

He shifted just slightly, pressing a kiss to her temple, the damp strands of her hair sticking to his lips. "Phoenix, love..."

She didn't answer, not with words. Instead, she pulled him closer, tucking herself against his chest, her fingers idly tracing circles against his skin.

He exhaled, letting the weight of the night settle between them. His arms tightened around her, solid and steady, as if he could keep everything else at bay for just a little while longer.

CHAPTER 14

Something was wrong.

It had been wrong for days—maybe since Rumatin, maybe before—but now, as they crossed the threshold into Almarijah, it wasn't just a whisper at the back of Farah's mind. It sank in, sharp and certain, like a blade pressed to the tender spot between her ribs.

The town unfolded before them, pale stone buildings huddled against the base of the hills, their rooftops catching the light. Farah breathed it in, steadying herself, but it did nothing to settle the gnawing disquiet in her chest.

This wasn't fear. Fear had a name, a shape, something she could sink her teeth into and fight. This was a pressure at the edges of her senses, like she was walking through a world slightly misaligned with itself, where every step felt just a breath too late.

The road curled into the heart of town, leading toward a square that should have been loud with traders shouting, laborers barking orders over the groan of heavy carts. But Almarijah was muted. Not silent, but held in the kind of hush that came when people had already seen something they wished they hadn't and had to pretend that all was well.

People still moved through the streets, a merchant's apprentice sweeping the stone steps, a pair of women drawing water from a well, men carrying sacks of grain toward a warehouse. But no one spoke above a murmur, and no one met their eyes for longer than a flicker of a glance.

Yasher nudged his horse closer to hers, his voice pitched low. "This place feel off to you?"

She barely inclined her head, her fingers tightening around the reins. "It's too quiet."

Mehran, riding at the front, cleared his throat. "We'll take the horses to the inn and stable them there. It'll be easier to keep them in one place."

"Good," Farah said. "We need to find the town steward before nightfall."

"Assuming they'll want to talk," Younis muttered.

She glanced at him. "They will." They would, or she'd make them.

The inn was a squat, sturdy building on the edge of the square, its thick wooden beams weathered from years of dust storms rolling off the hills. A sloping roof of pale clay tiles gleamed in the evening light, and beside it, a stable yard housed a few other travelers' horses. The scent of hay and sweat and animal musk was thick in the cooling air.

Pari, curled up in the cart with her rucksack still

hugged to her chest, peered up at the inn. "Are we staying here?"

"Just for the night, Little Divine," Yasher said, dismounting. He reached up to help Pari down, lifting her easily before setting her on her feet.

Farah dismounted, leading her horse toward the stable, but the moment she stepped forward, the unease sharpened, becoming a physical discomfort. The bracelet on her wrist spun a bit faster.

She ignored it, swallowing against the tightness in her throat. She had to.

The innkeeper stood in the doorway, a wiry man with a salt-and-pepper beard and the cautious air of someone who had learned to measure his words. He wasn't afraid of them, not exactly, but there was something wary in the way his fingers tightened around the rag he was using to wipe down a pewter pitcher.

His gaze swept over them—Yasher first, then the soldiers, then finally her. And then it lingered. Not on her face, but on her coat, the embroidered edges that marked it as something finer than a traveler's garb, something from the Citadel.

Recognition flickered in his eyes, quick and uncertain. Like he was weighing something, some calculation shifting behind his careful expression.

His fingers twitched on the rag in his hands. A subtle movement, but enough. Enough for her to see that whatever had settled into this town's bones had already reached the people in it.

The innkeeper's gaze darted, for just a second, toward the road leading out of town.

He knew something.

Farah took a measured step closer. "We need rooms for the night and space in the stable for our horses."

The innkeeper hesitated, glancing over their group again, before finally nodding. "Two silvers a night, food included."

She could feel something pressing against her. Not a presence, not a force, but something in herself that felt… distant.

Like she was wrapped in layers she couldn't shed, muffled from her own instincts. She had thought—foolishly—that last night would settle something inside her. That if she reached for Yasher, pulled him into her, she'd feel solid again. That it would press out the static crawling beneath her skin.

But it wasn't just the road.

It wasn't just the silence in this town.

It was her.

She had initiated things last night—not because she'd wanted comfort, not because of anything deep, but because she wanted to feel something she couldn't seem to grasp within anymore. And she had felt Yasher, felt his warmth, the solid weight of him, but it hadn't settled the wrongness coiling inside her. It had been like grasping at smoke.

And, somewhere in the back of her mind, she wondered if that damn merchant woman's flirtations had pushed her into it.

She scowled at herself. That wasn't the reason. It shouldn't be the reason. She knew better than that.

She forced herself back to the present, to the

innkeeper who was still watching them too carefully, too measuring.

"We'll take the rooms."

The innkeeper hesitated again, then nodded toward the stable yard. "You'll find space there. Food will be ready within the hour."

She handed her reins off to Younis and turned toward Yasher. "Get the horses settled. I'll be back."

His brows lifted. "Where are you going?"

"To find someone who actually wants to tell me what the hell is going on in this town."

Yasher let out a breath, rubbing the back of his neck. "You think they will?"

"They won't have a choice."

He held her gaze for a long moment, something knowing in his eyes. Then he gave her a wry grin, tilting his head toward the street.

"Go break them, Phoenix." Yasher's smirk was easy, but his gaze wasn't. "I'll make sure your bed's waiting when you're done shaking answers out of them."

She should have rolled her eyes. Instead, she just nodded.

THE STEWARD'S home was tucked into the western edge of the square, a modest stone building with thick wooden shutters and a heavy iron-banded door. It was meant to project stability, authority. But the lanterns inside were dim, the air thick with the scent of old parchment and ink, and the man behind the desk, Aqa Darvishi, if the plaque on his desk was to be believed, looked more tired than anything else.

Farah had dealt with men like him before. Not corrupt or cruel—just small. The kind of man who had spent a lifetime keeping his town from collapsing under the weight of greater forces, all while knowing he would never be strong enough to hold it together. He wasn't incompetent. He was resigned.

The steward's office was small, cramped with ledgers and half-melted candles that left trails of wax down their holders. Darvishi, sat behind a heavy wooden desk, his fingers tapping idly against the pages of an open ledger. He was older than she'd expected, his beard streaked with gray, his eyes shrewd and calculating.

His gaze flicked over her, not just a glance, but a calculation. It was subtle, the way his fingers tightened over the edge of his ledger, the way his shoulders straightened ever so slightly. Not fear. Not yet. But recognition.

"You're from the Citadel," he said, voice flat. Not a question.

Farah didn't confirm it, but she didn't deny it either.

Darvishi sighed, setting his quill aside with slow, deliberate movements. "I assume you're not here about taxes."

Farah wasn't in the mood for games. "I need to know about Sakasan."

The steward's posture remained relaxed, but something in his gaze sharpened. He folded his hands over the desk, considering her.

"You'd do better heading inland, avoiding the Cliffs,"

he said. "Tamidh's roads are rougher, but safer. More traveled."

She leaned against the edge of the desk, unimpressed. "Safer from what?"

Darvishi exhaled sharply, his fingers drumming against the desk. His gaze flicked toward the door. Then, finally, "You know what."

Farah held his stare, unyielding. "Say it."

His fingers twitched. He sat back in his chair. "The governor of Sakasan has locked down the town. No one in or out. Claims it's to contain an illness."

A chill slid down her spine, but she kept her face carefully neutral. "You don't believe it."

Darvishi hesitated, then shook his head. "It's not my place to say what I believe. But I know that it started with disappearances. A few people at first. Then whole families. No bodies. No explanations."

She inhaled slowly. "And the governor? Who gave the order?"

Darvishi's lips thinned. "If I had to guess? Someone influencing him. That man is popular, but one of the most ineffectual governors I've seen in ages. It was the kind of order you don't question unless you want to disappear yourself, the way that it was written, which was definitely not by his hand."

The scent of old parchment and melted wax had grown cloying. The office felt smaller than when she entered, the stacked ledgers pressing in, the dim light making every shadow heavier. She clenched her teeth, her patience thinning like overdrawn metal. She had been willing to let him skirt around the truth, to let him ease his way toward an answer, but now he was just wasting her time.

"You're not going to turn back, are you?" Darvishi asked, resignation creeping into his voice.

"No."

His sigh was slow, his fingers twitched as he adjusted a ledger on his desk, a nervous tell he probably wasn't aware of. "Then don't make camp near the cliffs."

Something in his tone shifted. Caution, and a tinge of fear.

Darvishi's mouth pressed into a thin line. His gaze flickered, not the way a liar's does, but the way a man does when he's seen something he knows he can never explain.

"The Asharan Cliffs stretch beyond Sakasan's northern edge." His voice dipped lower, quieter. "Travelers say the wind carries voices. That the shadows... move wrong." A pause. A flicker of something in his eyes.

"And that they take those who walk too close."

Her pulse kicked up, the words needling at her temper in the worst way. This man had known something was wrong for who knew how long and had said nothing to the Citadel.

"Let me make sure I understand," she said, voice taut. "A town has been locked down under suspicious circumstances. People are vanishing. You're hearing whispers about shadows moving wrong, about voices in the wind. And yet, no one has thought to send word to the Citadel, the Mashya?"

Darvishi stiffened, the lines in his face deepening. "I serve Almarijah, not Sakasan. It is not my business to question a governor's orders, nor to involve the Crown where it is not needed."

She laughed, but there was nothing warm in it.

"Not needed?" She took a step toward his desk, planting her palms flat against the wood. The metal inkwell vibrated. "Do you think whatever is happening in Sakasan is just going to stay there?"

Darvishi's expression darkened. "You act as if the Citadel hasn't ignored worse."

Farah's jaw locked, but she forced her voice to remain level. "The Citadel is no longer under Behnaz's rule. The Mashya wants to rebuild Emari, not let it rot piece by piece because some bureaucrats are too cowardly to face the truth."

The steward's lips thinned, but he didn't back down.

"The truth," he repeated. "The truth is that we've learned to look after our own. Those of us who remember what happened to the people who asked too many questions when her Glorious Radiance was still the power on the throne."

His meaning was clear. The Mashyana had ruled Emari for decades, even if Enayat had been by her side through most of it, and under her reign, power had been hoarded, suffering had been dismissed, and those who pushed too hard had been silenced.

Farah forced herself to take a slow breath. That was the past. The Mashya was trying to fix it. She was trying to fix it. But men like Darvishi—men who had survived by keeping their heads down and their mouths shut— were going to make it difficult.

"And what do you think is going to happen when

whatever's inside Sakasan decides it's not enough? That it needs more? You aren't too far away that it would see you as an option." she asked coldly.

Darvishi hesitated.

She shook her head, pushing off the desk.

"Stay out of our way," she said, stepping back. "Because whether you like it or not, the Citadel is involved now."

She turned, striding for the door. She didn't wait for his approval. She didn't need it.

But just as her hand touched the brass handle, his voice stopped her.

"Khānum." Low. Measured. Weighted with something not quite pity, not quite warning. "Not all things are meant to be disturbed."

Farah clenched her jaw.

She stepped into the night air without another word.

Her hands curled into fists, the metal at her belt humming faintly, as if it knew what she intended.

I'm not here to disturb the darkness. I'm here to burn it out.

Farah barely restrained herself from slamming the door behind her as she stepped out of the steward's home, fingers tightening around the cool brass handle before she let it swing closed with more force than necessary. The air outside was crisp, carrying the lingering scent of damp earth and the distant, smokey tang of wood fires. It did little to temper the heat simmering beneath her skin.

Mehran stood by the low stone wall bordering the home, arms loosely crossed, but his gaze sharpened the moment he saw her expression. He straightened instinctively, pushing off the wall as she strode past him. He was a soldier, he knew the look of someone barely holding onto their temper.

Her boots hit the cobbled path in clipped steps as she headed down the street, her fists tightening at her sides. "I cannot stand men like that."

Mehran fell into step beside her, glancing back toward the steward's house. "Like what?"

"Someone who has spent his whole life mistaking silence for wisdom." The words came out like a curse, bitter on her tongue. "One who survives by keeping his head down and convincing himself that his inaction makes him neutral, and not a waste of time."

Mehran let out a quiet hum of acknowledgment, but didn't interrupt.

"They knew, Mehran," she continued, her voice low and sharp. "They knew something was wrong, and they let it fester. And why? Because it didn't affect them. Because it wasn't their business. Because they didn't want to 'involve the Crown.'"

The words felt like acid.

The well-kept street faded into narrower roads, the light from the occasional lantern casting long, wavering shadows across the dirt path. She kept her strides purposeful, but there was an edge to her movements—something too rigid, too coiled.

Mehran adjusted the strap of his belt, flicking a glance her way. "You think he was lying?"

Farah scoffed. "No. That's the worst part. He believes every word."

That was what made men like Darvishi dangerous. Not outright malice, not ambition—the steadfast belief that ignoring a problem would make it go away. That fear and superstition were good enough reasons to let people suffer.

They walked in tense silence for a few moments, the sounds of the town settling around them. A dog barked somewhere in the distance. A door creaked open, spilling the soft murmur of conversation from a house before closing again, muffling the voices inside.

"You going to tell Yasher?" Mehran finally asked, his voice lighter, almost wry.

Farah shot him a sharp look. "Of course I am."

Mehran smirked, shaking his head. "Good. He'll love that."

She narrowed her eyes. "What is that supposed to mean?"

Mehran shrugged, adjusting his sword belt. "Means he's about as fond of the word 'no' as you are."

She huffed a breath, shoving her hands into the folds of her coat.

"Darvishi thinks Sakasan is lost," she muttered, the weight of it pressing against her ribs. "Like whatever is inside has already taken root too deeply."

Mehran's expression darkened, his usual easy confidence hardening into something grimmer.

If Sakasan was lost, that meant the people still inside had been abandoned.

They turned a corner, the warm glow of the inn's lanterns finally coming into view as the sun sank. The air smelled of roasted meat and spiced tea, the comforting scent wrapping around them, at odds with the unease still clinging to her skin.

Mehran exhaled, stretching his arms over his head as if shaking off the conversation. "So, are we ignoring his advice, then?"

She shot him a pointed look.

Mehran chuckled. "Right. Silly question."

She wasn't turning back. If the Darkness had taken root in Sakasan, she would burn it down to stop it from spreading.

CHAPTER 15

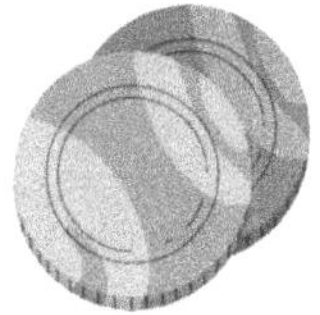

THE TAVERN WAS WARM, thick with the scent of spiced lamb, old wood, and the sharp bite of cheap liquor. The air carried the easy, familiar chaos of men drinking after a long day's work—quiet laughter, the scrape of chairs, the wet slap of a losing hand in cards. While the town itself seemed to be too quiet, the room tried very hard to forget that.

Yasher let himself sink into it, stretching out his legs beneath the table, rolling a coin between his fingers. The last few days had been nothing but tension, but this? This was familiar.

Across from him, Taj scowled, eyes flicking between the cards in his hand and the growing pile of winnings at Yasher's side. "You're cheating."

He smirked, resting his elbow on the table as he lazily flipped another card. "I don't need to cheat. I'm just lucky."

Younis let out a quiet chuckle beside him, nursing a cup of tea rather than the stronger fare most of the other patrons indulged in. Taj muttered something under his breath, reaching for his drink.

Yasher stretched his arms out, tilting his head back slightly. The weight of travel still clung to him, the long days in the saddle leaving his muscles tight, but for the first time in days, the tension in his chest had eased.

His gaze flicked toward the stairs leading to their rented rooms. Pari had gone up earlier, too tired to fight the inevitable. She'd barely managed a murmur before all but collapsing into her blankets. The road had gotten to her as well.

Yasher, on the other hand, wasn't ready to turn in yet. Not when there was still the matter of what they were walking towards tomorrow.

He drummed his fingers against the table absently. Mehran and Farah had been gone longer than he liked. He wasn't worried, not really—Farah could handle herself better than anyone he knew—but something in his gut twisted with unease.

Maybe it was the way Farah had been since they left Rumatin. The way she kept locking him out, even as she pulled him close. A contradiction that dug under his skin.

Or maybe it was the road itself.

Or maybe—and this was the part he hated most—it was just that feeling again. That wrongness. That quiet prickle beneath his skin, like something waiting in the dark.

The door swung open, spilling cool night air and tension into the tavern as Mehran and Farah stepped inside. He didn't need to study her long to see the signs

—shoulders too tight, fingers curled like she was still gripping something invisible.

Taj followed his gaze and let out a low whistle. "Well, that's not a good look."

She moved like a blade—controlled, deliberate—but he saw the crack in the edge. Something had riled her up.

He leaned his arms on the table as she reached them, his smirk sharp but easy. "Judging by that expression, I'm guessing the steward wasn't falling over himself to be helpful."

Farah exhaled, shaking off more than just cold air. "Not here."

He nodded once and rose smoothly, slipping his winnings into his pocket as Taj made a noise of protest.

Younis stood as well, tossing a few coins onto the table for their drinks before following them up the stairs, letting Mehran get something to eat after quietly updating the older soldier.

Farah was already moving ahead, Younis close behind. Yasher followed, his senses sharpening, the warm comfort of the tavern fading behind him as the weight of whatever awaited them settled in.

They reached the top of the stairs, and Yasher's hand went to the door handle before he stopped short, remembering. Pari.

He exhaled sharply through his nose and turned back toward Farah before she could open the door. "Shit, can't go in there if you've got news."

Farah frowned. "What?"

"Pari's in there, sleeping," he said, tilting his head toward the room.

Understanding flickered across her face, followed swiftly by a sigh. She pinched the bridge of her nose. "Outside, then."

Without another word, she pivoted and led them back down the stairs and through the side door of the tavern. The cool night air settled around them as they stepped into the alley, the scents of damp stone and cedar drifting in from the forest beyond. The muffled hum of conversation from inside faded behind the heavy wooden door.

Farah crossed her arms, staring out at the empty street beyond the alley. Yasher leaned against the stone wall beside her, waiting. Younis stayed a few paces back, his arms clasped behind him, his stance alert.

He gave her a few seconds before nudging her lightly with his shoulder. "Alright, Phoenix. Let's have it."

She inhaled deeply, then exhaled slowly, her fingers tightening around her arms before she spoke. "The steward wants us to turn around."

Yasher lifted a brow. "Not surprising. We already figured they wouldn't be thrilled about us heading toward Sakasan."

"It's more than that." She turned to face him fully, her gaze sharp. "He recognized I was from the Crown, even if he didn't know exactly who I was. And still, he tried to send me away. He didn't even give me the usual lip service about how it's 'dangerous' or how 'it's not a good time for travel.' He was direct. And yet still cagey as hell."

That was a bad sign. "What did he say, exactly?"

"He warned me that Sakasan is locked down because

of an unexplained illness, which we already knew from the merchants." Farah's jaw tightened. "But the way he spoke… he wasn't just worried about us going. He was worried about what we might find."

That sent a prickling sensation down his spine. "What, does he think we'll be coming back with some terrible news he doesn't want to deal with?"

Farah huffed a bitter laugh. "That's what it felt like. He wasn't concerned about us getting sick. He was concerned about what we might uncover if we ignored his warning."

He ran a hand through his hair. "Alright," he said, more serious now. "So, he's scared. The question is, of what?"

Farah shook her head. "He wouldn't say exactly. I'm not sure if he even really knows. But whatever's happening in Sakasan, it's bad enough that a man who should be grateful for Crown support was trying to send me back to the Citadel rather than risk me seeing it firsthand."

Younis, who had remained quiet until now, finally spoke.

"It means we need to be prepared." His voice was level, steady. "We have no idea what we're walking into."

Yasher sighed, rubbing the back of his neck. "We never do."

Her eyes flicked to him, searching. "You don't have to come."

Yasher let out a sharp, incredulous laugh.

"Phoenix." He stepped forward, tilting his head as he

met her stare. "You know damn well that's not happening."

She studied him for a moment, then let out a slow breath. "I had to say it."

"No, you didn't." His voice softened, and he reached out, brushing his knuckles against hers before pulling back. "So, do we leave at first light?"

Farah hesitated. "There's something else."

Yasher straightened. "Of course there is."

Farah reached into her coat, and before he even saw it, he felt it.

A whisper of wrongness. Crawling up his spine like ice and pressure, settling low in his gut. His mouth flattened instinctively, his body knowing what his mind hadn't yet caught up to.

Then she pulled it free. That damn wooden box. That damned relic.

Farah ran a finger along the lid, her voice quieter now. "Whatever's happening in Sakasan... I think this is connected. This thing is... I don't know, whispering? Whenever the shadows are mentioned."

His gaze flicked from her face to the relic, then back again. His mouth pressed into a thin line. "And you're carrying that thing around? For how long?"

Farah's brows drew together. "I need to figure out what it is."

He huffed, shaking his head.

"Maybe. But are you sure that's a good idea?" His voice lowered. "Phoenix, you've been off since we left Rumatin. You don't feel it?"

Farah went very still, her fingers tightening around the box. "What are you implying?"

He hesitated, but then exhaled, deciding there was no use in dancing around it. "You're different," he admitted. "Not yourself. Distant. I'd lay money it's because it's in your pocket instead of the strongbox where it's supposed to be."

Her expression didn't change, but her shoulders pulled tighter. "We're on the road. We have a task ahead of us. That's all."

Yasher wasn't blind to the pull of power, his own Talent had made damn sure of that. Even if he tried not to lean on it, even if it had been erratic lately, the awareness was always there, like a second sense prickling at the edges of his perception. And right now, it was screaming at him. He didn't like this thing. He didn't like the way it sat in her pocket, like a whisper in the dark, or the way she was gripping it now, like she needed it.

Farah must have seen something in his expression because she sighed, rubbing her temple before relenting. "I'm careful with it."

That wasn't enough to settle him, but he could tell he wasn't going to win this with one conversation. "Alright. But if that thing so much as twitches, I'm throwing it into the sea."

Farah gave him a flat look. "I'd like to see you try."

That made him grin, the tension breaking just a little. "Oh, you'll see."

Younis cleared his throat. "If we're done arguing over ancient relics, we should make sure the others are ready. First light, then?"

She tucked the box away and nodded. "First light."

Yasher exhaled, rolling his shoulders. "Guess we'd better get some rest, then."

As they stepped back inside, the tavern's warmth felt hollow. Like it wasn't quite reaching his skin.

His mind wouldn't let it go. The whisper of wrongness. The way Farah had held that box. The way she had clutched it.

He didn't trust that relic.

And for the first time since they met, he wasn't sure if he trusted Farah's grip on herself.

THE MORNING AIR bit at his skin, crisp and sharp as a knife's edge. Yasher exhaled, watching the faint mist of his breath disappear into the chill. Soon, the heat would rise, burning away the cold, but for now, everything felt still, edged with something quiet and waiting.

Familiar sounds filled the space around him—the soft chuff of breath through flared nostrils, the rhythmic scrape of hooves against packed dirt, the low murmur of stable hands moving through their morning tasks. Routine. Predictable.

And yet, not quite right.

Younis was already done, checking over the ox and cart to make sure everything was secured, while Taj, naturally, was taking his time, fussing over his horse like she was some fine-bred royal charger instead of a sturdy road mount. He murmured something to her, smoothing a hand along her muzzle before glancing up, catching Yasher watching him.

"She's not gonna like us being ready before her." Taj grinned, tossing him an easy smirk.

Yasher raised a brow, tightening the last strap on his saddle. "Who says we're leaving without her?"

Taj gave an exaggerated shrug. "Just saying. Mehran took her, what, half an hour ago? She'll be pissed if we're packed and ready before she gets back."

Younis let out a low chuckle, pulling himself into the saddle. "That would require her to actually be surprised by something we do."

He snorted, shaking his head. They weren't wrong. Farah had a way of anticipating things before they even thought to act. It was part of what made her terrifyingly competent—and, at times, infuriating.

Something about this whole thing sat wrong. Not in any obvious way, not yet—but in the way Yasher felt the weight of it pressing against his ribs, settling deep in his gut like a hand curling around his luck and squeezing.

Farah had been quiet last night. Too quiet. Even when she curled up next to him, even when her body had softened against his, it was like she was somewhere else entirely. A step removed, her mind running ahead into places he couldn't follow.

She hadn't reached for the relic again, not that he'd noticed, but that didn't mean she wasn't thinking about it. He'd seen the way she handled it before, fingers curling around it like it tightly, something grounding her even as it unraveled her. It wasn't like her.

Farah wasn't someone who needed to be anchored.

She was the anchor—unshakable, immovable, the force that bent the world to her will. And yet...

He frowned, adjusting his coat. *Twelve hells.*

Taj swung up onto his horse, stretching his arms above his head. "So, we're just gonna ride in and hope for the best?"

Younis let out a dry snort as he secured the last of the packs to the cart. "That's usually how this goes."

He sighed, throwing a leg over his saddle. "Wouldn't be the first time."

Younis gave him a long, measured look. "You think this is worse than we're expecting?"

Yasher didn't answer immediately. He just glanced toward the road where Farah, Pari, and Mehran had disappeared into the thinning morning mist, that unease curling tighter around his ribs.

"...Yeah," he admitted, voice low. "I do."

The others fell quiet.

Even the horses seemed to shift uneasily, ears flicking, hooves scuffing against the dirt.

He flexed his fingers against the reins.

Farah was strong. Unyielding. If there was something wrong, she would push through it, force herself forward the way she always did.

But he had a sick feeling in his gut that whatever they were riding toward—whatever had left Sakasan so damned silent—wasn't something she could just push through. The thought chilled him more than the mountain air ever could.

The sound of footsteps and the low creak of a wooden cart pulled Yasher from his thoughts. He turned just in time to see Farah and Pari making their way up the road, Mehran trailing slightly behind, balancing a bundle of supplies in his arms. The little girl was humming softly, shifting a small sack over her shoulder, her braids bouncing with each step. Farah, on the other hand, looked as composed as ever, her expression giving away nothing.

She moved with effortless efficiency, securing the parcels in the supply cart, tying the ropes with practiced ease. Pari climbed up onto the cart, settling herself onto the edge, already picking apart the folds of a cloth-wrapped package that smelled faintly of dried fruit.

Yasher dismounted before he'd even decided to move. His boots hit the ground, and he reached for her, fingers closing warm and solid around her wrist before she could slip away.

Farah stilled, turning towards him.

He tugged her closer, sliding his hands around her waist, feeling the slight tension coiled beneath the layers of her coat. He didn't press, didn't try to make her meet his gaze—just held her, anchoring himself in the warmth of her body, in the familiar press of her against him.

For a breath—a single breath—she let herself lean into him. Just long enough for him to feel the tension ease in her shoulders, just long enough for his fingers to brush over the small of her back, anchoring her.

Then, like water slipping through his fingers, she was gone. It wasn't much, barely a few inches.

But he felt it like a chasm.

Her fingers brushed over his coat, a quick, absent gesture, before she murmured, "We should get moving."

Yasher studied her, trying to see past the veil she'd drawn over herself, but her expression was smooth, unreadable. Her lips had softened into something close to a smile. It was meant for him, but it wasn't real.

He let her go, though it took more effort than it should have.

She turned back to the cart, checking the knots one last time, her hands quick and methodical. Pari shot him a curious look, but Yasher just ruffled the girl's hair before stepping back, forcing himself to shake off the lingering unease crawling up his spine.

"Ready?" Mehran asked, already mounting his horse.

Yasher swung himself back into the saddle. "As we'll ever be."

But just as he turned his horse toward the road, a familiar voice cut through the morning air.

"Well, well, looks like we caught you just in time."

Yasher twisted in his saddle, eyebrows lifting.

The sound of hooves and jingling bells announced them first.

Lelah strode up the road, grinning like she was arriving at a long-lost lover's doorstep. Her amber eyes gleamed with easy mischief, the same confident sway in her step as before. Behind her, Samir followed with measured calm, his sharp gaze flicking over their group with a merchant's quiet efficiency—reading, assessing, calculating.

"You weren't going to leave without saying goodbye, were you?" Lelah teased, sauntering forward, the bells on her sash jingling lightly. "That would've been just rude."

Farah straightened, rolling her shoulders. "I assumed you were long gone."

Lelah gave a dramatic sigh. "We were supposed to be. But turns out, fixing a wagon wheel doesn't do much good if your driver decides to drink himself into a stupor the night it's fixed." She tossed a glare over her shoulder at one of the younger men behind her, who looked properly sheepish. "So, we're a bit delayed."

Yasher smirked, shaking his head. "And here I thought you just couldn't stand to be away from me."

Lelah grinned, stepping closer. "Caught me."

Farah exhaled through her nose, not quite a sigh, not quite amusement.

Samir, less interested in Yasher's flirtations, eyed the loaded cart before flicking his gaze to Farah. "You're still going to Sakasan?"

Farah's expression didn't change. "That's the plan."

Samir rubbed a hand over his jaw. "Then I'd tread carefully."

"We always tread carefully," Yasher said, shifting his weight in the saddle. "Why? Something new?"

Samir and Lelah exchanged a look—one of those quiet, knowing glances that people who knew each other well share.

Lelah's easy demeanor sobered just slightly. "We heard more talk last night from others heading to Rumatin. Quiet talk. About people trying to leave and not making it past the gates."

He frowned. "People disappearing?"

"Not sure." Lelah's lips pursed. "No one knows where

they went. Just that they left, and no one's heard from them since."

Yasher glanced at Farah, who was already staring at the road ahead, her jaw set. She didn't have to say anything. They were still going.

Yasher exhaled, adjusting his reins. "Well. That's comforting."

Lelah tilted her head, watching him. "You could come with us instead. Safer, easier, less strange disappearances."

He barked a laugh. "As tempting as that is, I think my luck would get me into trouble one way or another."

Lelah grinned. "Shame. You would've made an excellent addition to our ranks."

He felt Farah's gaze flick toward him, sharp and unreadable.

He just smirked. "Don't doubt it."

Samir folded his arms, looking at Farah. "You're still just as stubborn, then."

Farah answered before Yasher could. "We don't have a choice."

Samir studied her for a moment, then nodded. "Then at least let us give you something for the road."

Lelah waved over one of the younger men in their group, who handed over a small satchel. She offered it to Yasher with a smile. "Nothing fancy, but it's always good to have extra rations."

Yasher took it, feeling the solid weight of dried meats and nuts inside. "Appreciate it."

Samir stepped back, gaze flicking between their group once more. "Be careful."

Farah dipped her chin in acknowledgment, but didn't say anything.

Lelah winked at Yasher before turning on her heel, already heading back to her caravan. "Try not to die, gorgeous!"

He grinned. "I'll do my best."

Farah nudged her horse forward, brushing past him without so much as a glance.

Yasher clicked his tongue, shaking his head as he fell into step beside her. "Now, if I didn't know any better, I'd say you're sulking."

She didn't answer. But her fingers tightened around the reins.

Good. That was something, at least.

CHAPTER 16

THE VILLAGE at the river's edge sat pressed against the water like a forgotten thing, the slow-moving current of the Dhayyan River licking at its crumbling docks, patient and endless. Weathered buildings leaned into one another, as if huddling for warmth against the creeping chill of the evening, their wooden shutters rattling in the steady wind rolling off the river. Smoke curled from chimneys in thin, hesitant threads, swallowed too quickly by the salt-thick air.

The water lapped against the docks in slow, uneven rhythms. Like something breathing. Like something waiting. Farah felt an echo of it in her head.

The ferry, little more than a flat raft secured by thick, barnacle-encrusted ropes, bobbed gently at its mooring, its lone operator watching their approach with the indifference of someone who had seen travelers come and go a thousand times before.

She barely registered any of it.

Everything felt wrong. Not just the silence of the

village. Not just the river's whispering pull, the air thick with brine and woodsmoke. Everything.

The wrongness curling at the edges of her mind was creeping in more and more, whispering with no voice, pressing with no hands. But it was there. A presence. A shadow pressing against the edges of her mind, curling beneath her ribs, twisting itself into knots she couldn't unravel. She could feel it like a splinter buried too deep in her skin to remove.

Farah forced herself to focus, guiding her horse toward the inn near the dock where Mehran had already dismounted.

"They're shutting down for the evening. We'll set up passage for the morning," he said, scanning the narrow, dirt-packed streets with a practiced eye. "We should be across first thing."

She gave a distracted nod, handing off her reins to a stable boy without much thought.

Pari hopped down from the supply cart, stretching her arms high above her head with an exaggerated groan.

"This place smells like fish," she muttered, scrunching her nose.

Taj ruffled her hair before she could duck away. "Eat enough of it, and you'll grow gills."

Pari shot him a skeptical look but allowed herself to be herded inside with the others.

The inn was modest but sturdy, its wooden beams dark with years of smoke and salt air. The common room was busy but not crowded, filled mostly with villagers finishing their evening meals. The scent of stewed vegetables and roasting fish filled the air, blending with the low hum of conversation.

Farah barely heard it.

The weight of Yasher's gaze pressed against her skin, quiet but unrelenting, following her every movement like he was searching for something. Waiting. For her to flinch. For her to break. For her to finally stop pretending that everything was fine when it wasn't.

"You're not eating?" he asked, voice mild, but his eyes were sharp.

"I'm not hungry."

A lie. But one he didn't call her on.

Instead, he just watched her, studying her in that way that made her stomach twist. Not with warmth or fondness, but with something uncomfortable, like he was peeling back her skin and seeing the splinter beneath.

She turned on her heel and headed for the stairs.

The small room overlooked the river, its single narrow window cracked open just enough to let the cool night air slip in. The ferry below creaked gently in the water, its thick ropes straining against the current.

Farah unfastened her belt, setting it aside, then shrugged out of her coat with slow, measured movements.

He followed her inside, closing the door behind him with quiet deliberation.

Then, softly, "What's wrong? It's that thing, isn't it?"

Farah's fingers stilled over the ties of her tunic.

She inhaled once, steadying herself, then turned to face him. "Nothing's wrong."

His brow lifted, his mouth pressing into a thin, unimpressed line.

"You sure about that?"

Her jaw clenched. "I'm tired, Yasher. I don't want to do this right now."

"Then when?" He crossed his arms over his chest, his voice even but edged with something sharp. "You've been closed off for days. You barely talk to me. You barely talk to anyone."

Farah exhaled through her nose, forcing herself to stay calm. "I have a lot on my mind."

"Yeah," Yasher said, too quickly. "And how much of that is coming from that damned relic you're carrying around, instead of the strongbox we carry explicitly for it? This isn't you, Phoenix."

Her spine went rigid. He saw it, saw the way her fingers curled around the fabric of her pocket, where the small box still rested.

"It's not—" she started, but he cut her off.

"You grip it like you need it. You're not sleeping, now you're not eating. You snap at everyone if you do speak. As if no one is necessary, we're only standing in your way."

The words hit like a slap.

She scowled, stepping forward before she could stop herself. "You think it's controlling me?"

"I think it's doing something to you," He shot back, voice low but unrelenting. "You're not yourself. And don't tell me you are, because I know you." His hands flexed at his sides. "You can barely connect to anything. You're in your own head, and I can't tell if it's because you're spiraling or because that thing is whispering to you at all hours."

Her breath came sharper now, her pulse a quick, agitated rhythm against her ribs.

She shouldn't say it. She knew that even as the words formed, sharp and reckless on her tongue.

"Maybe that's what you hate, isn't it?" Her voice was sharp, the words slipping out before she could stop them. "That I don't need you."

She saw the way his face stilled, how the line of his jaw went taut—but he didn't react, not right away.

Good. Let him feel it.

His expression darkened. "What the hell is that supposed to mean?"

She scoffed. "Come on, Yasher. You act like you're worried, like you're so concerned, but you don't really want me to focus on anything but you, do you?"

He took a slow breath, steadying himself. "That's not fair."

Farah wasn't interested in fair. She was angry—at him, at herself, at the weight of everything pressing down on her.

So, she pushed.

"Maybe that merchant... Lelah, was right."

His breath stilled. His shoulders went taut—not from anger.

From something else.

"You could be free, couldn't you? No more risking your neck for a country that isn't yours. Joining the caravan, playing cards, trading stories, instead of standing with me, supporting me, supporting our task. You could just—go."

A beat of silence. Thicker than the river. He stared at her, blue eyes flat, his mouth pressing into something unreadable.

Then, slowly, deliberately, he stepped back.

Without a word, he crossed the room, grabbed his bag, and slung it over his shoulder.

Farah's stomach twisted. The words had already left her mouth—there was no pulling them back.

"Yasher—" whatever she could say to try and make this right stuck in her throat.

He slung his bag over his shoulder. Didn't look at her. Didn't need to.

"I'll stay with the soldiers tonight." Not a question. Not a fight. A decision.

He reached for the door. Stopped. Paused.

For one, fleeting moment, she thought he might say something.

He stepped out and closed the door behind him.

And just like that, he was gone.

Farah stood in the middle of the room, it felt colder without him, the walls pressing in, the air too still, too empty.

The river murmured below, endless, uncaring.

And finally—finally—something inside her cracked, the wall that had been wrapped around her shattering, and she felt everything.

Farah tightened the last strap on her saddlebags with precise, efficient movements, forcing her hands to remain steady. The morning air was crisp, carrying the scent of lingering smoke from the inn's hearth. She exhaled slowly, rolling her shoulders, pushing away the stiffness that had settled there overnight.

Sleep had been a shallow, restless thing. It had come in fits, unraveling before it could take hold, leaving her trapped in that place between exhaustion and awareness.

Not because of the fight—though that wound still ached, raw beneath the surface, waiting for her to acknowledge it. Because of everything.

Because of the space Yasher had left beside her.

The weight of the relic. The unease burrowing beneath her skin. The way her mind felt distant, detached, like something was pressing against the edges of her thoughts, keeping her from feeling anything clearly. Even when she had lain down, exhaustion heavy in her bones, it had taken too long to close her eyes. Too long to stop the replay of Yasher's voice, the quiet hurt beneath the frustration.

She had wanted to go after him. To smooth over the sharp edges of their words, to tell him that it wasn't him —that she was wrong. Off.

But she hadn't. Instead, she'd curled into herself, staring at the ceiling for what felt like hours, waiting for the tightness in her chest to ease. It hadn't. It sat there still, aching in a way she didn't know how to fix.

At some point in the night, Pari had crawled into bed beside her, tucking herself into Farah's side without a word. A small warmth in the cold. Farah had curled an arm around her automatically, as if it were instinct. The girl had said nothing, just nestled in closer, her breathing steady.

Farah had stayed awake long after, listening to the soft rise and fall of Pari's breaths, staring at the ceiling, her mind filled with thoughts that wouldn't quiet.

Now, in the morning light, it was easier to shove it all down. To focus on the task at hand. To remind herself that whatever unease had settled into her bones—whatever Yasher had seen in her last night—was secondary to what lay ahead.

She straightened, adjusting the fall of her coat as she pulled her composure into place. She couldn't afford distractions now. Not when they were heading toward something that none of them understood.

The scent of wet earth and morning frost clung to the air as she descended the stairs, her steps measured, her expression carefully schooled into something neutral. She stepped into the courtyard where the others had already gathered, tending to their final preparations.

Mehran was tightening the girth on his horse's saddle, speaking in low tones to Younis. Taj stood off to the side, rolling his shoulders as if shaking off the last of sleep. Pari was by the cart, double-checking the provisions, her small fingers quick as she secured the sacks in place with the practiced efficiency of someone far older than her nine years.

And Yasher—

Yasher worked in silence, his movements sharp,

methodical, distant. The familiar ease—the casual quips, the effortless teasing—was absent.

Farah had expected that. What she hadn't expected was how much it hurt. The space between them felt too wide. Too cold. Too final.

She tried to ignore it. Ignore the sting, the part of her that had wanted to wake up and pretend none of it had happened. Instead, she walked past him, toward Pari and the cart.

Just as she passed the group, she heard it.

"—lover's spat?" Taj's voice cut through the crisp morning air, light, teasing, completely unaware of the knife he had just twisted. "Didn't think you two actually fought."

The silence that followed wasn't sharp. It was worse.

It was dead.

Yasher didn't look at her. Didn't react. Didn't acknowledge it at all. And that—that was worse than if he had.

Mehran sighed, walked up behind Taj, and smacked him upside the head. "*Ahmagh,* you idiot. I swear by the Unnamed Gods you were dropped on your head as a child."

She didn't pause, just kept walking, her expression unreadable, her shoulders squared.

Farah kept moving, her boots crunching against the damp earth. The others fell into motion around her, finishing the last of their preparations. The quiet efficiency of it should have been grounding, but her unease had settled too deep. The relic pulsed faintly against her side, a sensation that wasn't quite touch but more like the hum of metal left too long in the forge, warping under unseen heat.

She exhaled slowly. *Focus.*

They set out from the inn in a steady line, leading their horses and the cart along the well-worn path toward the ferry. The early morning quiet was punctuated only by the occasional clink of tack and the murmured exchanges between Mehran and Younis up ahead. Taj led the oxen, while Pari walked beside her, small and steady, her hands tucked into the sleeves of her coat against the morning chill.

Farah kept her gaze ahead, refusing to let it stray to him.

He was close—she could sense him even without looking. His presence was something she had grown used to, something she had learned to place even in the dark, even in a crowd. But now there was a distance between them, an edge to the air that hadn't been there before. And she hated it.

The walk to the ferry was quiet save for the rhythmic tread of hooves and wheels against damp earth. They reached the dock just as the boatman began untying the mooring lines, the wooden ferry rocking gently with the river's slow current.

Farah handed off her horse to one of the workers and stepped onto the ferry's planks with the others. The wood groaned under the shift in weight as the last of their group boarded. The boatman gave a nod, pushing off, and the ferry drifted into the river's flow, the water lapping against its sides in steady, unhurried movements.

Only then did Farah lift her gaze toward the few other passengers already seated on the benches lining the deck, surveying for anything out of the ordinary as she always did, stopping on a figure who shouldn't be there, should be far, far away on her own journey.

Jeta Veseli, lounging near the stern, draped across the wooden bench like she had carved the seat for herself, one leg crossed over the other, her braid curling over her shoulder like a waiting viper. Her coat was dusted with the remnants of a long journey, but there was nothing weary in her posture. She looked completely at ease, the way only someone who knew they were always exactly where they were meant to be could.

The moment stretched, taut and unbroken.

Then Jeta smiled. "You look like you've seen a ghost."

Farah didn't react. Didn't let herself glance toward Yasher.

Instead, she exhaled slowly, adjusting the weight of her coat as she stepped further onto the deck.

"We left you in Rumatin," she said flatly.

Jeta lifted a single brow, amused. "Yes, yes you did. And now I am here."

Farah narrowed her eyes. The river wind tugged at the loose strands of her hair, cold against the heat creeping into her skin.

Beside her, Pari made a small sound that wasn't quite surprise, wasn't quite expectation.

Farah didn't move.

Neither did Yasher.

Jeta's smile deepened as she shifted, patting the empty space beside her. "Well then. Are you going to sit, or are we going to keep pretending this isn't an interesting coincidence?"

The ferry rocked gently beneath them, the water lapping in steady rhythm against its wooden hull. Pari sat comfortably beside Jeta, her small frame tucked against the older woman's side, legs kicking idly over the edge of the bench.

Jeta, ever at ease, propped her chin in her palm and regarded Pari with lazy amusement. "Well, little herald," she murmured, "why don't you tell me what I've missed while they remember how words work?"

Pari's dark eyes flicked up, assessing in that way that always made Farah uneasy—like the girl was weighing something unseen. But then, just as quickly, she brightened, fingers curling in the fabric of her coat.

"Well," Pari began, voice slipping into the easy cadence of a storyteller, "first, we nearly lost Yasher."

Farah resisted the urge to sigh.

Jeta made a thoughtful sound, barely glancing at Yasher before returning her attention to Pari. "Did you?"

Pari nodded. "He fell off his horse."

Jeta turned fully toward Yasher, brows raised. "Really?"

Yasher rolled his shoulders in a lazy stretch, feigning complete indifference. "Not my fault the damn thing spooked."

Pari scrunched her nose. "That's *exactly* your fault."

Jeta's lips twitched. "I'm inclined to agree."

Farah crossed her arms. "We didn't almost lose him. He just—" She waved a hand. "Fell."

"I rolled," Yasher corrected.

"You ate dirt," Pari said.

Jeta exhaled a quiet laugh. "A tragedy, I'm sure. He still looks to be in one piece, at least."

Pari continued, unfazed. "Then, we almost got caught by those men at the crossroads, but Farah scared them off."

Farah pressed her fingers against the bridge of her nose. "I didn't scare them. I warned them."

Pari blinked up at her, entirely unconvinced. "Your warning included your daggers."

Jeta let out a pleased hum. "Good girl."

Farah sighed.

Pari kicked her legs absently, thinking. "Oh! Mehran let me use his tent since I didn't have one."

Jeta arched a brow. "And why didn't you have a tent?"

Pari shrugged. "No one expected me to come."

Jeta's gaze flickered, something unreadable passing behind her eyes.

"No," she murmured. "I suppose they didn't."

Farah shifted. There was something in Jeta's tone she didn't like.

Pari, oblivious to the moment, continued. "Mehran said he didn't mind sleeping outside. But he also said if he didn't, I'd probably steal Yasher's, but he and Farah share the tent, so I wouldn't do that. Then he said that Taj didn't really need his."

Jeta laughed. "Smart man."

Farah felt Yasher move before he spoke, the sound of his voice sharp against the hush that had followed them all morning.

"How did you find us?"

But she had opened her mouth at the same time—"Where did you..."

They both stopped.

The silence that followed was heavier than it should've been. Not awkward—something quieter. Sharper. The kind of silence that came after raised voices and words you couldn't take back.

Farah turned toward him, catching the brief flicker of surprise in his eyes before it smoothed over into something unreadable. His jaw was set just a little too tight, his hands loose at his sides in that calculated way of his.

She could've pushed. Could've finished the sentence and kept going like nothing sat between them.

But she didn't. Instead, she inclined her head. A small, deliberate gesture. Not surrender. Not apology.

Just space.

A signal. She wasn't ready to fight again.

Yasher caught it, his expression shifting slightly before he turned back to Jeta.

"How did you find us?"

Jeta stretched her arms above her head, unbothered, unhurried, completely in control.

"Oh, you know me," she mused, voice dripping with amusement. "Always taking the scenic route."

Yasher's jaw tightened. Farah saw it—just a flicker, just a moment.

Jeta saw it too.

"That's not an answer."

"No," Jeta agreed, "but it's a rather charming deflection, don't you think?"

Yasher let out a slow breath, visibly reining himself in. "Where are you going, Jeta?"

"Tamidh," she answered easily.

Yasher frowned. "And you're taking the leisurely, southern route there."

"I said I was going to Tamidh," Jeta corrected. "You assumed I meant *directly*."

Farah's fingers flexed at her sides. "So, what? You just happened to be on this ferry at the same time as us?"

Jeta's lips curled, something sharp in her amusement. "What can I say? I had a feeling. Those fickle gods decided that plans needed to change."

Yasher's patience was thinning—Farah could see it in the set of his shoulders, the way his fingers flexed at his sides. "You don't just follow feelings, Jeta, do you?"

Jeta arched a brow. "And you don't just happen upon Luck, do you?"

He stilled.

The river stretched wide and unbothered around them.

Farah felt the shift in the air, the quiet hum of something bigger pressing at the edges of the moment.

Jeta leaned back against the railing, stretching her arms lazily. "Besides," she said lightly, "I thought you might need a little support."

Farah frowned. "For what?"

"Oh," she murmured, tipping her head back to glance at the sky, as if the answer were written in the clouds.

"I imagine we'll find out soon enough."

And something in her tone made Farah wish they wouldn't.

CHAPTER 17

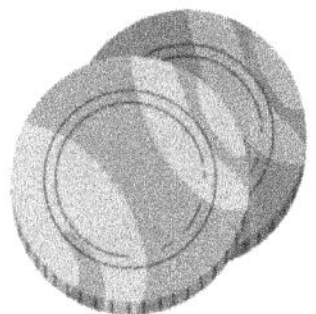

YASHER HADN'T SLEPT. That had to be why he felt everything flipped backwards.

And it wasn't just the kind of restless night where you wake up groggy, rub the exhaustion from your eyes, and move on. No, this was something thicker, something weighing him down like stones in his chest.

Every muscle ached from a night spent on the cold floor of the soldiers' room, his spine stiff from lying on rolled-up blankets that did nothing to stop the knots from forming. He had counted every creak of the wood, every shift of the wind outside, every damn breath that wasn't hers.

And now, this morning, every muscle in his body ached from the floorboards, exhaustion clinging to him like damp wool. But worse than that—far worse than that—was the silence.

Farah hadn't looked at him once. It shouldn't have bothered him. But it did, so much more than he wanted to admit.

He wanted to be mad. He was mad. But the anger tangled too easily with something else—something heavier, something he didn't want to name.

So, he ignored it. Just like she was ignoring him.

Which was fine. *Fine.*

Except that now—as if the morning couldn't get any worse—he had to deal with Jeta *fucking* Veseli, sitting there on the ferry like she'd been waiting for them all along.

A muscle ticked in Yasher's jaw. He crossed his arms, glaring at her, exhaustion sharpening his words.

Yasher exhaled sharply through his nose, arms crossing tight over his chest. "You really can't find your own boats, can you?"

Jeta turned, her dark eyes gleaming like she had been waiting for him to say that. She stretched against the railing, a cat in the sun, every movement deliberate, easy, calculated.

"What can I say?" she murmured, lips curling. "I like the company."

Jeta's head tilted, dark eyes studying him.

Pari, still silent, tilted her head too, mirroring Jeta's movement.

He looked away first.

It wasn't like he'd been surprised when she left. She had warned them, made it clear that Tamidh was where she was headed. But deep down, some stupid part of him had felt like her departure had been an indictment.

Like she'd taken one look at him—his Luck spiraling out of control, his complete lack of understanding of it— and decided he wasn't worth the effort.

That thought had festered, whether he admitted it or not.

And now she was here, back as if nothing had happened.

Pari shifted slightly, still watching. He had the distinct, uncomfortable feeling that she was filing this moment away for later.

"You said you were going to Tamidh."

Jeta didn't respond immediately. Instead, she stretched again, shifting easily with the sway of the ferry. "Still am," she finally said.

Pari breathed in softly, like she'd expected that answer.

Yasher's patience, already gone, wore even thinner. "Then what are you doing here?"

Jeta turned back toward the water, unbothered. "Taking the long way."

Pari let out a quiet hmm.

Yasher shot her a look. "What?"

Pari just shrugged. "That's what people say when they're not telling the whole truth."

Jeta let out a pleased little chuckle. "Sharp girl."

Pari smirked.

Jeta only smiled wider.

Yasher dragged a hand down his face, resisting the urge to groan. Too tired for this. Too tired for Jeta. Too tired for Farah standing stiff-backed at the front of the ferry, refusing to look at him where she'd moved to be away from him.

Jeta must have seen something in his expression,

because her smile shifted—not quite gone, but something quieter now, unreadable.

Pari shifted too, her small hands tightening where they rested in her lap.

He hated that, too.

Jeta was always watching, always weighing things in that way of hers, Pari joining her.

"I thought you didn't need help." Jeta didn't just say it. She dropped it like a blade.

Pari stilled.

Yasher's hands flexed at his sides, jaw tightening.

"I don't," he said.

Pari blinked up at him, entirely unconvinced.

"Ah. That's right." Jeta shifted again, draping her arm across the back of the bench like she was settling into some kind of performance. "Because you've got it all under control. It does look like everything's going so well."

Yasher felt the words hit exactly where they were meant to. Not just about his Luck, but also at the wall of silence between him and Farah.

Pari's eyes flicked to Jeta, then back to him, like she could sense it too.

Yasher turned away before she could say anything.

"You're still talking in riddles," he muttered.

Jeta chuckled, the sound low and pleased. "And you're still pretending you don't need answers."

Pari inhaled, as if she were about to say something, then stopped.

Yasher caught it. Noticed.

He let out a slow breath, shifting his weight, forcing himself to focus on anything else.

Farah still hadn't turned around since acknowledging the old woman. Not once.

She was ignoring him as if last night had meant nothing. As if the things they'd said—the hurt buried beneath the anger—hadn't settled into her bones the way it had in his.

She was good at that. At pushing things down until they looked like they weren't there at all.

Pari glanced at her, then back to Yasher, as if marking that too.

Jeta shifted beside him, her expression still calm, unreadable.

The ferry rocked gently, the water carrying them forward.

Jeta leaned back and exhaled. "Well," she mused, "at least I was right."

Yasher's head turned slightly. "About what?"

Jeta smiled, slow and knowing. "That you'd need a little support. At times the gods do pay at least a little attention to us lowly souls here."

Pari exhaled softly, her small hands unclenching.

He moved away from the old woman and little girl, starting to move to stand next to Farah as he usually would, then spun back to the horses and the soldiers.

The ferry finally bumped gently against the dock, ropes tightening as the ferryman secured them to the wooden posts. The planks groaned under the shifting weight of the horses, the cart, the passengers.

Yasher stepped onto solid ground, rolling his shoulders, trying to work out the stiffness from a morning spent standing too tense, too still.

They should have been moving already. Instead, they were wasting time.

Because Jeta was here.

And worse—she was staying.

Pari tugged at Jeta's sleeve, looking up at her with that bright, knowing expression she always had when she was getting what she wanted. "You can sit with me in the cart," she said, as if it had already been decided.

Jeta made a thoughtful sound. "That so?"

Pari nodded, entirely confident.

Yasher resisted the urge to sigh.

Jeta, for her part, only grinned. "Well, how can I say no to such a generous offer?" She ruffled Pari's hair before stepping past Yasher, not sparing him a glance.

Farah, who had remained silent for the entirety of the ferry ride, adjusted the strap of her saddlebags before finally breaking her silence. "We should get moving."

Yasher caught the flicker of something in her expression—relief, maybe, at finally getting off that damn boat.

He understood the feeling.

Mehran and the other soldiers had already started getting the horses settled, murmuring among themselves, but they straightened when Jeta approached.

And then, in the span of three sentences, she had all of them smiling.

The scowl he couldn't stop seemed to be staying around for a while.

She clapped Mehran on the back, asked Younis about his stiff leg, teased Taj about his eternally bad luck with cards. And they responded like she belonged here. Like she had always belonged here, never in a moment questioning how she knew any of these things.

Yasher's irritation only deepened.

"Enjoying yourself?" he muttered when she finally made her way back toward the cart.

Jeta shot him a smile. "Immensely."

He frowned, glancing at Farah, who stood beside him. She looked equally unimpressed. That, at least, was something they could still share.

Yasher exhaled, letting his frustration settle into something sharper. "Since you're in such a good mood, maybe you can finally answer a question for us."

Jeta climbed into the cart with easy grace, stretching her legs out in front of her. "I answer lots of questions."

"Not the ones that matter," Farah said, voice clipped.

Jeta smirked. "Matter to whom?"

Yasher's fingers curled at his sides. "Why are you here, Jeta?"

Jeta leaned back, arms draped over the side of the cart like a queen surveying her kingdom. "Right now? To keep our little herald company, obviously. Later on? We will have to see."

"You left for Tamidh," Farah said, tone flat. "Then you appeared on a ferry. You said we might need support. Support for what, exactly?"

Jeta smiled like they were discussing the weather. "Oh, I imagine we'll find out soon enough."

Yasher gritted his teeth. "See? This. This is exactly what I mean."

Jeta lifted a brow, amused. "What do you mean, *saqalu*?"

"I mean the cryptic bullshit," he snapped. "Every time we ask you something, you dance around it like we're playing a game we don't know the rules to."

Jeta rested her chin in her palm. "Maybe you should learn the rules, then."

Farah sighed sharply. "Jeta."

Jeta held up her hands in mock surrender. "What do you want me to say? That I had a feeling? That I listened to my instincts? That the Damned Divine yanked me up by my heels and placed me on the ferry? What would make you feel better?"

Yasher scoffed. "That's not an answer."

Jeta grinned. "It's my answer."

Yasher stared at her, debating if it was even worth it to keep pushing. Because he already knew how this worked—Jeta wouldn't say anything until she decided it was time.

And no amount of irritation, exhaustion, or perfectly reasonable frustration would make her talk faster.

He exhaled hard, rubbing a hand over his face. His patience was gone. His energy was gone.

"Fine. Be difficult. That's all you're ever going to be, isn't it?"

Jeta's laughter wasn't sharp. It was just amused.

Farah, apparently not done yet, crossed her arms. "Is this about my mission?"

Jeta made an appreciative sound. "Which one?"

Farah's eyes narrowed. "You know which one."

Jeta tilted her head, considering. "Well, it's certainly possible."

Farah exhaled, sharp and slow. "You don't know, do you?"

Jeta lifted a shoulder. "I know many things. Some are just... more interesting than others."

Farah didn't roll her eyes, but Yasher could feel the deep, unwavering temptation behind her expression.

He took a little bit of pleasure in that, though he shouldn't.

Jeta stretched again, settling further into the cart. Completely at ease. Completely unbothered. Like she had already seen this moment before.

"We should get moving." She tipped her head back slightly, sighing as if at some private joke. "I'd hate to keep the road waiting."

And Yasher—exhausted, frustrated, on edge—hated how much she made it sound like fate.

Pari kicked her legs idly. "Will you tell me a story?"

Jeta grinned. "That depends. Would you like one about luck, fate, or destiny?"

Pari considered. "What's the difference?"

Jeta's smile was slow, thoughtful. "An excellent question."

Yasher ran a hand over his face again, sparing a glance before he thought about it to Farah in askance.

She didn't say anything.

It was going to be a long fucking day.

THEY STOPPED at a bend in the road where the trees began to thin, giving way to open stretches of dry, wind-carved stone after a few hours of travel to rest the horses and themselves. The cedars that had crowded the riverbanks behind them were now scattered, their dark-green needles breaking apart into patches of scraggly brush and exposed rock. The scent of pine and damp earth was fading, replaced by something drier—the sharp tang of sun-warmed stone, the faint bite of salt in the air carried inland by the wind.

The road ahead twisted through the hills, winding toward Sakasan.

It wasn't quite desert here, but it was getting there.

Yasher stepped off the road, rolling his shoulders, but the ache stayed lodged deep—not just from the miles or the saddle, but from the damn silence.

His Luck curled at the edges of his senses, not like a guide, but like something pressing against him, warning him. Off-kilter. Wrong.

Behind him, the soldiers were tending to the horses, checking girths, adjusting packs, loosening straps to let the animals breathe. Pari was still in the cart, swinging her legs idly, watching everything with sharp eyes that took in more than she let on. Jeta had descended from the cart and was stretching out her back.

Farah stood a little apart from them, adjusting the strap of her saddlebags, her movements precise, practiced—something to occupy herself. She was close enough that Yasher could feel her presence, but still too far to acknowledge him.

Which was still fine. *Fine.*

Jeta clapped her hands together. "Alright, little herald," she said, turning to Pari. "Why don't you go help the soldiers with the horses?"

Pari frowned up at her, clearly reluctant to leave. "Why?"

Jeta smiled. "Because I asked nicely, and I need to speak with those two before they decide to poison the rest of us so we can join in on their sulking."

"They had a fight last night, and they don't want to say sorry." Pari replied, looking between himself and Farah. After a moment, she let out a dramatic sigh and slid off the cart, trotting over to Mehran and Younis. She called for Taj loudly, her voice carrying, and the soldier turned with an exaggerated groan, already bracing for whatever task she was about to assign herself.

That left just the three of them.

Yasher sighed, already bracing for whatever Jeta had planned, but she turned away from him and looked at Farah with a glare. She stepped forward, closing the space between them and holding out her hand—palm up, fingers relaxed—toward Farah.

Farah blinked at her, stiffening slightly. "What?"

Jeta didn't answer. Didn't move. Just waited, hand still extended.

Farah's eyes flicked down, wary. "What are you doing?"

Jeta tilted her head. "Holding out my hand."

"I can see that."

"And yet, you're still not giving me what I asked for."

Farah's shoulders squared. "You didn't ask for anything."

Jeta exhaled, long-suffering. "Farahnaz."

Farah crossed her arms. "Jeta."

Jeta arched a brow, unimpressed, then glanced toward Yasher. "Still being a difficult one, I see."

He couldn't help the sharp laugh that escaped. "Oh, absolutely."

Farah shot him a glare.

Jeta only smiled, turning back to her. "Give it to me."

Farah's jaw tightened. "Give what to you?"

Jeta's smile faded, just slightly. "The fragment of the Veil, Farah."

Something in the air shifted. How had she known about any of this?

He wisely kept his mouth shut because he wanted anyone other than Farah to carry it, but the questions came into his mind fast. *How did Jeta know anything about the Veil? Did she really understand what it was doing to Farah? Would Farah give it over? Would Jeta fix what was wrong with her?*

Farah's fingers curled slightly, but she didn't move. "It's fine where it is."

Jeta sighed, shaking her head. "It's not healthy to keep a corruption that close to you. It won't stay separate from you for long."

Farah stiffened as he automatically stepped closer, the word sinking in his gut like a bad draw at the card table, ready to rip the box from her and not have her hate him forever.

Jeta tilted her hand slightly, expectant, ignoring him, fully focused on Farah. "You know I'm right."

Farah didn't answer immediately, and it was obvious to the world that she didn't want to answer at all.

And that was what made him so uneasy.

Because Farah wasn't the kind of person who second-guessed things. She didn't hesitate. She didn't waver. Standing there, clutching that relic like it was a part of her—she was hesitating.

Slowly, reluctantly, Farah pulled the lacquered box from her vest, fingers brushing over the worn wood like she didn't want to let it go.

Jeta took it from her without ceremony, turning it over in her hands, feeling the weight of it.

She hummed softly. "Stubborn, bull-headed thing, aren't you?"

He wasn't sure if she was talking to Farah or the relic.

Jeta turned and walked to the cart, moving without hurry, and placed the relic inside the strongbox buried beneath the supplies. She clicked the latch shut, drew something over it, then dusted her hands off and turned back to them like it was done.

Farah's arms remained crossed, her posture rigid.

She took a few steps closer, her gaze shifting between the two of them.

He didn't like that look. He knew that look.

"Now," she said, her voice lighter, more amused, "while we're dealing with problems, I think it's about time you two work yours out. That thing shouldn't bother you any longer."

Farah's expression darkened instantly. "We don't have a problem."

Jeta lifted a brow. "Oh? That's interesting, because

you still aren't looking at each other, like petulant children, neither wanting to take the first step to an honest apology for whatever ill words you threw at one another. While that," she waved towards the strongbox. "More than likely made it worse, you're just making each other and the rest of us miserable. For that, I do blame both of you, not just that ugly thing in the box."

Yasher opened his mouth, then shut it.

Jeta smiled like she had already won.

Farah turned slightly, not looking at him, but not quite ignoring him either. "We're handling it."

"Sure," Jeta said. "By brooding separately and letting it splinter into something worse. Ach, you are both so young."

Farah's jaw tensed.

Yasher rubbed at his temples. "Look, Jeta—"

"No, you look," she interrupted, suddenly serious. "You two may think you can function like this, but you're wrong. Whatever's festering between you is going to break something beyond repair if you don't deal with it now. I don't know what was said, nor do I really care, but act like you are not children, and I shall stop treating you as such."

Farah's arms remained tightly crossed, but she didn't argue.

Jeta smiled, slow and knowing. "See? You know I'm right."

He sighed, dragging a hand down his face. "So what, you want us to sit in a circle and talk about our feelings?"

Jeta grinned. "Wouldn't that be fun?"

Farah scowled. "Not happening."

Jeta let out an exaggerated sigh. "Fine. You don't have to talk now. But if you let this turn into something bigger, don't say I didn't warn you."

She clapped Yasher on the shoulder as she passed, dropping her voice just for him. "And if you ever want real advice about women, you know where to find me."

Yasher scowled. "Gods help me."

Jeta just laughed, walking back toward the cart where Pari was waiting.

Yasher exhaled, watching her go.

Farah was still standing there, still not looking at him.

And the worst part? Jeta was right.

This was going to break something if they didn't figure it out, and he had no idea how to fix it. He would apologize for anything that he did to her, gladly... but it wouldn't actually fix anything.

The air between them had been heavy since last night, since the words had come too fast, too sharp, slicing deeper than either of them had meant. Yasher knew—logically—that the relic had been twisting Farah up, pressing into her thoughts like rot beneath the skin, but that didn't erase what she'd said. And it didn't erase the way it had felt.

He wanted to shake it off, to let it slide away like he had with a thousand other fights in his life. He wanted to shove it down, drown it out, pretend that none of it mattered. But this was Farah. This was much more painful.

Farah hadn't moved. She was standing with her arms

crossed, gaze fixed on the horizon, her fingers curled slightly against her sleeves.

He let out a slow, deliberate breath, dragging a hand through his hair. "Anything to say?"

No response. Not even a glance.

He let out a sharp, humorless laugh, shaking his head. "Alright. I guess we're just gonna stand here in silence until one of us drops dead, then."

Her shoulders pulled tighter, like a bowstring drawn too far back.

For a moment, he thought she wouldn't answer.

Then she shifted, fingers brushing absently over the strap of her belt, a movement too practiced to be casual. "It wasn't me, not... everything."

Yasher let out a sharp breath that wasn't quite a laugh. "I know."

She hesitated. "Do you?"

He turned toward her, tilting his head. "I just said I do, didn't I?"

Her fingers stilled against her sleeve.

He sighed, raking a hand through his hair. "Look, I get it. The relic was messing with you. It got in your head, and—" He shook his head. "Doesn't change the fact that you meant what you said. I know you too well."

Farah's arms tightened around herself.

The words had been cutting, precise. A strike made to land where it hurt most. That's what she's best at, aiming right for the place with the most damage.

Because it was true. The truest thing about him.

He had spent his whole life knowing it, hearing it from his father, from his brothers, from even himself.

That he was the kind of man who ran before the walls could close in. That he was good at slipping through cracks, at making sure no place ever got too permanent, no bond ever got too tight.

But he had never heard it from her.

Farah had never had that choice. She had never run. She had stood and fought and stayed, because that was who she was.

She had always known that about him, he knew that. Clocked it the moment she saved him from a beating in the tavern by the docks over a year ago. She had just never said it since then.

Until last night, when she had thrown it at him like a perfectly balanced knife right into his heart.

He exhaled through his teeth, slow and careful. "You think I don't know that's who I am?"

Her gaze finally lifted. Her dark eyes were guarded, wary.

"That's not—" She stopped herself, shaking her head. "That's not what I meant."

"Yeah?" His voice was rougher than he intended. "Didn't sound that way."

Farah pressed her lips together, arms still crossed. She wasn't looking away now, but she was still holding something back, something locked behind her ribs, and he wasn't sure if it was worth trying to pry it free.

She looked tired. More than that—she looked guilty.

Yasher sighed again, quieter this time. "You wanna know what the worst part is?"

She said nothing, but she was listening now. He could feel it.

"The worst part is," he continued, voice lower, "that you weren't wrong, no matter how much it stung."

Farah flinched. It was quick, barely there, but Yasher caught it anyway.

He huffed a small, humorless laugh. "You think I don't see it? My father used to say I was born with one foot already out the door. My brothers—" He exhaled, shaking his head. "Doesn't matter. Point is, it's not news to me, Farah."

Her throat worked as she swallowed. "Yasher."

He shook his head. "It's fine. Really. You just happened to say it out loud this time."

"It's not fine."

He looked at her again, searching her face. She was stubborn, always had been, but the expression she wore now was something else—something softer, something that looked an awful lot like regret.

"You don't run from everything." The words came slowly, like she wasn't sure she should be saying them.

He tilted his head, voice low. "No?"

Farah's fingers curled into the fabric of her sleeves. She let out a slow breath, then—soft, certain—"Not from me."

Something in his chest tightened.

Not from me.

He let out a slow breath, scraping a hand down his face. "Twelve hells, Farah."

She didn't say anything.

He glanced away, staring out toward the thinning trees, toward the rocky hills that stretched ahead of them. Toward the road that led them both deeper into whatever mess they had gotten themselves into.

He could have left a hundred times by now.

There had been moments—so many moments—when it would have been easier to slip away. He had told himself, in the beginning, that he was just waiting for the right time. That as soon as things got too messy, too tangled, too real, he'd be gone.

Except—he wasn't. And maybe that meant something.

Maybe that meant everything.

He dragged in another breath, slower this time. "You really think that?"

She held his gaze. "I know it."

The words should have felt heavier, but instead, they settled somewhere solid in his chest.

He let out another slow exhale, shaking his head. "You are really terrible at apologies, you know that?"

Farah's lips twitched. "I wasn't apologizing."

He huffed a laugh. "Could've fooled me."

She didn't argue.

Instead, she reached for his hand. Not quickly. Not carelessly.

Her fingers curled lightly around his, a tentative warmth against his skin.

Not pulling. Not demanding. Just... there, hopeful.

If he chose to take it.

He stared at their hands for a beat too long, then exhaled, and chose to tighten his grip in return.

Maybe they were both terrible at apologies, but maybe that didn't matter.

Not when there were things that didn't need to be said.

Not when they knew.

A voice called from the cart, breaking the moment. "If you two are done brooding, we'd love to get moving before the next century! I am not getting any younger."

Yasher groaned, tipping his head back. "Jeta, I swear—"

Farah sighed but didn't let go of his hand.

Yasher glanced at her again, a slow grin tugging at his lips. "See? Look at us, working our problems out, both wanting to strangle the same old woman and toss her body to the wolves."

Farah huffed a quiet laugh. "Shut up and get on your horse."

Yasher smirked, pulling her hand up to his lips first before letting go.

CHAPTER 18

THE FIRE BURNED LOW, embers pulsing like a slow heartbeat, their glow flickering against the dark stretch of land around them. The scent of charred wood mingled with the distant brine of the sea, salt carried inland by the restless wind. Beyond the firelight, the cliffs rose in jagged relief, a wall of black rock against the vast emptiness beyond.

Farah stretched her hands toward the warmth, letting it sink into her skin. It was better now. The tight coil in her chest had loosened, the strange weight in her thoughts finally gone. It had lifted while Jeta locked up the relic and she breathed easier, her mind clearer than it had been in days.

She curled her fingers, stretching her arms up above her head as if shaking off the last remnants of tension. For a moment, the warmth seemed to pass through her rather than settle—but it was nothing. Just the lingering effect of exhaustion, of long nights spent carrying too much in her thoughts.

The fire flickered. The embers glowed bright, then softened into a slow, steady burn. Normal.

She exhaled. The weight had passed. The corruption, whatever it had been, had quieted. She was back to herself.

Jeta sat across from her, stretched out in the firelight, one arm draped lazily over her knee, looking as if she had always belonged there.

"You can share my tent," Pari announced, serious as anything. "As long as Mehran agrees. It is his tent after all."

Jeta tilted her head, considering. "And if Mehran is not agreeable?"

Pari shrugged. "Then we'll just have to convince him."

Jeta's lips curled, pleased. "I do like the way you think, little herald."

Pari grinned, already certain Mehran would agree.

Taj, ever attentive, perked up from where he had been adjusting the kettle over the fire. "Do you need extra blankets? I have one. And if the ground's too rough, I can—"

Yasher cut in, shaking his head. "Taj, you cannot just go around trusting Jeta like this." He leaned back, arms stretched lazily behind him. "She's going to convince you to steal horses or sell your soul for a story. Probably both."

Taj hesitated, glancing at Jeta as if genuinely considering whether she was capable of such things.

Jeta sighed, long-suffering. "What a reputation I have."

Farah smirked. "Because it's earned."

Younis, seated on a nearby rock, let out a quiet chuckle. "She's not denying it, though."

Jeta pressed a hand to her chest, eyes full of false innocence. "Why, Younis-*jan*, if you keep speaking such truths, I might grow fond of you."

Mehran snorted. "That's what worries us."

The shift had happened faster than Farah would have expected, but not in a way that felt forced. The old woman had slipped into their ranks like she had always been there, not by demanding space, but by filling it seamlessly—never overstepping, never forcing her presence, just fitting herself into the natural rhythm of the soldiers' banter with an ease that felt almost practiced.

By the time *Ostad* slipped into the conversation, the honorific for elder teacher, it wasn't abrupt. It didn't feel like an offering handed to an outsider. It was something earned.

Jeta didn't react—no false modesty, no sharp amusement. Just quiet acceptance, like she had expected it.

Like it was already hers.

Pari sighed contentedly, curling further into her coat. "*Ostad* should tell another story."

Jeta's gaze flickered toward her.

"Is that a request, little herald?"

Yasher groaned. "You see what I mean? She's already got Pari under her spell."

Jeta smiled, slow and knowing. "And you, *saqalu*?"

"Oh, I don't fall for tricks that easily."

Farah raised an eyebrow. "Says the man currently letting me use him as a pillow."

He didn't look remotely ashamed. "That's different."

Jeta only laughed, tilting her head toward Pari. "And what story do you expect, little herald?"

Pari considered for a long moment before answering. "A story about Luck. You know even more than Yasher does about it."

Farah felt the shift. A small thing, barely there—the way the air seemed to still, the way the fire crackled a little softer, the way his fingers against her hesitated, just for a breath.

Jeta smiled, slow and knowing.

"Ah," she murmured. "Luck."

The way she said it was different than how most did. Not as an abstract thing, not as chance or fate. Like it was something real. Something she had seen, something she had touched.

Jeta rested her elbow on her knee, chin in her hand, watching the firelight flicker between them. When she spoke, her voice was softer, almost thoughtful.

The fire burned low, its glow flickering across the faces of those gathered around it. The scent of charred wood clung to the cold night air, mixing with the distant brine of the unseen sea. Somewhere beyond the cliffs, the water whispered against the shore, a rhythm older than any kingdom, older than the gods themselves.

Farah sat with her hands outstretched toward the warmth, fingers loose, her expression unreadable. The relic was gone—locked away, out of reach—and the weight that had pressed against her mind for days had lifted. She felt clearer now. Lighter. She told herself it had only been residual, that whatever unease had settled into her was nothing more than the strain of the journey.

And yet, when Jeta began to speak, a sliver of tension curled between her ribs.

"Long ago, before the first kingdom rose, before the first coin was struck, before the bickering gods had decided to leave this plane, there was a man who walked the world with luck stitched into his bones," Jeta said, her voice unhurried, her dark eyes flickering in the firelight. "He was not a king. He was not a soldier. He had no name worth remembering, and yet his shadow stretched across the lands, wherever he went."

Farah barely moved, but Jeta's gaze flickered toward her.

"He was the kind of man who should have died a hundred times, but never did," Jeta continued, her voice dipping into something softer, something deliberate. "Arrows missed him by the width of a breath. Bridges collapsed the moment he had stepped off them. When the sea rose to swallow the land, the water never touched his feet."

Jeta paused—just slightly, just enough for the silence to settle between them. Then she tilted her head, looking straight at Farah.

"You've met men like that, haven't you?"

It was not a question.

The fire popped. Farah inhaled, slow and measured, her face carefully still.

"People called him favored. Chosen. Touched by the gods, though he had never prayed a day in his life. Mind you, this was before the Talents were given to man by the gods as their parting gift, so no one quite understood what was happening to him, least of all him."

Farah felt Yasher shift beside her. Not much. Just enough.

"For what little he did understand, the man knew one thing. This was not a gift." Jeta's gaze had not left her.

"Because for every time the world bent to let him pass, it took from those around him. A soldier who stepped where he had stood was struck by an arrow meant for him. A woman who walked beside him drowned where he did not. And when the world burned, he walked through the ashes, untouched, while those behind him fell."

Jeta's voice was steady, but there was something else beneath it. Something sharp. Something meant for Farah alone.

"His Luck was not a blessing," Jeta murmured. "It was a weight he carried wherever he went."

The words sat heavy in the night air. The fire crackled, sending up a slow drift of embers. The others listened, intent, but Farah was aware of Jeta's focus—of the way the other woman was waiting for something.

A reaction. A flicker of something unguarded.

Pari, who had been curled against Jeta's side, let out a small breath. "That's not fair," she said, her voice soft but certain.

Jeta glanced at her, the sharpness in her gaze easing. "No?"

Pari shook her head. "The man never asked for it. It wasn't his fault."

Jeta's lips curled, something almost approving in the expression. "You are right, this was not something he asked for, and yet he still carried it. Many things in this world are not fair, little herald. That doesn't mean they don't come with a cost regardless."

Pari frowned, considering that. Then, after a long moment, she asked, "What happened to him?"

Jeta tilted her head slightly. "No one knows. Some say that he still wanders through Emari, never getting the reprieve of walking the Chinvat Bridge, to be judged. Sowing chaos here and there, changing things to his favor regardless of whether he wants them to."

Pari wrinkled her nose. "That's a bad ending."

Jeta's lips curled. "Who said it ended?"

The fire crackled softly, sending a slow drift of embers into the night air.

Pari shifted closer, wrapping her arms around her knees. "But the gods made the mistake, not him. If they forgot him, they should have to fix it."

Jeta's eyes gleamed, catching the firelight. "And do you think the gods admit their mistakes, little herald?"

Pari hesitated, then made a face. "...No. They just forget us and what they did."

Jeta chuckled, ruffling Pari's hair. "Smart girl. We should always be wary when it comes to gods. Their gifts are not always worth the pain that they cost, and rarely do they take back what it is they've given."

Farah inhaled slowly, staring into the fire.

She told herself she wasn't thinking about it.

She wasn't thinking about the way Jeta had spoken,

about how the story felt too close to something else, about the way Yasher had gone quiet beside her.

She wasn't thinking about luck, or curses, or the way the gods do not take back their gifts.

She wasn't thinking about how her instincts had faltered—and sowed chaos.

Instead, she let herself settle into Yasher's warmth, his arm still resting against her waist, still steady, still present. She let the night close in around them, let the fire burn low, and told herself it meant nothing.

THE CAMP HAD SETTLED into quiet. Taj stretched with a satisfied groan before retreating to his tent. Mehran and Younis stood at the edge of the clearing, speaking in low voices as they sorted the watch shifts. Jeta murmured something to Pari before following the girl into their shared tent, the sound of fabric rustling as they disappeared inside.

Farah remained by the fire, watching the glow flicker against the dark silhouettes of their tents, feeling the last warmth against her skin before the night fully took hold.

Then, Yasher's fingers brushed against hers.

A light touch, barely there, but enough.

Enough to say, *Come with me.*

She followed without hesitation, stepping inside the tent and letting the canvas fall closed behind them.

The air inside was warmer, thick with the scent of leather and dust, something familiar and grounding. Yasher shrugged off his coat, tossing it aside as he sat down on the bedroll, stretching his legs out with a tired sigh.

Farah hesitated, standing just inside, fingers curled at the edges of her sleeves. The fight from the night before still lingered between them, a thin thread of tension neither had fully pulled free from yet.

Yasher glanced up at her, his expression softer now, but still searching.

"You're thinking too much again," he murmured.

She let out a slow breath, feeling the rise and fall of her chest with more awareness than usual, like she had to remind herself to match the rhythm of the space around her. "I usually do."

His lips curved slightly, but it wasn't quite a smile. His head tipped back against the bedroll, eyes unreadable in the dim glow of the embers outside. The silence between them stretched, warm but unspoken, the fight from the night before lingering like the last wisps of smoke in the air—thinned but not quite gone.

"I don't want that fight to sit between us," he murmured.

Neither did she, but the pause before she answered was just a fraction too long.

She stepped closer, lowering herself beside him. Their knees brushed —a quiet, grounding touch—but she didn't reach for him yet.

"I know it sounds like an excuse to blame the relic," she said quietly, her voice measured, careful. "But it was. And I hate that."

Yasher's gaze flicked to hers, sharp with something unreadable.

She exhaled, forcing herself to hold his eyes. "I felt it twisting inside me, changing the way I thought, the way I reacted. And even knowing that, I still don't get to take back the things I said. I still don't get to pretend it wasn't me."

His fingers flexed against his knee, thoughtful rather than tense. "You don't have to pretend anything."

She swallowed. "I never want to hurt you."

His expression softened, the sharp edges of it easing, but he didn't speak right away. He just looked at her, the firelight catching in his blue eyes, flickering like something unspoken rested just beneath the surface.

When he finally spoke, his voice was quieter. "Then don't."

She inhaled slowly, the words settling deep in her chest.

Not an accusation. Not a demand. Just a simple, steady truth.

She had been trained to hurt people, first by weapons, and then by words as well thanks to the environment that the Beloveds existed in. To wield herself like a weapon, to cut and never hesitate. But he was something different. She didn't want her words to land like blades with him, didn't want the things she carried to become wounds in him.

Her fingers twitched, then lifted, brushing along the line of his jaw, her touch barely there. His stubble was rough beneath her fingertips, grounding. Real. A reminder of something solid.

His hand reached for hers, his grip warm and steady. He didn't pull, didn't press, just held her there.

"You know that's not who you are," he murmured.

She let out a slow breath. "I do."

He tilted his head slightly, studying her. "Then why do you look like you're afraid?"

She blinked, caught off guard.

"I'm not afraid," she said, but the words felt flimsy even as she said them.

His fingers traced over the inside of her wrist, slow and thoughtful. "You always do that when you lie."

Farah let out a short, breathy laugh, shaking her head. "You think you know me that well?"

Yasher huffed softly, tilting his head toward her. "I know that if I told you I'd leave tomorrow, you'd tell me you'd be fine, even if it was the last thing you wanted me to do."

Her breath hitched, because he wasn't wrong.

She would say it, wouldn't she? Just like she always did. Just like she had before, when he made jokes about slipping away in the night, or when he acted like he was just a passing storm in her life, not something permanent.

And every time he did, she let it pass. Because the truth was terrifying.

She had been fine before him. She had survived before him. She would survive after him. But fine and whole were not the same thing. If Yasher left, it would shear off a piece of her soul.

Farah's fingers curled slightly, tightening around his. "Don't joke about that."

Yasher went still.

Then, softer, "Phoenix—"

She shook her head. "Just don't."

The words had come out sharper than she intended, but she couldn't bring herself to take them back.

He exhaled, shifting closer, his forehead brushing against hers. His voice dropped lower, gentler. "I wouldn't."

She closed her eyes, willing herself to breathe evenly.

She could feel his warmth, the steady rise and fall of his breath, the way he wasn't pulling away.

When she spoke again, it was barely above a whisper. "You always act like you could just disappear, like it wouldn't matter."

He tensed slightly beneath her touch, but he didn't interrupt.

Farah swallowed, opening her eyes again. "It would matter."

The silence between them stretched, not heavy, but filled with something fragile, something unspoken but deeply understood.

Yasher's grip on her wrist tightened slightly, grounding. "I know."

She exhaled, and this time, the tension in her shoulders loosened.

"Good," she murmured.

Yasher let out a soft chuckle, shaking his head. "You're really bad at being vulnerable, you know that?"

She hesitated, then exhaled, a quiet breath that carried something unspoken. "I'm not used to it."

He tilted his head, watching her. Waiting.

Farah's fingers traced absently over the back of his

hand. "It's not how I was raised. It's not... safe to show anything but strength."

Yasher didn't speak, but his grip on her wrist tightened slightly—steady, grounding.

She inhaled slowly, letting her fingers settle over his. "But you—" She swallowed, feeling the weight of it before saying, quieter, "You make it feel safe."

Yasher's expression shifted, something unreadable flickering in his eyes.

For a long moment, he just looked at her.

Then, finally, he smiled—smaller than before, softer. "Phoenix."

Farah huffed, rolling her eyes even as warmth curled in her chest. "Don't let it go to your head."

Yasher's grin widened slightly, his thumb brushing over her knuckles. "Too late."

She sighed, shaking her head, but she didn't let go. Didn't want to.

And when he kissed her, slow and certain, it was not a question.

It was an answer.

"The relic," he murmured, his voice quiet but fierce after they broke apart. "Is it... has it let you loose?"

Her fingers twitched against the fabric of her vest. The movement was small, something even she might not have noticed if not for the sharp way his gaze flicked to it —too quick, too knowing.

She had felt it before, in Rumatin, on the road, in the quiet moments where she had clutched it without realizing. But now?

Now it was gone. And yet—

Farah exhaled, rolling her shoulders, forcing herself to relax beneath his stare but she couldn't help but look away. "It's... quieter now."

"Not gone?" The words slid between them like a blade eased into its sheath—dangerous in what they might mean.

Farah hesitated. It was only for a moment. A blink. A breath.

Then she shook her head. "Not entirely. Not yet. It's been getting better since Jeta took it away, but there are... memories more than anything, fading to the background, like an echo."

He turned her to face him directly, and she met his gaze, steady. "I'm myself again. Mostly."

His brows furrowed slightly, like he didn't love that answer.

"Hey," she said, reaching up to brush her thumb against his cheek. "It's not in my hands anymore."

Yasher exhaled slowly. "But it was in your head for days."

Farah nodded. "And I'm telling you—I'm here, Yasher. I know what's real."

His fingers trailed up her arm, slowly, until he was cupping her face, his thumb resting at the hollow of her jaw. His gaze held hers, searching.

Then, finally, he let out a quiet breath. "Okay."

Farah let the tension slip from her shoulders, leaning into his touch.

Yasher's thumb traced along her jaw, thoughtful. "I never saw you hesitate before."

Farah huffed a small breath, lips curving wryly. "I'm allowed to hesitate sometimes."

"Not you," he murmured. "You always know exactly what to do."

She let her fingers slide into his hair, tilting his face toward hers. "Not always."

Yasher kissed her softly at first, testing. A slow press of lips, warm and familiar. She exhaled against him, the tension in her shoulders loosening as she kissed him back, deeper this time, letting the last of the lingering distance between them fade.

Yasher's hands moved to her waist, pulling her closer until their bodies were flush against each other. His warmth pressed into her, grounding, solid.

Farah sighed into him as his lips moved from her mouth to her jaw, down to the curve of her throat. His breath was warm against her skin, his hands tracing slow, familiar paths over her back, her sides. There was no rush—just slow certainty, just the warmth of knowing each other.

She let her hands slide into his hair, tilting his face toward hers again, capturing his mouth with hers. The kiss deepened, slow and searching, as if they were relearning each other, relearning the spaces between them.

He pulled her down with him, the bedroll shifting beneath them. His hands skated over her waist, tugging at her tunic, and she helped him pull it over her head before reaching for the fastenings of his shirt.

Yasher smiled against her lips. "Eager?"

Farah huffed. "Shut up."

He laughed softly, catching her wrist and pressing a kiss to the inside of it before rolling her beneath him.

His lips traced over her collarbone, her shoulder, hands exploring the curves of her body like he was memorizing them all over again. She arched into his touch, sighing as his fingers traced down her spine, slow and reverent.

She tugged at his shirt until it was gone, her hands smoothing over his bare skin. The warmth of him, the weight of him, the familiar way he fit against her—it all settled something inside her that had been fraying at the edges.

Yasher's hands found her hips, his lips pressing against the side of her throat as he whispered, "You're here."

Farah ran her fingers down his back, breathing him in. "I'm here."

Nothing was desperate or rushed. It was something gentle, something that neither of them had to think about.

Something that simply was.

The tension from the night before melted away into warmth, into the quiet hush of hands on skin, lips against lips, breath mingling in the still air.

Yasher's name slipped past her lips in a whisper, and he exhaled, pressing his forehead against hers, his fingers tangling with hers where their hands rested against the bedroll.

They moved together, slow and unhurried, a quiet mending of something frayed but never broken.

A promise, without words. A shared breath. A soft sigh.

And when they finally stilled, when Yasher let his weight settle against her and Farah's arms curled around him, there was nothing left between them but warmth.

No fight. No relic. No distance.

Just them.

Yasher pressed a kiss against her shoulder, his breath steadying. "Sleep, love."

Farah closed her eyes, feeling the warmth of him, the steady rise and fall of his breathing.

And for the first time in days, sleep came easy.

CHAPTER 19

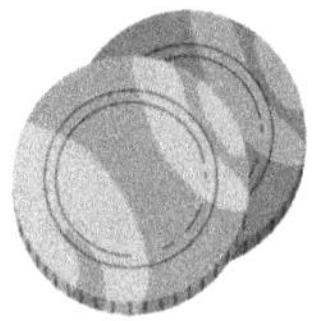

THE WIND HAD SHIFTED.

It wasn't anything obvious—no sudden gusts, no scent of rain—but Yasher felt it all the same. A quiet wrongness curled through the air, pressing against his skin like the weight of an unthrown dice.

The land here felt scraped bare, as if the world had stretched too thin along the cliffs, leaving nothing but stone and silence.

Ahead, Sakasan loomed along the jagged coastline, its white-stone walls catching the last burn of the sinking sun. From a distance, it should have looked like any other town.

But it didn't. It looked untouched. Too untouched.

No crumbling edges from sea winds battering the cliffs. No scars of repairs along the walls, no uneven stonework where damage had been hastily patched. The torches in the watchtowers stood unlit, their iron sconces rusting in place, as if no hand had tended them in weeks. The gates hung open—welcoming, undisturbed.

The roads bore the marks of travel—wagon ruts, hoof prints, the pressed-down grooves of decades of steady foot traffic. *But where were the travelers?*

Where were the sounds of life?

His skin prickled. The town looked alive. But it wasn't.

It stood like a painting, like something frozen in time.

His grip on the reins tightened. *This wasn't right.* The wind had shifted the closer they rode, carrying not the expected scents of salt and hearth smoke, but something thinner. The air itself felt wrong.

Like the city was watching them back.

He exhaled slowly, the hair at the nape of his neck standing on end. The silence was the worst part. No distant hammering from a blacksmith. No voices rising from the market. No echo of waves against boats down at the harbor.

Just stillness.

Yasher's stomach twisted.

He pulled his horse to a stop at the crest of a low ridge, where the path sloped downward toward the city's outskirts. The others followed suit, the cart creaking to a halt towards the back. The soldiers shifted in their saddles, scanning the town as if waiting for something—anything—to reveal itself. Nothing did.

Farah pulled up beside him, but she didn't look at him.

Her gaze was locked on the city, her shoulders drawn taut beneath her coat. She wasn't just watching—she was reading it, picking apart the edges of something unseen, something only she could sense.

He had spent enough time with her to know when she was wary and when she was certain something was wrong. This wasn't the quick, assessing glance of a soldier scanning for an ambush. It wasn't even the sharpened focus she took on before a fight.

This was different. She flexed her fingers against the reins.

"What do you think?" she asked, her voice controlled, but not quite steady.

He exhaled, scanning the town again, hoping to see someone, anyone, or at least hear children playing or a guard coughing. Instead, there was nothing.

"Looks normal," he said, testing the words. "If you had never seen another person in your life, ever."

Her grip on the reins tightened.

He glanced at her. "You feel it too?"

She didn't answer right away. That, more than anything, set something uneasy crawling beneath his ribs.

Not denial. Not uncertainty.

Something worse.

Recognition.

Yasher watched the slow tension coil through her shoulders, the way her jaw set, the way her eyes flickered —not with wariness, but with the quiet, locked-in focus of someone seeing a thing they had hoped not to see again.

She knew exactly what was wrong. And she wasn't saying it.

His mouth went dry. "Phoenix?"

Still, nothing.

Then, finally—too soft, too quiet:

"Something's off. Aren't the gates supposed to be closed?"

He glanced at Farah again, but she wasn't looking at him. She was looking at the town. There was something close to dread in her expression.

Before she could say anything else, Pari's voice cut through the quiet.

"It feels wrong," she said. Her voice was quieter than usual, more thoughtful. "Thick."

Yasher turned in his saddle, frowning. "Thick?"

Pari nodded from the cart, her small fingers curled tight into the edge of the bench. "Like when the air gets heavy before a storm. Or when you try to walk through water that's too deep."

A slow dread curled in his gut. He trusted Pari's instincts—always had. She wasn't one to spook easily. If she felt something was wrong, it wasn't just nerves.

Farah sat straighter, scanning the town again. "We shouldn't just walk in blind," she said. "If something's wrong, I want to know before we're in the middle of it."

Jeta shifted where she sat beside Pari in the cart, her arms draped lazily over her knees.

"Well," she said, voice light. "I suppose that depends on how much you want to know before it's too late."

He rolled his eyes. "Oh, thank you. That's very reassuring."

Jeta only smiled. Twelve hells, how he hated that smile.

Mehran rode forward, his expression tight. "No obvious signs of trouble, but I don't like it." His gaze flicked toward Farah. "What's the call?"

Farah hesitated, thinking through the options.

Yasher gave her about three seconds before he made the choice for her.

"I'll go first."

Farah's head snapped toward him. "What?"

He gestured vaguely toward the town. "Someone's got to get a closer look, and I'm the best suited for it. I can walk in, ask a few questions, get a read on things before we roll in with this full caravan and let them know we're here."

Farah's jaw tightened. "That's not—"

He held up a hand. "Before you say something about how that's reckless, let me remind you—this is exactly what I do."

Farah's mouth pressed into a thin line. "It's not the same."

He raised a brow. "How is it not the same?"

She turned in her saddle, facing him fully. "This isn't a tavern in Banima, Yasher. This isn't some merchant caravan where you can slip in, cheat a few dice rolls, and slip out if it goes south." She gestured toward the town. "We don't know what's waiting in there."

"That's why I should go in first," he pointed out.

She shook her head. "I don't like it."

Yasher sighed. "Farah, you're not sending me in like some sacrificial lamb. I'm volunteering."

"That doesn't make it better."

"Come on. I've talked my way in and out of worse."

He flashed a grin, but it didn't land the way he wanted. Farah's expression didn't waver.

"You're not invincible."

He let out a breath. "Ye of little faith."

Her fingers twitched against her reins, and he could see her debating, weighing the options against her instincts. She didn't think of his Luck as something reliable, something that could be used like a weapon or a tool. And she didn't think of him as something to throw in front of danger.

Which was exactly why he had to make this call.

The shift came too fast. Too strong.

One second, Yasher was weighing options, feeling for the pendulum of Luck to swing. The next, he was already leaning forward, his grip tightening on the reins as his body moved before his mind caught up.

A pull, deep in his ribs, winding like a thread through his bones.

Not a whisper. Not a suggestion. A demand.

His throat went dry. The feeling coiled tighter, winding toward Sakasan, dragging him toward it, a tide he could no more fight than the pull of gravity itself. It was like stepping away would be—

Wrong.

Not a choice. Not a risk. A necessity.

IIis fingers curled tightly against his reins, nails pressing into the leather. His gut churned, instincts screaming to move forward, to close the distance, to see.

Because something was waiting for him in that city.

And it already knew he was coming.

THE SILENCE of Sakasan wasn't the silence of emptiness. It wasn't the raw wound of a town gutted by war, nor the slow decay of a village lost to sickness and time. Pari was right in calling it thick, like breath held just beneath the surface of water. It pressed against Yasher's skin, wormed into the spaces between sounds, coiled in the hollows where noise should have been.

Yasher had walked into plenty of bad situations in his life, had slipped into places he wasn't supposed to be, had stood at the edge of a decision and felt the weight of his Luck press down on him, making a choice for him before he even knew it needed to be made. But this? This was different.

The town shouldn't have felt like this.

His horse's hooves clattered softly against the stone-paved streets, each sound ringing too sharp, too clean, swallowed too quickly by the hush that pressed in from all sides. A place like this—nestled against the cliffs, a waypoint between the southern route of Emari and ships coming through Bailla Straits—should have been alive. Full of movement, full of sound, full of the daily churn of life. But the air sat still. The streets stretched empty before him. Nothing stirred.

Yet Sakasan wasn't dead.

The market stalls were still laden with goods, baskets brimming with dried fruit and grain—too full, as if no one had ever taken from them, as if hunger had never pressed against this place.

The air smelled wrong, stale. As though nothing in

Sakasan had moved, had changed, in longer than it should have.

The pieces of life were all here, but the people weren't.

Yasher's fingers flexed against the reins as his horse snorted sharply, its ears swiveling, tail flicking once before going rigid. The muscles beneath the saddle twitched—not the restless energy of a long ride, but something else. A subtle, creeping stiffness, as if the air had wound too tight around them.

He exhaled slowly, shifting his weight in the saddle. This wasn't just a bad feeling. Bad feelings could be shaken off, could be blamed on an empty stomach or an unlucky hand. This was deeper, more certain. This was his Luck, watching, just as still as the town around him.

He scanned the town, gaze drifting over the open doors, the still signs of movement halted mid-gesture, the subtle wrongness in the way everything had been left behind.

His Luck *tightened* inside him, a breath caught mid-draw. It wasn't pushing him forward or dragging him back, but it was watching, pressing against his ribs like a hand against a locked door, testing for a weakness. A decision had to be made, and it was letting him make it for now.

Something moved.

Quick. Darting. Small.

Not a shadow, not a trick of the light. Too deliberate.

Yasher's fingers twitched toward his belt, but he didn't reach for his dagger just yet. His Luck sat heavy in

his ribs, watching. Not warning. Not urging. Just...
waiting.

He reined his horse to a stop, sliding down from the saddle in one smooth motion. His boots hit the stone, and the town swallowed the sound faster than it should have, like the world around him had already expected him to be here.

He kept his posture loose, like a man who had wandered in by accident, like someone who had nothing to fear as he walked his horse. But the weight of the silence pressed against his skin, and he had the distinct, crawling feeling that someone was watching.

Not just one person. Many.

"Not looking for trouble," he said, voice smooth. "Just looking for a conversation."

A pause. A breath.

Then, from behind a stack of empty crates, a boy stepped out.

His movements weren't the hesitant steps of a child who had been caught lurking. There was no startle in his expression, no guilt in the way he squared his thin shoulders.

He had been waiting.

The boy was young—eight, maybe nine. Dark curls in a tangle, arms too thin for his tunic, but not desperate. Not hollow-cheeked or starving. His clothes were dust-streaked but not torn, too big but not ragged.

He didn't speak. Didn't move closer. Just stood there, watching. Measuring.

Yasher had spent his life reading people, catching the things they didn't want seen—the flicker of a lie in a gambler's eyes, the tightness in a mark's grip when their coin purse was light, the hesitation of a player who was about to fold.

But this boy...

There was nothing to read. Just quiet patience. Just waiting.

Yasher tilted his head, adjusting the fall of his coat, his usual smirk softening into something more thoughtful. "You got a name?"

A pause. The slightest flicker of something.

Then, quiet—"Ardin."

Yasher offered a small, easy nod. "Alright, Ardin. Are you alone out here?"

The boy didn't answer right away. His dark eyes flicked past Yasher—watching something. Listening.

Something cold coiled low in Yasher's stomach. His Luck hadn't shifted—not forward, not back—but it wasn't sitting easy anymore.

He kept his voice steady. "Ardin, who else is here?"

Ardin's fingers twitched against his tunic, gripping at something unseen, something not there. His throat bobbed with a swallow too forced, too careful—a boy who had learned that hesitation cost more than words. His dark eyes flicked past Yasher, just for a breath, toward something unseen behind him.

Then he turned and walked away.

Yasher didn't look over his shoulder to where the boy's eyes had flicked.

His Luck stayed silent. That was almost worse.

He had learned to listen when it pushed him into

things, just as much as when it pulled him away. Leaving the decision up to him, dammit.

He let out a slow breath, adjusting the weight on his heels before following.

The little boy led him through the streets. Past neat rows of houses with their shutters cracked open. Past storefronts that looked ready for business but stood untouched. Every step brought them deeper into the town, and still—no one appeared.

The only sound was the wind, whispering through empty spaces.

Yasher's free hand curled at his side.

Then, finally, they reached the town center.

Yasher stopped mid-stride, his mind not able to process what he was seeing.

Because the town wasn't empty.

They were all here.

Dozens of people. Standing still.

Too still.

A woman near a fruit stall had a basket of apples balanced against her hip. A merchant stood beside his cart, hand resting on his wares. A child clutched the hem of his father's coat, head tilted slightly.

But none of them moved.

They stood as if waiting for something.

A tight coil of instinct pulled through Yasher's ribs. The kind that told him to step lightly, to breathe slow, to be careful.

He let his breath out slowly.

Then, he took a step forward.

The moment his foot met stone at the edge of the

square, the town *exhaled*. A single breath, stretched across a dozen bodies, a movement too smooth, too rehearsed. The woman adjusted her basket, but her hands didn't quite settle naturally, her fingers lingering a fraction too long against the wicker before completing the motion. The merchant wiped his tunic, but his knuckles paled with the force of it, like the action was too deliberate. The child tugged at his father's coat, but the father hesitated—a heartbeat too long—before reacting.

It was a performance. A scene resetting itself after a missed cue.

Yasher didn't let himself react, didn't let the unease coil too tightly in his spine, didn't let his breath catch the way it wanted to. He had spent his whole life learning how to listen—not just with his ears, but with his skin, his bones, the air around him. The shift of a gambler's weight before they bluffed. The flicker of a guard's fingers near their blade. The way a room could change shape around him, a hundred silent conversations threading through the air unseen.

And right now, Sakasan was saying all the things that it didn't a moment ago.

His horse shifted beside him, snorting softly, the only thing that felt real in the town square. Yasher gave its neck a quick, grounding pat, his fingers brushing through the coarse mane before he moved forward at a slow, even pace, letting his gaze drift over the crowd.

No one was staring at him. No one acknowledged him at all.

They weren't avoiding him, weren't whispering

behind hands or darting glances his way like an outsider might expect in a small town. They were simply... acting normal. Going about their lives. A man near the well filled a bucket with steady, practiced motions. A group of women gathered under the shade of an awning, speaking in quiet tones, their hands gesturing over what looked like a basket of mended cloth. A boy crouched near a stall, absently tracing shapes into the dust at his feet.

Yasher had seen plenty of strange things in his life, had slipped between the cracks of places that weren't quite what they seemed, had felt his Luck steer him toward choices he didn't always understand. But this?

This was something else entirely.

Yasher flexed his fingers against his thigh, resisting the urge to exhale too sharply. His pulse had slowed, steady and even, but that was only because he had learned to breathe past instinct, to shove it down when it tried to claw its way out of his chest.

He didn't trust silence. And he didn't trust his Luck when it stopped playing.

But he knew how to play his own games.

He strolled toward the well, easy and unbothered, a man walking through a town he had no reason to doubt. His shoulders stayed loose, his hands empty, his face set in that familiar half-smile that made men underestimate him at the card tables and let him walk away with their coin.

The man at the well was older, his skin lined by years of sun and salt, his sleeves rolled past his elbows as he worked. A picture of normalcy, in a town that was anything but.

Yasher stopped a few paces away, letting the man notice him first, let the moment land naturally before speaking.

"Afternoon," he said, his voice slipping into something warm, familiar, belonging. "I was hoping to get a drink."

The man didn't pause, didn't look up sharply or react as if surprised by a stranger's voice. He simply nodded. As if Yasher had always been there. As if Yasher should be here.

"Plenty of water," the man said, lifting the bucket. "Help yourself."

Yasher stepped forward, studying the man the way he studied gamblers at a table—watching for the tell, the giveaway, the little flicker of something underneath the surface. But there was nothing. No tension, no wariness. Just emptiness. Not like a man keeping a secret, but like a man with nothing to keep.

He reached for the ladle, the wood cool beneath his fingers, and dipped it into the bucket. The water was clean, clear, still. He lifted it to his lips, taking a slow sip, letting the silence stretch before speaking.

"You all seem quiet."

The man wiped his hands on his tunic. "Nothing to be loud about."

He said it like it was a fact. A certainty. Like he had never even considered the possibility of noise.

"I passed through Rumatin a few days ago," Yasher said, keeping his voice light, casual. The kind of tone that got people to trust you without realizing why. "Heard talk that things might not be safe out this way."

The man's fingers tightened slightly against the rim of the bucket. Not tense. Just... aware.

Then, smooth as anything, he let go, straightened his spine, and said, "Sakasan is safe."

Not a reassurance. Not a dismissal.

A statement. Flat and absolute.

He set the ladle back into the bucket, his fingers loose, his stance relaxed—but his pulse a fraction too fast.

"Good to hear," he murmured.

The man nodded then turned back to his task, his hands moving in the exact same rhythm as before, the same way they would have even if Yasher had never spoken to him at all.

Like nothing had changed. Like nothing could change.

He let his gaze sweep the square again, searching for Ardin.

The boy was nowhere to be seen.

His gut tightened slightly, but he didn't show it.

He let himself move, let himself blend in. The act came naturally. He walked past the market stalls, past the idle conversations, past the too-perfect normalcy of a town that had been frozen in time, and yet no one so much as glanced at him.

And that should have been a relief. It should have made him feel like he could walk away, turn back toward the ridge, return to Farah and the others and tell them to burn Sakasan to the ground as soon as possible.

But he didn't.

The street curved ahead, leading deeper into town, and without thinking, without hesitating, Yasher followed it.

His fingers twitched at his sides. Not quite reaching for a weapon. Not quite relaxing, either.

Alright, then.

He wasn't walking away.

Which meant he had to figure out why.

THE TOWN CARRIED on around him, the rhythm of movement seamless, effortless, too perfect. The people of Sakasan moved with the ease of a life uninterrupted. They were not reacting to him. They weren't looking at him.

But they knew he was there. This was a held breath, a coiled moment, a stillness that was not indecision but calculation.

And then—She arrived.

At first, it was only the color of her coat that set her apart. A black so deep it refused the light, devouring it in a way that was not shadow but something worse. A void sewn into fabric, not empty but full—full of something unseen, something shifting beneath its surface like the pulse of something vast, contained, waiting.

She moved not like a person stepping forward, adjusting their weight, shifting through space. No, she moved like her presence folded closer without effort.

That was when Yasher saw the embroidery.

At first, it was nothing—black against black, a subtle texture meant to be overlooked. But as the fabric shifted with her steps, something moved beneath it. A flicker—not metal, but something alive. Not stitched into the fabric, but woven into its very being, pulsing like light pressing against the skin of the world, struggling to be seen.

His fingers twitched at his side, a reflex he didn't fully register. A part of him had already decided that this was something to be wary of—something that should be left alone. Something itched at the back of his mind of almost familiarity as he watched her.

The town, no the world, was bending around her like it had been waiting for her arrival.

His gambler's gut twisted, that deep, quiet instinct that had kept him alive when his Luck wavered or was silent as it was now, when the cards in his hands had been stacked against him. This wasn't just a bad hand. This was a rigged table.

She was too perfect. Her skin was untouched by the sun, unmarked by time or wind, smooth as polished quartz. But it wasn't just that. It was the way she stood, the way she existed.

The way the world seemed to shape itself to her presence, rather than the other way around.

He had walked into plenty of bad situations before. Had sidled up to danger with a grin and a well-placed bluff. This wasn't something he could talk his way out of, because this woman wasn't just another player at the table.

She was the house. And the house always won.

She moved toward him.

No—she was already there.

The space between them folded too easily, too smoothly, like distance meant nothing, like the world itself had shifted to accommodate her, to put her exactly where she wanted to be.

She was too close. Not in the way that people pressed too near in a crowded street, their presence unavoidable but unintentional. Not in the way men loomed over a card table, hoping to unnerve their opponents with sheer proximity. Not even in the way of lovers, where closeness was a deliberate, whispered thing, an understanding built between bodies.

This was intimacy without invitation.

The world felt thin around her. The air itself seemed to move differently, slower somehow, as if the space between them had become something tangible, something he had unknowingly stepped into without realizing it. The sensation wasn't suffocating—not quite—but it was pressing, like standing at the edge of a tide just before the wave broke, the undertow already curling around his ankles, waiting to pull him forward.

But Yasher wasn't pulled into this enchantment. He had learned long ago that just because something felt inevitable, just because it moved like it belonged, didn't mean it was safe.

She was watching him now, still and patient, her lips just barely curved into the kind of smile that wasn't meant to be reassuring, but disarming. As if he were something interesting to her, something worth taking a moment to study, to observe.

Then—she breathed in.

He felt the prickle along his spine before he even fully understood what was happening. He knew what it was to be sized up, assessed, but this wasn't that. This wasn't someone trying to figure out his worth, his value, whether or not he was useful or dangerous.

She was smelling him. No, not him.

Something on him.

A flicker passed behind her gaze, something that didn't quite reach the surface of her expression—recognition.

Yasher felt the shift in his Luck before he felt the shift in himself. A static hum, deep in the back of his mind, the way a storm felt before the first crack of thunder, the weight of something rolling through him, just beneath his skin. It wasn't a pull, wasn't a push, just an awareness, a breath of pressure that hadn't existed before, a thread tightening around something unseen.

He had to tread carefully. He slowly stepped back, away from this woman and put up an easy smile.

"Hello there," he said, letting the words roll easy, practiced, slipping into the space between them like water filling a cup.

"Welcome traveler. Sakasan does not turn away guests," she continued. "A traveler like yourself must be weary. There's always food, a place to rest."

He felt his mouth opening before he could stop it, words slipping into place, as if the weight of them had already formed in his chest. He almost said it—almost said he had people waiting for him, that he was traveling with others, that he wasn't alone.

His Luck crackled inside his mind, not a sound, not a thought, but a fracture of noise, a brief, jarring shift, as if the world had knocked out of place for a single, painful moment. A brief, staggering drop before a fall.

He didn't say it.

Didn't give up Farah. Didn't give up Pari. Didn't let her know there were others.

Instead, he exhaled, slow and steady, as if nothing had shifted at all.

"A kind offer," he said, voice smooth, unbothered, wrapping around the space where the wrong words had almost fallen. "But I prefer to keep moving. Wouldn't want to overstay my welcome."

She watched him.

Then, without breaking his gaze, she inhaled once more.

Slow. Deliberate. As if memorizing something.

And then she said, softer this time, almost gentle—

"Go back to your friends, Yasher Gavrilov."

His name.

It shouldn't have felt like an attack, but it landed like one—like the final move in a game he hadn't even realized he was playing.

The breath left his lungs in something too measured, too careful, as if his body was trying to convince itself this was fine.

The silence stretched between them, thin as a wire pulled taut.

She had not moved. Had not pressed forward, had

not reached for him, had not done anything at all. And yet, he felt as though she had taken something from him. As though something had shifted in the space between them, in the space inside him.

I should say something.

He didn't.

Instead, he exhaled, steady, even. "Didn't realize I was famous."

The faintest hint of amusement flickered at the edges of her too-perfect mouth. "Oh, you're not."

Yasher's fingers twitched at his sides. "Then how do you know my name?"

She inhaled, slow, deliberate. "Names carry echoes. Some more than others."

He didn't flinch. Didn't let himself react. But the way his Luck tightened—sharp, immediate—told him everything he needed to know. He needed to leave, now.

His pulse didn't spike, didn't betray him, but his body felt hyper-aware of itself, of her, of every breath between them. He knew he needed to leave, to get out of this cursed town, but couldn't move.

Then she tilted her head, her too-dark eyes drinking in the light. "It's an interesting thing, Luck."

She smiled. Slow. Knowing. As if she could taste the shift in the air.

"It always leaves a trail."

The space between them felt thinner, tighter, the world pressing in at the edges of his vision, waiting for the next move.

Yasher had spent years standing at the edges of

things, slipping through cracks before they could close around him.

This time, he didn't wait for the walls to fall.

He turned and walked away, and did not look back.

CHAPTER 20

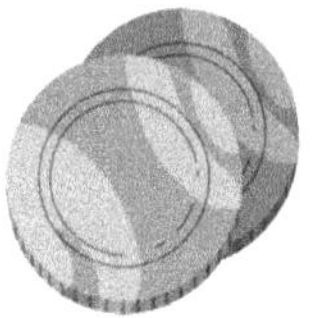

THE RIDE back passed in an instant, the world blurring at the edges, Yasher's mind still caught in the moment he had left Sakasan behind. It was as if time had bent not only in the town but in the space between, twisting itself into something unrecognizable.

His horse's breath was heavy beneath him, warm against the cooling air. The sweat lathering its flanks should have been a sign of hard riding, of hours spent on the road, but Yasher couldn't remember pushing the beast that hard. He had left at a walk, a steady pace, but the way the horse moved now, the tired, dragging weight in its gait, told him that it had carried him for miles he did not recall.

He felt it in his bones, in the hollowness in his chest, in the way his thoughts felt a step behind his own breath, like his body had moved through something his mind couldn't follow.

The air didn't feel right.

The light had shifted, shadows stretching longer, the

sky washing into the first hues of evening. The heat of the afternoon was gone, replaced by the creeping chill of dusk, settling like a weight he hadn't noticed pressing down on him until now.

As the camp came into view, he caught sight of them —figures standing too still, watching the path, their shapes taut with waiting, not frozen in the moment like the townspeople. The wagon sat anchored in its place, their horses tethered loosely to a low stretch of sparse cedar. The embers of the fire smoldered, an occasional flicker of light crackling from within the darkened wood. The sea beyond the cliffs churned slow and steady, its scent mixing with the damp earth, the cool weight of evening creeping in.

He barely had time to swing himself down before Farah was on him.

Her fingers twisted into the worn fabric of his coat, tight, desperate, searching, like she was bracing against a storm only she could feel. Like she needed the solid weight of him beneath her hands to prove he hadn't slipped through her fingers.

There was no hesitation. No careful control. No distance.

Only fear. Bare, raw, unguarded fear.

"Yasher."

His name left her lips rough, like it had been caught in her throat too long, like she had spent the last several hours trying not to speak it.

And then she was touching him, checking him, her hands sliding over his arms, his chest, pressing against his sides as if expecting to find some hidden injury, some evidence of where he had been, what had been done to him.

His breath hitched, his body instinctively stilling beneath her hands. The way she was looking at him now—like she had almost lost him, like she hadn't been sure he'd come back—was doing something sharp and terrible to his insides.

"I'm here," he murmured, but his voice didn't hold its usual ease. He swallowed hard, glancing past her toward the others. "What—?"

"You were gone for hours," Mehran said, his tone clipped, his arms folded tight over his chest, his expression dark.

Yasher frowned. "That's not—"

"It's nearly dusk," Younis muttered, shifting where he stood. "You left before noon."

He had left the camp not more than an hour ago. Had walked into the town, spoken to the woman, left before anything else could take hold.

That crispness of evening settling in, the subtle shift in temperature, the slow breath of the sea air curling against the cliffs. The fire had burned down to embers, no longer fresh, no longer stoked. His horse—his poor, tired beast—was spent.

Time had bent for him. And it had stretched for them.

His hands curled slightly, resisting the urge to reach for the coin, to roll it between his fingers, to press into the weight of his Luck and demand it explain itself.

But his Luck had already spoken. It had stolen his words in Sakasan.

It had let time slip through his fingers like sand.

And now, it was silent. Not gone, but waiting.

Instead, he forced himself to look at Farah again.

She was still gripping him, though her hold had loosened slightly, her fingers twitching against the fabric of his coat, as if caught between letting go and holding on for dear life.

"What happened here?" he asked, his voice quieter now, more careful.

Farah exhaled sharply, but it wasn't relief—it was exhaustion.

"There was something in the air," Farah murmured, her voice taut, like she wasn't sure if she should be speaking it aloud.

"The trees shifted, but there was no wind. The fire—it wouldn't stay lit. We stoked it, fed it, kept the embers alive, but it kept trying to go out. Like something was smothering it."

Yasher's breath hitched.

Pari, still curled in the cart, lifted her head, her small fingers tightening around the fabric of her coat.

"It wasn't just watching," she whispered. "It was waiting. With us, for you to come back."

Yasher's breath hitched.

Jeta, who had been unnervingly quiet up until now, shifted slightly where she sat, her gaze flicking toward Pari, something unreadable in her expression. Taj stood a little apart, arms folded, his usually relaxed posture stiff with unease, while Mehran and Younis both exchanged glances, their own tension mirrored in the way their hands hovered too close to their weapons.

They hadn't just been waiting for him. They had been holding the line.

And he had no idea what they had been holding it against.

A muscle ticked in Yasher's jaw.

He looked back at Farah.

She was still watching him, still searching his face, her fingers still curled against his arm. He had seen her in battle, seen her face down enemies, watched her stand unwavering beneath the weight of court expectations. He had never seen her like this.

He shouldn't have made her feel this way. Shouldn't have let her worry, shouldn't have left her with nothing but time and fear while he disappeared into a town that had swallowed hours from the world and spat him back out whole.

Yasher reached up, brushing his knuckles lightly against Farah's cheek, the barest touch, as if reassuring himself as much as her.

"Yeah," he murmured. "I'm here."

The wind shifted, curling against the cliffs, pushing past them like a breath taken in, slow and steady.

The fire still flickered, uneasy, as if resisting something unseen.

<hr>

Yasher knew he should eat, knew the dried rations in his hands were the only thing keeping his body moving, but the taste was nothing. His jaw worked mechanically, barely registering the coarse texture of the bread, the salted meat, his thoughts still tangled with everything he had seen, everything he had felt. The sky had deepened into its full night-black, the stars stretching endless above them, their cold, unfeeling light stark against the darkness. The cliffs loomed in the distance, sharp and jagged against the horizon, the town of Sakasan hidden beyond, waiting in its unnatural quiet.

His body was his. His breath was his. His mind was his.

But something had brushed against him in that town, and he wasn't entirely sure it had let go. He started saying to the group that they should burn the town to the ground, damn the consequences so many times but something stopped him it became a mantra in his head.

He wasn't the only one feeling it.

Farah sat next to him, her posture deceptively relaxed, but her fingers had been pulling apart the same piece of bread for the last ten minutes, the small crumbs falling unheeded to her lap. She would randomly pat his knee, as if proving to herself that he was back.

Mehran and Younis remained close, their usual ease abandoned in favor of sharp glances toward the trees, their hands resting a little too naturally near their weapons. Taj sat with his arms folded, one leg bouncing slightly. Pari, curled up with a blanket, had fallen asleep on the other side of Yasher, her small hands tucked beneath her cheek, her breath slow and even, as if his return made it acceptable to finally calm and sleep.

Jeta sat with her hands folded together across from him, her gaze trained on the fire, the flickering light making the lines of her face look deeper, sharper. She hadn't spoken since he'd returned, hadn't offered any of her usual cryptic remarks or half-smiles, only watched, listening in a way that felt more knowing than anything else.

The silence between them had stretched too long. They needed answers, and he was the only one who could give them. He shifted, rubbing a hand over his face before letting it drop to rest on his knee, exhaling slowly before speaking.

"Well," he said, breaking the quiet, "I suppose you lot want to hear what I saw now that we've had a moment."

Farah's gaze snapped to him, the others immediately straightening, their attention sharp. He didn't hesitate.

He told them everything.

The town, the people who stood frozen, the way they only moved after he had entered their sight, resuming their lives as if nothing had happened, their movements too precise, too controlled, too deliberate. He told them about the boy, the one who led him to the square, and about her.

The woman who had been waiting.

His voice was steady as he described her, but something in his chest tightened as he spoke, as if giving form to the memory would only make it more real. He told them of the way she carried herself, the unnatural elegance of her stillness, the near-living texture of her coat embroidered in dark, glimmering threads, shifting with the light like starlit silk. He described her voice, the slow, deliberate way she spoke, as if her words were more than just sounds, as if they were written into the world itself, truths that could not be unwound.

Farah shifted closer, her hand laid on his leg fully now. She didn't look at him directly, but he felt her there, steady and certain, even as the weight of his words settled around them. He wasn't sure if she reached for him first, or if he moved without thinking, but his pinky brushed against hers, the smallest connection.

"She told me to go back to you," he said, shifting where he sat, rolling out the tension in his shoulders, though it didn't leave. He reached for her then, not for show, not for anyone else, just for himself—fingers curling gently around hers, pulling her hand toward him in a quiet reassurance, in something unspoken but understood. "Didn't try to stop me, didn't threaten me. She seemed to smell you on me, and decided I'd be back."

Her fingers tightened, just barely.

The fire crackled, but no one spoke immediately. His words settled over them, pressing against the silence.

Jeta was the first to speak.

"She knew you'd return," she murmured.

"You sound sure of that," he said.

The old woman didn't look at him—just watched the fire, the flames flickering in her eyes like old memories. Her voice was low, certain. "Because things like her don't let go until they're finished. She found something on you she wants, and she won't let that go."

Farah's fingers curled against his, her posture still deceptively loose. "Why? Why shouldn't we raze the town completely and bury whatever it was that trapped him there?" she asked.

Jeta sighed, stretching out one leg before crossing her arms over her chest. "Tearing that town down won't do anything to her. Some people chase fate like it's a thing to earn," she said. "Others move like they've already claimed it—like it was always theirs."

Farah's voice came quiet, thoughtful. "She moved like that from what Yasher said."

Jeta nodded slowly. "Exactly."

Mehran exhaled slowly, rubbing a hand along his jaw. "That doesn't explain what she is."

"No," Jeta admitted, her voice still too measured. "It doesn't."

The wind picked up, rustling the trees, sending the firelight flickering higher for a moment—too high, too sharp, like something had breathed against it.

Farah hadn't reacted immediately when Jeta spoke, hadn't questioned her outright, but Yasher saw it—the sharp way her fingers curled against her knee, the way her shoulders locked as if something had settled too neatly into place in her mind.

"Do we send for reinforcements?"

Farah's question cut through the tension like a blade, calm on the surface—but Yasher could hear the strain beneath it. She wasn't posturing. She was weighing. Calculating.

Yasher rubbed a hand down the back of his neck. "Depends what we're walking into," he said, voice low. "The Mashya didn't send us here to raise banners."

"No," Younis said grimly, "he sent us to stop whatever this is from reaching the gates of the Citadel. Which means we don't wait for proof. That town isn't clean. And it isn't done."

Taj's fingers drummed once against his knee. "The

refugees already told us what they saw. What they ran from. We just didn't listen."

The silence that followed wasn't passive.

It was agreement. It was dread.

He looked at Farah again, and for a second, they were aligned—two people staring down the edge of something they didn't know how to fight.

And no one—not one of them—wanted to be the one to say what they all felt.

That reinforcements might already be too late, even if they could fight something like this.

Jeta, in that maddeningly even tone of hers, said, "The Darkness moves quickly when no one is looking. We're watching it now, aware of it. That means it will act against us. What that looks like is the question."

He froze at the same time as Farah, fear racing up his spine. The others didn't know the name of the Darkness was Mazdavir. Not really. Not like they did.

Not the way it had been whispered to Farah by Rashnu himself.

Not the way it had taken hold of Behnaz, twisting her until she was unrecognizable.

Not the way it had nearly taken Farah, too with that damned relic they carried in the strongbox.

And now Jeta—who wasn't privy to any of those things—was speaking about it like it was already walking the roads ahead of them.

His fingers curled into a fist, his coin still cold in his palm. He didn't ask how she knew. Because if Jeta had answers, she'd only share them when it suited her.

Farah recovered first, her expression neutral, though

he could see the sharp focus in her eyes, the way she was turning Jeta's words over in her mind. "Do you think we need more people?"

Jeta tilted her head, eyes reflecting the firelight. "That depends on what you think this really is."

Farah's brow creased. "Meaning?"

Jeta's gaze didn't waver. "If you believe this can be solved with swords and soldiers… if you think this is just another battle, you'll need more of both."

She paused, the silence thick between them.

"But if it's not just a battle of people," she added softly, "if it's something older… darker… then you'll need more than steel."

Farah's voice was steady. "And what exactly would that be?"

Jeta's lips curved faintly—not quite a smile.

"You'll need understanding. The right people. And a willingness to walk roads most don't come back from."

Jeta reached forward and stirred the fire once, embers catching in the night air like sparks looking for a fuse.

"So, which kind of battle is this is the better question."

The fire crackled, throwing wild shadows across their faces.

Younis cleared his throat, breaking the tension. "We'll talk strategy in the morning. For now, we need eyes on the perimeter." He cast a glance toward the dark tree line. "I'll take first with Mehran. Second goes to Taj and—"

"I'll take second with Taj," Farah said, her voice steady.

Younis looked at her, surprise flickering across his face. "Hand, that's not necessary—"

"It is," she said flatly. "You forget I spent years with the Beloveds. This isn't new to me. We need extra eyes tonight, that much is plain."

Younis hesitated, clearly weighing the argument. But she didn't give him room to object again. She was already rising, checking her blades.

Yasher didn't say a word. He knew that tone. There was no changing her mind. Telling Farah not to do something was the fastest way to make sure she did it anyway, so he didn't say a damn thing.

Instead, he pushed himself to his feet, stretching out his legs, rolling his shoulders as he moved toward the cart where their gear was stowed. The decision had been made before the fire was even built—no tents tonight. The woods had been unsettled since they arrived, and while they'd seen no movement beyond the trees, they all felt it. It was safer to sleep in the open, near the fire, near each other.

Yasher grabbed the bedrolls, unrolling his own beside Pari, then paused. Farah stood across the fire, expression unreadable.

Without speaking, she crossed the space between them and laid her bedroll down beside his, her movements quiet but deliberate.

He waited for her to settle, then turned toward her. He didn't ask. He just reached—slow, certain—and when his hand found the curve of her back, she leaned closer to him.

He sighed at the look he saw cross her face, pressing a lingering kiss to her forehead.

"I'm fine." Then, after a beat, his lips quirked against her skin. "Not saying I wasn't about to be swallowed by a cursed town and turned into a statue, but look at me—still moving, still devastatingly handsome."

She let out a slow breath, her fingers still curled into his shirt. "Debatable."

He huffed, tilting his head slightly to glance down at her. "Wow. Not even a full minute of relief before you cut me down?"

She didn't look up, but he could feel the weight of her exhaustion pressing into him, the edge of something still unsettled in the way her hand clung just a little tighter than usual.

"I was relieved," she murmured, quieter now. "Still am." A pause. Then, dry, "Doesn't mean you're not insufferable."

Yasher grinned, his breath warm against her hair. "That's the closest thing to affection I've gotten all day. I'll take it."

She sighed, exasperated but unwilling to move away. "Sleep, *ashgh*."

He smirked at her balance of irritation yet calling him lover. "See? That's how I know you really missed me."

She didn't answer, only curled closer, her fingers curling tighter against his chest. She'd be up soon enough to stand watch, so he'd take the time to hold her close.

He let his own breath settle, but he didn't feel like sleep would come easy for him tonight.

CHAPTER 21

THE MORNING MIST still clung low to the ground, curling like restless ghosts around the trunks of the thinning trees. The scent of damp earth and fading embers mingled with the sharp tang of salt carried inland from the sea. The cliffs in the distance stood stark against the sky, dark shapes rising from the land like broken teeth, their jagged edges still half-shrouded in the thinning fog. Beyond them, Sakasan waited.

Farah stood at the edge of camp, arms folded tight, her stance balanced out of habit more than necessity. The night had done nothing to loosen the knot in her chest. If anything, it had settled deeper—something cold and persistent lodged beneath the surface of her breath. She had spent years learning how to sense danger before it showed its teeth. But this wasn't a threat she could outmaneuver or draw her sword against. Nothing came upon them during the night, but that didn't mean anything when they entered the town.

Something in that town had touched Yasher.

Changed him, maybe. She hadn't asked. But the way he looked when he returned, hollow around the edges, something tight wound behind his eyes... it gnawed at her.

Behind her, the others were moving through the quiet rhythm of morning preparations. Jeta remained cross-legged atop a supply crate, hands resting lightly on her knees, watching with that same unreadable calm she always carried as Pari packed up her drawings.

Yasher was beside her, rolling up his bedroll with practiced ease, his fingers moving in a rhythm too smooth, too deliberate, the familiarity of motion without the ease. He hadn't spoken much since waking, his usual remarks absent, his teasing forgotten. Even his silence felt off, not the lazy quiet he often wore like a second skin, but something tighter, something stretched too thin.

She exhaled slowly, pushing the thoughts aside. They needed to move forward.

"We need to send word back even if we don't request reinforcements," she said at last, glancing toward the others. "Taj."

Taj, caught mid-stretch, blinked in surprise. "Me?"

Farah nodded, keeping her tone measured. "You're the fastest rider," she said simply. "And you know how to deliver a message in a way that will make them listen."

He grinned, shaking off the stiffness in his shoulders as he straightened.

"Finally, some recognition," he said, placing a dramatic hand over his chest. "And here I thought you just wanted to get rid of me."

Farah huffed a quiet breath, shaking her head. "Not quite."

Younis, adjusting his saddle, didn't look up. "Get there fast, tell the Mashya what we've found, and make sure Rostam hears it first."

Taj's amusement faded slightly, replaced by something sharper, more serious. He nodded once. "I'll make sure of it," he said, adjusting the straps on his saddle before glancing back toward her. "What exactly am I telling them?"

Farah hesitated for a brief moment, organizing her thoughts before answering. "Everything. Tell them about the town, the way the people moved—the way they didn't move until Yasher saw them." She clenched her arms tighter against herself, the memory twisting in her gut. "Tell them about the woman."

Taj gave a slow nod, already turning back toward his horse, adjusting the straps, preparing to leave.

And then her gaze shifted.

Pari sat near the cart, her small hands idly flipping through her stack of parchment, her fingertips ghosting over the edges as if reading something in the paper itself. She had been too quiet this morning. This was her chance to protect.

"Pari," Farah said, stepping toward her, keeping her voice steady. "I want you to go with Taj."

The girl's hands stilled.

Then, slowly, she lifted her head, dark eyes narrowing slightly as if she hadn't heard correctly.

Farah took a careful step closer, trying to meet her where she was. "It isn't safe in Sakasan. We don't know what we're walking into, and we don't know how dangerous it is. If you go back to the Citadel, you'll be safe—"

"No."

The refusal came fast, sharp as a drawn blade, cutting through the morning air with no hesitation.

Not a protest. Not a question. Not the wavering defiance of a child unwilling to follow orders.

A fact.

Farah frowned. "Pari—"

"I said no," the girl repeated, her voice firm. Certain. "I have to stay."

She inhaled slowly, forcing patience. "You promised me that you would do what I said. Pari, this isn't a game—"

"I know it's not a game. My drawings have shown me."

Pari reached for her satchel, fingers already flipping through parchment—quick, practiced. She found the one she wanted and stood, stepping forward. Her expression didn't change, but there was something in her eyes now. Not fear. Not even sadness.

She held the drawing out between them.

Farah hesitated. Even before her fingers brushed the paper, she felt it—that strange tension that always came with Pari's drawings when they were more than just drawings. A pressure behind her eyes, a warning in her bones.

And then she looked.

The breath caught sharp in her throat.

This wasn't the cliffs. Not the town. Not what she had expected.

It was a cavern.

Dark and wide, stretching across the page in uneven lines and heavy shadows. The rock formations were jagged, drawn in charcoal-thick strokes, looming at the edges like teeth. The shadows pressed in from the corners of the parchment.

Alive. Reaching. Curling around the figures like smoke with weight.

There were people—six of them. Just enough. Farah recognized the shape of her own figure beside Yasher's, the detail uncanny even in crude strokes. Jeta. Mehran. Younis. All grappling or fighting shadows.

And Pari, standing slightly apart from the others, her arm extended.

Reaching toward another figure, different from the rest.

It was massive. Shrouded in dark ink and thick charcoal lines, the shape twisted, faceless but unmistakably present—larger than anything else on the page, impossible to ignore. The way Pari's hand reached for it made something cold knot in her stomach.

But Pari's voice filled the silence, low and certain.

"I have to be here," she said again. "I have to see it through."

Farah gritted her teeth, gripping the parchment tighter. "I don't like this, Pari. I need to keep you safe."

"I don't either," Yasher muttered, stepping beside her. He exhaled, rubbing a hand down his face before glancing between the drawing and Pari. "But she's not changing her mind."

She hated it. Hated how much it felt like the truth. Pari wasn't afraid.

She wasn't afraid because she already knew what was going to happen.

She opened her mouth to push again, but before she could—

Jeta.

"You can't argue with fate," Jeta said, her voice slipping back into that familiar, knowing rhythm, the hint of amusement curling at the edges.

Farah turned to her, scowling. "She's a child."

Jeta exhaled, slow and considering, before leaning forward slightly, her gaze sharper now, less distant. "And yet, fate and that pompous bird don't seem to care what you think about this, do they?"

"You can ignore it. You can fight it." Jeta tilted her head, her eyes flicking between Farah and Pari, reading something unspoken between them. "But that's never worked for you before, has it?"

She pressed her fingers against her temple, giving up on this argument.

"Fine," she muttered. "Fine."

Pari smiled, something small, something relieved.

Taj, who had been watching all of this with the air of a man who wanted no part in it, cleared his throat. "Right. Well. If the tiny oracle is staying, I guess I'm heading off alone."

Yasher clapped him on the shoulder. "Ride fast, be safe."

Taj swung into the saddle, adjusting his grip on the reins, his usual easy grin tempered by awareness. He wasn't just delivering a message—he was leaving them behind.

"Try not to get cursed while I'm gone," he muttered.

She didn't rise to the bait. "Just ride fast."

He nodded, once, then spurred his horse forward.

Within moments, he was nothing but a silhouette against the morning light, swallowed by the mist and the waiting road.

She exhaled.

Yasher touched her arm lightly, grounding her. "We should move, Phoenix."

Farah nodded, looking towards the silent town.

The choice had been made, but it didn't feel like theirs anymore.

It felt like they had stepped into something already waiting, something already shaped, something known.

Now, there was only one path left to walk.

***

SAKASAN STRETCHED OUT BEFORE THEM, framed by cliffs and sea, the scent of brine curling through the streets and settling into the sun-warmed clay of its buildings. The town moved with a practiced rhythm, its market alive with the rustle of fabric and the echo of laughter. And yet, there was something too measured about it—like the scene had been built to look right, not to feel right. Every detail was perfect. A little too perfect.

The dust from their passage through the streets had

barely settled when the marketplace swallowed them whole, voices rising and falling in the steady cadence of life unchanged. Farah felt it settle against her skin—something unseen pressing at the edges of her awareness, as if the town itself was watching without ever turning its head, just as Yasher had said.

Farah kept her posture even, her grip on the reins light, but her attention swept over every detail, cataloging them with a quiet, sharpened focus. This was not the town Yasher had described. There were no frozen figures waiting for notice, no lingering presence in the air. The townspeople moved. They breathed. And that, more than anything, set her on edge.

At the center of it all, she was waiting for them.

The woman stood poised, her presence woven into the square as naturally as the stone beneath her feet. She was just as he'd described.

The woman's gaze moved slowly over them, unhurried, but perceptive. She took in Younis and Mehran first, reading them like an idle scholar passing over a text she had studied before. When her eyes flickered toward Jeta and Pari in the cart, she lingered on the little girl, ignoring Jeta all together. Just a curious pause, like one might give a riddle they hadn't expected to find. Pari tilted her head at the same time, eyes narrowed, gaze steady. Not fearful. Assessing.

Then, she saw Yasher.

Her lips curled slightly, the barest ghost of a smile.

"Ah," she murmured, her voice carrying easily across the square despite its softness. "Gharib. You return with your friends."

She felt Yasher's posture shift, their horses side by side. His grip on the reins did not tighten, but she knew the tension was there, hiding beneath the easy tilt of his frame. He was a man who knew when to put on a performance, when to lean into charm or wit, but he seemed to freeze for a moment before loosening his frame, looking just a little bored.

"Didn't expect me, did you?" he asked, his tone light, but without its usual warmth. "Thought I'd gone for good."

The woman exhaled, something close to amusement flickering behind her dark eyes.

"No, gharib," she said simply. "I knew you would return. I only wondered how long it would take."

The woman's gaze slid from Yasher, falling on Farah like a hammer. It pressed against her like the first touch of a blade against skin, not yet cutting, but capable. Testing.

A flicker of something crawled down her spine—cold, unmistakable, and far too familiar. Recognition. It was the same quiet wrongness she had carried for weeks when the relic sat too close to her skin. The same whisper behind her thoughts, the same hunger curling in the shadows of her mind, pressing her toward silence, obedience, power.

Farah exhaled, slow and steady. She didn't acknowledge the familiarity aloud—didn't dare. But it clung to her like the scent of forge smoke.

The relic might be gone. But whatever this was... it came from the same place, she could feel it curling around her.

No. She was herself again, in control of herself again. She was sure of it.

The woman's expression did not change, but there was something about the way she was looking at her, something unreadable beneath the surface of those dark eyes. It wasn't suspicion. It wasn't hostility. It was knowing.

Farah inhaled slowly, pushing down the discomfort curling beneath her ribs.

"You must be weary from the road," the woman said, her voice like a quiet current in still water. "Come—let us offer you rest."

Yasher shifted slightly beside her, just enough for her to feel it. He was waiting for her to decide.

Farah flicked a glance toward the cart, kicking herself for not sending Pari away with Taj. Back to safety, away from this woman, this town.

Jeta sat perched atop the strongbox, her green coat dulled from the road, its fabric dust-caked and thread-bare at the cuffs. It seemed to have weathered in the brief ride out of the wood.

The way Jeta held herself—shoulders hunched, spine slightly bowed, legs drawn close beneath her—caught her attention the most. An old woman making herself smaller, older, weaker.

Farah had seen Jeta stand tall before unruly Beloveds, before nobles, before the Mashyana. Now she was folding in like a figure in a child's puppet theater—still visible, but less. Meant to be overlooked.

Farah's gaze dropped lower, just briefly, catching the subtle shift of fabric to cover the box just a little more, but making it look as though she was just an old weak woman sick of the road.

Jeta knew what this place was. She knew what was waiting for them. And for the first time since Farah had met her as a small child—Jeta Veseli looked like a completely different person.

Farah turned back to the woman, feeling the weight of the moment coil tight around her ribs, making sure to keep her posture and face clear or realizing what Jeta had done.

They had to play along, to find out how to purge this town of whatever was afflicting it.

Farah inhaled slowly, steadying herself.

"Lead the way."

EVEN THE QUIETEST settlements Farah had passed through had a rhythm—boots against stone, murmured greetings between doorways, the clang of iron from a forge or the cry of a vendor haggling too loud. Life always made noise.

But here, the silences swallowed the sound. The wind blew soft but didn't rustle the drying herbs overhead. Doors opened and shut without creak. The town moved around them—normal, orderly, paced —and yet it felt like they were intruding on a stage, one whose actors had already rehearsed the moment of their arrival.

She heard the scuff of her boots too clearly, the leather creak of Yasher's saddle straps, the soft exhale of a horse. Every small noise felt wrong for how alone it sounded.

Something should have filled the spaces between the sound. Laughter. Gossip. Barking dogs. Instead, it felt like the town had made just enough noise to seem real— and no more.

The woman's presence did not demand attention the way a ruler's might. She did not carry herself with the rigid authority of nobility, nor did she wield the easy command of a general. She was the kind of person people turned toward without realizing why. The kind of presence that settled at the edges of a room and made it hers without speaking a word.

Then, she looked at Farah as if she was an old friend, long separated.

"I never gave you my name," The woman said, voice even, slipping into the air like the hush before an unsheathed blade.

"No, you didn't."

She smiled as if that answer pleased her. "I am Afsoun. And you," she murmured, not asking, not wondering, just knowing—"are Farahnaz Rahnema, Hand of the Mashyana... Oh, yes, the Mashya now."

She kept her breath steady. "You seem sure of that."

Afsoun tilted her head slightly, dark eyes flickering with something unreadable. "Names carry weight," she said simply. "And yours is not light, nor your burdens."

Farah met her gaze evenly, though something cold traced the base of her spine.

She had been measured before. Weighed in the eyes

of rulers, of soldiers, of those who wanted something from her—power, obedience, loyalty.

Afsoun did not look at her like she wanted something. She looked at her like she knew her.

No, not knew. Like she had been waiting for her.

The feeling crawled beneath Farah's skin, not sharp enough to be called fear, not heavy enough to be called warning—just a quiet, curling certainty. Afsoun saw something in her that Farah could not see in herself.

Afsoun let the moment settle before turning forward again, as if satisfied.

The road narrowed into a quieter part of town, the air thick with the scent of drying herbs, damp stone, and the distant, sharp brine of the sea curling between the alleyways. The occasional figure passed them, their steps easy, unhurried. But they moved with an unnatural ease, as if they were following a rhythm that no one else could hear. There was no hesitation in their gait, no absent-minded glances, no muttered complaints or quiet greetings. Their movements were not wrong, not unnatural— just practiced.

Too smooth. Too content.

And when one of them looked her way, just for a flicker of a second—she could have sworn they had been looking before she even turned her head.

Farah kept her breathing steady, but the weight at the base of her skull did not lift. She had been to war, had stood before rulers with their sentences already decided, had stepped into dark rooms with the understanding that she may not step out again. But this was different.

It did not feel like walking into a battle. It felt like she had already lost.

And yet, the thought did not send a shiver down her spine the way it should have. It did not make her breath catch or her pulse quicken. It only settled, familiar and quiet, like a thing she had always known.

Afsoun led them toward a small inn. The entrance was framed by an archway of carved stone, a single unlit lantern swaying just beyond the door. The door opened before Afsoun had fully reached it.

She swung down from her saddle, her boots landing against the packed earth with a soft thud. The others followed suit, dismounting in smooth, practiced motions, though Yasher took a breath before moving, his fingers lingering just a little longer on the reins, as if grounding himself in something tangible before stepping forward. Mehran and Younis kept hold of their horses, but their movements were clipped, wary.

Pari climbed down from the cart with ease, her small hands gripping the wooden side as she jumped the last step onto the ground. Jeta followed, but carefully. Too carefully.

She lowered herself with the slowness of an older person measuring every step to prevent a fall. When she reached the ground, she let out a slow, quiet breath, her hand drifted toward her ribs, pressing lightly as if to calm her racing heart.

Inside, the air cooled. The scent of fresh dough and saffron curled through the space, mingling with the quiet hum of the dimly lit room. The stone walls bore the weight of time, thick enough to keep the heat at bay, the flickering oil lamps casting a golden haze against the smooth surfaces.

At the far counter, an older woman kneaded dough. When she looked up, there was no flicker of surprise—only calm acceptance, as if she had been waiting for them too.

"These travelers will take rooms," Afsoun said, her voice low and certain. "They rest under the grace of the town."

The phrase echoed like a decree, like the closing of a door. It was phrased like a kindness, but it felt like a collar.

The innkeeper's hesitation was barely perceptible, just the briefest pause before she nodded, dusting her hands against her apron.

"Of course," she murmured. "There are rooms upstairs."

Farah let her arms cross loosely over her chest, though it was the only part of her that remained relaxed. Every instinct she had was on edge, but she didn't let it show—not in her face, not in her posture, her training, both formal and informal, taking over to suppress everything in her mind.

"You speak for the town," she said, tone measured, carefully weighed. "But you're not its governor."

Afsoun met her gaze without pause.

"No," she said simply. "But I serve where I am needed."

Farah didn't blink, but something inside her coiled tighter. The woman wasn't lying. That was the problem. She wasn't bluffing or performing. This was someone used to stepping into a role—and being obeyed without question.

"The governor, like many others, fell ill when the sickness swept through Sakasan. In his absence, someone must ensure the town endures."

"The sickness?" Farah asked carefully.

Afsoun studied her for a moment before answering.

"It has passed," she said, voice light. "For the most part. We are still... recovering in places."

Her fingers drifted over the embroidery of her sleeve, the gesture as absent as it was deliberate. "We were careful," Afsoun continued. "We let no one in. And when the worst had passed, we opened our gates again for you. But we endure."

She turned slightly, her attention still fixed primarily on Farah, the dark depths of her eyes unreadable.

"You and your companions are welcome in the governor's house for the evening meal," she said. "But for now, I'll leave you to rest and take the road off of you."

She inclined her head in a measured nod. "That's generous of you."

Afsoun smiled at that—an expression more observed than felt—before turning with fluid ease, stepping away into the hush of the inn.

Yasher lingered just long enough to murmur under his breath, "I know I say this a lot, but I really don't like this."

Farah let her fingers brush against his wrist, a brief, grounding touch.

Neither did she.

CHAPTER 22

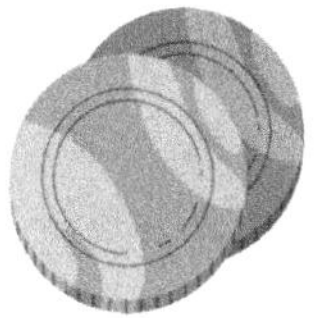

THE ROOMS WERE SMALL. That, at least, felt normal in this wholly not normal town.

The scent of old wood and faintly lingering spice filled the air, a mix of dried coriander and something sweeter, like honeyed dates long since eaten but leaving their memory behind. The wooden walls bore the weight of time, smooth where countless hands had pressed against them, rough where the grain had been left untouched. The single narrow window let in little light, and the furniture was sparse—just a bed, a basin of water, and a low wooden table near the door.

He inhaled slowly, rubbing a hand over his face. The cold splash of water against his skin had chased some of the exhaustion from his body, but it hadn't helped the tension winding through his chest.

And Afsoun...

His hands curled slightly against the edge of the basin.

She had welcomed him back. But she had barely

spared him a glance after that, his role complete. Instead, her focus had settled on Farah, sharp and deliberate— she was the one she'd been waiting for.

He didn't like that, though he was hard-pressed to find anything that he did like about this place.

A knock at the door pulled him from his thoughts. He glanced up, already knowing who it would be.

"Door's open," he called, stepping back.

He turned just as Mehran stepped inside, Younis close behind. Jeta followed, moving carefully, slowly, the way she had since they had arrived, but Yasher didn't miss the way the tension in her shoulders shifted the moment the door was shut. Pari trailed behind her, eyes darting between them.

They filled the small space quickly, the air shifting as bodies settled into place.

Jeta and Pari took the bed, Pari curling her legs beneath her as Jeta lowered herself with slow, deliberate motions. She let out a breath as she did, reaching up to smooth the edges of her headscarf in a way that was almost absent, almost thoughtful.

Yasher leaned against the edge of the table, watching her.

"You noticed," Jeta murmured, her tone just wry enough to be amused.

He snorted. "Hard not to. You've been moving like you've had a bad hip you've neglected to share with us for ages since we crossed the gates."

Jeta hummed, and he caught the brief flicker of a smile before it was gone.

Farah stood from the lone chair, moving to stand next to him. "Did she seem fooled?"

Reaching into the satchel at Pari's hip, Jeta pulled free a piece of charcoal. Pari made a small noise, but Jeta only gave her a brief nod. "I'll return it, little herald."

Then, without another word, she rose from the bed and crossed to the far wall.

The movement was smooth now, no hesitation or stiffness. She crouched with ease, pressing the tip of the charcoal to the wooden surface and beginning to draw. The strokes were deliberate, confident—lines that seemed to echo something older than ink, older than language. A sigil not taught, but remembered.

Yasher frowned. He didn't recognize it, but something about it felt... buried, a secret etched into the world's bones.

She moved to the next wall. Then the door. Then the window, marking the same symbol at each point. Each repetition deepened the unease in the room—the charcoal marks stark against wood, each one drawn with a reverence that made the space feel less like a room and more like a warded cell.

The air shifted, subtle but unmistakable. Not just silence—but a dampening. As if something beyond the walls had paused, then turned away.

Jeta wiped her fingers against her sleeve, brushing away the charcoal dust like ashes. "It won't stop her," she said, voice low. "But it might slow her down."

Yasher exhaled through his nose, shifting where he leaned. "Afsoun?"

Jeta inclined her head. "Whatever she is."

A chill brushed along the back of his neck.

Farah's expression remained unreadable. "What do you mean?"

Jeta hesitated, then met her gaze fully. "Afsoun is not what she appears to be."

Silence stretched.

Mehran frowned, arms folded across his chest. "Not what she appears to be?"

Jeta inhaled slowly, weighing her words before she spoke them. "She walks among people, speaks as they do, but that does not mean she is one of them. I'd lay good money on that."

His stomach twisted. He had felt something strange about her the moment he had stepped into the town square the day before. The moment she had stood in front of him, the way she moved, so still, so measured. He hadn't had the words for it then. He barely had them now.

But Jeta had just given him one.

Farah, still composed, still steady, said, "I've met a god, and she isn't that. She's human, if a strange one."

Jeta exhaled. Then, so softly it could have been mistaken for a breath, "She wears the shape of one well."

A tension filled the space between all of them.

Mehran shifted. Younis let out a slow breath.

Farah didn't move.

Jeta studied her for a long moment. "You carried the relic. You know what it feels like. Similar, isn't it, to that woman?"

Farah's voice came too quickly. "I don't remember."

Yasher's head turned before he could stop it. Not at

the words, but at the *tone*—too quick, too clean. A perfect answer delivered an instant too fast.

And her hand—

He saw it. The way her fingers twitched against her leg. The way her shoulders stayed perfectly still, too still, like she was *holding something in.*

His stomach dropped.

That was a lie.

His breath caught—just for a moment, just enough for his chest to tighten like something had slipped beneath his ribs.

But then she exhaled, calm again. Composed. Her gaze fixed ahead like nothing had shifted.

You're tired, he told himself. *Overthinking. She's fine.*

She had to be.

Jeta's gaze flickered—not toward the floor, but toward the door. The sigil she'd drawn there. Then, softly, like peeling back a truth she didn't want to share: "She knows you carried it."

Yasher's fingers curled against the edge of the table. "But she never saw it on us."

Jeta hesitated.

His Luck twitched—silent still, but tense, alert.

"No," she said at last, and this time, her voice held none of its usual calm. "She didn't need to."

Yasher's stomach twisted. "Then how—?"

"Because things like her don't need to see. They... recognize." Jeta's voice thinned, like even she was dancing too close to something.

She turned back to Farah, something sharper in her gaze now. "And they don't forget what they recognize."

The weight of those words pressed deep, and for the first time in hours, Yasher felt his Luck shift—like dice tumbling across a table, not landing yet, just spinning.

Farah's jaw tightened. "How?"

Jeta held Farah's gaze, her expression carefully blank, she already knew the words would land too heavy no matter how she said them.

"Things like her…" She let the words hang, the weight of them stretching out between them, pressing into the air. Then locked eyes with Farah, "They don't need to see with their eyes."

The room felt smaller.

The firelight from the hall outside flickered at the edges of the closed door, casting a long, shifting shadow across Jeta's face. It made her look like something else for a moment—something unknowable.

He didn't realize his fingers had curled slightly against the table's edge.

Farah was silent for a long moment. Then, "The relic… is it safe?"

Jeta weighed the words before she gave them away. "It is."

Farah frowned. "Safe where?"

Jeta met her gaze. Unblinking. Unshaken. "Somewhere she cannot reach."

The old woman dusted the charcoal from her fingers, her gaze settling on Farah. Not just looking at her— watching her.

Yasher felt the shift before he even understood it.

"We need to be careful." Her voice was measured,

deliberate. "Afsoun plays a game we don't yet know the rules to."

Then, she tilted her head slightly. "And if you aren't careful, you'll start playing without realizing it."

She was still looking at Farah. "That's how it starts. Small. Easy. The world around you shifts, and before you know it, you've changed with it."

That was when he moved.

Subtle, just half a step—not quite blocking, but close. His hand curled around Farah's, a quiet, grounding touch. He wasn't sure if he was holding her steady or keeping her back.

Jeta's lips curled slightly, but the expression didn't quite reach her eyes. "Watch for it, *saqalu*," she murmured. "You won't see it coming."

The fire crackled. The room felt smaller. He exhaled slowly, letting his fingers tighten around Farah's. She was warm. The way she always was. But something about that warmth felt different.

He didn't like the way Jeta was looking at Farah, like someone taking measure of a cost.

And he didn't like what she wasn't saying. He didn't like that, yet again since setting foot in this cursed town, his Luck wasn't whispering in the back of his mind. It wasn't tugging at his ribs or guiding his steps. It wasn't doing anything at all, other than random twinges and full stops. He had lived by it—trusted it to catch him when reason couldn't. It had always been there. A thread beneath the skin, the gut-deep certainty before a coin landed.

But now? Now it felt like a door had been shut from the inside.

Like something had seen him coming and closed the path before he ever reached it.

It wasn't Farah. It was this place.

He had felt the profound wrongness of people moving too smoothly, speaking without hesitation.

And now, the stillness had slipped into his bones, curled around something deeper. His Luck was absent.

Like it was being held back. Like something had set the pieces before he ever stepped onto the board.

He swallowed against the knot in his throat, and forced a smirk, slipping back into something easy, something he knew.

"Well, dear hearts," he drawled, "let's hope this isn't our last dinner."

Farah didn't smile or roll her eyes. Didn't even nudge him the way she usually did when he tried to cut through the tension with humor.

She stood beside him, too still, her arms folded, her gaze fixed somewhere ahead — not on him.

Yasher shifted slightly, close enough for their shoulders to brush. He let his fingers graze hers — just a small touch, a habit more than anything. She didn't pull away.

But she didn't take his hand, either.

She just let it hang there, cool and quiet between them.

He told himself it was nothing. That she was just tired, that they all were, and they were only beginning. But the way she didn't move...

That stayed with him.

THE STREETS of Sakasan carried a hush that burrowed into Yasher's bones.

Evening in a town should have been filled with soft sounds—the murmur of voices drifting through shuttered windows, the rhythmic scrape of boots against worn stone, the distant clang of metal as merchants packed up their wares or locked their doors for the night. There should have been the faint call of a street vendor lingering too long at his stall, the laughter of a child dodging between carts, the slow, steady breath of a place winding down into its own rhythm of rest. But here, there was none of that. Only the low whisper of the wind curling through the alleyways, carrying the scent of old spice and cooling clay, the distant brine of the sea mixing with something he couldn't quite name.

The innkeeper led them forward, her back straight, her steps measured, never once glancing back to ensure they followed. She had barely spoken since they left the inn, her silence stretching like a cord between them, taut and unbroken.

He kept his stride loose, shoulders relaxed, but his mind stayed sharp, cataloging every flicker of movement in the shadows, every shift in the air as they passed. The unease that he carried since stepping into this town hadn't faded. It sat beneath his ribs, heavy and unwelcome, a certainty rather than an uncertainty.

He didn't need to look to know that Farah felt it, too.

She walked beside him, steady and poised, but her gaze flicked across the rooftops and alleyways with careful precision. Not like someone seeking a threat with their hand hovering near a blade, but in the way of a person who had learned to see even when there was nothing to look at, not needing her hand on her blade to know she would be ready.

Without thinking, he let their hands brush as they moved, the touch brief.

Ahead, Jeta had somehow acquired her cane again, one he hadn't seen since Rumatin.

He nearly smirked at the sight. He hadn't seen her take it, hadn't seen where she might have found it, let alone where she grabbed it before they left the inn, but there it was—dark wood polished smooth from years of use, the handle carved in intricate rose vines, the delicate petals twisting along the curve in exquisite detail. She leaned on it just enough to sell the illusion of frailty, her posture slightly stooped, her fingers curled carefully around the worn handle. Pari walked beside her, one small hand brushing against Jeta's sleeve, the other gripping the strap of her satchel.

A perfectly played lie that honestly made him truly appreciate Jeta.

The governor's house rose ahead of them.

For a town's seat of authority, it was modest. Two stories of weathered stone, softened by the passage of years and the breath of the sea air that swept inland from the cliffs. A low wall framed the courtyard, the wrought-iron gate standing slightly ajar, unguarded, its hinges silent in the stillness. The windows were narrow, their shutters closed against the deepening evening, the golden flicker of lantern light escaping only through the thin slats, shifting with the movement inside.

And in front of the entrance, waiting, stood Afsoun.

Her gaze swept over them, though did not linger on the soldiers or Pari and Jeta. She barely spared a glance at Yasher, though her lips curved ever so slightly when her eyes met his.

And then, as always, her focus settled on Farah.

"Welcome, travelers," Afsoun said, her voice smooth as river-worn stone. "I hope the inn is to your liking."

"It is suitable to our needs," Farah replied evenly.

Afsoun smiled—if it could even be called that. The expression was almost warmth, almost familiarity, but it did not move beyond her mouth.

"Good," she murmured. "I would have expected nothing less."

She turned slightly, gesturing toward the door with a slow, fluid motion, one that felt less like an invitation and more like the final page of a script unfolding exactly as it was meant to.

"The governor has been expecting you."

Farah hesitated only a fraction of a breath—just long enough that he knew she was considering, measuring— but then she inclined her head and stepped past Afsoun, crossing through the threshold of the governor's house.

Afsoun did not move.

Instead, she watched Farah go, her expression unreadable, her gaze lingering on the space where she had stood, as if committing the exact moment to memory.

Then, slowly, she turned her head—and looked at Yasher.

A single glance. Unhurried. Knowing.

Yasher held her gaze, letting his own remain unreadable, letting his expression settle into something easy, something unbothered. He had spent years perfecting the art of keeping his face still, of playing the fool when it suited him, of making people underestimate what he saw and what he knew.

After a breath—just long enough to make it clear that she had chosen to linger—she turned and stepped through the doorway, vanishing into the house beyond.

His fingers flexed at his sides before stilling, tension settling low in his spine. He glanced at Jeta.

She had said Afsoun wore the shape of a human but was not necessarily one. He had thought of that once already, but now, standing here in the dimming evening, watching the last flickers of lantern light play against the smooth stone, he realized something else. Afsoun didn't just move like she was learning how to be human instead of being one. She watched them like she was waiting for them to realize it.

The weight in his chest coiled tighter.

He turned—and found Farah looking at him.

For the first time since entering Sakasan, something in her expression had cracked. Not enough for the others to see. Not enough for anyone to understand.

But he saw it.

Worry.

Not for herself, never for herself. For him, and the rest of them.

Before he could think, he reached for her hand, his fingers brushing hers, warmth against warmth, grounding and steady. Her palm turned into his, her grip curling around him, something wordless passing between them.

"I'm right here," he murmured, too low for anyone else to hear.

She didn't answer but her eyes softened as she nodded.

But after a breath, she let him go.

And he followed her inside.

The air inside the governor's house felt thicker than it had outside, pressing in with a weight that was hard to name. It wasn't just the warmth of the lanterns or the lingering scent of burning resin—it was something else, something more insidious.

The dining hall was modest, its beauty understated. The walls were carved with curling waves and vines, their details softened by years of careful upkeep, though the stone itself seemed old—older than the rest of the town, perhaps. A long table, cushions ringing around it, low and polished to a dark sheen, stretched across the center of the room.

At the far end, seated in the place of honor, was the governor.

Yasher had been expecting someone like the Mashya —a man of quiet power, still sharp despite his years, someone whose authority had been built through experience and will, recovering from an illness. But the man before him was neither of those things.

The governor's skin was thin, stretched over sharp

bones, his once-dark hair now faded to gray at the temples. His eyes, sunken into his face, held shadows that no lantern light could soften. His robes, deep blue and embroidered in fine golden thread, pooled around him like a shell that had been left behind by something far greater than what remained within it.

He looked wrong.

Not in the way Afsoun did, with her too-fluid grace and too-careful smiles, but in the way the rest of the town did, the way that spoke of something drained. Like a man who had given too much of himself away and had nothing left to reclaim.

Yasher took his seat, crossing his legs as if he were entirely at ease. A lie, but a convincing one. Across from him, Farah settled onto the cushions with a quiet grace, her hands resting lightly in her lap.

Afsoun remained standing, not taking a seat at the table.

Instead, she stood near the far wall, poised beside a servant, her hands clasped lightly in front of her. She looked as though she belonged everywhere and nowhere at once.

Her eyes swept the table as the food was served, though Yasher noted she gave no instruction. None was needed. The servant moved, already anticipating what was expected, setting down plates of saffron rice, slow-cooked lamb, flatbreads warm from the oven. The scent of cumin and coriander curled in the air, mingling with the sharper tang of something pickled, something preserved.

It should have been comforting.

The spread was generous—too generous. Dishes placed with the precision of a staged tableau, food that smelled right but felt wrong. He couldn't name it. Couldn't point to a single thing on the table and say *this, this is what's off.*

But his stomach had already answered for him. He wasn't hungry. He was never full of nerves before a meal, never this still. But something about this meal, this room, these people, had made the thought of chewing feel like a performance.

Around him, no one else moved either. The flatware gleamed untouched. Plates stayed full. Even the scent of spices couldn't mask the hesitation clinging to the air.

Mehran finally lifted his fork, but Yasher watched the way his hand moved—careful, almost forced. A man making a decision, not a man satisfying hunger.

The governor, for all his hospitality, ate nothing.

Afsoun, who had prepared their place at this table, had not prepared one for herself.

Yasher's appetite shrank.

"We had feared the worst," Mehran said, breaking the silence with practiced ease. His voice was light, conversational, though Yasher could hear the careful weight beneath it. "When word came that Sakasan had closed its gates, there were rumors the town had been lost."

The governor exhaled softly, slow and measured. "The sickness struck quickly, but we did what was necessary to protect our people. Isolation was our only choice."

Farah turned her cup slowly between her fingers,

studying the man at the head of the table. "How many did you lose?"

A pause.

The governor's expression didn't change. His fingers remained still against his lap, unmoving.

"Too many," he answered finally.

Younis shook his head, his voice low. "And yet the town stands."

The governor nodded slowly, "Endurance is what remains when all else is taken," he said.

A pause. His hands remained still in his lap, his gaze not quite meeting theirs.

"We did not survive," he added, quieter now. "We... adjusted."

Yasher felt something tighten in his chest. *Adjusted.* Like a mechanism. Like a town tuned to someone else's rhythm.

Afsoun moved to the servant, murmuring something too soft for him to hear. She gestured toward the table, but did not look at any of them as she did. Her attention, though subtle, was elsewhere.

Farah was watching her too, though she kept her movements careful, her expression unreadable.

The meal continued, but he hardly tasted it.

Every bite, every sip, every motion felt rehearsed— not by the people at the table, but by the scene itself.

The rhythm of it was too exact.

Cups refilled a breath before they emptied. Answers delivered without hesitation, as if the questions had been handed out earlier. Even the silences had structure.

His fingers curled slightly against the cushion

beneath him. This wasn't hospitality. This was performance, just like everything else in this town. The worst part was he didn't know if they were the guests, the audience, or the actors.

When Afsoun finally turned, murmuring something low to the servant before stepping from the room, he took his chance.

Something shifted.

Not in the light, not in the sounds—but in the people. In the governor.

He saw it first in the man's shoulders, how they slumped ever so slightly, like a man released from invisible bindings. His fingers, which had remained perfectly still throughout the meal, moved—just once—tapping against his knee like a habit resumed only in her absence.

He didn't look toward the door. Didn't follow her with his eyes. He didn't dare.

And that, more than anything, told Yasher what he needed to know.

This wasn't respect. It wasn't duty. It was fear. Afsoun had exited the room with grace, but the aftertaste she left behind was sharp, bitter.

The room breathed again when she left.

The governor, once ghostlike, had shifted—just barely—but enough to prove it.

He leaned forward slightly, resting an arm against his knee, his gaze shifting toward the governor.

"She doesn't sit," he said, keeping his tone easy, almost amused. "She serves. But I get the feeling that's not her place."

The governor's gaze slid toward him, his expression as unreadable as before.

"Afsoun is…" A pause. A measured breath. "A guiding hand in Sakasan."

He arched a brow. "A guiding hand who doesn't take a seat at the table?"

The governor's lips twitched, though it wasn't a smile. More a movement.

"She prefers to remain where she is needed," he said carefully. "To ensure that all things… proceed as they should."

He felt the weight of that answer settle deep in his ribs.

Not as they must. Not as they are meant to.

As they should.

His grip on the piece of bread in his hands tightened slightly.

Farah spoke, her voice smooth and level. "And where, exactly, is she needed?"

"Everywhere," the governor replied. Not hesitant. Not evasive. Just… sure.

The word echoed too loudly in his mind.

Silence stretched across the table like a drawn blade.

Yasher shifted just slightly, not enough to draw attention, but enough to angle toward Farah. He didn't look at her, but he saw her peripheral glance, the faint twitch of her fingers against her knee. And then slowly her hand moved. Not toward food. Not toward a cup. Toward him.

Her fingers brushed his thigh under the table, a fleeting touch that grounded him in a way no words could. No show of strength. No clever retort. Just a reminder. She was still here. She was still her. He let his hand settle atop hers and let their fingers intertwine, anchoring himself. For a breath, the room didn't feel quite so small, quite so heavy.

Mehran reached for his cup, his movements slow. "The sickness—it has passed? Earlier Afsoun said that it had mostly gone."

The governor nodded once. "For now."

The words landed like a stone in the quiet.

He did not say it with relief. He did not say it with caution. He said it the way a man might speak of a tide—something inevitable, something that would always return.

He let out a slow breath, shifting slightly where he sat, rolling out the tension in his shoulders, though it didn't leave.

Whatever power held Sakasan wasn't seated at this table.

It was standing outside the door.

THE MEAL HAD BEEN a formality from the start, a slow exchange of words and pleasantries meant to steady the ground between them, but Yasher had never been one for such careful dances. He preferred to read a man in the flick of his gaze, the twitch of his fingers, the shift of his weight in his chair, all the things that spoke the truth long before his mouth ever formed the words.

But the governor gave him nothing.

His frail hands lay motionless against the heavy folds of his robes, fingers curled slightly, as though frozen mid-thought. His posture did not shift, not even to adjust the fabric or ease the weight of sitting. There was no unconscious motion, no subtle flicker of discomfort, no absent-minded gestures that marked a man as human. He could have been a statue, sculpted into place and left to gather dust—except for his eyes. They did not drift or wander, did not glaze over with fatigue or dull with distraction. They were fixed, locked in place, as though the act of looking was not a choice but a command imprinted into his very being.

Farah beside him, her presence steady, her expression measured as she picked at her own meal with practiced control. The line between her brows had deepened the longer the meal went on, her fingers lingering on the edge of her plate without truly moving.

He knew she saw it too.

For what, he wasn't sure yet, but the silence had stretched long enough. The feeling creeping up his spine, settling low in his ribs, had grown unbearable, and he wasn't one to ignore instinct when it screamed at him. He leaned forward slightly, resting an arm against his knee in what looked like an easy, relaxed motion, but there was a sharpness behind it. His words, when they came, were casual in tone, but pointed beneath the surface.

"You never said how you fared, governor. During the sickness."

For a moment, there was nothing. Then, slowly, the governor blinked, the motion measured in a way that made his skin prickle. His head turned slightly, as though he had to search for the meaning behind the question before answering it.

"I endured," he said at last.

Before he could press further, Farah's voice came, steady and firm. "The Unnamed Gods have smiled on you for your endurance."

A pause.

The governor's lips parted. But no sound came.

His throat moved, his jaw working slightly, the barest twitch of movement in his face. His mouth was forming the shape of a word, but the sound—whatever it was—would not come. The silence pressed tighter, wrapping around him like a hand at his throat. The pulse in Yasher's own ribs quickened, his instincts screaming at him to move, to act, to do something, but he didn't know what.

And then, at last, in a voice that was barely more than a whisper, the word escaped.

"Yes."

It was the kind of answer given not by a man recalling truth, but by a man forcing the words past something else.

Farah's fingers barely shifted as she set her cup down on the table, her gaze locked on the governor. "And the others?"

Again, that pause.

He felt it before he saw it—the smallest crack forming.

The governor's expression twitched. A flicker of something behind his eyes, a breath that wasn't quite right, a ripple beneath still water. His lips parted slightly, as if he meant to speak, but nothing came.

Something was wrong.

The hair at the back of Yasher's neck lifted.

The governor's throat bobbed, and for the first time, his jaw tensed.

Yasher recognized what that was.

It was panic.

The governor's breath came too shallowly now, his fingers tightening imperceptibly against his lap. He looked across the table, his gaze flickering as though trying to focus on something unseen, his lips barely parting—

"I—"

The sound that left him was strangled, raw. He jerked forward slightly, as though something inside him was being pushed down, suffocated before it could escape.

Mehran moved first, his instincts driving him to reach forward, but Yasher caught the slight motion from the corner of his eye and shifted just enough to stop him. The instinct was good, but something in Yasher screamed not to touch the man.

The governor shuddered.

Something—someone—inside him was trying to speak.

And then—it broke.

"Not all of them."

The whisper slipped from the governor's mouth like a breath he hadn't meant to speak— barely there, almost too soft to catch, but undeniable.

It didn't sound forced.

It sounded... broken.

Like a thought he'd held too long in his mouth finally cracked apart. Like something deep inside him had splintered around the truth, leaking through before it could be buried again.

Yasher had seen hesitation before. Had seen men choke on lies or falter under the weight of their own guilt. But this—this was something else. Not struggle. Not remorse.

A fracture.

His body jerked, his breath stuttering, his hands clenching suddenly, violently, into the fabric of his robes. Yasher felt his pulse lurch in response, the unnaturalness of it settling like ice in his chest.

Pari let out a soft, startled breath, her small hands tightening around Jeta's sleeve.

Then, just as suddenly—the moment passed.

The governor went still.

Too still.

He'd seen men faint before, had seen the way exhaustion and heat could pull a man's consciousness from him like water from a broken jug—but this wasn't that.

The governor's chest rose and fell slowly. His fingers loosened.

And when he lifted his head again, the moment of panic was gone.

His breath was weak but steady once more. His hands no longer trembled. His posture had returned to its unnatural stillness.

He lifted his cup to his lips, took a slow, measured

sip, and when he set it down again, it was as though none of it had ever happened.

"We endured," he said, his voice as smooth as it had been at the start of the meal.

From the edge of his vision, Yasher caught the twitch of Jeta's hand—fingers tightening around the carved head of her cane like she was anchoring herself.

He didn't need to see her face to know she had clocked the same thing he had. Maybe more. And if Jeta Veseli was rattled—really rattled—it meant the rest of them should've been running miles ago.

"Not all of them," she echoed, softer than before, but the edge of the words carried weight.

She was staring at the governor.

Not shocked. Not unsettled.

Watching. As if recognizing something she hadn't seen in centuries—and had hoped never to see again.

The governor sat back against the cushions, his body perfectly at ease. The tension that had cracked through him only moments before was erased, as if it had never existed.

Yasher glanced at Farah, his pulse a steady beat in his ears.

She was watching the governor the same way he was.

After a breath, Farah leaned forward slightly, her voice steady. "So many lost? That is a tragedy."

The governor met her gaze, his dark eyes empty of hesitation.

Too smooth, too controlled.

"Too many," he answered.

And then—he smiled. As if that had always been the answer. As if nothing had ever been wrong at all.

The silence in the dining hall was thick enough to choke on, pressing against Yasher's ribs like a slow-moving tide that refused to recede. The words that had slipped from the governor's mouth moments before—*Not all of them*—still echoed in Yasher's mind, a stark contrast to the lifeless calm that had settled over the old man once more. The moment had been real, too raw to be anything else, but now it was gone, smoothed over like a footprint in shifting sand, erased by something unseen, something Yasher could feel but couldn't name.

The scent of resin-heavy smoke from the braziers mixed with the slow-cooling spices of the untouched meal, layering the air with something both cloying and stale. The lamb, fragrant with saffron and coriander, had gone cold on their plates, the rich oil congealing at the edges, but no one had the stomach to reach for another bite. Even Mehran, who rarely let unease get in the way of a full meal, sat stiff-backed, his hands unmoving against his thighs, his dark eyes flicking between the governor and Farah as if waiting for one of them to break the spell that had settled over the room.

But it was not Farah who ended the silence.

The door opened and Afsoun stepped through.

The lamplight softened the sharp planes of her face, her expression composed, her dark eyes drifting over the table's occupants with that same unreadable gaze she always wore. Her gaze, as always, found Farah before anyone else.

The corners of her lips curved into a faint smile.

"A fine evening," she murmured, her tone light, almost conversational, but there was a weight beneath the words, something that pressed against the air between them, subtle yet suffocating. "I trust the governor has been an excellent host."

Farah did not immediately respond. She did not return the smile, nor did she let her expression waver, but Yasher saw the careful way she adjusted her posture, the shift in her weight. It was the smallest tell, an invisible armor being fastened into place, the kind of preparation that came when sensing the presence of something dangerous and not yet knowing which direction the first strike would come from.

Farah met Afsoun's gaze, the moment stretching between them, silent, weighted, unreadable. And then, with the same careful control she had wielded her entire life, she spoke.

"The conversation has been enlightening."

Afsoun tilted her head, just slightly. The smallest shift of weight, the slightest narrowing of her gaze—like a blade being drawn but never fully unsheathed.

Then, after a pause meant to make them feel it, she smiled.

"I am glad."

Afsoun was testing her footing. Farah was doing the same.

The woman folded her hands together, her fingers resting lightly over each other, her nails short but polished, neat, not a single rough edge to them.

"But I am afraid the evening grows late," she continued, her tone as gentle as a lullaby, yet carrying the undeniable weight of something final. "The road has taken much from you, and while we are honored by your presence, it would be best if you returned to the inn before night deepens too much."

The words settled in the room like a thick fog, curling between them, creeping into the spaces between their ribs.

Not *it would be best if you rested.* Not *it would be best to retire for the night.*

It would be best if you left. Before night grew too late.

And then there was that pause at the end, the deliberate space between her last syllable and the silence that followed, like something else should have come after it, something unspoken, something that, if said aloud, might unravel whatever kept the bones of this town standing upright.

He glanced at Farah, but she had not moved.

She was still watching Afsoun, her own gaze just as steady, just as quiet, just as measuring.

And then, slowly, carefully, she inclined her head. "Thank you for your hospitality. May the Unnamed Gods keep you, governor," she said, each syllable wrapped in careful politeness.

"Of course," she murmured, answering for the governor, the warmth in her voice only a shade deep. "We will see you again soon."

His pulse pounded a little harder, a steady beat against his ribs.

No one moved for a moment, but then Mehran was rising, his large frame unfolding with the slow, careful ease of a man trained to move deliberately, while Younis followed, his usual sharpness tempered by caution. Jeta reached for her cane, not a single flicker of her performance faltering even as she let out a small, tired exhale, the kind an old woman might give after too many hours sitting upright. Pari clung to Jeta's side, her small hands gripping the older woman's sleeve as they moved, her large dark eyes unreadable in the low light of the dining hall.

Yasher rose as well, stretching just slightly, forcing his movements to remain easy, unbothered, though every muscle in his body was wound tight. He knew Farah could feel it, could sense the tension rolling beneath his skin the same way he could sense the slow, methodical way she was keeping her breathing even.

As they stepped past Afsoun, he could feel her watching them.

Her presence didn't press against him the way it had the first time they met, didn't feel like hands curling over his skin or fingers trailing along the threads of his Luck, but there was something just as unsettling about the way she let them go.

CHAPTER 23

THE AIR CLUNG thick with the dampness of night, heavy with the mingled scents of cold stone, dried ash, and something faintly metallic—like old blood left too long in the sun. The buildings loomed close, their walls worn smooth by time, their silent facades pressing in as though they leaned closer with every step she took. Farah moved without hesitation, her boots whispering against the packed earth and stone, but the hush around her was unnatural. Not the gentle quiet of a town asleep —but the brittle stillness of a held breath, the kind that comes just before something breaks.

She exhaled softly, pulling her coat tighter around her shoulders as she stepped out into the empty street, her boots barely whispering against the worn dirt path. The wind from the cliffs stirred against the edges of her coat, cool and thin, carrying the scent of salt and something else—something deeper, something older.

Sleep had abandoned her long before the sky had begun to pale, leaving her trapped in the weight of her own thoughts. The deep blues and silvers of false dawn stretched over the horizon, but they brought no comfort, no sense of renewal. The unease had settled inside her, threading through the marrow of her bones like a silent, unanswered summons. Something pressing at the edges of her thoughts, whispering along the contours of her mind like a tide tugging at the shore. Yasher's warmth comforted her in the small bed, his breath slow and even in sleep, one arm draped carelessly across his stomach, the faintest furrow between his brows even in rest.

She had studied his face in the low light, had let herself memorize the way the faintest shadow of stubble darkened his jaw, the way the soft crease of his lips never quite smoothed out, even in sleep. A part of her had wanted to stay, to press her forehead against his and let herself breathe him in, to let herself feel something *solid*.

But the restlessness had won.

It was not just the heaviness of the previous day. It was something deeper humming beneath her skin, something *waiting*.

The further she walked, the more she felt it.

It was not the same cloying pull of the relic—not the slow, insidious whisper of something spoiled—but it was close. It settled into the edges of her mind, the weight of it so subtle she might have mistaken it for something else, might have told herself she had imagined it, if she had not recognized the feeling for what it was.

Control.

She had been raised to believe control was the key to survival. That only through absolute mastery of herself

—her actions, her mind, her *will*—could she carve a place in the world that could not be taken from her. It had been the lesson drilled into her in the Mashyana's court, in the years of training, in the years of standing beside Behnaz as both weapon and witness. It had been the truth she had clung to when she had raised a blade for the first time, when she had made her first kill in the shadows, when she had become the Hand of the Mashyana.

And yet, here she did not feel in control. She felt as if there was a battle between control and chaos in her soul.

The feeling crawled over her skin, slow and insidious, like the brush of unseen fingertips tracing too close. Not Afsoun, not the governor.

No, this was different. It was woven into the bones of the town itself, humming beneath the worn stones, curling through the empty streets. Not a presence, not a single set of eyes peering from a window or watching from an alley. It was all of it. The walls, the streets, the air. The town itself.

And the worst part wasn't that it slowed feeling unnatural. Control and chaos were coming to an agreement within her. As if it was inevitable.

She did not let her pace falter, though the sensation crawled over her skin like unseen hands trailing too close. Instead, she let her steps slow only slightly as she passed the empty market stalls, her fingers brushing against the worn wooden edges of a table left abandoned in the cool hush of morning.

The street curved ahead, narrowing into a tight

passage between buildings, and before she could take another breath—she knew.

Afsoun was waiting, as she had expected to find her.

She stood just beyond the threshold of an arched entryway, half in shadow, half caught in the pale slant of light creeping into the street. The hem of her coat stirred slightly in the cold wind, the embroidered thread catching the faintest gleam of movement.

Farah did not tense.

She did not allow herself to react at all.

She simply met Afsoun's gaze, steady, unmoving, waiting.

Afsoun's lips curved, the faintest hint of amusement threading through her voice. "You are not the first to walk these streets before dawn, Farahnaz."

Farah exhaled slowly. "And yet I seem to be the only one here tonight, until you."

Afsoun tilted her head just slightly. "Are you?"

The wind shifted, and for a moment, she thought she saw movement in the farthest reaches of her vision, beyond the narrow mouth of an alleyway. But when she looked, there was nothing.

She turned back to Afsoun, whose gaze had not wavered.

"You're restless," Afsoun observed, her tone light, unassuming. "That does not surprise me."

"You feel it, don't you?" Afsoun asked—not curious, but certain. She stepped forward, the faint rustle of her coat the only sound in the narrow street. "The way the town settles around your bones. Like it was waiting for you."

Her voice didn't sharpen. It softened.

"You don't have to name it. Not yet. But it knows you. And you—" her gaze flickered, sharp beneath the calm "—you've always known it."

She should have felt the shiver that ran down her spine, but it was dulled. But her bracelet spun on her wrist, a comforting weight.

Afsoun's smile didn't change. "Control isn't the absence of change. It's the decision of how you'll be changed. You already feel the difference, don't you?"

She didn't wait for an answer.

"The day is coming," she said gently, almost affectionately, "when you will stop resisting the shape of who you are meant to be. I only hope, when it arrives, you recognize yourself."

She held her ground as Afsoun turned, her dark coat trailing behind her as she slipped away into the shadows of the narrow street.

She let the wind curl through the empty street, cold against her skin, and ignored the way her pulse still thundered beneath it, not moving.

She stood in the empty street long after Afsoun had disappeared, the words left behind curling in the cold morning air like the last embers of a dying fire.

She should have turned back. She should have walked the same path she had taken from the inn, returned to Yasher's warmth before he stirred.

But she didn't.

Instead, she stood rooted in place, staring down the narrow alley where Afsoun had disappeared, the shadows swallowing her whole without a whisper of movement, without a trace left behind. She should turn back. Should shake this off as another manipulation, another battle of words meant to set her off-balance.

But the weight of Afsoun's voice still lingered in her mind, curling like ink through water, impossible to separate from the parts of her that had already begun to change.

Control isn't the absence of change. It's the decision of how you'll be changed.

The words settled over her like a second skin, pressing into the spaces she had once guarded, sinking deep into the places she had once held as her own.

Her Talent had been honed by discipline, by sheer, unrelenting will. She had mastered her abilities not because they had been gifted to her freely, but because she had bled for them, because she had shaped them with her own hands, her own mind.

And yet—

The relic had touched her.

Even now, with it locked away in Jeta's possession, the echo of it still lingered beneath her ribs, an aftertaste, a whisper.

And Afsoun had seen it.

Farah exhaled sharply, pressing her fingers into the thick fabric of her sleeves, grounding herself in the sensation. She had no patience for riddles, no time for this slow unraveling that Afsoun seemed intent on weaving.

Farah turned on her heel, her boots pressing into the dirt as she made her way back toward the inn. The streets remained empty, as though the very bones of Sakasan were holding their breath.

The inn was still wrapped in shadows when she reached it, the faint glow of an oil lamp flickering just inside the common room where the old innkeeper had likely woken before the sun, moving through his morning tasks with the slow steadiness of a man who had done the same thing for years. She slipped past the door with practiced ease, her steps making no sound against the wooden floorboards as she climbed the narrow stairs leading to their rooms.

The latch on her door was loose when she pressed against it. Yasher was sitting on the edge of the bed, his back to her, scars standing out from his skin in moonlight, his hands braced against his knees. His hair was slightly disheveled from sleep, though the tension in his shoulders told her that he had not truly rested, that he had woken the moment she had left.

A slow, steady breath escaped him before he turned his head just enough to glance at her over his shoulder.

"You weren't exactly subtle," he murmured, his voice rough with sleep, but edged with something else.

She shut the door behind her, keeping her movements controlled. "Didn't think I needed to be."

He shook his head slightly as he leaned back, stretching his arms out behind him before running a hand through his hair, pushing it away from his face.

"Where did you go?"

She hesitated, unsure if she wanted to give him this answer.

She stepped closer, kneeling on the bed beside him,

her fingers brushing against his skin before slipping down to find his wrist, tracing the line of his pulse with absent familiarity.

He tilted his head slightly, watching her.

She could tell him. Could explain that she had woken with something pressing against her thoughts, something pulling, and that she had followed it. That she had found Afsoun waiting for her like a carefully placed stone in her path.

But that would mean admitting that something was happening to her, that she had changed. Whatever battle was happening within her had come to a conclusion.

Instead, she let out a slow breath and said, "I couldn't sleep."

He hummed, a low, skeptical sound, but he didn't press immediately. His free hand reached up, catching her fingers against his own, thumb smoothing over her knuckles. It was an absent gesture, something natural between them, but this time it lingered, as if he were measuring her against the moment.

"What's really happening with you?" he murmured, watching her carefully now.

Farah hesitated. "Nothing. It's just this town."

He arched a brow. "Liar."

It wasn't an accusation. But it wasn't playful, either.

Farah exhaled softly, curling her fingers around his wrist. "You're imagining things."

His lips parted slightly, as if he wanted to argue, but something in her face must have made him change his mind. He shifted, twisting to fully face her now, their knees brushing.

"Phoenix," he said quietly, her name a weight between them.

She held his gaze.

For a moment, neither of them spoke.

He sighed, the edge in his voice softening into something quieter. He pressed his forehead to hers, his breath brushing her skin.

"You'll tell me," he murmured, barely more than a breath. "When you're ready."

She closed her eyes. She should have told him. She should have said something—anything—to ease the weight behind his words.

But instead, she leaned in. Her lips found his, slow and certain, not out of need but out of defiance.

She kissed him like silence. Like closing a door. Like setting down a truth she wasn't ready to hold.

He didn't resist. His hands slid around her waist, drawing her closer, his body warm and steady beneath her palms. A place to rest.

She pressed harder into him, fingers curling into the fabric of his shirt, not out of desire but out of desperation. As if she could bury Afsoun's voice beneath his breath. As if Yasher's skin could shield her from what she already knew.

The day is coming, Farahnaz.

She kissed him again. Fiercer this time.

He held her, and she let herself believe, for just a moment, that this could be enough. That if she didn't speak it, the truth wouldn't exist.

She didn't want answers today. She only wanted to forget she needed them.

THE SCENT of fresh bread clung to the air in the common room, mixing with the sharper, spiced aroma of Jeta's tea. The light filtering through the windows was pale, weak, struggling to break through the overcast sky, casting long, thin shadows across the worn wooden floorboards. The place was empty save for them, the hush so complete that Farah could hear the faintest scratch of charcoal from the other room where Pari must have been drawing.

But all of it—the warmth of the hearth, the quiet rituals of morning, the muffled movements of the town outside—felt like nothing more than a thin veil stretched over something deeper, something colder.

Because Jeta sat there at the small wooden table, her hands cradling a cup of tea as though she had all the time in the world, as though she wasn't keeping something from her that *belonged* to her.

She took a slow breath, pressing down the sharp coil of irritation twisting in her chest, tamping down the instinct to demand outright, to take rather than ask, to remove the obstacle rather than negotiate around it. Instead, she kept her steps measured, controlled, her face unreadable as she approached the table.

"I need it," she said, the words sharper than she meant, too fast, too loud, like they'd broken free before she could leash them.

She hadn't meant to sound desperate.

But the desperation wasn't about the relic. Not really. It was about the whisper she'd felt under her skin since the moment she let it go. About the weight she hadn't stopped carrying, the one that wasn't in the box but in her own bones.

Jeta exhaled softly—not a sigh, but something quieter. Sadder. Like she already knew.

She finally lifted her gaze from the cup, calm and unshaken.

There was no surprise in her expression, as if she had been waiting for this moment, expecting it. She made no move to acknowledge the request immediately, only studied Farah with an unnerving patience, the kind that made her skin prickle, the kind that suggested Jeta already knew the answer to a question Farah had not yet asked.

"I'm sure you do," Jeta murmured at last, her fingers tapping absently against the ceramic, "but that doesn't mean you're getting it."

The quiet, measured response only stoked the slow-burning frustration curling in her gut, like embers stirring to life with each passing moment. She forced herself to stay still, to keep her breathing even, to resist the sharp urge to seize control of the conversation before it unraveled into something neither of them could walk back from.

"It's mine," she said, her voice clipped, the edge in it sharper than she intended.

Jeta's expression shifted just slightly, something flickering in her green eyes. Pity.

And then, as if the words themselves tasted bitter on her tongue, she let out a short breath and murmured, "Yours?"

She tilted her head, considering her for a long moment before shaking it slightly, as though disappointed. "I wasn't aware corruption had an owner."

The words landed like a strike, subtle yet undeniable, an accusation wrapped in the guise of casual conversation.

Her fingers twitched, an involuntary motion, her fists curling in the fabric of her sleeves. "I can control it," she said, more forcefully this time, the certainty in her voice unshaken, unwavering. "It is needed."

Jeta set her cup down with deliberate care, the soft clink of ceramic against wood sounding much too loud in the quiet of the room. She leaned back, her gaze never leaving Farah's, a considering look crossing her face, one that sent an odd, unpleasant sensation curling beneath Farah's skin.

"I was hoping," Jeta said finally, her tone almost wistful, "that it hadn't gotten its claws in you yet. But I was foolhardy in that thought."

The slow, creeping frustration inside Farah flared. "I am *fine*."

Jeta studied her for a long moment before her eyes flickered, just for an instant, toward Farah's hands, as if she had already seen what Farah herself could not, as if she already knew what lay beneath her skin, wrapped around her bones, threading into the spaces between her thoughts.

She sighed again, softer this time, and said, "Are you? You seem to be fighting it still, but He does like to play with his... food."

Farah stepped forward, closing the distance between

them in a single breath, the slow coil of restraint slipping, unraveling. She was tired of Jeta's riddles, of her insufferable *waiting*, of the way she always seemed to think she knew more than everyone else but refused to give up anything useful.

"Give it to me."

Jeta did not move. Did not blink. "No."

The single word was quiet, but it might as well have been a blade to the throat.

Something inside Farah snapped, the tightness in her chest bursting into something swift and searing. The heat of it was almost a relief, as if the pressure had been waiting to break free, waiting for an outlet.

Her hand shot out, gripping the front of Jeta's coat, yanking her forward until there was barely space for breath between them. The green fabric bunched beneath her fingers, the scent of road dust and the faint, lingering spice of Jeta's tea filling her nose as she met the older woman's gaze, her own pulse hammering behind her ribs.

The old woman had *forced* this. Had pushed her into it. She had only reacted accordingly.

Jeta's expression did not change. She did not fight, did not struggle, did not so much as flinch.

She only looked at Farah as if she already knew exactly how this was going to play out.

"You don't get to keep it from me," Farah said, venom threading through the words. "You're afraid because you don't understand what it is. But I do."

Something in Jeta's gaze darkened, something deep

and knowing, something that should not have made Farah feel *seen* in the way that it did.

"And that," Jeta said, her voice softer now, heavier, "is exactly why you can't have it."

The air between them felt charged, brittle, the weight of those words pressing into the narrow space that separated them.

A hand closed gently around her wrist.

Yasher.

The contact wasn't sudden. It was quiet. Certain. Like he'd already known where this was going the moment she stood.

He didn't pull her away. Didn't say her name like a scolding. He just held her, fingers warm, steady, anchoring—not to stop her, but to remind her she didn't need to prove anything.

"Farah."

Her name came low, breathless, like he was afraid of what he'd seen in her face before she turned.

She held Jeta's gaze for a long breath, her pulse thudding in her ears like footsteps echoing down an empty hall. Something in the older woman's face wasn't resistance—it was reflection. Like she had seen this before, and already knew how it would end.

And in that moment, Farah saw herself—not just in the now, but where this path could lead.

It wasn't Yasher's voice or Jeta's calm that made her let go.

It was the cold press of her own restraint fraying.

She released her grip—not out of defeat, but out of

the terrifying realization that she *could* have gone further.

Jeta exhaled, brushing off her coat as if nothing had happened, as if she had already put this behind her. But Farah could see it—the shift.

The quiet certainty in Jeta's eyes. The knowledge that she had been right.

Farah turned, her gaze snapping to Yasher's.

His blue eyes were darker than usual, shadowed by something she didn't want to name. He studied her, closely, too closely, the way he always did when he was trying to read the truth beneath her silences.

"I'm fine," she said, quieter than she meant to.

He didn't answer. Didn't move.

Just stood there, holding her in that gaze that always made it feel like he saw more than he should. And for a heartbeat, just one, she thought he didn't believe her. Thought he might say something, call her on it, pull at the thread until it unraveled.

But he didn't.

After a long moment, he stepped back, his fingers letting go of her wrist with quiet care.

And that should have been a relief, but it wasn't.

Because she knew what it meant to be seen—and looked past anyway.

And that was the part she couldn't shake. Not Jeta's pity. Not even the sharp coil of anger still winding beneath her skin.

But the way Yasher had looked at her, like he had seen something she hadn't.

The room tightened around her like a noose, every breath heavier than the last. The low scrape of Jeta adjusting her coat, the soft hush of Yasher's breathing—it all pressed in too close, too sharp. Her vision narrowed, not from tears, but from something colder, harder. A recoil.

He was still watching her. She could feel it, even without looking. Not accusation. Not anger. Something worse. Expectation.

Jeta's silence burned worse than her refusal. She wasn't angry. She wasn't rattled. She was waiting as if Farah would come to the conclusion she'd already reached on her own.

That she had crossed a line. That she wasn't sure where the line had even been.

Her fingers twitched at her side, and for a breath, she didn't know if she wanted to lash out or fall to her knees.

She turned and walked out of the room.

Because if she stayed a second longer, she wasn't sure who she would be, who she'd already become.

Her pulse pounded in her ears, her footsteps unnaturally loud against the uneven stone as she stepped outside into the thin, biting morning air.

She kept walking.

The streets blurred around her, every footstep striking harder than it needed to. She didn't stop to see if anyone stirred behind a shutter. She didn't care. The silence wrapped around her shoulders like a chain of silk —soft, cloying, impossible to break.

She didn't remember choosing the road to the cliffs. Her legs had simply taken her there, as if the wind had pulled at her bones until she couldn't turn another way.

And then—the sea.

It opened in front of her, vast and endless, its dark waves gnawing at the cliffs like they had always been hungry. The cold wind slammed into her, tangling her hair, yanking at her coat, forcing her to draw a breath that scraped against her lungs.

Only then did the heat hit.

Not from outside. From within.

A tight, awful pulse of fury.

She had nearly *hurt* Jeta, and would have turned on Yasher possibly.

Not out of defense. Not out of reason.

Out of want.

Out of power.

Her fingers curled into fists at her sides, sleeves twisting beneath her grip. Her jaw clenched.

I am fine, she had said. Lied.

He hadn't believed her. Not really. She saw it in the way his gaze had lingered, searching, *worried*.

The wind howled around her, lifting her hair like loose thread, the taste of salt sharp on her tongue. It filled the silence with a sound that didn't ask questions, didn't wait for answers.

She closed her eyes.

Control is a choice. Power is the ability to wield it.

Afsoun's words slipped into her again, unbidden. They felt like truth. They felt like poison.

Farah pressed both hands to her face. *Get it together.*

She had spent her life building who she was from the ground up, hammering herself into something sharp, something unshakable. She had bled to become what she was.

But that wasn't what Yasher had seen in her eyes.

And that... *that* was what scared her.

She stood at the edge, the cliffs steady beneath her boots, her Talent spinning her bracelet absently, and stared out at the sea until the numbness settled back into place.

Until she could believe, just for a moment, that she was still herself.

CHAPTER 24

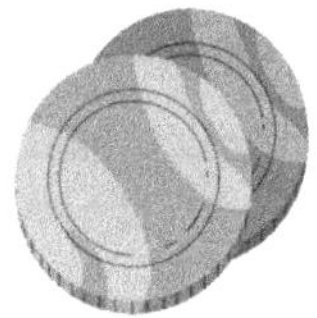

THE DOOR SLAMMED SHUT behind her, and the silence she left behind was heavier than her presence had ever been. Yasher didn't move. Just stared at the door like glaring might summon her back. She'd left like something in her was about to break, and he couldn't tell if it was anger, shame, or something else curling sharp and unfamiliar beneath her skin.

His pulse thrummed in his ears, sharp and uneven, but he ignored it, dragging a slow, controlled breath into his lungs. The room smelled of tea, of the faint remnants of last night's supper, of damp wool and woodsmoke, but beneath it all, there was still the lingering scent of her—of metal and cedar, of something sharp and steady that had always felt like *Farah*. And now, it was just another reminder that she wasn't standing in front of him, wasn't sitting beside him, wasn't within reach to pull back from the edge she seemed determined to jump toward.

Across the room, Jeta sat at the table, fingers curled

around the ceramic cup that had long gone cold, the steam no longer rising from its surface. She wasn't drinking it, wasn't even pretending to, just staring at the door with that unreadable expression of hers, something sharp but distant settling in her green eyes. The quiet stretched between them, the only sound the faint rustle of fabric as the old woman shifted just enough to lift her cup before setting it back down without taking a sip.

He rolled his shoulders, but the tension didn't shake loose. It sat in his chest, tight and unmoving, an iron weight pressing down. He dragged a hand through his hair, fingers catching in the tangles, gripping too hard before forcing himself to drop it.

"She just—" The words caught in his throat, burning at the edges. He ran a hand through his hair again, rough this time. "She knows better than this."

The words sounded thin. Fragile. He was trying to convince himself as much, if not more than Jeta.

Her fingers tapped lightly against her cup, the rhythm maddening in its calm. "Does she?"

His jaw tightened. Because what he'd seen—that *wasn't* Farah. Not the way she reached for Jeta, not the way she'd moved like something was owed to her. Like she had the right to lay hands on an old woman. He didn't want to say it. Didn't want to believe it. But the truth gnawed at him anyway, steady and quiet. She had scared him.

"She's not—" He stopped, breathing harshly through his nose. Not yet. Not entirely. But the words wouldn't come, wouldn't shape themselves into something real. Because how was he supposed to say it? That he had seen something shift in her, something slipping, something breaking? That the way she had reached for Jeta wasn't in anger, wasn't even in desperation—but in possession?

That thought made his stomach twist, sharp and sick.

Jeta's gaze didn't waver. She didn't soften, didn't hesitate.

"She thinks she's doing the right thing," she said softly, her eyes fixed on the door Farah had vanished through. "She always does. That's what made her a good Beloved, an excellent Hand. That's what makes this all so dangerous."

A pause.

"Because when Farah believes she's in the right, she doesn't stop to ask if she's hurting herself in the process."

The words landed like iron—heavy, unmovable, impossible to shake.

His fingers curled into his palms before pulling at his bracelet. He needed something solid, something real, because everything about this conversation made his chest feel hollow.

He exhaled sharply through his nose, dragging a hand through his hair, frustration tightening like a coil in his chest. "And what the hell is it that she thinks she's doing?"

She went quiet again, her gaze flickering—not to him, but to the door Farah had left through. As if she could still see her standing there, still hear the tension in her voice.

Finally, she let out a slow breath. "That," she murmured, voice softer, weightier, "is the part she hasn't figured out yet. When she does, it could go... poorly."

A knot twisted tight in his gut. Because he had seen that look before—too many times, in too many places. In Farah's eyes when she was bleeding but refused to fall. In the set of her jaw when she was faced with an impossible choice and didn't hesitate to make it anyway. In the quiet moments, when no one else was watching, when the stressors of everything pressed against her and she carried it without complaint.

Because she never stopped. Not when she should. Not when it mattered. Not even for herself.

He shook his head, but the unease remained lodged deep in his chest, an immovable weight pressing against his ribs. He wanted to believe this was temporary—that Farah would shake it off, that this wasn't anything they couldn't fix.

But Jeta had seen it. And so had he.

Yasher flexed his fingers, forcing them to loosen, to stop curling into fists at his sides. "She's strong enough to—"

"To fight it?" Jeta cut in smoothly, her gaze steady, sharp. "To control it?"

She tilted her head slightly. "That's what she believes too, isn't it? You want to pull her back," she continued, voice quieter now, "but you don't even know what you're pulling her back from, do you?"

He clenched his teeth, forced himself to breathe. The common room felt too small, the dim lantern light too heavy, the walls too close, pressing inward with each passing second. He shifted his weight, the wood beneath his boots creaking in protest, but none of it shook the feeling lodged deep in his ribs.

"...It should've left her, it was supposed to be gone, done," Yasher muttered, barely above a whisper. The words hit the air like a confession, like he'd peeled something raw and unfinished out of his chest and couldn't take it back.

"The relic—when you took it, Jeta. It should've let her go. She wasn't holding it anymore. It should've... stopped."

She didn't answer immediately. She just watched him, the sharp green of her gaze unreadable, her fingers curling around her cooling cup of tea.

"It should have, but I may have been too late," she said at last. And that, somehow, was worse.

"It can't be too late, she can't..." His hands shook. He forced them still. He hadn't wanted to say it because saying it made it real. Because if the corruption had stayed—if it had sunk its claws into Farah even after the relic was gone, he didn't know how to fix that.

Jeta sighed, shaking her head. "She's been off for some time now, but I had hoped that it was just an echo."

"No," he admitted. "I've known. I just..." He looked away, jaw tightening. "Didn't want to believe it."

Didn't want to admit that he had hoped, even prayed to whoever would listen, that he was wrong.

She studied him for a long moment before sighing again, rubbing her temple with two fingers. "That's what you're trying to pull her back from, *saqalu*. And it's already got its claws in deep."

A beat. Then softer, "He always does."

He hated that there wasn't a single damn thing he could say in response.

That was the part that made his hands tighten into fists, that made his jaw lock, that sent something unsteady rushing through him. Because if he didn't know what she was running toward, if he didn't understand what was gripping her so tightly beneath her skin, then how the hell was he supposed to stop it?

Jeta rubbed the bridge of her nose as if she were just as tired of this conversation as he was.

"You can't make someone let you help them," she said, her voice low, threaded with a sadness she rarely let show. "Not until they decide they want to be helped. You can only hope they decide before it's too late."

He hated how much her words made sense. The common room felt like it was closing in on him—lantern light too dim, air too thick, walls leaning just a little too close.

He dragged a hand through his hair, his breath tight in his chest.

"That sounds like the kind of bullshit people say when they've already given up," he muttered, but there was no fire in it—just the hollow echo of something he couldn't fix.

Jeta let out a short, dry laugh, shaking her head. "Probably. But it's still true."

The silence between them stretched again, but it wasn't the usual silence—the quiet of travel, of long nights on the road, of unspoken agreements. This was something else. This was something neither of them had an answer for.

He forced himself to think. He hated this. Every part of him wanted to go after her, to stop her before she got too far, before the distance between them became something real.

But Farah wasn't a problem to be solved. She wasn't a battle to be won or an enemy to outmaneuver. She was Farah, his Phoenix. And if he pushed her now, if he tried to drag her back when she wasn't ready, he knew exactly how that would end.

She'd fight him. Not with words or reason—but with that unrelenting, break-before-she-bends stubbornness that had kept her alive this long.

He had spent his whole life trusting his instincts. They had saved him more times than he could count, had pulled him back from the edge of disaster more times than he deserved. But right now?

Right now, every instinct screamed at him to follow her.

Jeta studied him for a long moment, as if already knowing what he was thinking, as if she could see the shape of his decisions before he had even made them. She exhaled, shaking her head. "You're still going after her, aren't you?"

He shrugged, but it wasn't casual. "Give her a head start."

Jeta snorted softly, shaking her head, but there was no real exasperation in it this time. "Idiots, both of you."

He stepped back, leaning against the wall near the

door, arms still folded, his fingers drumming lightly against the fabric of his coat, as if he was counting cards instead of counting down.

She'd come back. She always did.

But he wasn't sure it would still be the version of her he loved, the one who reached for his hand in the dark.

And that was the part that scared him the most.

THE WIND HAD PICKED up by the time Yasher finally pushed himself off the wall he leaned on to let her have a moment. It curled through the narrow streets, carrying the scent of damp stone and the faintest trace of salt from the cliffs beyond.

Farah had been gone too long.

He'd told himself to wait. That she needed space, that she needed time. That after what had happened in the inn, after the way she had looked at Jeta, after the way her voice had hardened when she demanded the relic, she needed a moment to put herself back together.

He had waited. But his Luck had begun to shift. Not a pull this time. A tremor.

At first, he thought he imagined it. Just nerves. But the feeling returned, gentle but persistent, like something brushing the edges of his awareness, testing for cracks. It wasn't guiding him. It was *wary*.

Find her, it murmured. A warning.

He ran a hand through his hair as he glanced toward the door before he started to move.

Jeta hadn't stopped him. Hadn't looked away. She

watched like someone counting seconds until a storm struck. That alone made his skin prickle.

He stepped outside, boots crunching against damp earth, and let his feet follow the pull in his chest.

It led him toward the cliffs.

The wind tore along the land, sharp and cold, laced with salt and sea-brine. It pulled at Farah's coat, catching the edges like it meant to unravel her. She stood with her arms crossed tight, not for warmth—no, it was something else. She was holding herself together by sheer force of will.

The sky was lit in slow gradients—violet to gray to washed-out blue—while the sea below battered the rock like it resented being kept out of the crevices in the stone.

He took a step closer, making sure his footsteps were deliberate, giving her space to flee if she needed it. But she didn't move. She stayed rooted, her fingers twitching slightly where they curled against her arms. Her hands, normally so steady, looked too pale in the half-light as they tightened and loosened over and over again on her arms.

He wanted to take them, to wrap them in his own, warm them with his breath, press them against his chest so she could feel that he was still here. But she had already pulled away once, and Yasher knew better than to reach for something when it wasn't being offered.

"Talk to me, tell me how I can help you. Let me," he finally said, his voice quieter than he intended, lost beneath the roar of the sea below.

She let out a breath in resignation. "I don't know,"

she admitted, and those words—gods, those words—settled into his ribs like a blade turned inward.

He dragged a hand through his hair, his fingers tightening at the nape of his neck as he forced himself to hold still, to keep his voice even.

"Farah." He didn't follow with anything else, just her name, as if saying it would be enough to pull her back, to remind her of everything that had come before, everything they had built together.

She swallowed, her throat bobbing once, her jaw tightening. "I need you to trust me."

His breath caught. He had trusted her, without question, without hesitation, through every fire they'd walked into together. But this wasn't that.

This wasn't the quiet faith of lovers who'd survived too much together.

She wasn't reaching for him, she was warning him to stay back.

He had spent his entire life knowing when to fold, when to slip away before the stakes grew too high. He had known when to press his Luck and when to keep his hands off the table. He wasn't a gambler who played blind.

Yet here he was, staring at the woman he loved, watching her walk to the edge of something that *felt* too much like a point of no return.

His instincts screamed at him.

His Luck *hummed*, that static charge at the base of his skull still lingering, still unsettled. His grip tightened at his sides, nails pressing half-moons into his palms. "Tell me what's happening to you."

Her gaze finally flickered toward him, dark eyes catching just enough of the morning light to gleam. "You already know."

He did. And that was the problem.

She thought it had left her when Jeta took it away. But he knew better. He had seen the shift in her, felt the weight of it in the way she had turned on Jeta in the inn, how she had spoken with that same unshakable certainty that had made Behnaz so dangerous.

Farah had told him, once, that Behnaz had believed herself necessary. That she had seen Emari as something only *she* could fix, only *she* could shape into something strong enough to survive. And when Yasher looked at Farah now, standing on the edge of the cliffs, he realized he had never truly understood what she meant until now.

His chest felt too tight, the weight of unspoken words pressing between them.

"I need you to talk to me," he said, stepping closer. "Not push me away. Not act like this is something you can carry on your own."

She let out a soft, humorless laugh, shaking her head. "What do you want me to say?"

"I want you to tell me that you *know* this isn't you."

Silence.

Her fingers twitched, the only break in her otherwise motionless stance. The hesitation was brief, barely enough to catch—but he saw it. Maybe, just maybe he could get her to listen. He reached for her hand, slow and careful, like if he moved too fast she might vanish.

Her fingers met his—just for a moment, just enough

for warmth to spark between their skin. But it wasn't grounding. It wasn't surrender. It was goodbye.

Then she let go.

Turned back toward the cliffs like the sea had offered her something he never could.

Yasher swallowed hard. "Don't do this alone, Phoenix."

Her voice came quiet, like the wind had stripped it bare. "It's easier, Yasher."

He froze.

She tilted her head slightly, just enough that he could see the edge of her profile, her dark lashes low, her mouth pressed into a firm line.

"It is," she continued, her voice barely more than the wind. "It's easier to just… let go. To stop fighting it. To lean into what makes sense."

His pulse pounded, and he let slip the only thing that she may listen to at this point. "That's what Behnaz did."

She inhaled sharply, her spine going rigid. He regretted the words the moment they left his mouth, but he didn't take them back. He *couldn't*.

She let out a slow, measured breath, steel in her voice. "I am not her."

"No," he agreed. "But you're standing in the same storm."

Her jaw clenched.

He reached for her again, this time cupping the back of her neck, turning her towards him to draw her closer, pressing his forehead against hers. "You don't have to walk into it alone."

Her breath hitched.

For a moment, just one moment, she softened.

Then it hit.

A snap behind his ribs—violent, wrong—like his Luck had been *caught*, not moved. Not pulled the way it always was, not nudged like a whisper on the wind. This wasn't his.

Something else had touched it.

He gasped, hand flying to his chest, like he could claw it back, like he could shield it from whatever had reached across the line. Every hair on his body lifted in alarm. His Luck didn't recoil—it *hid*.

She staggered back, her eyes going wide—not with shock, but with recognition. Like she'd touched something *familiar* and hated that she had.

A tremor ran through her, deeper than a shiver, like her body trying to shake off a memory it didn't want to name.

Her hands hovered at her sides, open, unsteady, and then curled into fists, tight, controlled.

He saw the way she fought it. The way she braced herself. And it scared him more than the tremor had.

He staggered, clutching at his chest, breath torn from his lungs like he'd been sucker-punched by a god. His Luck didn't just lurch—it *cringed*. Like it had been *seen*.

His Luck had been the thing he trusted when the world didn't make sense. It had whispered in the back of his mind, pulled his hand away from flame, guided his blade without explanation. It had been his secret weapon, his compass.

Now it recoiled like a wounded thing.

Whatever had brushed against him—it didn't just notice him. It noticed the *thread*. And it *wanted* it.

He'd felt fear before. Real, pulsing, fight-or-die fear. But this? This was different. This was knowing something had looked past him, past Farah, past everything he thought he could protect—and marked it all anyway.

And if it could reach his Luck?

Then it was already too close.

<hr>

THEY WALKED BACK toward the town in silence, the wind at their backs, the cliffs fading behind them as the path narrowed between the rising hills. Yasher couldn't shake the weight pressing against his ribs, the nagging pull of his Luck curling at the edges of his thoughts. It wasn't gone, but it wasn't settled either, still hiding from whatever it was that happened at the cliffs.

Farah walked ahead, her pace steady, her spine impossibly straight. She had agreed, finally, to come back to the inn, to try to listen, to let him help. He wasn't sure if he could trust it, trust her, but he wouldn't let himself let go of her.

There was no sign of the woman who had staggered back at the cliffs, who had looked at him with uncertainty just an hour ago. Whatever had shaken her, it had been packed away. Now she moved like she was wearing her own shape too tightly, every motion clean, efficient, dangerous. Like she'd chosen a mask and wasn't planning to take it off.

She had slowed, just barely, her posture shifting in

that subtle way he recognized from years of fighting beside her. She wasn't tensing for battle, but she was watching, waiting, reading the space around them like a map written in movements and absences.

Yasher caught up to her, lowering his voice. "You feel it too. Something's changed."

She didn't look at him, her dark eyes flicking toward the buildings. "It's different than yesterday."

People moved through the square, carrying baskets of fresh bread and cloth-wrapped bundles. Merchants swept their stalls with identical motions, every arm raised in near-perfect rhythm, every smile landing just a breath too late. It was convincing from a distance, but wrong the moment he leaned in. A group of children darted between doorways, kicking a leather ball, laughing at the same intervals.

Farah turned her head slightly toward him. "Yesterday, they were acting like people."

Yasher's pulse ticked up. "And now they aren't."

Her lips pressed together, her eyes dark and unreadable.

Yasher scanned the square again, looking for something—anything—that might tell him what had changed. Then he saw her.

Afsoun.

She was standing near the entrance of the governor's home, her hands folded neatly in front of her, as if she had simply been waiting for them to return. Her coat—deep, dark fabric embroidered with shimmering thread—caught the weak light, shifting like water, like something alive.

Her eyes found Farah immediately.

Yasher felt the shift before he saw it.

Afsoun smiled like someone welcoming back a runaway piece of herself. "Farahnaz."

Farah didn't flinch—but he saw the way her hand closed into a loose fist, like she was catching something before it slipped too far.

He barely bit back a curse before stepping forward, next to Farah, but Afsoun's gaze didn't flick to him, didn't acknowledge him at all, though he knew she had seen him. She only had eyes for Farah, her expression polite, too welcoming.

Afsoun gestured toward the governor's house. "I trust your walk was... enlightening."

Farah didn't answer immediately.

He forced a grin, stepping slightly in front of Farah, just enough to shift Afsoun's focus. "Not much of a morning walk kind of person, but this place is growing on me."

Afsoun's gaze flicked to him, only briefly, before sliding back to Farah. "I doubt that, gharib."

His smile didn't falter, but his muscles coiled. She hadn't spoken like that yesterday. She had played polite, welcoming. But now? Now she spoke to him like he was a slight annoyance, standing between what she wanted.

Farah finally spoke, her voice steady. "We should check on the governor."

Afsoun's lips curved, though it wasn't quite a smile.

"Yes," she murmured, stepping aside. "That would be best."

She turned, leading them toward the door, and the

shift came like a hand on his shoulder—firm, unexpected. Not a nudge, not a whisper. Something reached for his Luck again, trying to draw it forward, like a player calling a card before it turned. His Luck pulled back into himself again, and his jaw clenched.

Farah moved first, her coat brushing against his as she passed him. Yasher followed, keeping close, his senses sharp, his body instinctively reading the space around him.

He didn't trust Afsoun.

He didn't trust this town.

And worst of all—he wasn't sure if Farah still trusted herself.

Because if she stopped... there'd be nothing left to pull her back.

CHAPTER 25

AFSOUN MOVED AHEAD of them through the governor's house, never once glancing back, as if she had no doubt that they would follow. Farah's steps were steady, measured, purposeful. She had walked through palaces and war camps, stood before rulers and executioners alike, faced men who had held her life in their hands and decided she was useful enough to let live. This woman, with all her careful grace and knowing smiles, did not intimidate her.

Yasher's presence was a steady, solid thing beside her, though she could feel the tension in the way he moved, the way his gaze flickered between Afsoun and the shadows stretching long across the floor. He had always been the cautious one, the one with an instinct for danger that had kept them alive more times than she could count. But where he saw a threat, Farah saw a test —one she was confident she would pass.

They entered the receiving hall, a space as unadorned as the rest of the house, its stone walls bare save for a few woven tapestries faded with age. A single brazier burned in the corner, its embers crackling softly, casting long shadows that flickered and danced across the floor. In the center of the room, seated on a cluster of silk-draped cushions, was the governor.

Farah's steps slowed.

The governor sat, surrounded by cushions to help him be comfortable, but he looked even smaller than he had the night prior, his body slumped deeper into the cushions as if he had been worn down by the passing hours. His skin, already thin and papery, seemed stretched too tight over his bones, the flickering lamp-light making him look almost hollowed out, as if the shadows beneath his eyes had sunk into his very skull.

She remembered how he had looked when she first saw him—frail, yes, but not like this. Something had drained him further, had settled into his bones. Yet his eyes, dark and restless, still carried that same recognition when they flickered up to her, as if he saw something in her that she had yet to name.

Farah met his gaze without hesitation, without uncertainty, without fear.

The breath that rattled from his chest was thin, barely more than a whisper, but the words that followed carried the weight of something heavy and known.

"She carries it," he rasped, his voice not quite his own. "He will be pleased. You have done well."

The silence that followed was sudden and absolute, pressing against the walls of the room like a living thing.

Afsoun's hand hesitated—a fraction of a moment, the pour of the tea slowing as if the liquid itself had thickened in the air. The movement was so slight, so imperceptible, that anyone else might have missed it. But Farah saw it. The reaction was fleeting, a flicker of something unreadable in the smooth lines of her face, glancing at Yasher before she turned her attention back to the governor with a measured slowness, her dark eyes gleaming in the firelight.

"What do you mean, honored one?" Afsoun's voice was soft, almost indulgent.

She felt Yasher shift beside her, a quiet movement, a preparation. He was waiting, bracing for the moment he would need to act. She could feel the tension radiating from him, the unspoken question in the way his fingers curled slightly at his sides, but she did not move. She placed a hand on his to calm him. She was in control here.

The governor's hands trembled slightly where they rested in his lap, his fingers twitching as if grasping at something just out of reach. His gaze flickered toward Afsoun, the slightest trace of unease slipping through his exhausted features. Then, he looked back to Farah. His lips parted, as if he meant to speak, as if there was more.

And then, his entire body shuddered.

His spine arched sharply, his breath catching in his throat as his fingers clenched into the fabric of his tunic. The teacup he had been holding slipped from his grasp, shattering against the stone floor, sending shards scattering in all directions.

Farah stepped forward instinctively, but Afsoun was already moving, already kneeling beside him, lowering him back against the cushions with a touch so careful, it might have been mistaken for tenderness.

The governor's body convulsed once, twice, and then the tremors stopped.

His chest rose and fell in uneven, gasping breaths, his fingers twitching weakly before stilling altogether. His eyelids fluttered. His body sagged, as if the tension had drained from him entirely.

Afsoun straightened, her hands lingering against the folds of the governor's tunic for just a moment longer than necessary before she turned her gaze back to Farah.

"The sickness has taken much from him," she said quietly. "He is not as strong as he once was."

For the first time since they had arrived, understanding settled inside of Farah. Afsoun was not stronger than her, not a threat, not something to fear. She was familiar. Resonant.

Behind her, Yasher shifted again, the movement subtle but unmistakable. She could feel his unease like a second pulse, the way his presence hovered just at the edge of hers, he was waiting for her to say something, to react, to push back.

She didn't. She let the silence stretch, let it speak for her.

Afsoun's lips curved slightly, just the faintest press of amusement, of acknowledgment. Then, she rose to her feet in a slow, fluid motion, adjusting the folds of her sleeves as she turned her attention back to the room as a whole.

"It is late," she said, her voice smooth as silk, calm as the still air before a storm. "You should return to the inn.

The shadows stretch long here, and there is a storm coming. Best not to lose yourself in it."

Farah turned, stepping away without hesitation, without lingering, without question. Yasher hesitated, but he followed.

As they stepped into the cool air, the streets stretching before them in empty quiet, Yasher's voice came low, quiet enough that only she would hear.

"It's like we're walking into a story that already knows its ending. Phoenix..." he began, his eyes filled with questions and concern.

Farah looked at him then, at the way the furrow in his brow had deepened, at the way his mouth had pressed into a tight line. His concern was there, etched into every line of his face, in the way his fingers hovered just at the edge of her sleeve, never quite touching but never straying far.

She reached up, her fingers brushing lightly against his cheek, the warmth of his skin grounding her.

"I'll take care of it," she murmured, the words slipping from her lips too easily, too smoothly, like a blade finding its mark.

His jaw tensed beneath her touch, but his eyes softened just slightly. "Farah—"

"I promise," she said, cutting off whatever argument was forming on his lips. "We'll see this through, and I'll make sure you all are safe."

She let her hand linger for a breath longer before drawing away, slipping her fingers into his for the briefest moment, squeezing once. A reassurance. A vow. But even as he squeezed back, she saw it. The flicker of hesitation in his eyes, the tightness at the corners of his mouth. He wanted to believe her. But part of him was still waiting for her to prove it.

She would protect him from the worst of it. Even if that meant protecting him from her.

THE SCENT of the inn clung to the air—aged wood and lingering spices from the evening's meal, the faint trace of damp wool that always seemed to settle into old buildings like this. It should have been comforting. The warmth of the hearth barely touched the coolness that had crept into Farah's bones, and the soft glow of lantern light stretching shadows across the walls felt more like an illusion of safety than the real thing.

Jeta was waiting for them.

She sat near the staircase leading to the rooms above, her cane resting across her lap, fingers curled loosely over the carved handle. Her face was composed, carefully neutral, but her eyes told a different story. Keen. Watchful. Measuring. Farah recognized the kind of scrutiny that came with someone weighing possibilities, turning over every detail, every movement.

Pari sat beside her, her usual restless energy subdued, charcoal dusting her fingertips, the edges of her sleeves already smudged from where she had wiped her hands absently. A half-finished drawing lay in front of her, but she wasn't focused on it. She was watching, small and quiet, the crease between her brows deepening when her gaze flicked over Farah, then to Yasher, then back again.

She stepped fully into the room, Yasher just behind her, his presence solid, a steady warmth in her periphery. Jeta inclined her head slightly, gaze flicking between them, settling on Farah as though she were studying something unseen.

"You took your time coming back."

The words were simple. Unassuming. But they made her pause, her shoulders tensing almost imperceptibly, the unspoken but important test that they held.

Behind her, Yasher shifted. If she turned her head just so, she would see the furrow forming between his brows, the way his mouth pressed into a tight line, concern etched into every part of him.

She met Jeta's eyes, tilting her chin slightly, keeping her expression smooth, unreadable. "There was a lot to see, much to understand."

Jeta hummed softly, a considering sound, her grip on her cane tightening just slightly. "And did you like what you saw?"

She felt the weight of it settle between them, the expectation hanging just beneath the surface of the words.

"I don't trust it," she admitted, careful, measured, each word deliberate. "But trust isn't necessary to understand something. To find out what you need from it."

Jeta's fingers tapped a slow rhythm against the wood of her cane, the motion as absent as it was thoughtful. "No, I suppose it isn't."

Something flickered in her gaze, a shift so subtle that

most wouldn't have noticed. Farah had spent years reading the most imperceptible of movements, trained to recognize the tightening of a jaw, the minute shift of weight that spoke louder than words. A breath of something not quite satisfaction, but not disappointment either.

Pari shifted beside her, her small hands pressing flat against the parchment, smearing the charcoal with the movement. Her dark eyes flicked between them, lingering on Farah too long, as if she could see what no one else could.

Jeta turned her head toward Yasher then, her voice easy. "And you?"

He let out a slow breath, rubbing a hand over his jaw before exhaling through his nose, his stance settling into something casual—except she knew him too well for that. His muscles were wound too tightly, his weight balanced in a way that meant he was bracing for something.

He didn't answer right away, only looked at Jeta for a long moment, his eyes darker than usual, mirroring the rough seas below the cliffs, shadowed by something heavier than frustration. "If you can see it, then do something about it."

Farah didn't turn to look at him. Couldn't. His voice —steady, certain, laced with that quiet desperation he never admitted aloud—cut too close. She wanted to say something. To reach for him, tell him that she had this under control. But something in her clenched instead.

Not now, a voice whispered. *Not if you want to hold on to what you've gained.*

She hated that she didn't know whether that voice was hers.

Jeta's fingers tightened around the cane.

His voice quieted but was unyielding, staring the old woman down. "The relic's out of her hands now, so fix it. Get rid of whatever it left behind."

Farah turned sharply toward him, shaking it off. "I don't need fixing. I am in control." The words were immediate, sharp-edged, but something about them didn't sound like defiance—it sounded like a warning.

Yasher didn't even glance at her. His gaze stayed locked on Jeta.

Jeta, who was watching him with something unreadable in her expression, something neither amused nor dismissive.

Her voice, when she finally spoke, was softer than expected. "You already know the answer to that, *saqalu*."

Yasher's jaw tightened.

Jeta inhaled slowly, as if she were choosing each word with care. "Only Farah can walk herself out of this at the moment. And I think we're in the way of that."

She stiffened.

Yasher exhaled sharply, rubbing a hand over his face. "You told me that before."

Jeta nodded once. "And it's still true."

Something heavy passed between them—Farah couldn't quite name it.

He rolled his shoulders, the muscles in his jaw twitching before he exhaled, long and slow. His irritation was tangible, but not sharp. She felt it run along her skin, but really didn't notice it.

"I don't like it when you test her," he muttered, quieter this time, the edge in his voice softened, but not gone.

Jeta tilted her head slightly, her sharp gaze flickering back to Farah. "Then perhaps she should stop giving me reasons to."

The words sat heavy between them, quiet but weighty.

Farah met her gaze, her heartbeat steady, measured. She didn't flinch from it. Didn't shy away. She understood what Jeta was implying, even if she didn't agree with it. She relaxed her shoulders, looking for all the world that she was cowed by the tutor.

Jeta exhaled slowly, adjusting her grip on her cane.

"You're still yourself," she said at last. A beat. A hesitation. "Mostly."

Her brow furrowed slightly. "Why wouldn't I be?"

She already knew the answer. Or she thought she did. But the question had slipped out anyway—she wanted to hear it said aloud.

Jeta's lips pressed into a thin line. "No reason."

Lie.

Farah knew it. Jeta knew she knew it. But neither of them pushed.

The silence stretched, taut and thin, until Pari's voice broke it.

"I don't like how it feels on you."

Farah turned her head sharply toward her, surprised by the quiet certainty in her words. Jeta's gaze flicked toward the child, her expression unreadable, but she softened. Just a fraction.

Farah took in Pari's small frame, the way she curled her hands into the fabric of her tunic, the tension in her thin shoulders. Something protective sparked in her chest—raw and immediate, a reflex as old as war. But beneath it, a coldness stirred. A flicker of irritation. She needed to protect her from that flicker, and she would.

She forced down that small piece. Swallowed hard. Pari's words weren't wrong. She just wasn't sure what to do about it.

Jeta's gaze settled back on her, something in it shifting, something deeper, something that wasn't just her usual cryptic amusement or teasing detachment.

"You should all get some rest," Jeta said finally, quiet but firm. "Tomorrow will be harder than today."

She should have asked what she meant by that. But she didn't. Because deep down, some part of her already understood.

And that part—the part she wasn't ready to name—wasn't afraid of what came next.

Just afraid of what it might cost.

Especially if Yasher saw it first.

CHAPTER 26

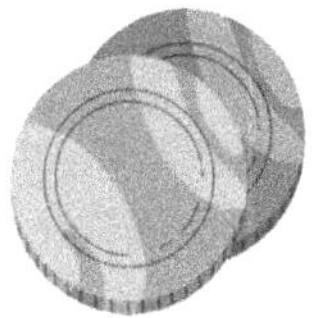

YASHER WOKE SLOWLY, the warmth of the bed pressed against his back, the quiet hum of morning settling over him. He didn't open his eyes right away, didn't need to. He knew where he was, knew the weight beside him, the shape of Farah curled in sleep, the rhythm of her breath.

For a few seconds, he let himself exist in that space, where everything felt untouched, unchanged.

But the feeling didn't last. Those feelings never did.

He turned his head slightly, enough to see her in the dim morning light. Even in rest, she carried tension, something tight around the corners of her mouth, the faint crease between her brows. She was dreaming, he could tell—her fingers twitched slightly against the sheets, her breathing shifting just enough to notice.

He reached for her before he thought better of it, brushing his fingertips lightly over her cheek. Warm. Steady. Alive.

Still Farah.

And yet.

Something gnawed at the edges of his thoughts, a deep, quiet knowing that wouldn't leave him alone. He had let himself believe it was gone—that the moment Jeta had taken the relic, whatever weight had settled on her shoulders had lifted.

It had been easier that way. Easier to convince himself that the sharpness in her voice, the way she carried herself just a little differently, was just exhaustion, just stress. Just the impossible task of trying to save a kingdom that had already been broken.

But that had been a lie, a selfish, desperate lie he had told himself because the truth was worse.

She wasn't back to normal. She was still carrying something. Still changing. He could see it in little tics on her face, small movements that were different.

He had seen it fully yesterday, in the way she had faced Jeta with that unyielding, impenetrable certainty, a certainty that reminded him too much of someone else. Of Behnaz, when she had made decisions that shaped the world in ways that could never be undone.

And he had stood there, like a fool, reassuring himself that it was over, that she had just needed time. That they had just needed time.

But time wasn't fixing this. And if time wouldn't fix it, then what the hell would?

She's still Farah, his Phoenix. But she wasn't only Farah anymore.

The thought twisted sharp in his chest, and he shook his head as if to argue with it.

Yasher clenched his jaw, staring at the ceiling, at the dim lines of morning stretching through the wooden slats of the inn's roof. He should say something. He should stop her. But how? If he pushed too hard, she'd pull away. If he waited too long, he'd lose her anyway.

What the hell was he supposed to do?

She stirred beside him, lashes fluttering as she shifted onto her back. Her lips parted slightly, her breathing changing, her body easing from sleep into wakefulness. He watched, caught in the quiet, waiting for her to open her eyes.

Dark, sharp, yet soft when she looked at him for just a moment, then changing to something more focused, further away. It was a look he knew, a look that meant she was already thinking, already moving past whatever rest she'd allowed herself to take. Already somewhere else, somewhere beyond this room, beyond him.

He swallowed against the ache rising in his chest, against the words that wanted to spill out, messy and desperate, before she could slip further away.

Stay. Stay with me, with us.

He didn't say it.

Instead, he exhaled slowly, his voice rough with sleep and something heavier, something too big for words.

"You know," he murmured, reaching out to brush his knuckles against her wrist, barely a touch at all, "I could spend a lifetime trying to convince you to stay here with me. Just us. Just this." He let his fingers trail down, a whisper of warmth against her skin. "No wars, no kings, no gods with their hands in our bones. Just waking up beside you every morning, learning how you look when you don't have the weight of the world on your shoulders. A little village, maybe in the mountains, away from everyone, and everything."

She blinked, and for a fraction of a second, something flickered in her expression. Something soft, something that might have been longing if she let it be.

She didn't let it be.

But the softness passed too quickly, like sunlight behind storm cloud. She was already gone again—somewhere behind her eyes, he couldn't follow.

"You'd get restless," she said, lips curving in a ghost of a smile, but the sharpness in her eyes didn't fade.

"Maybe," he admitted, tilting his head slightly before cupping her face in his hands, his thumbs brushing just lightly along the edges of her jaw. "Maybe a small village there instead, with a single tavern to play a few hands. But I'd always come back to you, every night."

She exhaled, a breath too quiet, too controlled. Without answering, she rolled onto her side, stretching before slipping out of bed, her bare feet making no sound against the worn wooden floor. Already moving. Already leaving him behind.

And Yasher?

He just watched her go, wondering how much of her he would still be able to hold onto when this was all over, if they survived whatever this town was going to throw at them next. Wondering if he'd even recognize her when it was.

He got dressed with mechanical motions, every piece of fabric feeling heavier than it should have. Something about the quiet between them, it wasn't rest. It was restraint. And it felt like standing too close to a fire, not sure if it would warm or consume.

Mehran and Younis sat at the table in the common room, speaking in low voices over their plates, their usual ease replaced with something heavier. Pari sat beside Jeta, her fingers curled around a piece of flatbread, though she wasn't eating. Jeta, for her part, looked weary, like she had spent more of the night thinking than sleeping.

Her gaze flicked to him as he pulled out a chair.

"Sleep well?" she asked.

He met her eyes and let out a noncommittal sound, pouring himself a cup of tea instead of answering.

He felt Farah settle beside him, her presence as steady as ever. If he hadn't spent so much of his life watching her this last year, knowing every shift of her weight, every flicker of her expression, he might have thought nothing had changed.

But he had spent the last year watching her, and he knew better.

Mehran cleared his throat, cutting through the quiet. "So what's the plan?"

Farah set her cup down with deliberate care. "We go back to the governor's house. We need to find where whatever it is that's controlling the town and purge it. Afsoun cannot be the only thing here that is... wrong."

He tensed. He had expected this, but hearing it spoken aloud still sent a chill up his spine.

Jeta leaned back slightly, tapping a slow rhythm against the table. "The governor is dying," she said, calm but firm. "There's nothing to be gained from questioning a dead man, especially when that thing is what's controlling him."

Farah met her gaze. "Then we talk to Afsoun."

Jeta's expression didn't change. "And what do you expect her to tell you?"

"The truth."

Jeta didn't blink. "And if it's not a truth you want to hear? While she is a large part of this, she is not the source."

Silence stretched between them, thick with things unspoken.

Farah exhaled, a slow, measured breath. "Then we deal with that when it happens."

He curled his fingers around his cup, his grip tight. He didn't like this. He didn't like how controlled she sounded, like the weight of the decision had already been made before anyone else had a say in it.

Jeta watched her for a long moment, then inclined her head just slightly. "I see."

The words carried weight. A test passed—or failed.

Pari shifted beside Jeta, the small crease between her brows deepening.

"It feels wrong," she murmured.

Farah turned to her, her expression softer. "What does?"

Pari hesitated, then shook her head. "Everything. There's something different from my drawings."

No one spoke.

Outside, the wind picked up, rattling against the shutters.

He let out a sharp breath and ran a hand through his

hair. "If we're going, then let's get it over with. Find out who to stab."

Farah didn't move. Instead, she turned to Younis. "Taj should be returning soon," she said, her voice steady, giving no hint that she expected argument. "I want you to ride out and wait for him outside the town gates. Make sure he made it back safely and see if he has any messages from the Mashya."

Younis nodded once, adjusting the belt at his waist.

Farah's gaze flicked toward Pari, and Yasher felt the shift before she even spoke again. "Take Pari with you."

Yasher's stomach twisted.

"No," he said, sharper than he meant to. "Wait—Farah, that's not right."

Farah didn't look at him. "It isn't safe for her here."

"That's exactly why she should stay with us," he pushed, stepping forward. "You want to send her off with one guard and no sense of what's coming while we walk into a storm we don't understand?"

Her eyes finally met his, and gods, there was distance in them he didn't recognize. "She'll be safer away from this."

"You don't know that," he said, quieter now but no less firm. "And I don't like what this place is doing to you. You want to protect her—so do I. But splitting us up doesn't feel like protection. It feels like a mistake."

Pari's head snapped up. "What?!"

Farah exhaled slowly, but her tone didn't soften. "It isn't safe for you here."

Pari shot up from the bench, her braid swinging

behind her as she planted her feet. "No! You said I could come. You said I belong here."

Farah, to her credit, didn't waver. "That was before I knew what we were walking into. I need you to be safe."

"So, I only belong here when *you* say so?" Pari's voice wasn't just sharp—it was edged with something more than a child's frustration but a warning.

Jeta, silent against the far wall, let out a low breath. Then, to Yasher's surprise, she nodded.

"Farah's right, little herald" she said. "This isn't where you need to be."

Pari turned on her, betrayal flashing across her face. "You too?"

"Pari—"

But the girl wasn't listening. "You all just want me gone. You don't trust me. Just because I said it was different than my drawings doesn't mean that I'm not needed here!"

Yasher stepped forward, crouching slightly so that his eyes met hers. "That's not true, Little Divine. We're just worried of what we're walking into. I don't like it either."

Pari turned away sharply, her hands curling into fists. "Then why are you making me leave?"

Yasher sighed, raking a hand through his hair before settling it lightly on her shoulder.

"Because we want to keep you safe." He squeezed gently. "We love you, Little Divine, and part of loving you is making sure that nothing bad happens."

She shook her head, eyes wet, but she didn't pull away.

Jeta moved closer, her cane tapping softly against the floor.

"No one is sending you away, child. Not forever. But you must go for now." Her voice was calm, smooth as still water, and she rested a light hand against Pari's head. "This road is not yours to walk."

Pari swallowed hard, her shoulders trembling.

Jeta exhaled softly, then reached out, her fingers brushing against Pari's wrist. "Do you remember what I gave you in Rumatin?"

Pari blinked, confusion flickering across her tear-streaked face. Slowly, she reached into the folds of her tunic and withdrew a small bead, smooth and dark as river stone, threaded onto a simple cord.

Jeta smiled faintly. "That bead has traveled far. It carries the memory of many roads, many places. And it will keep you close, no matter how far you go."

Pari clutched the bead tightly, her breathing unsteady. "I don't want to go."

Yasher glanced at Jeta, then back at the girl. "Taj will be waiting, and you know he'll let you talk his ear off the whole way back."

Pari sniffed. "I wanted to stay."

Yasher's throat tightened. She sounded so small, and gods help him, he wanted to say yes—wanted to promise that she'd be safe, that they could protect her without sending her away. But he couldn't lie to her. Not now. Not about this.

"I know," Yasher said, voice low. "But you trust me, don't you?"

For a long moment, Pari said nothing. Then, finally, she gave a single, reluctant nod.

Farah watched from the doorway, silent—setting herself apart from them—but he caught the flicker of relief beneath the steel in her gaze.

Jeta gave Pari's shoulder a gentle squeeze before stepping back. "Go get your things," she said. "And be quick about it, little herald."

Pari hesitated, then turned and walked toward the stairs, her steps slower than usual, but she didn't fight it anymore.

Farah let out a slow breath, nodding once to Younis. "Go as soon as she's ready, and take the camp equipment. I don't want her here for this."

Younis gave a sharp nod before following Pari to gather his own things.

Only when the door swung shut behind them did Farah turn to Yasher.

"That's done." Then, smoothly, like nothing had just changed, like she hadn't just broken the little girl's heart. "Let's go."

As they left the inn, stepping out into the gray morning, he exhaled sharply. He had spent his whole life trusting his instincts, trusting his Luck before he even had the idea that this Talent existed. They had never failed him. And right now, every instinct screamed at him to stop this. To stop her before she would do something that couldn't be taken back.

He had ignored it before. He wouldn't ignore it again.

Farah thought she could handle this alone. Even Jeta thought she could, at least that's what it seemed like, it was next to impossible to know what Jeta was thinking at any given time.

She was wrong.

He wasn't letting this happen to her.

She always came back to him. But this time, his Luck wasn't so sure. And Yasher had learned—when his instincts faltered, when the gods stayed silent—he'd have to be the one to find her, pull her back. Hold the line before she destroyed herself.

THE STREETS of Sakasan stretched before them, quiet beneath the morning light. The sky had taken on even more rolling clouds than yesterday, the air thick with the scent of the tide rolling in from the cliffs beyond the town and a true threat of rain.

He glanced at Farah, walking beside him. She hadn't spoken much since they left the inn, but her posture said enough. Her shoulders were tight, her hands flexing ever so slightly as if resisting the urge to clench.

They passed through the narrow alleys toward the governor's residence. The buildings here were tall and old, their walls worn smooth by salt air and time. No one stood in the doorways, no market stalls had been set up, no voices carried through the air save for the distant crash of waves against the cliffs.

Farah must have sensed his unease because she finally broke the silence. "You're quiet."

He let out a breath, slow and measured. "Just thinking."

She cast him a sidelong glance. "Dangerous habit."

He huffed a quiet laugh but didn't disagree. Almost normal. Almost.

They turned a corner, and there she was.

Afsoun stood at the base of the governor's house, poised, waiting for them. She did not nod in greeting, nor did she feign surprise. She only lifted her chin slightly—*a queen before her court.*

Her gaze landed on Farah first, and for a moment, Yasher could have sworn the world narrowed. The weight of it settled, not in the way of someone looking, but of someone knowing.

Farah did not hesitate. "Afsoun," she greeted, her voice smooth, controlled. "We need to speak."

Afsoun smiled, tilting her head ever so slightly. "Farahnaz. Of course."

His gut twisted. The name sounded too intimate coming from her lips, too deliberate.

Farah barely reacted. "May we speak inside?"

Afsoun considered them both, her eyes flicking briefly to him before settling once more on Farah. Then, with a small incline of her head, she turned and gestured toward the entrance.

"Of course," she said. "I have been expecting you."

Yasher had no doubt that she had.

The heavy wooden doors of the governor's residence groaned softly as Afsoun pushed them open, stepping inside without another word. Yasher hesitated. Not for show, not out of caution—his gut that told him stepping inside was a mistake. *A bad hand, already dealt.* But Farah moved without hesitation, so he forced himself forward, his boots whispering over the smooth stone.

The air inside was cooler than the streets, thick with the scent of aged wood and dried herbs that burned in a brass dish along the far wall. The silence stretched across the space, vast and waiting.

Afsoun moved ahead of them, her coat flowing like ink, her hands loose at her sides.

Farah moved forward without hesitation, her posture steady, her chin lifted just enough to remind anyone watching that she had never been afraid of walking into unknowns.

He kept his hands loose at his sides, resisting the urge to thumb the coin in his pocket. His Luck should have settled by now, come back to him after that assault yesterday. What little he could feel from it was like a timid dog, beat too often, crawled into a corner. It wasn't just stretched thin. It was fraying at the edges, slipping like sand through his fingers. *Unsteady. Wrong.*

He wanted to believe the tightness in his ribs was just nerves, just the fear he was holding from what was happening with Farah, but Luck wasn't nerves. It was his instinct. And right now, every other part of him was telling him to turn around, pull her with him, and leave this cursed town.

The light in the house was strange, filtering in at angles that didn't seem quite right, catching against the dust that drifted lazily in the still air.

Afsoun led them to a chamber that overlooked the town square. A low table sat at its center, cushions arranged neatly around it. The walls bore the same intricate carvings as the rest of the house, patterns that wove together like the knots of a story half-forgotten.

She turned to them then, her expression serene. "Sit."

Farah didn't move immediately, watching her with the sharp, assessing gaze Yasher had seen her use before interrogations. But after a beat, she stepped forward and lowered herself onto one of the cushions.

Yasher took the one beside her. He didn't miss the way Afsoun's eyes lingered on Farah as she moved, her expression unreadable.

Afsoun settled across from them with the kind of grace that felt practiced, deliberate.

"You came with questions," she said smoothly, folding her hands in her lap. "Ask them."

Farah didn't waste a breath. "The governor. What's wrong with him?"

Afsoun tilted her head slightly. "Illness takes many shapes."

He scoffed. "That's not an answer."

Afsoun smiled. "It is the only one I will give."

Farah's jaw tightened, but she pressed on. "The town —when we arrived, it felt abandoned. But now it seems... normal. What changed?"

Afsoun's dark eyes gleamed. "Nothing."

He narrowed his gaze. "That's bullshit."

Afsoun regarded him with something that might have been amusement, but it was laced with something colder, something that sent a slow chill crawling beneath his skin.

"Gharib." Afsoun let the word settle between them, tasting it like something she already owned. "Always so eager to name the shape of things before you've seen their true form."

Farah's fingers brushed against his wrist—a light, grounding touch—but her attention never left Afsoun.

"If nothing has changed," Farah said evenly, "then tell me what's already here."

Afsoun exhaled softly, leaning forward just slightly. "This town," she said, her voice gentle, almost reverent, "has simply learned not to fear its shadows."

Something cold curled in his stomach.

Farah's expression remained unreadable. "And you? What have you learned, Afsoun?"

Afsoun's lips curved just slightly, as if she found the question amusing.

"I have learned," she said softly, "that fear is a choice. One I do not wish to make."

The weight of her words settled in the air like smoke, curling into the spaces between them. He fought the urge to shift where he sat, to roll out the tension in his shoulders. He had spent years knowing when a game was rigged, when a hand had already been played before he even touched the cards. This was one of those times.

Farah sat still beside him, her expression composed, but he could see the way her fingers twitched slightly, and the bracelet rubbed against the fabric of her sleeve. She had always been good at masking her thoughts, at schooling her features into something unreadable, but Yasher had spent enough time watching her, memorizing the small tells, the little betrayals of movement. She didn't like this any more than he did.

Afsoun watched them both, calm, composed, waiting.

He exhaled through his nose. "Fear isn't a choice," he said. "It's a warning."

Afsoun smiled faintly, as if she found that amusing. "Warnings are just another kind of story," she said. "Ones people tell themselves to keep their world small. To keep their truths from changing."

Yasher's jaw tightened. "Or maybe it's the one thing that keeps them alive."

Afsoun tilted her head slightly, her gaze lingering on him just long enough to feel like a needle pressed against his ribs. "You are still here. You have not abandoned them, or her. That is your choice, chosen."

The words sent something cold curling along his spine.

Farah finally spoke, her voice measured. "What do you want from this town, Afsoun?"

The woman exhaled softly, leaning back, her hands resting lightly in her lap. "Want?" she echoed, as if the question was unfamiliar to her.

Farah didn't move, didn't let the silence settle. "This place, it's changed. Its people changed. But you aren't from here, are you?"

Afsoun's lips curved at the edges, the hint of a smile that never quite reached her eyes. "I am simply here, as it has always been."

He scoffed once again.

Afsoun's gaze flicked toward him, unreadable. "And what answer would you prefer?"

Yasher clenched his teeth, fighting the urge to get up,

to move, to get them both the hell out of this suffocating room. There was something about her presence that pressed against him, something just beyond his understanding, like standing at the edge of a cliff and not knowing how far the drop went.

Farah, though—Farah was still watching Afsoun carefully, weighing each word, each pause, as if piecing together a puzzle.

Yasher saw the moment she decided to change tactics.

"You said the town learned not to fear its shadows," Farah said. "But shadows don't just disappear. They only shift."

Afsoun considered her for a long moment before answering. "Perhaps."

Farah's eyes darkened. "And when the sun moves, when it is gone—what do they become?"

Afsoun smiled, slow and deliberate. "That depends," she murmured. "On whether you are standing in the light."

A silence settled over them, thick and full of meaning that Yasher couldn't quite place but could feel, deep in his bones.

He hated this.

Farah, to her credit, didn't waver. "The governor," she said, shifting the conversation.

Afsoun nodded once, a slow, deliberate motion. "Yes."

Farah's voice remained steady. "I would like to see him."

He stiffened beside her. He knew that tone, that

unwavering command wrapped in something that still managed to sound like a request. Farah wasn't asking.

Afsoun considered her for a long moment, something unreadable passing through her gaze. Then, with a quiet exhale, she rose to her feet.

"Very well," she said smoothly. "Come. He has been… struggling since you last spoke."

He hesitated, feeling the shift in the air. The conversation had played out like a game, but he had the sickening feeling that Afsoun had been the one holding the cards the entire time.

Farah stood, her back straight, her movements controlled. She glanced at him once, a flicker of something soft, something grounding, before she turned toward the door.

Yasher stood as well, rolling his shoulders as he forced himself to follow.

Afsoun was already walking ahead of them, leading them deeper into the governor's house.

And Yasher couldn't shake the feeling that whatever lay ahead was something they weren't meant to see.

The air in the governor's house was heavier than it had been. The house had been dim then, but now, as Afsoun led them deeper inside, it felt darker, more stifling.

Something had changed.

They had spoken with the governor just yesterday. He had been frail, exhausted, just a little worse than their first meeting, his words had come slow and had seemed to require a lot of effort, but he had spoken. He had looked at them, had acknowledged them, was aware of them. Now, as Afsoun pushed open the chamber door, Yasher felt a cold thread of unease curl tight in his ribs.

The man on the cushions wasn't the same. He was not well.

His robes hung off him like they had been draped over a skeleton rather than a living man. His skin had grown even more waxen, his cheekbones sharper, as if whatever life he had left was being siphoned away. His breath was thinner, his chest rising and falling in slow, rattling motions, each inhale stretched too far apart, each exhale barely making a sound.

Yasher felt something heavy settle in his gut.

Farah stepped forward, her movements careful, controlled. He could see the tension in her shoulders, the way she carried herself like she was preparing for a fight, though there was no enemy in sight.

"What happened to him?" Her voice was even, but there was a sharpness to it.

Afsoun exhaled softly, her face placid. "Time moves differently for some."

Yasher clenched his jaw. "He didn't look like this yesterday."

Afsoun tilted her head slightly, her dark eyes gleaming. "He is unwell, as I said."

He hated the way she said it. Like none of this was strange. Like none of this should be questioned.

Farah crouched beside the governor, her movements controlled, and slow as if not to spook the old man. Yasher knew that stillness, had seen it before, when she was pushing through something stronger than she wanted to admit. The firelight caught the sharp angles of her face as she studied the governor, her jaw clenched, fingers curled just slightly at her sides.

"Has he spoken?" she asked, voice steady. But he heard the breath she had to take before saying it.

Afsoun hummed. "Not today."

He exhaled sharply. "Yesterday, he still had his mind. His voice. If this was sickness, it wouldn't have eaten away at him this quickly."

Afsoun smiled faintly. "Perhaps he has simply given in, finally."

Farah's fingers curled into her sleeve. "Given in to what?"

Afsoun did not answer.

Yasher's skin prickled.

Silence stretched, thick and suffocating. Then—

A shift. A twitch of the governor's fingers against the fabric of his robes.

Yasher went still.

Farah didn't move, her eyes locked on him.

Then, slowly, the governor's head lifted.

It was wrong. Too slow, too stiff, like something long unused was forcing itself to function again. The dim light cast shadows over his face, sinking into the hollows of his eyes.

The governor's lips parted, but the breath that came wasn't a gasp. It was *a sigh*, like something slipping free.

"Too late. It's all too late. He comes."

The words landed in the still air like a verdict, like a truth written in stone long before they arrived.

Yasher's pulse hammered in his ears.

Farah's jaw tightened. "What?"

The governor's throat worked, a shallow, struggling inhale. His mouth barely moved, but the words came anyway.

"The door..." His voice cracked, dry as brittle paper. "Already... opening."

His Luck didn't move. Didn't twist or coil or warn. It was just... absent.

Farah leaned in, her tone sharp. "What door? What does that mean?"

But the governor's breath hitched—

Then stopped.

The silence that followed was absolute.

Yasher's breath hitched, a sharp, involuntary thing, like a blade scraping against his ribs. Cold sweat prickled at the back of his neck, a damp chill crawling beneath the collar of his shirt. The air in the room was too thick, pressing against his skin like something alive. His fingers twitched, instinct screaming at him to move, to do something, but all he could do was watch as the governor sagged, watch as his wheezing breaths turned shallow, watch as the silence swallowed him whole.

Farah didn't move. Didn't speak. He didn't know what he expected—shock, sorrow, even rage—but there was nothing. Just that same calm, quiet focus. That same terrifying composure.

Afsoun sighed—a slow, measured breath, as though she had been waiting for this very moment. Her lips curved, but it wasn't a smile of surprise or concern. She tilted her head slightly, her dark eyes gleaming, and for the first time, he realized, she wasn't reacting to the old man's death. She was confirming it happened.

Like this had all been inevitable.

***

THE ROOM WAS TOO QUIET. Not the silence of reverence or mourning, but something else—something hollow. The embers in the brazier still smoldered, their heat barely touching the cold weight that had settled over the chamber. The scent of burning herbs clung to the air, thick and cloying, as if it were trying to mask something deeper, something rotting beneath the surface.

Yasher's gaze flicked toward the governor's withered body, his face slack, his skin ashen. Just yesterday, this man had been speaking to them, his voice thin but steady. And now, he was nothing more than a shell.

Afsoun stood beside him, unmoving, her hands folded before her. She didn't look at the body with sorrow or reverence. Not even indifference. Just... expectation. Like the dead were only useful once they stopped breathing.

Farah took a slow step forward. She inhaled, then spoke with the quiet weight of tradition—a prayer used to comfort those left behind. Something to hold onto in a room that felt like it was slipping sideways.

"May the Unnamed Gods guide his soul to the Bridge, and may his soul be weighed with mercy."

Afsoun exhaled, a small sound, barely a breath of acknowledgment. She lifted one hand in an absent, almost dismissive gesture.

"Indeed," she murmured.

Nothing more.

No weight. No respect. Just a vague, indifferent acceptance, as if she were humoring a child's recitation rather than standing in the presence of the dead.

His jaw tightened.

Farah's gaze lingered on Afsoun for a fraction longer, her dark eyes sharp and searching. Then, without a word, she turned, her posture rigid as she stepped away from the body.

Afsoun followed her movements with quiet interest, her expression smooth. "We will hold his Leaving tonight."

Farah's steps halted. "Tonight?"

Afsoun inclined her head slightly. "It is necessary."

Yasher frowned. "Necessary for what?"

"The illness has taken too many," Afsoun said, her voice calm, measured. "We must be certain it does not linger."

The words were reasonable, caution for the need to protect the living, but something about the way Afsoun spoke them sent a wrongness curling deep in his gut. As if this had always been inevitable.

"You think it will come back," Farah said. Not a question. A statement.

Afsoun's smile was slight, barely more than a breath of amusement. "All things should be anticipated," she said smoothly, as if correcting them rather than answering.

"Then we will be there," she said, voice steady. She didn't look at him. Didn't wait for his input. He felt it again—that slow slide away from *we* into *she*. A line he wasn't sure how to cross anymore.

Afsoun's smile lingered, pleased, expectant. "Of course."

The silence stretched again, wrapping around them like something unseen.

Then, with an elegant motion, Afsoun turned, stepping toward the doorway, gesturing lightly for them to follow.

"The town will need to prepare," she said. "You should take what rest you can before the evening."

Rest. As if any of them would find it.

Farah's expression didn't shift, but he saw it—the barely-there hesitation, a flicker of something deep in her gaze before she turned away. A breath later, she strode past Afsoun, her boots striking the stone with quiet precision, as if forcing the doubt out of every step.

Yasher hesitated for a moment longer, his eyes flicking back to the governor's still form, the way his hands lay limp against the folds of his robe, as though they had never moved at all.

Then he followed.

As the door whispered shut behind them, Yasher felt it still clinging to him—Afsoun's voice, her presence, the echo of a gaze that knew too much.

CHAPTER 27

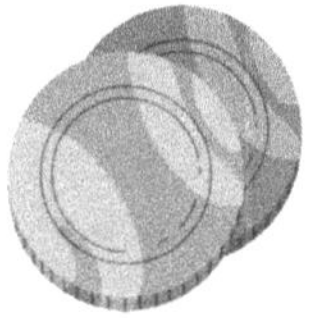

THE WALK back to the inn felt longer than it should have, with each step slowed by the weight of things neither of them said, though Yasher wanted to take her hand and just leave this place.

It wasn't the kind of silence that came with comfort, with knowing someone so well that words weren't necessary. It wasn't even the silence of tension before a game of cards, the air thick with possibility, with chance, with the thrill of the unknown.

Farah walked ahead of him, her pace measured, her posture stiff. There was an edge to her, a sharpness like a blade between them that hadn't dulled since they left Afsoun at the governor's house.

He could still hear her voice   smooth, placid, utterly unshaken. *It is only a precaution, to ensure the sickness does not return.*

His pulse thrummed against his chest, uneven and restless. He rolled his shoulders, trying to shake the tension crawling up his spine, but it stuck—tight, unrelenting.

The door creaked on its hinges as they stepped inside, and the warm scent of tea and burning wood wrapped around them, a stark contrast to the tight coil of unease that had been following them since the morning.

Mehran and Jeta were seated at the low table near the fire, a deck of cards spread between them, a quiet game playing out in the flickering light. Mehran's expression was unreadable, his fingers deft as he placed a card down, his focus entirely on the game. Jeta, on the other hand, was watching him with the faintest curve of amusement on her lips, as if she already knew how this was going to end. A small clay cup of tea rested at her elbow, steam curling lazily from its rim.

She didn't look up immediately, but he knew better. She'd been waiting for them. She placed her cards down slowly, deliberately, as if the game had never really mattered.

"You're back earlier than I expected," she murmured, finally lifting her gaze.

Farah moved to the table but didn't sit, just ran a hand through her hair, exhaling softly. "The governor is dead."

He felt the room still around those words. Even the fire seemed to quiet.

Jeta's fingers stilled against the edge of her cards. Mehran looked up then, his brows pulling together slightly, though he didn't speak.

Yasher lowered himself onto the cushion beside

Farah, stretching out his legs. "His Leaving is tonight. Afsoun's orders."

Jeta let out a slow breath, setting her cards aside. "That soon? That's not tradition."

Farah nodded, her fingers tapping lightly against the table, the spoon next to Jeta's tea quivered slightly. "She said it was necessary. That they couldn't risk waiting."

Jeta's gaze flicked toward the window, the firelight catching in her dark eyes. "Death moves strangely in this place," she murmured.

The door slammed open with enough force to rattle the shutters.

Younis.

He strode inside, breath ragged, tunic damp with sweat. His usually steady hands were clenched into fists, and for the first time since Yasher had known him, he looked shaken. Truly shaken.

Mehran was already standing, his chair scraping back against the floor. "What is it?"

"The gates were closed," Younis said, voice rough from exertion.

Farah straightened. "What?"

"When I took Pari out of the city," Younis said, running a hand through his hair, "we reached the gates, but they were locked. No guards, no movement. Just shut."

Yasher felt something cold coil in his gut.

"I left Pari on the horse," Younis continued, his words clipped, quick, as if forcing himself to stay calm. "Told her to stay put while I checked if I could unlatch them or find someone to open them."

He swallowed, his fists clenching.

Younis swallowed, his breath uneven. "I heard something." His voice dropped lower, strained. "Turned just in time to see a boy—dark-haired, maybe ten, maybe younger. He had Pari's hand before I could stop him."

Yasher's stomach twisted, something cold sliding between his ribs.

"And then?" Farah pressed, voice dangerously steady.

Younis shook his head, frustration flickering in his eyes. "Then they were gone, lost in the alleys."

Farah's expression darkened. "Where is she?"

Younis exhaled sharply, frustration evident in every movement. "They disappeared into the alleys. I searched everywhere. I couldn't find her. So, I came straight here."

Mehran swore under his breath. Jeta remained still, but her expression shifted, something sharpening in her eyes.

Silence settled over the room like a stone sinking into deep water.

Yasher was already standing, his heart hammering against his ribs.

The boy from the square.

Too calm. Too knowing. He hadn't just found Yasher that day. He'd chosen him. Moved him like a piece on a board.

And now, he'd taken Pari.

Yasher's breath came slow, steady, controlled.

He was going to find them. And they were going to regret it.

THE TOWN PRESSED in around them, its silence suffocating, a living thing that coiled tighter with each step Yasher took. He breathed in, but the air—heavy, stagnant—seemed to crawl down his throat, as though the world itself was holding its breath. The storm loomed overhead, a slow, creeping presence, dark clouds sliding across the sky like the wings of something vast and waiting. The daylight struggled to hold its ground, flickering between the breaks in the clouds, casting the streets in a sickly, washed-out glow. Windows were sealed tight, doors shut with a finality that made his skin prickle. No sounds, no movement, not even the echo of his footsteps. Nothing. No sign of Pari.

That alone was enough to feel like a blade at his throat, stealing his breath.

His boots scuffed against the worn cobblestone as they moved, his body coiled with the kind of tension he hadn't felt in years. Not since he was a boy, waiting for a fight he couldn't predict, something he didn't know the rules to. His gut twisted. Something unseen watching from the edges.

And this town? It was watching.

The wind had picked up in anticipation of bringing in the storm that he could see at the horizon, mirroring the anxiety that grew every minute they couldn't find Pari.

Farah moved beside him, her presence a steady point in the unraveling thread of his thoughts, but even she had changed. There was a sharpness to her steps, a new way she held her shoulders, as if she were preparing for a fight she wasn't sure she would win. It wasn't the confidence he was used to—wasn't the calculated surety of the Hand of the Mashyana. This was something else, something more brittle. At least somewhere in there she still cared about Pari.

Something he didn't recognize.

Younis and Mehran were stone-faced, moving with an efficiency that made Yasher feel like a damned amateur. Their training was evident in every step, in the way they kept their hands loose but ready, their eyes never stopping. *Good soldiers*, he thought grimly. And yet even they weren't at ease. They knew something was wrong here, too.

They just didn't know just how very wrong it was.

But Jeta did.

The moment she stopped moving, Mehran and Younis responded like wolves sensing a change in the wind. They shifted seamlessly, Mehran angling toward the rear while Younis took the side, both instinctively guarding their flanks. Yasher halted a half-second later, his breath stilling in his chest.

His Luck should have been pulling him forward, guiding him. Instead, it writhed—tangled, splintering apart the moment he tried to grasp it. It was like trying to follow a thread only to find it fraying in his hands, pulling him in a dozen directions at once. Wrong. Everything felt *wrong*. Every step he took, the pull of it flickered and faded, dragging him forward, then twisting sideways, like something unseen was pulling him apart thread by thread.

He clenched his teeth, pushing through the static in his head.

Jeta caught the shift in his expression. "Nothing?" she murmured, quiet enough that only he could hear.

Yasher shook his head. "It's pulling me in every damn direction," he muttered under his breath. "I can't tell what's real and what's not."

Jeta hummed, something thoughtful in the sound, but she didn't press further. Instead, she turned to Farah. "Where would they take her?"

Farah exhaled slowly, her gaze flicking toward the center of town, where the square sat empty.

"Somewhere hidden. Somewhere people wouldn't stumble upon." She paused, fingers curling slightly at her side. "If they were going to hurt her, they wouldn't have taken her at all. They need her for something."

A prickle crawled up the back of Yasher's neck.

"They closed the gates to keep people in," Mehran said, voice low. "Not out. They've been planning something."

Younis, still scanning the alleys, clicked his tongue softly. "And the town is too quiet. They're watching us."

No one argued.

Jeta was looking toward the cliffs.

"The cliffs?" Younis' brow furrowed, voice low but firm. "Why would they—"

Jeta cut him off.

"Because it's where Mazdavir's influence began from. Probably an old sanctuary of his that was supposed to have died out three hundred years ago."

Silence slammed into them like a hammer.

Yasher's stomach twisted. His pulse kicked hard against his ribs.

Jeta had *never* said that name before, let anyone know that she knew exactly what, or who, they were going against.

His fingers curled into a fist at his side. "What did you just say?"

Jeta met his gaze evenly, her eyes dark, unreadable. "You heard me. I may be old, but I didn't mumble. The Divine Rot stinks all over this place."

Farah tensed beside him. Her hand hovered near her belt, not touching a weapon, but close enough. "How do you know about Mazdavir?"

Mehran and Younis exchanged glances, unreadable expressions shifting between them. They weren't strangers to whispers of the *Darkness*, the slow rot that had seeped through Emari over the years. But Mazdavir? That was something else.

Jeta exhaled slowly, then stood—not just rising, but unfolding, like something waking from its disguise. A blade drawn. A truth unhidden. The slight tremor in her fingers vanished. The weight on her shoulders was gone. And for the first time, Yasher realized just how carefully she had been playing them.

She didn't hunch her shoulders. Didn't lean against the cane like she had back at the inn, instead holding it as if ready to use it as a weapon. And for one breathless moment, Yasher's Luck went still—like it was holding its breath. Like it recognized her before he did.

The subtle shake in her movements vanished, and for the first time since Yasher had met her, she stood in full, unyielding presence—not a frail traveler, not a kindly teacher.

Something older. Something solid. Something that didn't belong here.

Farah's fingers flexed slightly. Yasher felt her shift beside him. Not enough to pull away, but enough to be aware.

Jeta turned toward Farah. "I knew you'd need support the moment I sniffed out what was on that relic you carried. I just wasn't sure about so many other things until now. Do you trust me?"

Farah's lips pressed into a thin line.

Yasher took a step forward, his voice sharper than he meant. "You're still speaking in riddles, old woman."

Jeta exhaled through her nose, almost tired.

"If I didn't," she said at last, her voice low, steady. "You wouldn't know I was still myself, *saqalu*."

Farah's gaze lingered on Jeta for a moment longer before she finally exhaled. "Fine."

Younis cleared his throat. "The cliffs, then."

Jeta nodded, then turned toward the cliffs.

"That's where they took her."

He glanced at Farah. She was still looking at Jeta. She wasn't doubting the woman, she was considering her, weighing her out as either an ally or an enemy.

A cold prickle ran down his spine.

He didn't trust it. Not for a damn second.

But he would find Pari. Even if he had to tear this cursed town to the ground with his bare hands, he would bring her back.

CHAPTER 28

THE CLIFFS SWALLOWED THE LIGHT, the jagged rocks rising around them like the ribs of some ancient beast, hollowed out and waiting. Every step forward felt heavier, the weight of something unseen pressing against her ribs, curling around the edges of her thoughts.

Pari was here.

Farah knew it with the kind of certainty that made her breath come sharper, that sent a low hum through her bones. Not instinct. Not logic. Something else. A pull that curled through her body, winding around her like unseen hands, guiding her forward. Stronger than doubt. Stronger than choice. But she didn't know if it was her certainty or something else's. Something that had wrapped itself around her thoughts, wearing them like a mask.

It felt right. But that didn't mean it was hers. She was meant to be here, she knew that much.

Ahead of them, Jeta walked with measured purpose,

leading them along the narrow path that wound between the cliffs. The woman no longer carried the weight of age in her stride—the quiet disguise she had worn since Rumatin now all but abandoned. The cane remained in her hand, its carved vines twisting along the wood, but she was wielding it more like a tool than a necessity now.

She watched her shift, the way the old woman straightened just a little too easily, the way the lines of weariness had faded from her face when she thought no one was looking. But here, in the growing gloom of the cliffs, it was more apparent than ever. Jeta was no more an aging scholar than Farah was an emissary of peace.

She had never claimed to be anything other than what she was—a tutor, a scholar, a guide. And yet.

Farah studied her now, the subtle yet undeniable changes drawing her attention. Her hair, once streaked liberally with gray, now carried only the faintest threads of silver. The fine lines at the corners of her eyes had softened, her face gaining an almost ageless quality that had not been there before. It wasn't dramatic—no one looking at her casually would think her transformed—but to Farah, who had been watching closely, who noticed the things that others dismissed, it was impossible to ignore.

But Farah had spent her life understanding the way metal whispered beneath her fingertips, how even the stillest blade hummed with potential if one knew how to listen. And this—this was not a trick. She never really knew what Jeta's Talent was, only that it allowed her to help strengthen and grow others' Talents. It seemed the old woman had some Talent that allowed it for herself as well.

Jeta moved with the certainty of someone who was not just familiar with the divine, but woven into it. A part of her wondered if Jeta had simply learned how to understand herself better than Farah had.

Her speech about Mazdavir and a long-dead sanctuary was more surprising than her transformation. Before Behnaz's deathbed confession, Farah had not known anything other than old folktales of the Darkness that sprang from the Unnamed Gods' wars before they left this plane. And for all that the old woman said, it was more than they'd known, and she was sure that she had more knowledge she wouldn't share without persuasion.

After they gathered Pari back from whatever this town was trying to do to her, she wanted a long talk with the old woman.

Yasher reached for her, his fingers brushing against hers—light, tentative, a question more than a touch. But when she didn't take it, his fingers curled slightly, as if resisting the instinct to pull her back to him. She wasn't just focused—she was fixed on bringing the little girl back to them, keeping her safe.

She wanted to take his hand. But some part of her—sharp, quiet, not hers—resented the idea.

It whispered that comfort was weakness. That softness would break them. That she had to carry this alone.

And the worst part? It still sounded like her. Her from before she'd met him.

She knew what he was thinking, could feel it in the

way his eyes lingered on her too often, the way he stayed close even when he didn't need to. Yasher was afraid for her. He thought she was slipping, thought she had already gone too far.

And maybe she had.

But what other choice did she have? She must keep the rest of them safe from whatever they were heading towards.

The wind shifted as they reached the mouth of the cave, as if pushing them away from it.

She stopped, her gaze tracing the jagged overhang of rock that framed the entrance.

It wasn't an entrance, it was something waiting for them.

Not in the way a cave should be. The thing inside knew her, had always known her, and was waiting for her to remember it back.

The stone should have been rough, worn by time, but it wasn't—it was too smooth in places, as if touched too often by hands that no longer exist. The carvings weren't just remnants, they were preserved, sharp-edged where they should have been eroded, as if the rock itself refused to let them fade. A door built to last. A door built to open.

It was a door.

Jeta stopped beside her, tilting her head slightly, considering the archway.

"No," she murmured, her voice quiet but absolute. "Not a cave. A door."

Yasher exhaled sharply. "Of course it is."

She ignored him, stepping forward, trailing her fingers lightly along the stone. Beneath her touch, the rock felt unnaturally cool, the pulse of something deeper thrumming beneath the surface.

A heartbeat. A presence.

She swallowed, steadying herself. "What is this place?"

Jeta was silent for a long moment, her gaze unreadable. Then, slowly, she said, "It is not a place meant to be found. It is a sanctuary of a memory. More than likely, where Behnaz put us all on this path."

Farah's stomach tightened.

Pari was inside. That much she knew. And she would save her.

Something stirred in the air around them, a shift in the pressure, a whisper against the skin, as if the very stone was holding its breath.

Mehran and Younis had drawn closer, their movements efficient, measured. They were trained soldiers, and their instincts were already bracing for what lay ahead.

Yasher shifted beside her, rolling his shoulders. "Do you hear that?"

Farah did.

The sound started as a whisper, barely audible beneath the rush of the wind. Then it thickened, layered, a hundred voices folding into each other, their rhythm not quite human. It wasn't coming from inside the cave.

It was coming from the stone itself.

She met Yasher's gaze.

Jeta's fingers tightened around the head of her cane.

Mehran and Younis exchanged a glance.

Farah turned back to the darkened mouth of the cave.

The voices in the stone weren't just calling.

They were welcoming her.

And for a breath, a heartbeat, she wanted to answer.

FARAH'S BREATH came slow and steady, but her pulse betrayed her, hammering against the cage of her ribs as she took in the cavern before her. The air was thick, the scent of damp stone and something faintly metallic lingering like the aftertaste of a storm. The darkness clung to the walls in uneven pools, the flickering light of scattered lanterns barely strong enough to cut through the gloom.

Pari was small in the center of it all. Farah forced herself to focus, cataloging every detail with the precision she had honed over the years—the slight tremor in the girl's frame, the way her fingers curled in tight fists against bound wrists, the slow, shallow rhythm of her breathing. Alive.

Farah's first thought should have been fear. Her second should have been action. But what pulsed through her instead—what twisted low in her chest—was something quieter, something curious. As if part of her already knew Pari was not in danger.

Not yet. Not until she made a mistake.

The space wasn't entirely silent, though it should have been. The quiet was too deep, too heavy, a waiting thing rather than an absence. And then, as if the shadows themselves had taken shape, Afsoun stepped forward.

Farah knew what she was supposed to feel. Rage. Fury sharp enough to carve through the stone beneath her feet, cold and unyielding as the metal that hummed in her blood. But she didn't.

Afsoun did not simply stand in this space—she filled it, as if the cavern itself had bent to accommodate her. As if the shadows at her feet stretched not away from her, but toward her, drawn like ink spilling into water. Farah's gut twisted. Afsoun did not wear this place like a woman standing in a room. She wore it like a second skin.

She watched the slow tilt of Afsoun's head, the way her lips curved into a smile that did not meet her eyes. It was not a human expression. It was something practiced, something learned, the way a child mimicked an adult's words without understanding their weight.

"You came," Afsoun said, her voice carrying across the cavern with a softness that did not belong in a place like this. "As I knew you would."

She did not move. She let the weight of the silence settle, let the air stretch tight around them. She wanted Afsoun to speak first. Wanted to see what shape her words took, what intention curled beneath them. But the longer she waited, the quieter her thoughts became. As if something deeper—something colder—was writing the script.

She didn't like how natural that felt. She fought against that feeling, focusing on bringing Pari out of this place.

Afsoun's smile remained, but something in it shifted, as if she had expected a different reaction, as if she had thought Farah would step forward, would engage, would take her place in whatever conversation had already been decided.

Behind her, she could feel Yasher's presence, the warmth of him just at her back, the steady pull of something grounding in the way he existed beside her. It was an unspoken thing, the knowledge that if she moved, he would move with her. If she struck, he would already be braced for the fallout.

But this was not a battle of blades. Not yet.

She lifted her chin, forcing herself to ease her stance, to let her body slip into something more neutral, more unreadable.

"Where else would I be?" she said, and her voice came smoother than she expected, free of the coiling at the base of her spine.

Afsoun's gaze flickered, something amused in the shift of her expression, as if she were pleased by Farah's response.

"You understand, then," Afsoun said, taking a slow step forward, the motion so fluid it barely seemed to disturb the ground beneath her. "That this was always meant to happen."

Farah wanted to scoff, to reject the shape of that fate outright. But another part of her—quieter, deeper—wanted to ask what it meant, curious to the response.

She chose to not speak.

The words slotted into a familiarity, too easy, settling alongside memories of other voices that had spoken with the same certainty, the same quiet authority. The Mashyana had spoken that way, once. Behnaz had shaped the world around her with words that left no space for doubt, no room for refusal.

But Farah had doubted. She had refused. And she would again. She would take this control and bend it to her will instead of the other way.

She exhaled slowly, tasting the damp air, the faint, acrid bite of oil from the lanterns, the distant scent of something that did not belong in a place of stone and silence. She let her eyes move, catching the faintest shift in the shadows behind Afsoun, the way they did not seem entirely her own. They split from her, creating a swirl of different variations of darkness.

Farah closed the distance between them by half. She felt the change in the air as she moved, the way the temperature seemed to shift, a slow, creeping warmth curling around the edges of the cold.

Pari let out a soft sound, a whisper of movement, and Farah's gaze flickered toward her, but she did not turn away from Afsoun fully.

"She is unharmed," Afsoun said smoothly, following Farah's glance. "For now."

Farah stilled. The words had been spoken lightly, almost carelessly, but they landed with weight.

The floor of the cavern felt steadier beneath her feet. The weight in her chest had settled, cold and sharp and clear.

Farah smiled, slow and deliberate, letting it form like a blade unsheathed.

"I think," she said quietly, "that you should choose your next words very carefully. She is precious to me."

Afsoun tilted her head, dark eyes gleaming in the flickering firelight. There was purpose to the stillness of her posture, she did not shift or sway as others did, as if she were rooted in the stone itself, a part of the cavern rather than merely standing within it.

The air in the cavern was thick, humid with the heat of too many bodies packed into the confined space, but there was a lingering chill that did not belong beneath it. It clung to the back of her neck, feather-light and insidious, the sensation of being watched not by Afsoun, but by the swirling darkness behind the woman.

From the corner of her eye, she caught the shift of movement behind Afsoun's shoulder. The walls were lined with figures, their faces lost to shadow. They did not fidget, did not murmur among themselves like any gathered group might. They were still—unnaturally still —as if waiting for permission to move.

Farah had spent too many years in the court of the Mashyana not to recognize a performance when she saw one.

Afsoun wanted her to see this.

She wanted Farah to know that she was not alone here. That she had an audience.

Farah did not rise to the bait. "Is that what this is? A show?"

Afsoun's lips curved—not quite a smile, but close.

"No," she said smoothly. "Not a show. A lesson. A call. An entrance."

Farah's fingers twitched at her side, the urge to reach

for her blade rising like a slow-building storm. Not yet. Not yet. She had to see the shape of this first, had to understand the game before she could upend the board.

Afsoun lifted a hand, trailing her fingers through the air as if feeling the texture of the space around them. And the air did shift, ever so slightly, a ripple that could not be seen, only felt—a distortion at the edges of perception.

"You feel it, don't you?" she murmured. "The shift beneath your feet. The way the world bends at its edges."

Farah clenched her jaw, forcing herself not to react.

She did feel it. Not just here. Not just now.

She had felt it from the moment she had touched the Veil fragment. From the moment she had carried it, let it seep into her veins, into her thoughts. And even now, with it locked away, with Jeta guarding it, she could still feel the faintest pull, like the ghost of a chain still wrapped around her wrist.

It had never fully left. Not even when Jeta locked it away while they were still on the road.

There were moments—small, precise—where she had thought things more quickly than she should. Responded before thought had caught up. Spoken with certainty that hadn't come from her.

Farah exhaled slowly. "I feel many things," she said evenly. "Mostly, I feel irritation."

Afsoun exhaled a quiet laugh. "You are bold, Farahnaz."

Afsoun lifted her hand, slow and deliberate, and the air around her seemed to thrum, a subtle vibration that was felt more than heard. It was not magic in the way

Farah knew magic—it was something else. Something older. Something that did not belong in this world.

Farah did not move.

Behind her, Yasher shifted, the sound of leather creaking softly as he adjusted his stance. He had not stepped forward, had not spoken, but she felt him like a weight at her back, steady and constant.

She did not need to look at him to know his expression.

"I wonder," Afsoun murmured, "if you believe you understand what is happening here."

Farah's gaze flicked to Pari, bound, small, and still in the vastness of the cavern.

A thread of heat coiled in her chest, a furious protectiveness that burned bright and sharp.

"I believe," she said, voice steady, "that you are going to release the girl. And then we are going to walk out of here."

Afsoun hummed, as if considering. "Is that so?"

Farah stepped forward again. The air changed around her, the temperature a strange thing—warm and cold at once, like standing at the threshold of a forge, feeling the heat licking at the edges but never quite touching the skin.

"You have begun something that I don't believe you understand," Farah continued. "You have taken that little girl, and I will not stand for that."

Afsoun studied her, dark lashes lowering ever so slightly, like the slow shuttering of a lantern's glow.

Then she turned her gaze toward the entrance of the cavern.

"Would you like to see why that cannot happen?" she asked, her voice a silken thread.

Farah's gut tightened.

Afsoun lifted her hand again, and the shadows along the walls seemed to deepen, shifting with unnatural ease.

A sound, low and rhythmic, echoed from the the dark sphere that the swirling darkness created.

Not footsteps. A presence. A force.

And then, from the blackness beyond the firelight, something unfolded itself from the dark.

At first, it was nothing—just an absence, an interruption in the shifting light. But then it moved, and Farah's stomach lurched, because she knew that motion. Not human. Not quite beast. Something between.

A figure, its form indistinct, its edges fraying like an ink-drenched page left to dissolve in water. It did not breathe, did not sway as a living thing would. It did not step forward so much as it was suddenly closer.

It had no eyes. No mouth. And yet she knew, with the certainty of a blade at her throat, that it saw her. It wasn't fully there, but would be soon enough.

Afsoun exhaled, almost fondly.

"You see, Farahnaz," she murmured. "You were always meant to come here."

The words didn't strike her like a lie. They settled—gently. Almost kindly. And for a moment, Farah did not reject them.

She simply… recognized them.

Her breath came slow and steady. Her mind cataloged everything at once—the positioning of the shadows, the weight of the cavern, the presence that stood just at its edge.

She let the steel of her resolve settle deep in her bones. She did not look at Yasher. She couldn't see his face and still push through.

She already knew how this was going to end.

She let it in.

CHAPTER 29

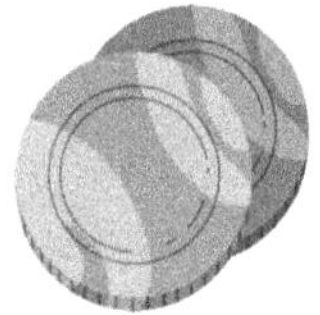

THE SHADOWS THICKENED at the edges of the firelight, stretching long and restless, moving as though stirred by an unfelt wind. The air hung heavy, thick with damp stone and something deeper, something that set Yasher's teeth on edge. The scent of burning tallow from the torches lined along the walls mixed with the distant tang of salt carried in from the sea beyond the cliffs, but underneath it all, there was a sharpness, a metallic note that felt like the taste of blood just before a wound breaks open.

He had spent a lifetime honing his instincts, trusting the whispers in his bones that told him when to press forward and when to turn away, when to push his Luck and when to let a hand pass him by. That same instinct was screaming now, loud and urgent, wrapping cold fingers around his spine, urging him to move, to act, to do something. And yet, for all that, he was rooted in place, standing on the threshold of something he did not yet understand, watching as the world bent in ways it shouldn't.

Afsoun stood at the heart of it, the only unmoving thing in a space that pulsed and twisted. Her eyes, dark and endless, were trained solely on Farah, and that was what made Yasher's stomach twist.

Because Afsoun wasn't looking at them as intruders or enemies. She wasn't looking at them as obstacles in her path.

She was looking at Farah as though she recognized her, not in the sense that they'd met recently, but that she'd known her for a very long time. Longer than should have been possible.

Farah was standing too still.

She was braced, steady, poised in that careful, deliberate way she always was before a strike—but there was no weapon in her hand, no blade she was readying, no enemy she had marked. Instead, there was something else. A tension coiling just beneath her skin—understanding.

The way she looked at Afsoun, the way she held herself, the way she wasn't recoiling from the shadows creeping at the edges of the cavern—it made Yasher's blood go cold.

And then, the shadows moved, some splitting off, creating something different. A void in the world.

A shape peeled itself from the darkness, slowly.

Yasher felt it before he truly saw it, the wrongness of it pressing against the edges of his senses like something twisting the very air around them. It wasn't a person. It wasn't even a thing. It was an absence, a wound torn into the shape of something that had never belonged in this world.

The figure was tall and thin, its form bleeding at the edges like ink spilling into water, shifting between shapes that never quite settled. It had no face, no eyes, no mouth, nothing that should have made Yasher feel watched—and yet he did.

His breath hitched—just for a second, just long enough to feel the tightness coil around his ribs, wrapping around his lungs like unseen hands squeezing, pressing. His body knew before his mind did. Every nerve, every instinct, every whisper of Luck in his blood screamed the same thing.

Run. Pull her back. Get her out of here.

But he couldn't move. Couldn't breathe right.

He had been in more dangerous situations than he could count, had faced enemies whose names he would never know, had felt the sharp edge of blades and the weight of danger pressing against his back more times than he cared to remember.

But this was different. This wasn't a game. This wasn't a gamble. This wasn't something he could talk his way out of, wasn't something he could manipulate into turning in his favor.

This was just wrong.

He felt his Luck stir, felt it shift and strain, the way it always did when something was about to tip the wrong way. Usually, it was a warning, a tug at his ribs that told him when a card was about to turn against him, when a step forward would lead him into a trap, when a roll of the dice would come up empty.

It wasn't just a warning. It was fear.

The air around them pulled inward, a breathless hush, a slow tightening that made the walls seem closer than they had been moments before. As if space itself had bent, waiting for her words.

"You see, Farahnaz," she murmured, the syllables drawn out, deliberate, final. She wasn't just speaking it. She was sealing it.

You were always meant to come here.

His chest felt tight, breath coming short as he glanced at Farah, at the way she was standing, unmoving, unshaken, her gaze locked on the thing in the dark. She wasn't afraid.

She should have been afraid.

His gut twisted, something deep and old and wrong crawling up the back of his spine, curling cold fingers around his throat.

And then, he saw it.

The thing that made his breath hitch, that sent a cold, clawing panic through his veins more than the dark figure behind Afsoun.

Farah wasn't recoiling. She wasn't stepping away.

She wasn't looking at the thing as something to be feared.

She was looking at it like something remembered, like something she had seen in a dream she couldn't forget.

Not awe. Not terror. Worse—acceptance.

His pulse pounded in his ears, and suddenly, he needed her to move.

He needed her to look at him, to shake off whatever hold this place had on her, to not let this happen.

"Farah," he said, voice low, steady, but pleading.

She blinked. The smallest crack.

He took a step forward, closing the space between them, not caring about the eyes watching, not caring about the thing in the dark, not caring about anything but getting her back.

His fingers twitched, instinct pulling at him, Luck rising to meet the moment, and before he could think, before he could second-guess himself, he reached for her.

His hand found hers.

Farah's breath hitched.

For a second, she hesitated.

For a second, Yasher felt the weight of her pulse against his fingertips, felt the warmth of her skin, felt her.

And then— She let go.

She let go, not with resistance. Not in anger, but with a softness that felt like goodbye.

His fingers twitched as the warmth of her skin disappeared, leaving behind only the cold press of air, the unsettling weight of something missing. Something being taken.

Farah didn't even look back.

Afsoun's fingers moved at her side, a subtle movement, barely perceptible, but the air responded. Shadows stretched and doubled, curling at the edges, their substance shifting between solid and incorporeal with each flicker of the firelight. The heat of the cavern thickened, pressing in around them, but there was a sharpness beneath it, cold and biting, like the breath of a winter storm before it broke over the cliffs.

His body knew before his mind did, every muscle coiling tight expecting a strike, anticipating an unseen blade poised just beyond the veil of flickering darkness. His Luck, unpredictable as it had been, roiled in his chest, a twisting thing that tugged at the edges of his perception, warning him.

The moment he moved, he felt it go wrong.

It was as if the ground had been pulled out from under him, but not in any way he understood. His balance faltered, his footing shifting in a way that made no sense, his pulse kicking against his ribs as the sensation of being redirected hit him like an unseen force. Not stopped—pushed.

Like his Luck had been unraveled and rewoven by someone else's hand. It made his skin crawl. His Luck had always been his—wild, yes, but his. Now it felt... borrowed. Bent to someone else's will.

He caught himself before he went sprawling, his breath a sharp inhale through his teeth, his body responding by pure instinct. His boots scuffed against the cavern floor, the rough stone biting through the worn leather, the sound lost beneath the low, rhythmic pulse of something unseen beyond the veil of flame and shadow.

And when he looked up, he met Afsoun's gaze.

She was watching him.

The curve of her lips was subtle, not quite a smirk, not quite a smile, but knowing, inevitable.

Yasher's fingers twitched toward the hilt of his blade,

the worn leather grip familiar beneath his fingertips, but he didn't draw it. Not yet. Not when Pari was still bound to that altar. Not when Farah was still standing too close to Afsoun.

His pulse beat against his ribs, too hard, too fast, but his voice was steady when he spoke. "Phoenix."

She didn't look at him.

Didn't even turn her head.

Her stance was unyielding, shoulders squared, breath measured, the unwavering confidence of someone who was exactly where they wanted to be. Where they thought they were meant to be.

Yasher felt something cold creep along the edges of his thoughts.

He took a step closer.

"Farah," he said again, lower this time, deliberate.

Her fingers twitched, just barely, before she finally turned to look at him.

And Yasher hated what he saw.

Because it was her.

But it was more.

Something unfamiliar. Something hungry.

His mouth went dry.

"Come with me," he said, and it wasn't a demand, wasn't even a request—it was a plea.

Farah tilted her head slightly, as if considering, her gaze searching his face, her brow drawing together in the faintest crease of confusion.

Then she exhaled, long and slow.

"I am exactly where I need to be," she said, and the words struck him harder than any blade.

Not only because she believed them, but because, deep down, so did he.

His stomach twisted, his grip tightening on his blade.

Behind him, Jeta shifted, her breath a quiet thing in the heavy air, but she didn't speak. Didn't interfere, as if they'd already lost. That, he would not accept.

And Afsoun—Afsoun laughed.

It was soft, smooth as silk unraveling beneath deft fingers, a hum of amusement that carried through the cavern like a whisper against stone.

Afsoun exhaled, long and slow, as if breathing in the moment she had been waiting for.

"Ah," she murmured, the sound almost fond, almost reverent.

And then she smiled.

"There you are."

Yasher's stomach twisted, but he forced himself to tear his gaze away—just for a breath, just long enough to flicker toward Pari. She was still bound, still small, still far too quiet. Her wrists, wrapped in thin restraints, had begun to redden, small bruises blooming like ink beneath her skin. Her shoulders trembled with the effort not to cry out, the tension in her small frame a silent scream held too long.

His foot shifted, barely a fraction, instinct screaming at him to move, to do something—

And then Farah turned.

Slowly. Deliberately. Not like she was answering a call, but like she already knew he would try. He could feel her slipping away.

Not all at once. Not in a way that was obvious to anyone else.

But he knew her.

He knew every flicker of thought that passed behind her eyes, every subtle shift of her expression that betrayed what she was feeling even when she didn't want to show it.

And right now, she was not looking at him the way she should have been.

Not the way she had always looked at him.

Not with fire, with exasperation, with that quiet, relentless pull that had tethered them together from the very beginning.

She was looking at him like she was seeing something distant.

Like she remembered him, but only in the way someone remembers the warmth of a fire they've long since walked away from.

Something that no longer mattered.

A hollow feeling opened in Yasher's chest.

This wasn't like her fight with Jeta. This wasn't like the anger, the sharpness, the way she'd been pulling away in pieces, slowly, the way he could feel something inside her shifting but had convinced himself he could hold her steady long enough to bring her back.

This was different. This was slipping.

This was losing.

He clenched his jaw, his hand tightening around the hilt of his blade, but he didn't draw it. Not yet. Not while Farah stood so still, so poised, as if she belonged here. Not while Pari's thin wrists were still bound, her small hands clenched into fists. The knots were intricate—deliberate. This wasn't a child taken for leverage. This was something ritualistic. He didn't know the shape of it yet—the rules, the lines drawn in shadow—but his gut told him this wasn't the end. It was the beginning of something.

Afsoun shifted slightly, her coat catching the light in a way that made its embroidery shimmer. The starlit lines along its edges seemed to pulse faintly, a rhythmic shimmer that wasn't just light—it was intention. Like the threads weren't stitched but bound. Like the coat didn't just belong to her, but obeyed her.

She exhaled softly, tilting her head, watching him. Not Farah—him.

"Still thinking you can win?" she murmured, voice laced with something that sent his stomach twisting. "Poor gharib. You don't even know what game you're playing."

She knew.

She had been waiting for this.

He would kill her for it. But this wasn't about Afsoun anymore. It was about Farah. About the woman who had once dragged him out of a crumbling cavern room with blood on her hands and fire in her eyes.

His fingers curled around the hilt of his blade. He didn't think. Didn't hesitate. He was going to move.

And then Afsoun snapped her fingers.

And the shadows surged.

Yasher's breath burned in his lungs, his ribs pressing tight against the unseen force that held him in place. The cavern was alive around him, the air thrumming with more than just power—something sentient, shifting, waiting.

And Farah had just stepped toward it.

The shadows surged.

They did not spread like ordinary darkness. They did not slither like smoke curling at the edges of firelight. They pulsed, as if the cavern itself had a heartbeat, as if the very act of Farah crossing that threshold had breathed life into something that had been lying in wait.

The weight against his chest tightened, pressing his back harder against the stone wall, pinning him down with an unseen force that felt neither solid nor incorporeal. His Luck twisted inside him, frayed and tangled, unable to slip between the cracks the way it always had. As if something else was holding the threads now.

He tried to move—tried to wrench himself free, to tear his body forward through sheer force of will—but the silver around his wrist burned colder, a tether he could not break. It wasn't just metal. It was her. And yet —not only her. It was the echo of whatever was threading through her will like fine wire, tightening its grip with every step she took.

The shadows shifted with intent, their edges stretching toward Farah—greeting her.

Yasher clenched his teeth, his pulse hammering against the inside of his skull. "Farah—" His voice broke, raw, his throat scraped dry by the weight of the air. "Don't—"

She hesitated.

For one breath.

For one single, fragile moment.

The world balanced on a knife's edge.

Then Afsoun spoke.

"You feel it, don't you?" Her voice curled through the space between them, wrapping around Farah. "The shape of it. The way it was always waiting for you."

Farah exhaled, and Yasher's stomach turned cold.

Because it was relief.

Not fear. Not hesitation. Not the fire of resistance he had expected.

It was acceptance. She took another step.

He wrenched against the invisible grip, his muscles screaming as though he were dragging his own body through wet sand, through tar, not meant to be fought. His breath turned ragged, his veins burning with effort, but the harder he fought, the tighter the pull became— as if it were learning, as if it were adapting to him.

And then the altar behind Afsoun began to glow.

A deep, unnatural light, one that did not flicker like fire, did not shine like the moon, but burned from within, casting long, stretched silhouettes against the cavern walls. Pari was still bound to it, her face pale, her breath too shallow.

She turned her head just slightly.

Her lips parted.

And she whispered one word.

A name.

"Jeta! Mehran! Younis!" he bellowed, his voice cracking through the cavern like a lash. "Get Pari!"

The reaction was instant.

Mehran surged forward, his soldier's instincts kicking in, reaching for the bindings around the girl's wrists. Pari's eyes were wide, frightened, but her breathing was steady—she wasn't crying, wasn't screaming, wasn't doing anything but watching.

Jeta had moved too, stepping toward the altar, though not as quickly, not as forcefully. Because she was watching something else.

Watching Farah.

And Farah—

Farah moved.

Not to stop him. Not to stop them.

But to step between them and Afsoun.

Yasher's stomach turned to ice. She was blocking Afsoun and the Darkness behind her, protecting them, sacrificing herself for them.

"Farah," he snarled, his voice low and tight, a raw thing in his throat.

"Take her." She whispered as she looked at him. Finally, finally. She was fully there for a breath, and the love in her eyes for him said all the apology that she possibly could with them. Then, they shuttered, her mahogany eyes disappearing behind a layer of the deepest black he'd ever seen.

And it shattered him.

Behind her, Afsoun exhaled softly, almost as if she was pleased. As if she had known all along that this moment would come.

He grabbed and tightened his grip on Farah's wrist, his pulse hammering in his throat. *Don't do this.* The words burned in his chest, but he didn't say them. He didn't need to. They were already in the way he held her, the way his fingers pressed against her skin as if he could anchor her, as if he could keep her from slipping away.

But she was already gone.

Because this was no longer a fight for her.

She wasn't resisting. She was *letting go*.

And that—that was what broke something in him. Not the fear. Not the shadows. But the way she looked at him like she released him.

"I can't hold it any longer, Yasher." She whispered again. "I'm so sorry."

The air hummed with tension. The walls of the cavern groaned, the ancient iron sconces along the stone flickering in the firelight as if something unseen had just exhaled. Metal scraped against rock, the sound sharp and grating, like the prelude to a collapse.

Yasher felt it before he saw it.

The pull. Deep. Not of this world.

Farah turned away from him.

And his world collapsed.

The cavern roared with the sound of iron and rock slamming into place. The tunnel behind them sealed shut, jagged slabs of stone crashing down in an avalanche of dust and noise. Yasher staggered back, shielding his face as debris scattered across the uneven ground, the thick, metallic taste of crushed earth coating his tongue.

Their only way out.

Gone.

He coughed, shaking off the weight of the dust,

already moving forward. Then his body wasn't his own anymore.

It happened too fast to fight. A force wrapped around him, sharp and unyielding. The buckles on his coat snapped taut, the small knives hidden in his sleeves jerked against his arms, the coins in his pockets clenched together in a violent rattle. His belt cinched tighter, pulling against his ribs, making it hard to breathe…

But the worst was the bracelet. The one she had given him.

The bracelet cinched around his wrist, metal biting into his skin like it had remembered its purpose. A gift turned shackle. A symbol of trust now pulling him down.

The metal burned, sinking into his skin, locking his bones in place. This wasn't some unseen force holding him down. This was her. Her will. Her Talent. Farah had put this on him, and now she was using it to keep him back.

Gods.

She had never let him go.

The metal burned cold against his skin, its weight suddenly unbearable.

She threw him back.

He barely had time to react before his own coat turned against him, wrenching him off his feet and slamming him into the cavern wall. His breath ripped from his lungs in a sharp, choking gasp, pain bursting through his ribs where the stone caught him. His head cracked against the rough surface, white spots exploding in his vision as his body threatened to fold in on itself.

For half a heartbeat, he couldn't move.

Then the weight of it pinned him down.

Not by hands. Not by shadows.

By her.

Through the ringing in his ears, he heard Afsoun's voice.

"Good," she murmured. "You see, Farahnaz? You were always meant for this."

Farah exhaled. Steady. Calm. Certain.

She didn't turn around, didn't look at him.

Something fractured in his chest. A raw, painful tearing.

He forced his hands against the stone, tried to push up, to break free, but the bracelet—her bracelet—still held him, the pull of it sinking into his skin, as if her touch had never truly left it, as if she had woven herself into it from the very beginning.

Yasher let out a low, shuddering breath.

The heat of blood pulsed at the back of his skull.

His heartbeat roared in his ears, but still—still—he called out to her, voice raw, broken.

"Farah."

She didn't stop.

Didn't answer.

She just stepped forward.

Straight toward Afsoun.

Straight into the darkness.

And Yasher, pinned and powerless, could do nothing but watch her leave him behind.

CHAPTER 30

THE AIR BURNED in her lungs, thick with the heat of too many bodies, the scent of sweat and old stone pressing against her skin. She had spent years learning to breathe through discomfort, to filter out distraction, to focus on what mattered. But this was different. This was something else entirely.

The moment stretched, slow and heavy, as if the cavern itself had drawn in a breath and refused to let it go. The weight of her actions pressed against her ribs, a dull ache that she refused to name, a sharp hook that she refused to acknowledge.

She had taken down Yasher. Let the shadows rise. Let herself become the thing she feared most in an attempt to save them.

She had done what she needed to do. Hadn't she?

She could still feel the echo of her Talent humming in her bones, the memory of it wrapping around the metal in the room, pulling it, bending it to her will, shaping the world to her design. She had acted without hesitation, without question, because she had to.

And yet.

Her pulse was unsteady. Her stomach twisted.

Yasher's eyes—still seared into the back of her mind.

She had expected anger, had braced for it. Expected him to shout, to curse her name, to demand answers. That, she could have handled. That, she could have fought back against. But what she saw in his eyes wasn't anger. It was devastation, raw and silent, something too deep for words and too sharp to ignore. Not just pain. Not just disbelief. Something hollowed out and left gaping.

Like she had broken something inside him.

Her hands curled into fists at her sides.

This was not the time to hesitate. She must do what she needed to do.

The cavern was still alive with movement, with flickering torchlight and the shifting presence of Afsoun's gathered followers, standing like silent sentinels along the walls. Waiting. For what, she wasn't sure. But she could feel them at the edges of her awareness, pressing inward, hemming her in.

Farah forced her focus forward, swallowing down the discomfort curling deep in her ribs.

Jeta.

The older woman was sprawled on the cavern floor, propped on one arm, her green coat gathered beneath her like fallen leaves. She wasn't hurt—not physically—but there was something in the way she stared at Farah that sent a strange, sharp feeling down her spine.

Jeta had never looked at her like this before.

There was no wry exasperation, no dry amusement, no lingering air of knowing.

Just... disappointment.

It settled on her shoulders heavier than any blade she had ever wielded.

Then—a sound as the old woman attempted to stand. The sharp clatter of something small and wooden against the cavern floor.

Farah's gaze snapped to the source, her chest tightening as she saw it.

The relic.

The box had tumbled free from Jeta's coat in the fall, its lacquered surface dull with dust, its brass latches glinting faintly in the firelight.

The air in the cavern shifted, subtle but insistent.

Her Talent surged through her like a reflex, reaching —grasping—pulling the relic to her before anyone could stop her.

But something moved faster.

Pari.

The little girl darted forward like a breath of wind, slipping between them in an instant, her small hands wrapping around the relic before it could reach Farah's outstretched power.

Her Talent hit a wall of resistance, her pull catching on something solid, something unmoving— No. Not unmoving. Unyielding.

Pari didn't hesitate. She moved like she was weight-less, a breath of wind through a battlefield, small hands latching onto the relic with a certainty that didn't belong to a child. She stood firm, her fingers locked around the wooden edges as if they were the only thing keeping the cavern from collapsing around her. Her stance was not wide, not powerful, not forceful—but it did not waver.

Farah's breath caught in her throat.

Her first instinct was to wrench the metal free, to pull harder, to take it back—

But she didn't. She couldn't. Something inside her wavered.

Pari was not afraid.

She wasn't trembling. Wasn't shrinking.

Just looking. Steady. Certain.

Not as a child looked at an elder, not as a follower looked at a leader, but as an equal.

And suddenly, it was Yasher's face in her mind again —the look of betrayal that had cut through the distance between them like a blade.

Farah's heart pounded against her ribs, a deep, aching rhythm she couldn't shake.

She could still feel the pull of the Veil fragment, still feel its call, even buried inside the box, even pressed against Pari's small frame.

But she didn't take it.

She could have. She should have.

Instead, she stood locked in place, her breath uneven, her fingers curling at her sides.

And Pari didn't move either.

She just held it there, clutching it tightly, standing between Farah and the thing she had wanted to take.

As if she had always been meant to.

A sudden, violent nausea twisted through her gut—

the undeniable knowledge that something had just shifted, something had just been decided. And it wasn't her decision anymore.

A ripple of awareness crawled down her spine, slow and cold.

Kill her. Make me whole. She heard from the shadows within her mind.

No, never. Not her.

For the first time since she had taken the relic into her hands, she realized she had never been holding it. Not truly. It had been holding her, guiding her choices, nesting in her bones. Its weight hadn't changed, but its presence had. She thought she had been watching it, measuring it, controlling it. But now, standing before Pari, the truth pressed against her ribs like a cold blade.

She really wasn't any better than Behnaz had been. She'd let it in, thinking she was stronger, better, and it had manipulated her just the same.

Pari's grip didn't loosen.

Her breath shuddered as she forced herself to step back. Behind her, she felt Yasher's eyes—still watching.

Still hoping.

And it hurt more than anything.

***

PARI'S small hands pressed the wooden box against her chest, her movements careful, deliberate, as if she understood the gravity of what she carried. Without hesitation, she crossed the cavern, the soft whisper of her footsteps barely audible over the tense hush that had settled over them. She held the box with both hands, cradling it the way one might hold something sacred, something fragile.

Jeta met her halfway, her fingers steady as they closed around the worn wood. She didn't move immediately, only stood there, still as stone, her thumb brushing against the grain of the lid. The lines of her face, so often marked by sharp wit and unshakable confidence, softened with something else—something deeper. Something almost hesitant. And then she exhaled. Slow and measured, like she was bracing herself for what came next.

She turned fully to Farah.

"I should have seen it earlier. You thought you were stronger than it, didn't you?" Jeta murmured, and her voice was not laced with disappointment, not barbed with accusation. It was softer than she had ever heard it. Raw. Unsteady. Regret, real and unyielding, shaped every syllable.

Jeta's fingers tightened around the relic, but her gaze never left Farah. There was no anger in it, no coldness, just something deeper, heavier, something that pressed against the air between them like the hush before a storm.

"I thought I understood you," Jeta continued, almost to herself. "I thought I knew your heart, even when you didn't know it yourself. I told myself you would find your way back. That you were stronger than whatever was pulling at you. But I was wrong. So, so wrong."

Her breath hitched, something twisting in her chest

—not guilt, not quite, but close, dangerous. She didn't want to hear this. She didn't want to be seen like this.

"I let you walk too far down this path," Jeta said, and this time, her voice wavered, but it did not break. "I should have stopped you sooner, should have fought harder. I should have let him help you more. Because now—" Her throat bobbed, as if swallowing something bitter. "Now, I don't know if I can bring you back at all."

A muscle in Jeta's jaw flexed, and then she exhaled, shaking her head slightly.

"I spent too long in the Citadel," she murmured, almost like a throwaway thought, but the weight of it settled into the space between them. "Too many years letting others do the dirty work. Watching from the edges. This is my hubris, thinking that you'd been put through so much hell from that bitch on the throne that you could survive anything."

She let out a slow breath, but her hands didn't waver, steady as they held the relic. "I was supposed to protect you," she whispered. "And I failed you, Farahnaz. I failed you by waiting too long. For that, I will carry my sorrow. I'm so sorry."

Then, with a grim, quiet certainty, she did what she should have done long before.

She took the choice away.

Farah felt it in the air first—a stillness, the breath before a storm. Her Talent pulsed once in recognition, not warning but readiness.

The vines that had curled around the carved rosewood of Jeta's cane stirred, quivering, as if roused from some deep slumber. And then they moved.

They stretched outward, twisting into the air, spiraling up Jeta's arms, unfurling. The embroidered roses on her coat—once threadbare, dulled from years on the road—shimmered. The vines in the pattern deepened in color, the green turning lush, the flowers blooming anew in luminous white, petals opening as if breathing for the first time.

And the scent—rich and ancient, like something pulled from the roots of the world. Not just roses, but life itself. Creation. Resurrection.

It was deep and rich, the earth after rainfall, the crisp bite of fresh leaves, the warm, heady perfume of blooming roses. The scent of something old, something vast.

Something eternal, a life-weaving like no other. *Ameretat.* Amesha Spenta, the goddess of Nature's Memory.

Farah staggered as the vines struck her, pulling her tightly towards the cavern floor, containing her in place.

Jeta lifted the box higher, her fingers curling tightly around it. And then she pulled.

The relic responded first. The black, writhing mass that had been coiled within the fragment twisted violently, a thing of shadows and sickness, its tendrils curling as if seeking escape. She could feel it thrashing, its presence a foul, cloying pressure in the air, wrong in a way that made her skin feel like it was being flayed off. Jeta did not hesitate.

The vines surged forward, winding tight, choking the writhing darkness in an unrelenting grip. The corruption convulsed, shrieking without sound, its tendrils lashing against the air as if trying to claw its way free. Jeta's fingers curled tighter, and the vines responded, coiling in, crushing. The shadow twisted—then cracked. Not like a branch or bone, but like a mountain. A deep, sickening vibration shuddered through the air as the corruption collapsed inward, folding into itself, shrinking, breaking apart. Flakes of darkness peeled away, crumbling like ash in a dying fire—until there was nothing left.

The relic fragment remained. No longer tainted, no longer twisted, only a piece of the Veil, gleaming faintly beneath Jeta's fingers.

The cavern pulsed—an uneven, thrumming force pressing against Farah's skin like the oppressive weight of an oncoming storm. The air itself seemed to tremble, its breath uneven, carrying the last echoes of Jeta's power and the remnants of something deeper, something that should have never been woken.

Afsoun lunged from somewhere behind her.

The moment snapped like a wire pulled too tight. Jeta reacted in an instant, her vines unfurling with deadly precision, lashing outward like whips of living emerald. They did not simply entangle Afsoun—they tore her from the air, yanked her mid-motion, sent her twisting, limbs flailing, dark coat shimmering in the dim light before she slammed against the cavern wall with a sickening, bone-crunching crack.

Stone groaned with the impact, dust shaking loose from the ceiling, drifting in thin, uneven rivulets through the air. Afsoun crumpled, her body flickering, unspooling at the edges, dark veins of shadow twisting from her form before she forced herself back together. Her head lolled forward, limbs twitching with a strange, unnatural delay, her body struggling to remember how to be.

The vines tightened for a breath, a heartbeat, then unwound just enough to free Farah's hands. She turned to Farah, her expression unreadable, her gaze steady—not with cruelty, not with anger, but with something more terrifying. Conviction.

Jeta reached for her and Farah couldn't stop her.

Pain. Not just pain. A deep, searing, all-consuming wound, not of flesh, but of a fundamental thing that had rooted itself into her, and it did not want to go. It fought. Clawing, twisting, resisting, sinking its talons deeper into the marrow of her bones, into the fragile spaces between breath and thought. It did not want to be cast out.

Farah convulsed, her spine bowing as she gasped, fingers clawing at Jeta's wrists, at anything solid, anything real. The force of it was unbearable, an unmaking that burned and shattered and tore through every piece of her that had once belonged to something else.

Afsoun screamed with her. Their pain shared a thread—unseen but unmistakable. What had bound them was unraveling, thread by cursed thread. Farah felt it snap inside her—like the breaking of a tether.

Farah struggled against the bindings coiled around her wrists, against the ache in her limbs, against the ragged pull of exhaustion that left her movements too slow, too weak. The corruption was gone, torn from her veins—but in its place was an echo. A silence. A hollowness that made her unsure where she ended and it had once begun. Every breath scraped against her ribs like splinters, her veins aching with absence. Hollow, empty —but not healed.

Farah forced her head up, her breath ragged, her vision swimming at the edges, and through the haze of agony she saw.

Afsoun was trembling, her hands clutching at herself as though she were the one being ripped apart, her breath coming in ragged gasps, her body shuddering. The connection between them, the festering, twisted thing that had bound them, was unraveling. Afsoun felt it. She was feeling all of it. The tearing. The loss. The absence.

Jeta's grip on Farah tightened. The vines constricted, bracing her as she finished what she had started.

But Afsoun moved.

Faster than she should have. Too fast.

Farah's breath stalled in her chest as shadow flickered, smooth as ink spilling through water, closing the space between them in the blink of an eye. Jeta barely had time to turn before Afsoun was there.

The strike landed in an instant.

Shadows solidified, sharp as the fangs of a starving beast, plunging deep. The sound was sickening, wet, a terrible, tearing thing that carved through flesh and something more.

Jeta's body jerked, her spine arching, her mouth parting on a breath that never fully came. The vines that had surged to meet Afsoun froze, shuddered, and then wilted. The roses along her sleeves, once luminous, curled inward, their petals blackening, shriveling, turning to dust.

The darkness did not just pierce her.

It took everything that lived.

Farah felt it, the pull in the air, the sharp, unnatural shift of life being ripped away. Jeta's eyes flickered, with something that made Farah's stomach lurch—understanding. Jeta knew. She had seen this before. And worse, she had known it was coming.

Farah opened her mouth, but no sound came. She couldn't move.

Jeta's hands twitched, her body trying to fight, trying to push back, but Afsoun's grip was relentless, her fingers curling, the shadows sinking deeper, taking.

Afsoun ripped her hand back and Jeta collapsed.

The vines that remained withered, curling into nothing, dissolving into dust as her body crumpled to the stone, her coat pooling around her like the last wilted petals of a dying bloom.

Farah roared.

A sound wrenched from somewhere deep, somewhere raw, somewhere jagged with fury and grief and something unnameable. Her vision blurred, the edges tunneling, her body moving before she could think, before she could breathe. Her limbs burned, her blood screamed, but she did not feel it. She did not feel the ground beneath her feet. Only the break in her ribs where grief had taken root. Only the fury.

All she saw was Jeta on the ground.

And Afsoun smiling.

CHAPTER 31

THE CAVERN SEEMED TO CONTRACT, the weight of Afsoun's presence pressing in, thick as smoke, curling through the space with the same quiet inevitability as the tide swallowing the shore. The air trembled with the echoes of Jeta's fall, the sharp tang of disturbed stone mingling with the scent of cut vines. The weight of it settled in Farah's ribs, twisting like a knife, but she did not move.

Afsoun stood at the center of it all, straight-backed, as though Jeta had done nothing to her. Her gaze, sharp and unwavering, locked onto Farah's, and in that moment, everything else—the fight, the blood, Yasher's presence behind her, the soldiers holding their ground at the cavern's edge—faded into nothing.

This was only for her.

Afsoun sighed, tilting her head just so, disappointment woven into every inch of her poise, every careful note of her voice.

"I had such hope for you, Farahnaz."

The name scraped against Farah's skin, deliberate,

precise. It was not the way Yasher said it, not the way Jeta murmured it or how the Mashya had spoken it with quiet approval. It was weighty, demanding. Afsoun wielded it like a blade, meant to remind Farah of something she was supposed to be.

"You carried it beautifully," Afsoun said, voice low, reverent, as if speaking of something sacred. She stepped forward with the elegance of someone who had already won. "You let it become part of you—no fear, no hesitation."

Her eyes softened—not with kindness, but with something gentler, more dangerous. Understanding.

"And now, you've let them peel it away. Let them fill your head with doubts and trembling hopes. They've made you fragile again."

She swallowed hard, but it did nothing to steady the hollow ache spreading through her chest, seeping into the spaces where something else had once lived. The last remnants of pain from Jeta's intervention still coiled beneath her skin—not sharp, not searing, but worse, it throbbed slow and deep, as if a limb had been severed and left phantom pain behind. The absence of the corruption felt like an open wound, raw and aching, pulsing with something she could not name.

She should have recoiled. Should have spat or laughed or met Afsoun's gaze with the same fire she had always carried into battle. But she didn't.

Because there was a thing inside her—quiet and coiled—that had once bloomed in the dark—remembered what it felt like to be sure. Not just strong. Untouchable.

The weight of her Talent singing in her bones, every step taken with conviction so sharp it cut doubt to ribbons. No questions. No fear. Only purpose, gilded and righteous, and hers.

She missed it.

The power. The certainty that what she did was right—because no one had been allowed to say otherwise.

And wasn't that the closest thing to peace?

"You don't have to mourn it," Afsoun murmured, her voice smooth as silk, offering something Farah hadn't realized she was waiting for. "You don't have to be lost. I can bring it back to you, stronger than before. You felt it, didn't you? How much easier everything was, how much clearer? The world is not kind to those who hesitate, Farahnaz. But it rewards those who take what is theirs."

Her breath came slow, controlled. She did not move, but she didn't pull away either.

Behind her, Yasher shifted—a scrape of boot on stone, barely audible. But she felt it. Felt *him*. The weight of his presence curled around her like a truth she wasn't ready to face, pressing against the raw edges of everything she had done, everything she had broken. It would be so easy to turn, to meet his gaze, to read the things she already knew she would find there—grief, anger, something softer beneath it all, that would undo her. But she didn't.

Coward.

The word coiled in her throat, bitter and burning. He was always there, steady and sure, standing in the wreckage she had left behind. And Farah—Farah, who had faced death, who had bled and fought and never once flinched in the face of pain—could not bring herself to look at him.

Afsoun's gaze flicked toward Yasher, a glance so brief, so dismissive, that it set Farah's teeth on edge. He was nothing to her, nothing worth even considering. But to Farah—

He was everything.

She hated that Afsoun knew it. Hated how easily she ignored him, how effortlessly she turned back to Farah with the same quiet, condescending certainty that had always poisoned her words.

"They don't understand," Afsoun murmured, taking another step forward. The movement was slow, deliberate, the way a hunter might approach a wounded animal, knowing the fight was already over. "They never have. They fear what they cannot control, what they cannot shape into their own image. You know this. You've always known it."

Farah's breath came sharp and shallow. She did not move, did not retreat, but she felt the space between them narrowing, suffocating, like unseen hands pressing against her ribs. Afsoun was too close.

"And yet you still let them shape you."

The words struck something raw inside her, a slow, curling ache that spread through her chest, deep and unbearable. No, no, she hadn't— but the thought twisted, tangled, wrapped itself in doubt. Hadn't she? Hadn't she let herself be undone, torn from the certainty that had once made everything so clear?

Her fingers curled into fists, nails biting into her palms, searching for something solid, something real.

"I decide who I am," she said. The words should have felt strong, unshakable. They weren't.

Afsoun's smile deepened, soft at the edges, full of knowing.

"Do you?"

A ripple of movement, so subtle it almost wasn't there. A shift in the air, an ancient, watchful thread slipping into the space between breath and silence.

Farah's spine went rigid. The cavern was wrong.

Not just the cavern. The very weight of the world around her.

Afsoun didn't notice, but Farah did.

A presence stirred through the air—not loud, not sudden, but slow and certain, like the first ripple of a storm reaching land. It was small, impossibly light, yet Farah felt it sink into the bones of the cavern, into the marrow of her spine, with the quiet authority of something that *should not* be ignored.

Pari.

She had been behind them, near the soldiers, cradled in the false safety of distance. A child—soft-spoken, wide-eyed, always drifting just at the edge of knowing. But so much more than that, carrying the expectations of a god within her small frame.

No footsteps. No sound. Just the steady pulse of something other.

Unnoticed. Unchallenged. Unafraid.

She did not understand how Afsoun hadn't felt the shift, hadn't turned to see the impossible weight that had settled into the air like ash after fire. But then again —Afsoun was always blind to anything she could not shape.

She stopped just at Afsoun's side, her small chin lifting, her expression too calm.

Farah's breath caught, her pulse a snarl in her ears.

Afsoun, lost in her own certainty, did not turn. She did not feel the quiet weight of something neither mortal nor divine settling into place.

Farah did.

Pari lifted her chin, her voice steady.

"Jeta wasn't the only one who could stop you."

Afsoun froze.

And then Pari reached out, and the air cracked.

The corruption wrenched free.

Afsoun howled.

Not a scream. Not pain. Not even rage, but deep, complete loss.

It ripped through the cavern, a raw, unhinged wail that sent vibrations shuddering through the stone, through the very marrow of the earth. The sound was wrong, jagged, splintering against the air. Shadows convulsed violently, lashing outward in wild, erratic tendrils, desperate, searching, unwilling to let go.

Farah felt it.

Not pain—not this time. A chain snapping. The hollow recoil of something unmade. The corruption had been inside her, but it had been inside Afsoun, too. And now, it was leaving her by force.

Afsoun's body buckled. Her fingers clawed at her chest, nails raking against her skin as if she could dig it back in, as if she could trap what was being torn away.

Her breath hitched, her pupils blown wide, unfocused, her lips parting in silent denial.

"No," she rasped, voice shattering like broken glass. "No, no—you can't."

Her limbs jerked, spasming as though whatever Pari was doing was pulling at the sinew itself, warping the structure of her body. Her coat, once a living thing, twisted wildly, the darkness writhing like it was trying to consume her instead. But there was nothing left for it to hold onto. Nothing left to anchor it to her.

It did not want to let go, but it had no choice.

Pari tilted her head, something ancient in her young face. "But I can."

And then she closed her fingers into a fist.

The corruption died.

Farah had not known silence could feel so immense. It pressed against her skin, thick as smoke, wrapping around the cavern like an unseen weight, suffocating in its completeness. The remnants of battle still hung in the air—the sharp tang of sweat and blood, the lingering metallic sting of power spent, the scent of something raw and ruined, as if the very stone of the cavern had been scorched by what had transpired. The shadows no longer moved at the edges of the torchlight. There was no more presence pushing against the fabric of the world, no more wrongness pressing at the seams of reality.

Afsoun did not fall. She came undone.

Not in body, but in essence—unraveling from the inside out, as if the idea of her had been revoked from this plane.

One heartbeat, she stood cloaked in darkness, the breath of Mazdavir pressed into every line of her being. The next—

Absence.

Her coat—no longer alive, no longer darkness—twitched like a dying thing before dissolving into ashless air. Her shape flickered once. Then again. Then collapsed inward, folding into a pinpoint of silence.

Not death. Not even ruin. Just... gone.

At the center of it all that once was Afsoun, like the husk of something shed, lay the Veil.

It should have felt like victory. Like purpose fulfilled. The thing she had chased across the kingdom, the thing that had nearly unmade her. The thing that had whispered to her, through her, until she could no longer tell where its hunger ended and hers began.

Now, it was silent.

But not cleanly so. Not like a wound healed or a prayer answered. The silence felt scorched, hollowed out, like the ringing quiet after a scream that had split the world open.

Farah reached for it—not with her hands, not yet, but with her senses, with the instinct she had honed around metal and memory and divine residue.

The Veil no longer whispered. No longer pulled.

But something in it still trembled. The faintest tremor, like a bell long since rung, its echo dying slow in the bones of the earth.

Mazdavir had been inside the relic. Created Afsoun *from it.*

And now... he was gone.

Not defeated. Not destroyed.

Just emptied.

Farah stared down at it, her breath slow, measured, as if breathing too hard might wake that which should stay dead. This was what she had bled for. This was what had driven her to the edge of herself.

And yet—

Her fingers twitched, reaching forward, not a decision but an inevitability, as if some unseen force still wove its threads through her veins, as if this moment had been waiting for her all along.

A small hand caught her wrist.

Warm. Steady. A presence so slight it should have meant nothing, and yet—

It stopped her.

Farah turned, breath catching in her throat. Pari's fingers, small but strong, curled around her wrist with no force, no demand, just the gentlest touch, like a thread spun from something far older than the girl herself. Her grip was light. Too light.

But she was smiling.

Not with joy. Not with relief. With knowing.

"I was needed here," she whispered. "To help you. He finally spoke to me again."

The breath in Farah's chest turned shallow. Something wasn't right.

Pari's fingers twitched. Her grip loosened.

Too fast.

And then—

She folded in on herself.

A soft exhale. A sway, barely a breath of movement,

then her knees gave way, her small frame crumpling in slow, soundless descent.

Farah lurched forward.

The silence that had felt so vast before now felt suffocating, like it had sunk into her chest, pressing into her ribs, thick and unrelenting. The soft thud of Pari's body hitting the stone sent a shock through her, raw and electric, like a blade dragged through exposed nerve.

Farah dropped to her knees beside her, the stone biting through the fabric of her trousers, cold and jagged, but she barely felt it. Her hands moved without thought, reaching, trembling, pressing into soft shoulders, a small chest that should have been rising, should have been moving— but wasn't.

Pari was warm. Still warm. That was the worst part. The warmth tricked her, lied to her, made her believe for one impossible second that this could all be undone, that whatever divine thread had been woven through the girl's blood might yet hold.

But it didn't.

Her fingers clutched at cloth and skin, frantic in their searching, as if she could anchor the girl back to the world with touch alone, as if willpower could stand in for breath. Her heartbeat thundered against her ribs like something trying to break free, but the silence inside Pari was louder.

No. Not like this.

Her breath caught on a sob that never made it past her throat, not because she held it back but because the world had constricted around her, pulled tight, too tight, until there was no room left for sound. The cavern was no longer a place—it was a tomb, a wound in the earth where all light and air had gone to die.

She pressed her forehead to Pari's shoulder, her hands trembling against the curve of the girl's ribs, as if memorizing the shape of a miracle that had burned itself out.

"Pari," she whispered, voice breaking.

Pari did not respond.

She was warm. She was soft. She was there.

And yet, something in the air had already shifted.

Something already gone to the bridge. To Rashnu.

The torches flickered, their light casting long, wavering shadows against the stone. The air smelled of char and dust, of old magic spent and something ancient lingering at the edges.

Farah's fingers clenched into the fabric of Pari's tunic, the small ridges of the embroidered thread biting into her palms.

FARAH BARELY REGISTERED the sound of footsteps pounding against the cavern floor, the sharp, hurried breaths of the others closing the distance between them. Her entire world had narrowed to the small, too-still form beneath her hands, to the unbearable silence where a heartbeat should have been.

Then Yasher was there.

A hand at her shoulder—firm, unyielding, not cruel but final. He pushed past her, not with fury, but with something colder. Something that said *you've done enough.*

She stumbled back, the breath catching in her throat as her palms lost contact with Pari's tunic, the warmth of the girl's body torn from her like a punishment.

Yasher did not look at her. Not once. As if she didn't deserve to be seen.

He fell to his knees beside Pari, cradling her head in his hands with a care so absolute it carved something jagged into Farah's ribs. His body curved protectively over the girl, as if she could still be sheltered, as if she could still be saved.

"Little Divine," he breathed, voice ragged, unraveling, barely more than air. His fingers—shaking, desperate—threaded through the girl's dark, tangled hair, her braids came loose, he smoothed it back from her face.

His thumb brushed against her temple, not just tender but pleading. His breath hitched, shallow and fractured, like he was trying to inhale through shattered ribs.

There was no Luck here. No charm. No glint in his eye.

Only a man who had nothing left.

Farah had seen death before. Had delivered it with her own hands. She had watched life drain from eyes that had once been bright, had heard the final, rattling exhale of those who would never take another breath. She had seen bodies broken, had walked through blood-soaked fields where the dead had been left to rot.

She had never—never—felt this before.

This weight, this unbearable pull in her chest, something was tearing her apart from the inside.

"Pari," he whispered again, his voice breaking. His movements were so careful, so gentle, afraid to shatter what little remained.

Her throat tightened. This wasn't happening. This couldn't be happening.

He inhaled sharply, his entire body shuddering, his grip tightening ever so slightly. His shoulders curled inward, trying to shield her, like holding her was the only thing keeping her from slipping further away.

She felt the breath leave her lungs, a slow, aching exhale, her vision tunneling in on the two of them, on the way Yasher's hand trembled against Pari's cheek, on the quiet, unbearable stillness of the girl in his arms.

This was her fault. Not Afsoun's. Not Mazdavir's.

Hers.

Pari had followed them with that too-knowing gaze and that terrible, beautiful trust. Had believed in Farah even when she no longer knew what she believed in.

The thought landed like iron in her gut. Dense and absolute, a weight her body couldn't seem to carry. Her chest ached as if a dagger had lodged between her ribs, sharp and unmoving.

She had carried the corruption. Let it root in her. Let it whisper through her choices, convinced she could wield it without cost.

And Pari had died for that lie.

Yasher's breath hitched—a sharp, unsteady inhale that never fully came, like something in his chest had broken, like the air itself had turned against him.

And then he let out a sound that shattered her.

Not a cry. Not a curse. Just breath.

A raw, broken exhale. The sound of a gambler who had just lost his final hand, of a man whose luck had finally run dry.

The world had gone silent.

The sort of silence that consumed.

A silence that stretched between the last breath that Pari had taken and the gaping, endless void where the next one should have been.

Farah had failed her.

Now she knelt there, frozen, while Yasher gathered Pari into his arms, his movements slow, trembling.

He did not speak to her. Did not look at her.

In the terrible, final silence between them.

She had not only lost Pari.

She had lost *him*.

Yasher whispered something against her brow, his voice so low, so hoarse, it was barely more than breath.

Pari had always been his in a way that had nothing to do with blood, nothing to do with fate, nothing to do with the strange, twisting paths that had led them here.

She had chosen Yasher, chosen Farah.

She had led them, followed them—not for power or purpose, but for love. And they had let her walk into a world that was never meant for someone like her.

She had been the only one without blood on her hands. The only one who had never taken a life, never compromised her soul to survive.

And still, she was the one who died.

Farah had promised herself she could carry the

weight, but she had passed it to a child. The thought burrowed into Farah's ribs, pressing sharp and deep, an agony she could not fight, could not contain, could not control.

Her breath hitched. She had felt pain before. Had been broken, had been beaten, had pushed past the threshold of endurance again and again.

But this—this was a wound unlike any she had ever borne.

No sword, no Talent, no force in the world could change what had already been done.

His entire body curled protectively around Pari's small frame, his arms still holding her like she might wake, like she might shift in his grasp and murmur something soft, something knowing, like she always did.

But she didn't.

And Yasher did not look at her.

He knew where the blame belonged.

His Luck had failed him.

And she had been the reason why.

She opened her mouth, but the air itself rejected her voice. The silence pressed in, thick and suffocating, like a cloak she could never shrug off.

There was nothing she could say.

Nothing she deserved to say.

And deep inside her, something knew—this would never leave her.

She would carry this silence. This failure.

It would follow her through every room she entered, settle into the cracks of every command she gave, linger behind every smile she forced.

A shadow not from the Darkness, but from herself.

Yasher let out a breath—raw, jagged, the sound of a man unraveling.

It was not a sob, not a scream, not anything loud enough to fill the cavern, but something quieter.

More broken.

A breath that sounded like surrender.

And it broke her all over again.

Something inside her gave way. Not loudly. Not visibly. But it cracked, deep and final—like a fault line that would never close again.

She did not cry. She did not scream.

She simply stayed there. Kneeling in the silence she had made.

CHAPTER 32

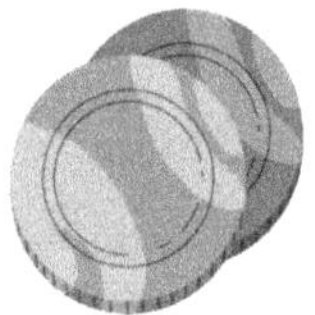

Yasher didn't know how long he had been sitting there. Maybe moments. Maybe hours. Maybe forever. His arms curled around Pari's small, still body, his thumb tracing slow circles at her temple—not because he believed, but because stopping would mean surrender.

His Luck, once a quiet presence just beneath his skin, was gone. Not dormant. Not silent. Hollow.

Like it had died with her.

The cavern might as well have been another world, distant and unreachable, the sounds around him muffled and meaningless. Voices stirred at the edges of his awareness—Mehran's, Younis's, the quiet rustle of movement, the shifting of stone—but they blurred together, indistinct, weightless. Even the flickering torchlight seemed unreal, too dim, too far away, like a memory half-remembered through water. None of it touched him. None of it mattered.

Farah moved beside him. Not close enough to touch, but close enough that her presence pressed against the edges of his awareness, sharp and uninvited.

The barricade she had thrown up dropped with a soft clatter, the sound too small to deserve the weight it carried.

She sat beside him.

He didn't look at her. Couldn't.

Because if he did—he'd see her face. And if he saw her face, he'd remember who let this happen. Who let *Pari* die.

She didn't touch him. Maybe she knew he would flinch.

His grip tightened around Pari. He knew he would have to move eventually, that he couldn't stay here forever, but the thought of letting go, of placing her down, of acknowledging that this was real, that she was truly gone, was too much.

So, he didn't move.

Didn't speak. Didn't breathe properly.

The world had been unsteady beneath his feet for days, twisting, shifting, refusing to follow the rules he had come to understand. But this—this was the worst of it.

This was the moment his Luck had truly failed him. The gods had failed them.

Not a close call, not a brush with death he could laugh about later. This wasn't a bluff gone wrong, a risk that hadn't paid off.

This was loss. Real, brutal, unchangeable. The kind no Luck in the world could undo.

It should have been him.

Not Pari. Not her bright eyes and sharp, knowing smiles. Not her endless curiosity. Not the girl who had followed them, who had chosen them, who had made herself part of them in a way he had never expected but had come to depend on.

His jaw clenched, his breath coming too shallow.

Farah was still beside him. Not speaking. Not touching. Just there.

It should have been comforting.

Yasher finally forced himself to look up, just enough to take in the cavern around them. Mehran and Younis stood near the entrance, their faces hard and unreadable, their movements efficient as they surveyed what was left. The last remnants of Afsoun's influence were fading, the shadows in the corners dissipating, leaving behind only the wreckage of what had happened here.

Afsoun was gone.

Jeta was dead.

Pari was dead.

And Yasher wasn't sure what he was anymore.

He exhaled sharply, the sound ragged, and bowed his head again, pressing his forehead to Pari's hair.

She still smelled like dust and charcoal and the faint sweetness of the tea she'd spilled on herself that morning—too strong, too sugary, the kind she insisted was perfect no matter how many times he teased her for it.

He could still feel the tug of her small hand dragging him through the market, hear the snap of her voice when she got impatient, see the way her brow furrowed when she pretended to be older than she was.

All of it still there.

All of it already gone.

A sound stirred behind him.

Soft.

A shift of fabric, a quiet inhale.

Yasher didn't move at first.

The cavern shifted. Not the crawling, rotted wrongness that had followed Afsoun like a second skin. Not that slick, suffocating press of corruption.

It prickled against his skin, but not with fear. With recognition. With memory that didn't belong to him.

A warmth, deep and old, rose through the air like the first breath of spring after a winter that had buried the world. Like the sun after a long night—not safe, but inevitable.

His Luck stirred—then stilled.

Something was waking.

Yasher's body tensed. He knew that feeling. That shift in the air, that silent pulse of something bending the world in a way it shouldn't.

The cavern shuddered in a way that Yasher felt deep in his bones, a shift that rippled through the air like the first breath of a storm breaking.

A scraping sound. Boots against stone.

Yasher's breath caught, something cold rushing through his veins, some instinct he couldn't name screaming at him that this was wrong. Not the wrongness of corruption, not the twisting presence of Mazdavir's influence, but something else.

Something old. Something vast. Something waking.

He lifted his head.

And saw her.

Jeta.

Not as she had been. Not broken, bloodied, and dead.

She stood at the mouth of the cavern, shaking dust from her coat like someone returning from a long journey.

He blinked slowly, his body too tired to flinch, his thoughts too splintered to catch up.

She looked younger. Cleaner. Not untouched—but unworn. Like time had slid off her like water from stone.

The lines that had settled into her face over years of living, of watching, of knowing, were gone, not softer, just gone. The gray that had streaked through her dark hair had vanished, leaving behind deep black waves, catching in the dim light. Even the way she held herself had shifted, no longer carrying the weight of years pressing into her bones.

It should have meant something. Should have sparked something in him.

But it didn't.

It was just one more thing that didn't make sense. Just one more reminder that the world had changed, and he hadn't kept up.

The gods could bring back Jeta.

But not Pari.

The thought should have filled him with awe. With hope. With some scrap of belief that all wasn't lost.

It didn't. It just made him feel... empty.

As if the divine had picked the wrong one.

Or worse— as if it had never been about right or wrong at all.

The cavern had gone silent again. Everyone was staring.

Jeta met their gazes, rolling her shoulders, settling back into her skin, her lips pressing into a thin line before she sighed, rubbing a hand down her face.

"Great Shining Halls," she muttered, voice low and rasping. "That bitch actually killed me."

The words barely reached Yasher.

He just stared at her.

Alive. Whole. Changed.

The air still didn't move. Pari's body was still in his arms.

And somewhere in the back of his mind, a thought flickered—small, quiet, weightless.

What if this was the gods' idea of mercy?

He didn't feel it.

He didn't feel anything at all.

JETA GROANED, the sound rasping through the cavern like stone dragged across stone—low, grinding, too solid for the body it came from.

She rolled her neck, and the crack of it was too loud, brittle and precise, like joints snapping into place that hadn't belonged to her a moment ago.

Her fingers flexed, stretched—too smooth, too fluid.

Yasher didn't flinch.

But he saw it.

The disconnect. The edges that didn't fit.

The way her body moved like it was remembering how to be *hers.*

"Damn it all," Jeta muttered, rolling her wrist like she was testing how the new shape of her bones sat beneath her skin. "I liked being an old woman. It was respectable. Dignified. Got me out of carrying things and everything."

She twisted her arm, tilting it to inspect the smooth, unlined skin beneath the cavern's dim glow. Her brows knitted together, and she let out a small, disapproving noise. "Now look at me. Young again. How inconvenient."

The words drifted into the heavy air, meant to be light, meant to be sharp enough to cut through the moment's jagged edges. It should have been funny. A day ago, he might have snorted, thrown something back at her—complained that she already made him carry everything anyway. But now—

Nothing.

No scoff from Mehran. No answering quip from him. No sound at all, save for the slow, uneven breaths filling the cavern, like no one wanted to be the first to break the silence.

The cavern held its breath. No one spoke, no one moved. The air stretched taut, thick with something wrong, something unnatural. Yasher had known silence in many forms—the sharp anticipation before a fight, the uneasy stillness of a hand hovering over a deck of cards, the void left behind after the dying had taken their last breath. But this wasn't like any of those.

This was the kind of silence that came when the world refused to make sense.

Jeta let out a breath, half a chuckle, but it died almost as soon as it left her lips. Even she could feel it—the weight pressing down, the wrongness of a body that shouldn't exist anymore standing there, shaking dust from her coat like she'd merely tripped and fallen rather than been split open, emptied, gone.

He should have said something. Should have asked her what the hell she was. But he couldn't. Because he already knew.

She was Jeta. She was alive again.

Her sharp gaze flicked over the cavern, over the remnants of what had been left behind—the scattered debris of a battle fought not just with steel, but with more. She took in the figures near the entrance, Mehran and Younis standing rigid, their hands still gripping their weapons, their expressions lined with something darker than grief, heavier than exhaustion. Her gaze passed over Farah, lingering for only a moment, before finally settling —fully, entirely—on Yasher.

On Pari.

The shift in her expression was immediate.

The sharpness in her features, the humor, the ease with which she carried herself—gone.

It drained from her, leaving something raw in its place. A shadow passed through her bright eyes, something deep and aching, as she took in the sight before her.

Slowly, she stepped forward. Not cautiously. Jeta had never been the kind of woman to hesitate, but with the kind of quiet certainty that belonged to people who had delivered bad news before. People who had sat beside the dying, watched the light leave their eyes, and still known what to say after.

He hated her for it.

His grip on Pari had loosened, but only because his arms were numb now, his fingers barely able to feel the fine threads of her tunic, the strands of her tangled curls. His body refused to register the truth his mind kept whispering. That she wasn't warming up, that she wasn't shifting in his hold, that he wasn't going to wake up in the morning and hear her scolding him for being reckless again, for being too slow, for thinking his Luck would last forever.

He wasn't ready.

Letting go meant accepting it. Letting go meant saying goodbye. And Yasher wasn't sure if he had ever learned how to do that, even after all the death, all the pain.

Jeta crouched beside him, her body lowering with the ease of someone who had done this before, who had knelt at the side of the fallen, who had reached for something that had already slipped beyond reach.

She hesitated.

Her fingers hovered just above Pari's forehead, motion suspended in the air like even time was holding its breath.

A heartbeat.

Two.

Then, finally, she let her hand settle. Her palm pressed lightly against the girl's cooling skin.

Her thumb traced the space between Pari's brows—soft, reverent.

Not healing. Not hope. Just the kind of touch people saved for the end.

And in that instant, he wasn't sure if the world had stopped—or if he had.

Her throat worked around something thick, something unsaid.

"She was too young," Jeta murmured, her voice quieter than Yasher had ever heard it. "Too small to take on that much. He shouldn't have put the burden on her."

Yasher felt his chest tighten, felt something in him break all over again, something already raw splitting further, deeper. His jaw clenched, his breath coming too shallow, his hands curling into the fabric of Pari's tunic.

Fix her.

The words never left his mouth.

They pulsed behind his teeth, pressed into the roof of his mouth, lodged like a blade at the base of his throat—too sharp to speak, too loud to silence.

He didn't say it. He couldn't.

But Jeta looked at him, and he knew...

She'd heard it anyway.

She turned her head, her expression heavy with emotions Yasher didn't want to name.

"She's gone," Jeta said, and it wasn't cold, wasn't dismissive. It was the truth, stripped bare. "I can't bring her back."

Yasher's breath hitched.

The words didn't hit like a blow, they landed like ash.

Soft. Final.

He'd never had anyone say it out loud before.

Not when the fires took his family. Not when he

stumbled through the remains of his home, soot in his throat and silence in every room.

No one said the words then.

They didn't need to.

He had seen what was left.

But hearing it now—spoken, confirmed, *real*—

It cracked something deep and old, something he thought had gone numb to years ago.

His breath hitched. His fingers spasmed against Pari's tunic, his pulse hammering against his ribs, too fast, too uneven. His mouth opened, closed, opened again.

He swallowed, tried to form something—anything—that would make sense of this, that would let him understand how the gods could let this happen.

"Why?"

It came out hoarse, wrong, like the word was torn from him rather than spoken.

He didn't even know what he was asking. Why her? Why now? Why had she burned so bright only to be snuffed out like she was nothing? Why had she trusted him when all he had done was fail her? Why—

His throat closed up.

He couldn't breathe.

Jeta exhaled, running a hand down her face, her own expression drawn tight with something heavy, something immovable. When she finally spoke, her voice carried none of the sharpness, none of the usual wit. Just resignation.

"I don't have that power," she said quietly. "Not for

something like this. Not for her. She's already walking the Bridge, *saqalu.*"

His vision blurred at the edges, the cavern twisting out of focus.

His mind locked up, recoiling from the word, from the truth pressing in around him like the walls of a collapsing tunnel.

No.

No, no, no—

His breath hitched. The tightness in his chest was unbearable, every inhale raw and uneven, as if his lungs had forgotten how to work without her laughter filling the air.

His forehead pressed against Pari's, his trembling fingers smoothing a stray curl behind her ear, a motion so small, so meaningless, and yet he clung to it like a prayer. Like if he just held her close enough, just stayed here long enough, she might come back.

Jeta withdrew her hand, her fingers curling into a loose fist against her knee as she straightened just slightly, still crouched at his side.

Her presence wasn't comforting. It wasn't meant to be.

She had nothing left to offer here.

Jeta's words settled over them like the final weight of stone sealing a tomb. There was no bargaining left, no last chance, no miracle that could change this. The world had turned, the decision had been made, and Pari was gone.

He exhaled, slow and shaky, his chest tight with a

feeling he couldn't even name anymore. He had always been able to move forward, to brush off the losses, to keep walking. It had been easier, once—before the first, before the worst. Before he lost his family to steel and fire, before he learned what it meant to stand in the ashes of everything that had ever tethered him to the world. Before he found a new home, new hands to pull him from the wreckage, only to watch them fall too—one by one, until there was nothing left but the hollow spaces where they had been. His adoptive mother, the woman who had given him something close to safety. Gone. The first person he had ever loved, whose laughter still ghosted through his mind in moments of quiet. Gone.

He had told himself, again and again, that he could survive it, that if he just kept moving, if he never let himself stop, he would never have to feel the full weight of it. But now, holding Pari's too-small, too-still body, he couldn't pretend anymore. This was the cost. This had always been the cost. And his Luck—his *damned* Luck—had never been enough to change it.

Pari had been his.

Not by blood. Not by duty.

Just—herself.

She'd chosen him. Walked into his life with those sharp eyes and that impossible faith, like she already knew where she belonged.

Like she *belonged with him.*

And he'd let her—

Gods.

He'd let her die for it.

The scrape of a boot against stone, deliberate but

hesitant. Then a breath, measured but weighted. Mehran cleared his throat, the sound rough, reluctant. When he spoke, it wasn't an order. It wasn't sharp. It wasn't the voice of a commander or a soldier or a man used to giving commands in the wake of bloodshed.

"We need to go," he said, quietly.

Yasher barely moved.

Mehran exhaled, then stepped forward—the caution of someone approaching wreckage, wary of disturbing whatever was still standing among the ruins. His usual sharpness had dulled, not absent but tucked away, his voice steady but lacking the familiar bite of impatience.

"Yasher," he tried again, softer now. "We can't stay here. Something happened to the town while we were down here."

The silence stretched.

Thick. Suffocating.

Yasher didn't lift his head. Didn't acknowledge the shadow that moved toward him.

A breath. A step. Another. Each one felt louder than it should've.

A weight beside him. Not intrusive. Not forceful. Just... there.

Mehran lowered himself slowly, his broad frame folding with more care than Yasher had ever seen from him. Like he was crouching beside something broken.

Like he knew he couldn't fix it.

Only witness it.

"You shouldn't have to do this alone," Mehran murmured. "Let me—"

"No." Yasher's voice was hoarse, barely above a whisper. His grip on Pari tightened, as if the mere suggestion that he relinquish her would make it real in a way he couldn't yet accept. "I have her."

Mehran studied him for a long moment, then nodded once. "All right." No argument, just quiet acceptance.

Still, Yasher didn't move.

He hadn't prayed. Not in years. Not since the fires.

But if the gods were real— If Pari was proof of anything—

Then what the hell was this?

Jeta got a second chance. A younger body. A divine rebirth he didn't understand and didn't want to.

And Pari?

Pari was cold in his arms.

No second chances. No miracle.

Just silence.

That's what the divine gave him. That's what they always gave him.

Not until Mehran reached out, a steady, grounding touch against his shoulder. Not pushing, not demanding. Just there.

"We'll do right by her," Mehran said, and his voice held a quiet certainty, the kind of promise that wasn't for show, wasn't empty. "I swear it."

Yasher closed his eyes. Swallowed hard.

Then, finally, he pushed himself up. His muscles screamed in protest, stiff from too long kneeling, his joints locking before they relented. Pari's weight was nothing—far too little, far too wrong, but she pressed against his chest like a stone. Heavy in all the ways that mattered.

She used to skip ahead on the trail, boots too big, hair catching the wind. Used to tug on his sleeve when she wanted to walk beside him. Used to fall asleep against his side like she belonged there.

Now she was still.

And his arms ached from holding her, though she weighed less than memory.

Mehran rose beside him, a step behind but not too far, like he was bracing himself to catch Yasher if he stumbled. Younis followed in grim, steady silence.

Jeta lingered, her fingers twitching like she wanted to reach out, to say something. But she didn't.

Farah still knelt where she had been.

Unmoving.

Her face was turned toward him, lit by the low flicker of the torches—but she wasn't hiding from him.

Not really.

She wasn't crying. Not in the way others might cry. No sobs. No sound.

But he saw it.

In the way her shoulders curved in, like she was holding herself together through sheer will. In the shine in her eyes, unspilled. In the tremble at the corner of her mouth that she hadn't managed to swallow back.

Her grief was there. So was her guilt.

And for all that she didn't move, didn't speak—she was breaking.

Not for the others to see. Just for him.

And gods help him—he had nothing left to give her.

Yasher looked away. And walked.

The path was uneven beneath his boots, but he

barely felt it. Each step was weightless, hollow, like walking through the memory of a moment rather than the moment itself. The world blurred at the edges, sound and light dulling as he carried Pari forward.

This wasn't how it was supposed to end.

His Luck had always saved him.

Gotten him out. Pulled him through. Bought him time.

But not this time.

Not her.

Not Pari.

And Yasher—

Yasher had nothing left to gamble.

CHAPTER 33

THE MORNING WAS QUIET, but not in the way that it should
have been.

It had been two days since the cavern.

Two days since Yasher had carried Pari's body out
into the light—his arms steady, his silence louder than
any scream. Since the Veil had been claimed. Since Jeta
had risen from death, not unchanged but remade. Since
the world had cracked open, and nothing had been put
back in the same place.

Two days since they emerged to a town destroyed
around them while they were in the cavern, ripped apart
by the storm that had raged while she thought she could
control the uncontrollable.

Farah sat on the edge of the bed, hands curled in her
lap, feet pressing into the uneven boards. The sheets
beside her were creased, the imprint of a body still
lingering in the fabric, but Yasher's presence had never
truly been there. He hadn't really moved the first day,
just staying in place there on the bed. She tried to pull

him towards her, holding him close, but he shrank away from her, his only real movement.

Even in stillness, his body had held the quiet tension of someone waiting for a blow that wouldn't come. And when she had shifted in the dark, just slightly, he had felt it—not her warmth, not her closeness, but the movement itself, the disturbance, as though he were bracing for something beyond her reach.

The pale, washed-out light slipping through the window barely reached him, casting only the faintest glow against the outline of his shoulders. Yasher stood at the washbasin, finally up. The water in the bowl sat still, untouched, as though it, too, was waiting. His back remained rigid, hands braced against the basin's edges, his head slightly bowed—not in prayer, not in thought, but in a stillness that was unlike him, unnatural. He had never been idle, never been a man who lingered too long in one place without purpose. But now, he was frozen. Not waiting. Not gathering himself. Just *there*. As if something inside him had finally gone quiet.

She wasn't sure if he knew she was watching, but she wasn't sure if it mattered to him.

Yasher had always carried himself with an easy sort of presence, a restless energy woven into the very fabric of his being. But now, that sharpness was dulled. He was simply there, unmoving, locked in place by something that had nothing to do with chains and everything to do with what had been lost.

She swallowed, her throat tight, the taste of ash and regret thick on her tongue. She turned her head slightly, letting her gaze sweep over him, taking in the way his shoulders tightened, the way the muscles in his back had tensed like he was bracing himself for something—something he couldn't see, something he couldn't stop.

Bruises bloomed in deep, aching shades along his arms, marks that she had put there, that her Talent had torn from him when she had wrenched the metals on his body, from his skin, from his bones. The memory of it curled in her gut like a hot iron, searing, burning. She had hurt him. Not just with words, not just with choices, but physically, with her own hands, with the power she had wielded like a blade aimed at his chest.

And still, still, that wasn't the worst of it.

The bruises would fade. She wasn't sure the rest of it would.

Farah inhaled slowly, steadying herself, before she finally spoke. "Yasher."

Her voice was quiet, measured, careful, but not hesitant. She had never been hesitant with him before. She wouldn't start now.

He didn't turn, didn't move.

But she saw the shift in his shoulders, the way his fingers tightened ever so slightly around the rim of the basin, as if grounding himself. As if steadying something that wasn't physical.

She pressed forward. "Talk to me."

He didn't move.

The silence stretched, slow and suffocating, like the breath before a final verdict.

She almost spoke again—almost filled the space with something, anything, just to keep it from swallowing her whole.

"What's there to say?" His voice wasn't cold. Wasn't cruel. Just stripped bare.

A hollow echo of the man who used to meet grief with defiance, who could laugh even when the sky was falling.

She stood, the movement slow, deliberate. She took a step toward him, close enough to see the tension ripple through his jaw, the shallow hitch in his breath, the grip of silence wrapped tight around him like armor.

"You haven't said anything since…," she murmured. "Not to me. Not to anyone."

He didn't turn. Didn't flinch.

"Pari is gone," he said, and the words—gods, the words—felt like a knife pressed against her ribs, not because of how he said them, but because of how empty they were.

She swallowed hard. "Yasher—"

Finally, he turned.

And the moment she met his eyes, her breath stilled in her throat.

This hollowed-out grief, something deep and unyielding, something carved into his very being in a way that could never be undone stole her breath. And beneath it—beneath all of it—there was something else. Blame. A thing that settled between them like an ocean too vast to cross.

Her stomach tightened, unease curling at the edges of her thoughts.

She took a step forward, reaching for him before she could think better of it, before she could stop herself. "Yasher, please—"

He stepped back.

Not far—barely a shift, just the weight of one foot sliding behind the other.

But it landed like a slap.

Her hand froze mid-reach, the air between them suddenly too wide to cross. Her fingers curled inward, as if scorched, and her chest constricted, a sharp ache radiating outward like a cracked bell.

She stared at him, a thousand words poised on the tip of her tongue, a thousand things she could say, should say...

"I need air," he muttered.

He turned before she could stop him, before she could say anything.

The door clicked shut behind him.

Farah sat motionless on the edge of the bed, her hands resting against her knees, fingers curled just enough to press into the fabric of her trousers. The air in the room was warm, thick with the scent of old wood and lingering candle smoke, the quiet weight of the morning settling over everything like a heavy shroud.

The silence that filled the space was unlike any she had ever known. It wasn't the expectant quiet before a battle, nor the tense hush of a negotiation where one wrong word could mean everything. This was stretched too thin, as if the very air between those walls had been stripped of meaning. It sat against her skin, seeped into the marrow of her bones, curling beneath her ribs and settling there, aching and persistent.

Her body was still, but inside, everything was twisting, shifting, pulling in too many directions at once. She should follow him. She should push past whatever fragile distance had settled between them, should find him and say *something*, anything, to bridge the widening gulf that neither of them had been willing to name.

But she stayed where she was. She hadn't earned his forgiveness. Not yet.

The sunlight crept slowly across the room, stretching in long, golden fingers through the uneven cracks of the wooden shutters, painting streaks of warmth against the cold stone floor. Dust swirled lazily in the beams, caught between movement and stillness, suspended in a space where neither belonged.

The town beyond was waking, slipping back into the rhythm of life as if nothing had changed. Conversations wove through the morning air, soft and unhurried, the kind of talk that belonged to those who still had the luxury of looking ahead as they repaired the physical damage the storm had brought them, and mental damage that Mazdavir did to the ones that survived.

They had seen horrors, had stood at the precipice of something terrible, but now they did what people always did—they survived, they endured, they moved forward. And yet, here, in this room, where the weight of last few days still pressed against her ribs, Farah could not. The world had already begun to settle, but she remained caught in the moment before the breaking, before every-thing unraveled, before she had to face what came next.

She wondered if Yasher was standing out there somewhere, watching the people rebuild, watching them sweep away the remnants of what had nearly claimed them. He had always been good at moving forward. He had always been light on his feet, slipping between moments as easily as he slipped between shadows. But now—now she wasn't sure where he was going.

And she wasn't sure if she was meant to follow.

She had made her choices. She had let the corruption in, hadn't she? Even if she hadn't welcomed it, even if she'd tried to fight it—it had still taken hold. She had carried it, let it whisper through her thoughts, let it shape the edge of her actions. That alone was enough. Enough to damn her.

Yasher had nearly died because of her. Jeta had died because of her. Pari had died for her.

And what had it bought them?

Another relic that wasn't really worth what it cost. A cause she had once clung to but could no longer define. Not in the same way. Not with blood still drying on their hands and silence wrapped around their hearts like a noose.

She had spent her whole life doing what was necessary, what was expected. But for the first time, the cost had become something she couldn't pay back. Something she couldn't fix.

And Yasher, who had fought for her, who had stayed through every storm, who had held fast when even she couldn't believe in herself—had turned away from her.

And maybe that was the quietest kind of end. The kind you didn't see coming until you were already standing in the ruins.

She had always believed that if she fought hard enough, endured long enough, she could hold onto what mattered. But not everything could be kept.

Not everything could be salvaged.

Some things, no matter how tightly you clung to them, still slipped through your fingers.

THE SOUND of hooves striking stone cut through the morning air the next day, a steady rhythm that seemed to echo the turmoil of the past few days. Farah turned at the sharp, familiar sound, her pulse quickening against her will, a hollow reminder of everything that had passed—the deaths, the battles, the choices. The weight of the world seemed to settle between her ribs, pushing her down as she watched the riders emerge from the gate, their formation sharp and disciplined.

They moved with purpose, the kind that only Emarian soldiers had, drilled and battle-hardened, answering to the Crown above all else. But it was Rostam who commanded her full attention, his presence unmistakable even through the early morning haze.

His arrival sent a ripple through the townspeople, startling them instead of freezing them. Their work stopped as soon as they saw him, their hands stilling over broken carts and debris while they were in the cavern. The murmurs faded into a thick, uneasy silence, the kind that came with the arrival of judgment wrapped in steel and authority.

Farah felt his gaze before she saw him—before he even spoke. It hit her like a weight pressing against her chest, the sharpness of it cutting through the space between them, carving through her like a blade.

"Farahnaz."

Her spine stiffened involuntarily, the muscles in her back tight with a tension she couldn't release. Her shoulders drew up, her breath catching as she watched him dismount, every movement precise, deliberate. He seemed untouched by the chaos, by the weight of the destruction around them.

She couldn't bring herself to meet his gaze—not fully. Not yet.

He would see it. He always did. He had always read her like an open book even when she had tried to keep her thoughts hidden. He knew what lay behind the walls she had built, and he had never hesitated to tear them down. What would he see in her now?

Would he still see the girl he had raised—the one he had taught, the one he had believed in? The one who had fought for something greater than herself? Or would he see the woman she had become—the woman who had let darkness creep into her soul, who had betrayed everything they had once stood for, everything they had once fought for together, lost the people she loved because of her own pride?

The weight of it pressed down on her, a suffocating awareness of the inevitable moment when he would see right through her—when he would read her as easily as he always had. The town was a reflection of what had happened, but it was nothing compared to the wreckage inside her. Her soul, shattered and twisted, would be clear to him. It would be a judgment, not of the town, but of her.

If he saw it, he would hate her.

And gods, she wasn't sure she could bear that after everything else she'd broken.

Her fingers curled into fists behind her back, nails pressing into her palms as she fought to keep the panic at bay, to hold herself together before he could see how badly she was unraveling.

Behind him, the other soldiers dismounted with the efficiency of men accustomed to war, their movements swift and instinctual, reaching for their weapons out of habit rather than immediate threat.

And just behind Rostam, halting his horse with a sharp, practiced movement, was Taj.

Farah's eyes met his, taking in the subtle shift in his expression, his mouth pulled tight, the furrow of his brow. He was whole, unscathed. That, at least, was something.

"You came back," she said, her voice carrying no emotion, as if the simple fact of his arrival should explain everything.

Taj let out a short, humorless breath and shook his head as he dismounted. "You have no idea what I had to do to get Rostam out here. The Citadel's in chaos. The Mashya is—" He cut himself off with a sharp exhale, jaw set, his voice quieting as something passed between them, something heavy with unspoken truths. "We'll talk later."

She held his gaze for a long moment, studying him— searching for something that would make sense of the cracks she could already see deep in his eyes. There was always more. There had to be.

Rostam's gaze sharpened as he focused fully on her.

"The gates were closed when we arrived for days they stayed that way, then they opened this morning." His voice was calm, controlled, but there was a sharp edge beneath it, a quiet command that cut through the air. He was asking for an explanation.

"The town wanted it that way," Farah replied, her arms folding tightly across her chest, a reflex against the growing tension. "We've been trying to get them open since... What we found here... it wasn't a town waiting for help, Rostam. It was something worse."

Rostam's expression remained unchanged, but the sharpness in his eyes betrayed the weight of his thoughts, the slight tightening at the corners of his mouth a sign of his recognition.

"And now?"

Farah turned her gaze toward the remnants of the town square. The survivors, faces worn with exhaustion, eyes empty from the weight of what they'd endured, slowly gathered in clusters. They were left to piece together lives that had been shattered, their once-familiar world reduced to rubble. She wondered if the survivors felt the same as she did, knowing what had happened without always being in control.

"They'll rebuild," she said, her voice quiet but firm. "Some of them will."

Rostam didn't press her further. With a subtle shift, he turned to one of his men and gave a quiet order to make camp in the open area near the square. The soldier nodded and moved off, his footsteps purposeful as he began to survey the wreckage of the town, the people left to face the aftermath.

Taj stepped forward, his voice barely a whisper. "Where's Pari? I brought her more paper and charcoal."

Farah's mouth opened, but the words stuck there, thick and suffocating. How could she possibly say them? How could she break the last thread of hope still clinging to his eyes?

Taj's face shifted, his jaw tightening as the reality of it settled in. It wasn't sudden. It wasn't clean. It was a slow descent, the truth sinking like stone into still water, spreading ripples he couldn't outrun.

"No, not her."

The words were so quiet, they barely made a sound.

Farah's gaze flickered away, unable to meet his eyes. Just for a moment, she turned, as if the simple act of looking away might make it hurt less, might give him space to grieve, might somehow undo what had already been torn apart.

The sound that escaped Taj was a low, raw exhale—a noise caught somewhere between a gasp and a curse. It struck her like a knife, the grief it carried so stripped of pretense, so unguarded, that it cut through the silence between them like a wound.

Farah's throat tightened. "Taj—"

But he didn't hear her. He had already turned away, his back a quiet wall between them. Another person that she'd broken.

Then, from behind her, a door creaked open.

Farah felt him before she heard him, the shift of wood was nothing compared to the weight of his presence. It pressed against her, pulling at her, filling the space with something too heavy to ignore. Yasher.

582

Her breath froze, caught somewhere deep in her chest, and she forced herself to exhale slowly. She didn't turn. Didn't move. But every part of her coiled, bracing herself for something she couldn't name, something that pressed too close to her soul.

He didn't speak.

He didn't step into the square right away, lingering in the threshold. His hesitation was brief, but long enough for the air to shift, for the space around him to feel heavier, thicker. Farah didn't turn. Not yet. Because if she did—if she met his eyes—she might find something she wasn't ready to see.

Taj inhaled sharply beside her. Rostam's gaze flicked toward the doorway, his expression unreadable. The soldiers with him stood back, their murmurs fading into the quiet, their presence felt but distant.

And then Yasher moved—slow, measured, hesitant, as though each step was a calculation. He had always moved with purpose, a restless energy in his bones. But now, each footfall felt heavier, deliberate, like he was testing the ground before committing to it.

And he didn't look at her. He didn't look at anyone.

He walked past her, heading to the cliffs, as he had done so often the last few days when he actually left the room.

She stood still, frozen in place, her chest tight and her breath caught somewhere deep inside. Every part of her wanted to reach out, to close the distance between them, but she couldn't. The air felt thick around her, and the silence—Gods, the silence between them—was enough to shatter everything she had left if she dared to break it.

"Farah," Rostam said quietly. "What happened?"

Tears filled her eyes, but she refused to let them fall. Instead, she began to tell Rostam everything, standing in the shadow of his horse as he listened with the same grim expression he always wore when war had left its mark somewhere new. He hadn't needed to say much. His presence had been enough. She had told him about Pari, Yasher, and even about Jeta. About herself, and all of her failures.

That had been the moment Rostam closed his eyes, only for a breath, before he had looked toward the others. When he turned back to her, it was not disgust, it was not hatred. In a way it was worse, as it was communion and sadness.

Mehran approached them to say that the Leaving was prepared.

She looked away from Rostam finally, letting the tears drop, and from the corner of her eye, finding the small figure of Yasher staring towards the sea silently, standing at the cliffs. His posture was tight, his hands at his sides. His face was stone. She left Rostam behind, his arm on hers before she turned to walk down the path to him.

The breath she took was slow, measured.

"Her Leaving is ready," she said, her voice quiet, steady.

She didn't say the words that came next, the ones that felt thick in her throat.

Yasher exhaled through his nose slowly and stepped forward.

Farah followed.

They walked in silence.

The dust stirred beneath their steps, the wind carrying the distant sound of voices, the shuffle of movement from those left behind. But here, on the path that led toward the pyre, there was only the crunch of boots on dry earth, only the weight of the air between them.

She wanted to say something.

But nothing would ease the ache of it. So, she did the only thing she could. She walked beside him.

When they reached the crest of the hill, the world stretched wide before them. The town lay below, small and weathered against the land. Beyond it, the road snaked toward the horizon, disappearing into the golden light of morning.

And before them, in a space where the land was soft and undisturbed, where the ground had been readied for the ritual—there, the wood had been stacked.

The Leaving pyre rose like a silent sentinel, stark against the pale morning sky, the carefully stacked cedar logs dark with oil, gleaming like something sacred—something unbearably final. Strips of pristine white cloth twisted gently in the breeze, their movements like quiet prayers, whispered but unheard, meant to guide a soul onward. The scent of saffron and cedar wrapped around Farah like a shroud, sharp and sweet, carrying the weight of every farewell she'd ever known and every regret she still carried.

Yasher's breath hitched, a tiny, fragile sound that she felt as if it were her own. Her awareness narrowed, every sense sharpening around him—the uneven rise of his chest, the faint twitch of his fingers at his sides, the way his jaw tightened with unspoken grief. She watched the subtle fracture behind his eyes, a glimpse of the pain he refused to fully reveal, and she clung to it, desperate and aching, as if memorizing even this—the way he hurt—could somehow hold him close for just a little longer.

Her fingers brushed his wrist, light, tentative. Not demanding. Just there. A touch that asked nothing, only offered.

For a moment, the warmth of him was there beneath her fingertips, the steady, quiet hum of his presence, the familiar weight of his existence beside hers. She had memorized the way his skin felt against hers, the way he always ran a little too warm, like some part of him burned brighter than the rest of the world.

He didn't pull away—but he didn't take her hand, either.

He stood unmoving, his gaze fixed stubbornly ahead, focusing on the pyre, the fluttering white cloth. She felt each shallow rise and fall of his breath as though they were her own, felt the subtle tension in his shoulders like a physical ache in her chest. She wanted desperately to reach further, to close the distance, to force him to acknowledge her—but she couldn't. She had lost that right.

So, she let her hand linger, just a moment longer, let her fingers rest against the pulse at his wrist, feeling the uneven beat beneath her touch. And then, with the same quiet grace with which she had reached for him, she withdrew.

She remained at his side, close enough that if he

turned, if he shifted even slightly, he would know she was there. That she was not leaving.

The wind twisted around them, carrying the scent of the faint oil that would send Pari's body onward, following her soul already in the House of Song. The smell of farewells filled the air—sharp, inevitable.

Yasher exhaled, slowly, as if releasing something that had been bound too tightly within him.

His hand, the one she had touched, trembled at his side, his fingers flexing as if searching for something he knew wasn't there.

He turned, just enough for Farah to see the flicker in his eyes, the brief softening of his gaze, a momentary crack in the stone wall he had built. His eyes fell to her hand, where it rested near him.

For a heartbeat, the world between them felt like it might break open. And then he reached out.

His fingers brushed her skin, feather-light, barely there—but it was enough to send a tremor through her chest, a familiar warmth she had forgotten she craved.

But it wasn't a reunion. It was a moment, fragile and fleeting, like the wind that carried their past, a past that had already slipped beyond their grasp.

His fingers slipped away, lingering just long enough to remind her of what had been, before he turned back to the pyre.

He did not pull away, but the space between them felt wider than ever.

And Farah stood there, her heart heavier than the pyre that awaited, as the wind whispered through the trees, carrying the scent of endings—ones she didn't know how to stop.

CHAPTER 34

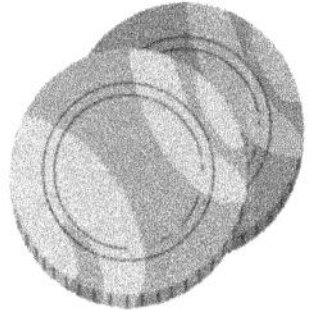

THE DAYS BLED TOGETHER, indistinguishable from one another. The town moved on, its rhythm steady despite the wreckage that the shadows had created while they fought their own war in the cavern. People resumed their routines, salvaging what they could, leaving the rest behind. The market reopened, bread and roasting meat perfuming the air, the streets once again alive with the hum of ordinary life. But for Yasher, there was nothing ordinary about it. Pari was gone. And he couldn't stop feeling the weight of her absence.

She had been small but bright, her presence filling every room without effort. Curious, certain—she pulled him into her world with ease. He still expected to hear her laughter, to feel her tiny hand tugging at him toward something new she had discovered. He listened for the scratch of charcoal against paper, for the hum she made while drawing, her hair falling across her eyes from where it had pulled out of her braids.

He had never been good at grief. Not the lingering

kind, the kind that ate at you day by day, like a wound that never quite closed. His whole life had been about pushing forward, never letting himself stop long enough to feel the weight of things lost. But this... This was Pari.

And with her gone, the silence felt unbearable.

He fell back into routine, his movements mechanical, disconnected. He spoke only when needed, a shadow among the others.

And then there was Farah.

Farah had become a ghost at the edge of his vision. He avoided her gaze, her touch, the intensity that once bound them now a wall between them during the day. Their exchanges were brief, clipped, and only when necessary, cold and distant.

At night, with darkness between them, he let himself get closer, close enough to feel her, to remember when there had been no distance between them. When trust had been effortless and the things said, the the things done could be put away, out of sight.

He still loved her. That had never changed, would never change. But every time he looked at her, the image of Pari's lifeless body in her arms haunted him. Farah had carried the corruption, trusted she could control it, yet again decided for the rest of them that she could do it without help, without them—and failed. He blamed her for that. More than he blamed himself.

He knew it wasn't fair. But the weight of it gnawed at him, a feeling that she had failed them both, something he couldn't forgive. He didn't know how to begin forgiving her, let alone forgive himself for failing to protect her, for trusting her when he had failed Pari.

"You should listen instead of getting stuck up in your head occasionally, *saqalu*," Jeta remarked once, her voice dry but gentle, not lifting her eyes from her cards as they played a game while others rebuilt the town around them. "Could learn something."

Yasher let out a quiet huff. "What, how to cheat?"

Jeta's lips curved faintly, but her gaze remained steady on her hand.

"You could stand to be better at it. You've lost your touch."

There was a brief pause before he sighed, taking another slow drag from his cup. "Not interested in learning tricks right now."

She studied him for a moment, her eyes still focused on her hand. "Suit yourself."

They fell into a rhythm, the hush of cards shuffling, the soft rustle of the wind outside. Simple, grounded sounds that filled the space between them without needing to fill it with words. He remained silent for the most part, and the not-old woman let him, his focus wavering between the game and the weight in his chest. At times he wanted to ask her about her transformation, felt the thought like an itch at the back of his mind, but there was a layer of mortar around most feelings these days.

The others, too, felt the weight of his silence. He kept his distance, retreating into his own world, silently playing cards with Jeta instead of going out and helping. Younis and Mehran tried to engage him during the day, discussing strategies for rebuilding and securing the area before heading back to the Citadel.

His responses were curt, measured, not out of rudeness but because the space between them felt too vast for anything more. When he did talk, it was about tasks, not about the rawness beneath the surface. It was easier that way. Easier than confronting what they all had lost.

Taj, however, sought him out more frequently, though he could tell that his friend from the road, from before, wasn't fooled by the quiet distance. Taj's eyes often lingered, as if waiting for him to speak, to open up. But he wasn't ready. He couldn't be. He wasn't ready to share the weight of the grief that kept him up at night, listening for Farah, both wanting her near and yet pushing her away when it happened. And the guilt—that gnawing guilt that made it impossible for him to trust himself with anyone.

One day, after another long round of work and minimal conversation, Taj stood next to Yasher, his posture stiff with unspoken frustration. "You're keeping yourself closed off," Taj said, his voice low but firm.

Yasher glanced at him, seeing the concern etched in his features, the way his friend was trying to reach him despite everything. "I'm fine."

Taj shook his head.

"You're not. And neither am I. Neither is anyone else." He paused before continuing, making a point to look towards Farah. "We can't keep pretending this is okay. We've all lost something, and you—" He stopped himself, jaw tightening. "It'll bury you if you don't let go."

He didn't respond at first, letting the words hang

between them. Finally, he spoke, his voice a quiet rasp. "I don't know what you want from me, Taj."

"I want you to let us in. I want you to stop pushing us away."

His throat tightened, his eyes going cold. "You don't understand."

"No," Taj said, his voice softening, "I do understand, at least a little bit. That little girl touched all of us, and we're all going through it in our own ways. But that doesn't mean I'm going to stand by and watch you drown in this because you refuse to hold out your hand."

He turned away, not wanting to confront the truth in Taj's eyes.

The inn was quiet in the hours after dusk, the kind of stillness that had started to comfort him. He sat at the small wooden table, fingers tracing the rim of his cup absentmindedly, the cold tea a reminder of how much had changed in so little time. The faint sounds of the inn, creaking floorboards, distant voices, seemed far away. Farah had already retreated to their room. He should follow, should try to make an effort to start to repair what felt unrepairable, but the words felt like stones in his throat, too heavy to swallow.

The door creaked open. He didn't need to turn to know it was Rostam.

The man's presence settled into the room, thick and unyielding, like a storm that had already passed but still left its weight in the air. He shut the door quietly behind him, his boots barely making a sound on the floor as he moved toward Yasher.

"Thought I might find you here," Rostam's voice

rumbled, calm, but with that edge—the question he wasn't asking.

Yasher didn't respond right away. He lifted the cup, took a sip of the cold tea, and set it down with a soft thud. Rostam waited, quiet, unblinking.

"Don't suppose you came to tell me how the camp's holding up," he muttered, his voice flat.

Rostam's gaze hardened, his posture still. "You're not fooling anyone."

His jaw tightened. "What's that supposed to mean?"

Rostam stepped closer, boots almost silent on the floor. "The silence. The detachment. You think you're hiding it, but you're not. You've never been good at lying to yourself. Others, yes, but not yourself."

He felt a tightening in his chest, a quick flash of irritation. "I'm fine," he muttered, the words tasting bitter before they even left his mouth.

"You're lying," Rostam said simply. His voice was steady, cutting through the thin veil he tried to hide behind. "You're falling apart in front of all of us, and you don't even see it."

His eyes flashed. His breath caught, the frustration sharp, but he couldn't quite push it away. "And what do you suggest I do, Rostam? To stand here and wallow in it with the others, singing songs and wailing to the sky? Pari is gone. There's nothing left but silence." The last words faltered before he could catch them, and the moment they escaped, he felt the weight of them crush him.

Rostam stood still for a moment, the silence settling

between them like a growing storm. He didn't step back. Didn't look away. "That's not what I meant."

His head snapped up, a laugh that wasn't really a laugh falling from his lips. "You want me to mourn like everyone else?" Yasher's voice had gone tight, edges fraying. "Want me to pretend it doesn't burn every time I think of her? That it will never not rip me apart every time?"

"No," Rostam said, and his voice softened, but only slightly. "I want you to stop running from it. From her. Farah... She cannot bear all of this alone. She can't carry everything on her shoulders and know there's no one to catch her when she falls. This isn't just about you, gharib."

He staggered back, his heart stuttering. He turned away quickly, eyes snapping to the window, where the pale moonlight cast long shadows across the town. Her. Farah. The weight of the words, of the implication, hit him harder than the loss of Pari itself. He stared out at the dim street, his chest tight, his breath shallow.

"I'm trying to..." he muttered, a bitter edge creeping into his voice. "I'm trying to survive this myself. To get through it on my own."

Rostam's voice dropped, but there was a certain fire in it, a hardness Yasher knew too well.

"Survive?" Rostam's tone sharpened. "You think this is about survival, Yasher? This is what happens when you let the darkness inside. And you've let it in. I'm not talking about the corruption, I'm talking about you— what you're doing to yourself and to her. You're doing more damage than Mazdavir ever could to her."

Yasher spun back to face him, fists clenched at his sides. "I didn't let this happen. Farah—"

"I know," Rostam interrupted. His words were like stone, unyielding, steady. "But you let yourself fall into it just the same. You are both one bad thought away from throwing yourselves into those rocks, instead of helping one another walk away from the edge."

A tremor shot through Yasher's chest as his eyes locked to him. Something raw broke through the anger, the walls he'd built, and his voice came out low, strained. "I love her," he whispered. "But she... she hid it. She didn't let us...let *me*...help her before it went too far."

Rostam nodded slowly, his eyes softer, but still knowing. "I know you do. But you're killing yourself if you think you can go back and fix something before it could happen. You're going to lose yourself before you lose her."

He turned away, trembling as he fought to hold himself together. His hands were shaking and he couldn't make them stop.

"What do I do about it?" The words were thick with frustration, almost choking him.

"Stop acting like you're in this alone," Rostam said firmly. "And start forgiving yourself, so you can forgive her."

He shook his head, the weight of it all pressing down on him. "I don't know if I can." His voice cracked, the pain impossible to hold back.

Rostam moved closer, his hand resting on Yasher's shoulder, a silent but powerful gesture. "I never said it would be easy. But it's the only way forward. For you. For her. For both of you." He squeezed his shoulder, the pressure grounding. "You're destroying both of you by pretending you're just destroying yourself."

He closed his eyes, a deep breath pulling through him, but the weight of it all suffocated him. His chest tightened, the room feeling smaller with every passing second.

"I'll try," he whispered, the words fragile, the uncertainty hanging in the air between them.

Rostam gave him a silent nod. "That's all any of us can do."

As Rostam turned to leave, he remained motionless. The weight of the words pressed down on him. *Try.* What did that even mean? How could he move forward when the past felt like it was buried under layers of rubble?

Could he forgive himself? Could he forgive Farah? He wasn't sure. Every time he thought about moving forward, the absence of Pari tightened around him, suffocating him in a way he couldn't escape.

He wasn't sure if he could ever leave the past behind. But he knew one thing. The man he had been before was gone.

Could he move on? Or would he be trapped, forever haunted by the choices that had defined them all?

YASHER STOOD at the edge of the courtyard, his eyes tracing the slow, methodical movements of those who remained. Farah was among them, speaking with

Mehran and Younis, their voices low and steady, discussing their return to the Citadel within the next few days. They moved with purpose, certainty. A certainty he couldn't find, not within himself. Not now.

The morning sun barely kissed the stone walls of the town, its weak light casting long, stretching shadows. The air was thick, laden with an unspoken weight, each breath harder than the last. His hands curled and uncurled at his sides in slow, tight motions, trying to find some semblance of control he knew was slipping through his fingers. His feet moved on their own accord, carrying him away from the scene, away from the faces of those who still had purpose, toward the only person who might offer him a way out—a way forward.

Jeta glanced up before he even reached her, as if she had been expecting him.

"Didn't think you were one for goodbyes," she mused, one brow lifting. "And I'm not leaving until tomorrow, *saqalu*. So if you wanted one more game lost under your belt, I'm happy to oblige."

He stopped a few paces away, shifting his weight from one foot to the other before forcing himself to stillness. "Not saying goodbye."

Jeta tilted her head slightly. "No?"

He shook his head, jaw tightening as a heavy ache settled into his chest.

"I want to go with you," he said quietly, the words feeling strangely final as they passed his lips. It was an escape. A desperate bid to outrun the grief that kept pressing closer, squeezing tighter with every passing day. Rostam could think him a coward, hell, he was a coward. He can't help anyone, let alone himself.

Something flickered across her face—curiosity, amusement, understanding. "To Tamidh?" she asked, though she already knew.

He nodded. "To train. To learn how to control this. I am… ready."

She didn't speak right away. Her gaze swept over him, taking him in, weighing him in a way that made his skin itch. Jeta had a way of seeing through people, of cutting straight to the things they tried to hide.

And Yasher was no longer good at hiding.

"You want to control it," she echoed, her voice even, but there was something in it, something questioning, something knowing.

He ran a hand through his hair before shaking his head. "I need to."

Jeta considered him for a long moment, the weight of her attention pressing against him. "And that's the only reason?"

He stiffened, but he should have known better than to think she wouldn't see it.

That she wouldn't see him.

Yasher forced a smirk, but it was weak, barely there. "You asking if I have ulterior motives?"

Jeta didn't smile. "I'm asking if you know them already, or if you're still lying to yourself."

His fingers twitched at his sides. He wanted to scoff, to brush it off, to turn away from the conversation entirely—but the words stuck, and he felt them press against something raw inside him.

He did know them, though he wanted to lie to himself still. This wasn't just about his Luck. Wasn't just about training, about understanding, about control.

It was about running.

Running from Pari's death, from the endless ache that followed in its wake. The hollow space she had left was sharp, jagged, and every time he breathed, he felt the guilt gripping his ribs—suffocating him. He could have done more. He should have. Every breath felt like failure, a reminder of the things he hadn't done, the life he hadn't been able to save.

He was running from the weight of it all.

From the grief that weighed him down. From the guilt that kept clawing at him. But most of all, from Farah.

Every time he looked at her, the tension between them was a living thing, thrumming between them like a chord stretched too tight. There had been trust, he had trusted her, and she had trusted him, but now there was a fracture, deep and raw.

He let out a breath, shaking his head.

"It doesn't matter," he said finally. "I need to do this."

"Then come," Jeta said simply, her voice calm but heavy with the weight of unspoken things. In those two words was a quiet camaraderie, one forged through shared losses.

He didn't need to explain things to Jeta. She knew, perhaps better than anyone, that sometimes the only thing you could do was keep moving forward. Even if it meant walking away from the people who remained, from everything you used to hold onto.

It should have made it easier.

Yasher swallowed hard, glancing back toward the courtyard, toward the others—toward Farah. She still stood where he had left her, speaking with Mehran, her posture straight, composed, focused. She was moving forward. She always had.

But Yasher—

Yasher wasn't. Not this time. He was just moving on, away, yet staying in this moment.

Jeta offered him a steady look. "We leave tomorrow. You'll have time to pack... and, well, figure out what comes next, *saqalu*."

He nodded.

She turned away, leaving him standing there with the weight of his decision settling like iron in his chest.

Tomorrow, he would leave, and a part of him questioned whether he could ever return. Not because of the distance, but because he wasn't sure there would be anything left of him to come back to. The life he was leaving behind felt as though it might slip away completely, like sand through his fingers.

He tried not to think about what that meant too deeply, not to imagine Farah standing alone, the space beside her empty because he had made the choice to leave it that way. Leaving now was a betrayal that would rip apart what little remained.

She had always deserved better than the broken pieces he was before, and what he'd become now was so much worse. And yet, there was a part of him—one that he couldn't quite silence—that wondered if leaving was the only thing that would give her the chance to find someone who could truly be there. Even if that meant he wasn't a part of her world any longer.

———

YASHER HAD ALWAYS KNOWN that leaving would hurt. He'd felt the ache building within him for days, heavy as iron, but he hadn't expected the sheer agony of standing here now, facing her, torn between the crushing need to escape and the desperate desire to stay. He had rehearsed this moment without realizing it since they left the cavern, but no preparation could shield him from the way Farah's eyes went still and dark when she realized he was leaving.

She stood in the doorway, the late afternoon light spilling behind her, casting her silhouette in gold while her eyes grew darker, deeper, unreadable as she took in the small, undeniable truths scattered throughout the room. His pack, already half-full. His coat tossed carelessly over the chair, waiting for him to pick it up.

He could feel her watching him, but he couldn't bring himself to meet her eyes just yet. Instead, he focused on the task in front of him, fingers tightening the straps of his pack, rolling a shirt with more care than was necessary, anything to keep his hands from shaking. He had spent too much time running to pretend that he wasn't doing it again now.

She had expected him to come back to the Citadel with her. She had hoped, that he might stay, to heal with her, to rebuild what had been shattered between them.

But the worst part—the part that knotted his gut and

dug deep into his chest—was the resignation in her eyes. She had known this moment was coming, had probably felt it long before he could even admit it to himself. And worse still, she had accepted it. She had already braced herself for this loss, for him leaving her—without anger, without demands, as if she knew, deep down, that she deserved it. And that quiet understanding, that acceptance, hollowed him out.

Farah always knew, didn't she? She saw the truth of it before he could even voice it, always one step ahead of him, always sharper. It was what made her brilliant, what kept her alive when others would have crumbled under the weight of it all. This was the first time he saw her mask she wore to the rest of the world falter, the first time that cold calculation of hers failed to conceal the hurt that lay just beneath, the first time in over a year that she'd felt the need to wear that mask, however poorly, to him.

He let out a breath, slow and steady, before finally forcing himself to really look at her.

"I need this, Farah."

His voice was quieter than he meant it to be, the weight of it settling between them like a stone sinking into deep water.

"I know," she said, her voice calm but heavy, the kind of quiet that spoke louder than any words could. There was no anger, no demand for an explanation, only an understanding so deep, so full of pain, it made him want to collapse under the weight of it.

She understood, she knew the truth.

He was leaving because *he couldn't bear it anymore.* He

couldn't bear the weight of what he had become—the man who failed, the man who couldn't save anyone. Running was the only thing that made sense, even if it wasn't right.

Farah shifted slightly, the wooden floor creaking beneath her.

She reached for him.

It was a quiet gesture—her fingers brushing softly against his wrist, tentative, uncertain. Yasher felt the contact like a brand against his skin, burning with the memory of every gentle touch, every whispered promise. He hesitated, torn between pulling away to spare them both and leaning into the warmth that still lingered, a lifeline he wasn't sure he deserved anymore. Her touch was an offering, unassuming but raw, a silent reminder of everything they had built, and everything he was now tearing apart.

The moment stretched between them, too heavy, too fragile. He could feel the warmth of her touch, the barest brush of her skin against his, a simple, human thing that should not have had the power to undo him any longer. But it did.

He turned his hand over, catching her fingers in his own, curling them together, holding on, even though he knew he was about to let go.

She inhaled, the sound barely more than a breath, and in that single exhale, he felt everything between them, everything that was being lost.

He pulled her to him, and she stepped forward without hesitation, pressing into his chest as if it were the only place she had ever truly belonged. Her arms tightened around him, fingers gripping his shirt like she was terrified to let go. His arms encircled her instinctively, holding her close enough to feel her heartbeat against his own—fast, uneven, echoing the quiet desperation of the moment.

She buried her face against his neck, her breath hot, unsteady, as though she could keep him here if she held on tightly enough. He closed his eyes, breathing her in, imprinting every detail—the warmth, the scent, the weight of her—knowing he'd carry the ache of this moment long after he had left her behind.

His lips found the top of her head, the crown of dark curls that had always carried the faint scent of oil and forge-smoke, the scent that was so distinctly hers.

She turned her face, her breath ghosting against his throat.

"Don't go," she whispered, her voice fracturing around the edges, quiet enough that the words felt like they might disappear before fully reaching him. Yasher's chest tightened, the plea twisting through him like a blade.

He wanted to say yes, gods did he want to promise her that he'd stay, that they'd find a way. He wanted to be strong enough for both of them, to erase the hurt, the soul-crushing loss he'd seen in her eyes from the moment Pari had fallen. But he wasn't strong, not now, not like this. And so, he stayed silent, holding her tighter instead.

Instead, he tilted her chin up, his fingers grazing the curve of her jaw, the touch slow and reverent, as if every inch of her mattered. His thumb brushed over her cheekbone, tender, lingering, and she leaned into his touch like she would never feel it again. Her lips parted, her breath hitching, her eyes dark and vulnerable, caught between hope and the terror of what was to come.

He kissed her. Slow. Deep. A kiss heavy with everything they had been, everything they had lost, and everything they could never say. It was desperate, but it was also goodbye.

Her hands slid up, threading through his hair, holding him there, keeping him close. She kissed him back just as deeply, just as fiercely, as if she could press herself into him, as if she could stay there, even if he left.

When they finally broke apart, it wasn't with distance. Their foreheads rested together, their breaths mingling, their hands still tangled.

"I'll come back," he murmured, his voice raw, but the words felt hollow in his mouth. "When I can. When I..."

Her fingers curled into his hair, her grip tightening just a little, as if holding onto something that was slipping away. She exhaled slowly, a soft, broken sound.

"I know," she whispered. "I know you will."

And neither of them spoke the truth they both felt, that when, or even if, he returned, the space between them would be a chasm too wide to bridge. The love they had would still be there, but it would be *different*—fragile, tarnished, and irrevocably changed.

CHAPTER 35

It was a brittle silence that started the morning, stretched thin like old glass, its edges sharp and fragile, threatening to break under the weight of everything left unsaid. Farah felt it in every breath, each inhale sharp, each exhale slow, as if the very air was too heavy. Her chest ached, and her throat tightened, but she held herself still, the quiet of the morning matching the quiet tension in her own heart, strained by the weight of all she had lost, all she had broken.

She stood at the edge of the town's main road, watching the horses being saddled, watching the dust rise in lazy swirls beneath shifting hooves, each movement a reminder of everything she was losing. The others were at a distance, their silence palpable, their eyes turned away, as if honoring something they couldn't quite name. Mehran and Younis murmured low, their voices barely above a whisper, pretending not to notice her. Rostam stood nearby, his posture rigid, arms crossed, his gaze unwavering but even without words, his eyes pressed into her like a reminder that she wasn't the only one witnessing this parting.

Taj, standing beside him, shifted uneasily, glancing between Yasher and Farah with something like hesitation, as if he wanted to say something, as if he thought he should say something. Before he could, Younis walked up and smacked him on the back of the head, muttering something sharp under his breath. Taj scowled, rubbing the spot, but before he could argue, Rostam cut them both a look—cool, sharp, commanding.

Neither of them said another word.

Instead, they fell into step behind him as he mounted his horse, the motion smooth, practiced. Taj hesitated for a fraction of a second longer, his gaze flicking once more toward Farah, but when Younis jerked his chin in the direction of their commander, he finally followed.

The villagers that remained moved through the square in slow, careful steps, trying to find their way now that the Darkness had left. The weight of loss sat heavy over everything, a suffocating presence woven into the very air. No one spoke more than necessary. No one dared to break the fragile quiet that clung to the morning like mist, delicate and threatening to shatter.

Jeta was already mounted, her posture loose, unhurried, though her sharp eyes tracked everything. She gave Yasher his space, letting him linger a moment longer with Farah. Maybe that was kindness. Maybe it was just inevitability.

Farah didn't know how to say goodbye.

She had thought, hoped against everything, maybe he would change his mind. Last night, when he had finally held her the way he used to, when his hands had trembled against her skin, when his breath had stuttered against her shoulder, that it had meant they could repair what had been broken. That maybe he would stay.

They had moved together in the dark, their bodies seeking what words could not say. His touch had been reverent, almost desperate, as if memorizing her, as if tracing every curve and line with the quiet understanding that this might be the last time. She had felt the weight of his grief in the way his hands had lingered, the way his fingers had curled into her skin like he was trying to hold on a little longer.

She had given herself to him, as she always had, as she always would, no matter how fractured things had become between them. She had pressed her lips to his, swallowing the sorrow there, had run her hands through his hair, feeling the way he shuddered beneath her touch. It had been slow, aching, a kind of devastation in itself. Not frantic, not angry, not something they could claim had been driven by grief alone. It had been love. A goodbye dressed as love.

And then, afterward, when their bodies were tangled and slick with sweat, when she had turned toward him, hoping—just *hoping*—he had stayed awake long enough to let her say something that might anchor him to her, she had felt it. The moment he had begun to pull away, the moment his arms had loosened, the moment he had shifted to face the wall instead of her.

She had known then.

She had known the moment his warmth had edged just slightly out of reach.

This was the end.

So now, she stood still, straight-backed and unread-able, watching as he gathered the last of his things, as he secured the straps on his horse, as he did everything but look at her.

She couldn't ask him to stay, not when she had been the reason they lost Pari. Not when every time he looked at her, she could feel the grief lingering just beneath his skin.

She had done this. Every time she saw his grief-shad-owed eyes, every time he pulled away, a part of her knew it was just. It was the price she had to pay for her arro-gance, for thinking she could wield something so dark without it consuming her. How could she ask him to stay? How could she demand his love when she had been the one to break everything they had?

She had been wrong.

Her fingers curled at her sides, nails pressing into the flesh of her palms as she exhaled slowly, willing herself to keep her breathing steady, to keep her face blank. Be the weapon again, not the woman breaking apart. He adjusted the strap on his satchel, his movements precise, focused. If he was feeling anything close to the storm inside her, he didn't show it.

He had always worn his heart so easily, so openly, except when it came to real pain. Except when it came to wounds that didn't heal right, to losses that weren't recoverable. Then, he buried it, let it settle deep, let it fester where no one else could see.

He was doing it now.

Finally, he turned to face her.

His blue eyes, so bright once, so full of mischief and warmth, were dark with something else. Something heavier. Something that she had put there.

She swallowed against the tightness in her throat, but it didn't ease.

"You'll be all right?" he asked, his voice quieter than it should have been.

It was a ridiculous question.

She was the Hand of the Mashya. The woman who had taken down rebels, who had walked through homes like a whisper, killing and taking what was needed. She had survived the worst of the Mashyana's trials. She had been chosen, been *made* for this.

The weight of his absence hadn't even settled yet in her heart, and she already knew she wouldn't be all right. It wouldn't be right again.

She nodded anyway, shuttering away her thoughts. "Of course."

Yasher's jaw tightened.

They had never been ones for pretty lies before, not between each other.

He reached for her, his hand hovering between them for a moment that stretched too long, too painfully. For a second, just a heartbeat, she thought he might pull her close again, that he might wrap his fingers around her waist, or cup the back of her neck, or press his forehead to hers the way he used to. But his hand faltered, just barely, and then—he let it fall.

The space between them grew colder.

Something cracked inside her, sharp and sudden, splintering beneath her ribs like shattered glass, the shards pressing deeper with each breath she forced herself to take. Every time she thought she was done breaking, that there was nothing left, something new cracked.

She wanted to scream, to beg, to force him to see her differently, to see her not as the destruction she had become, but as the woman he had once loved. The woman who had loved him without reservation, without fear. To remind him of what they had been, of what they could still be—if only she could reach him.

He watched her warily, as if expecting a fight, as if bracing for the sharp edge of her fury, the weight of her defiance. But she did not raise her voice, she just looked at him.

Her gaze swept over the lines of his face, memorizing them, cataloging every shadow and every sharp edge that grief had carved into him. The man she had loved. The man she still loved. The man she had fought beside, laughed with, stolen moments of warmth and tenderness with in the dark hours of the night. The man who had seen her at her worst and still stayed. Until now.

She finally reached for him, her hand steady, deliberate. She cupped his cheek, her palm fitting against the roughness of his unshaven jaw, her fingers curling slightly against his skin. He didn't flinch, but he was still as marble.

Slowly, as if pulled by some force neither of them could name, he lifted his own hand. His fingers ghosted along her jaw, his palm warm as it came to rest against her cheek, mirroring her touch with the same aching reverence. His thumb brushed over her skin, the barest, most fleeting motion, but it was enough. It was everything.

His eyes, so guarded, so unreadable, softened just enough for her to see it, to see him. The grief, the love, the unbearable weight of all that had come between them. He still loved her. As much as she still loved him.

And then, softly, so softly it was nearly lost to the morning wind, she said, "Mu Ashta Za E."

The words were ancient, an offering that stretched back through centuries, carrying the weight of an unspoken vow she had never dared voice before. It was a confession, a promise, and a final plea, all wrapped in a single phrase, *my heart is yours*. Farah's heart, her love, was laid bare in those words, even if he couldn't understand them fully.

His expression shifted for the briefest of moments. A flicker of something deep passed through his eyes. It was as though the weight of her words, the depth of her feelings, had struck him, even without fully knowing what she had said. Something inside him seemed to crack just for a moment and then it was gone, swallowed up by the distance between them.

And that, too, was a goodbye.

His mouth pressed into a tight line. His shoulders straightened. And then, after a long, lingering beat, he dipped his head low, stepping back.

But just as he reached for the reins, just as the weight of their parting settled between them, heavy and inescapable, he hesitated. His fingers curled around the worn leather, knuckles white with tension, and then he said,

"We will find each other, Phoenix."

Her breath caught. It was not a promise. Not quite. But it was something.

And as he swung into the saddle, as he turned his horse toward the horizon where Jeta already waited, Farah let those words settle deep inside her, let them carve themselves into the hollow ache in her chest.

Because no matter what had broken between them, no matter how far he rode, how much distance stretched between them—She believed him.

And then, with a sharp pull on the reins, he was gone.

She stood, unmoving, as the dust curled in the air, as he rode away—until he was nothing but a dark shape against the horizon.

Until he was gone.

Only then, when she was certain no one could see, did her breath shudder.

Did her fingers tremble.

Did she press a hand to her stomach, as if she could hold together the pieces of herself that had just broken apart.

Now, standing in the silence left by Yasher's departure, Farah knew this was her punishment. Losing him was not only inevitable, it was what she deserved.

THE ROAD STRETCHED ENDLESSLY AHEAD, the dust curling beneath the horses' hooves, each step a reminder of the miles between them and Sakasan. The town, heavy with unfinished memories, receded behind them, a weight that clung to her shoulders, pressing down with every breath she took.

Farah rode at the front of their company through the growing cedars, her hands on the reins, but her grip was tight, rigid. Every movement was a conscious effort to stay composed, to not let herself slip.

But now, she only felt the hollowness where he had been.

She kept her eyes on the road ahead, but the ache in her chest did not fade.

The small complement of soldiers that had arrived with Rostam rode in formation, disciplined, efficient. They moved like a single being, a shifting mass of armor and stee.

Taj, for all his sharp-eyed watchfulness, had the sense not to try to comfort her. But he didn't let her disappear into silence, either.

"Gods, it's too quiet," Taj muttered beside her after an hour of steady riding, his voice pitched just enough for her to hear over the wind. "I'm going to die of boredom. Someone start a fight. Or a song. Or a passionate monologue about fate. Anything."

Farah ignored him, staring straight ahead.

Taj exhaled sharply. "You know, most people would at least humor me."

Still nothing.

Taj shook his head, clicking his tongue. "Fine. How about a story? A tragic tale of woe and bad decisions. A man falls in love with someone wildly unattainable. He makes a fool of himself, ruins everything, and is forced to challenge a horse to single combat to prove his worth."

Farah's fingers twitched on the reins, but she gave no other indication that she had heard him.

Taj sighed dramatically, dragging a hand down his face. "By the Seven, you people are impossible. I am a gift, you know. A treasure. A light in the darkness."

Behind them, Mehran let out a quiet snort, and Younis muttered something that sounded suspiciously like, "A headache."

Taj gasped, placing a hand over his heart. "Really, Younis? I'm just trying to lighten the mood, fill this damned divine silence."

She exhaled slowly through her nose, her focus unshaken, but she could feel the weight of Taj's expectant stare, could hear the smirk in his voice as he said,

"You're smiling, aren't you?"

She wasn't. But she hated that he had even suggested it.

Taj clicked his tongue. "Look, I'm trying, okay?"

She heard Mehran chuckle behind them.

Younis, ever the serious one, muttered something under his breath again, and Taj let out a wounded huff. "You think I should stop trying? You? The man who has never smiled in his life?"

She let the conversation fade into the background, let it become nothing more than a hum of voices behind her.

Ahead of them, the road stretched endlessly, winding through rolling hills that would eventually give way to the familiar, sun-worn paths leading back to the Citadel. She focused on the rhythm of her horse's gait, on the distant scent of rain in the wind, on the way the light cut through the thinning clouds in long, pale fingers.

The road stretched on, unchanging.

Beside her, Rostam had been silent for a long time. He had let Taj attempt his foolishness at lifting the mood, had let the others murmur among themselves, had let the hush settle between them.

But now, as the road stretched before them and the sky grew a shade darker, he finally spoke.

"Get out of your head, you'll just end up hating yourself," his voice low but certain. "You need to say something, otherwise Taj will just keep trying to get that scowl off your face."

She exhaled slowly, her grip tightening ever so slightly. "There's nothing to say."

Rostam hummed, unconvinced. "There is always something to say."

She didn't answer.

Then, after some time, Rostam spoke again, his voice edged with something knowing.

"You love him. I don't understand why still, but it is what it is." Rostam's words were simple, but there was a knowing in his voice, as if he had seen this kind of pain before.

Her fingers tightened around the reins, but her throat was tight, her chest heavy with something she couldn't name. "It doesn't matter now. It's too late for that."

"It does," Rostam said simply. "It always does."

She turned her head slightly, frowning at him. He met her gaze with the same steady patience he always had, the kind that had made him impossible to fool since she was young.

He sighed, shifting in his saddle, his eyes tracing the horizon. "I know what it is to love someone and lose them. To let go because you believe it is the only choice. To wonder, afterward, if you should have fought harder. If you should have walked away before it was too late."

Farah swallowed against the sudden, sharp weight in her throat. "But you didn't lose him."

"No," Rostam murmured. "Not in the end, but I thought I had."

She turned her gaze fully to him now, watching him closely. There was something different in his expression, something softer than she was used to.

"You spent years apart," she said.

Rostam exhaled, a quiet chuckle beneath his breath.

"I did." His mouth pressed into a wry line. "And for years, I told myself I had done the right thing. That Enayat had his kingdom, his duty, his responsibilities, and I had mine. That what we were, what we had, was something that had to be left behind, for the good of the kingdom, for the good of him."

He looked down at his reins, his gloved fingers flexing slightly. "And now?"

"Now," he said, softer, "I know I was a fool for ever thinking that we were stronger separate than we are together."

Rostam's voice dropped lower, like he wasn't just speaking to her but to some past version of himself. "We are older now. We have made mistakes, lost time we can never recover. But in the end, we found our way back to each other. And sometimes, I wonder if I should have fought harder for him back then, if I should have followed him when duty pulled us apart. But I know this. If I had left, if I had abandoned my station completely to move on without him, I wouldn't have been there when he needed me most. I wouldn't have been able to stand between him and the blade meant to end him."

His jaw tightened slightly, and when he looked at her again, his expression was unwavering. "Maybe the time apart was wasted. Maybe it was necessary. But what I do know is this. Love does not erase the choices we make, nor does it undo the roads we walk. We can only decide, when the moment comes, if we will meet each other again."

He let out a quiet breath, shaking his head just slightly. "And when that moment came, I was still close enough to reach him. I was still in the place where I could protect him, stand beside him, fight for him."

His gaze settled on her, knowing and steady. "If you want to find him again, if you want there to be a path back, you cannot go so far that he will never reach you."

She inhaled sharply, his words settling deep in her chest, in the place where grief and love tangled so tightly she could no longer tell where one ended and the other began.

Farah turned away, her throat tight, willing the tears blurring her vision to stay, not to drop.

"Some people find their way back," Rostam murmured, his voice even, like he was stating a truth rather than offering comfort. "Even after war. After duty. After choices that pull them apart."

He was quiet for a moment, letting the rhythm of their horses' hooves fill the space between them. Then, softer, more certain:

"But that only happens if you don't let the distance swallow you first."

She tightened her grip on the reins, her spine straight. The road ahead stretched long and empty, the hills rolling out before them, the weight of the past few days pressing down on her shoulders like an unseen yoke. She kept her eyes forward, unwilling to look at him, unwilling to see whatever patience or expectation lingered in his gaze.

Rostam didn't press. He never did. But his presence beside her carried its own weight, the weight of a man who had lived enough to know the difference between time lost and time wasted. She wasn't sure which one this was yet.

"I'll be honest with you, *dokhtar*," Rostam said after a beat, his voice quieter, more measured. "I didn't trust him when I first met him. By the Seven, I don't really know if I trust him now."

"Too much charm. Too much ease. A man who could slip in and out of places without leaving a mark... those kinds of men don't last long in this world, and the ones who do leave only wreckage behind." He exhaled, shaking his head slightly. "I thought he would be a passing thing, a distraction you'd outgrow, as I saw you do when you were younger. And for a long time, I wanted that to be true."

She inhaled sharply, her shoulders drawing tighter, but Rostam only continued, steady as ever.

"But he didn't leave. Not when things got difficult. Not when you pushed him away. Not when it would've been easier for him to slip through the cracks and pretend he was never here at all."

He turned his head slightly, finally meeting her gaze, his expression unreadable. "And now, for better or worse, I know this. Yasher might be reckless. He might be stubborn. He might be a damn fool." A pause. "But even I can't deny that if there is one thing that I can attest doesn't change like the weather for him, it's his dedication for you."

"And that counts for something," Rostam admitted, grudging but honest. "It's rare enough to find someone willing to love another without condition, to take them for all that they are, the sharp edges and the broken pieces." He glanced at her, and for all his bluntness, his expression was softer than she expected. A muscle in her jaw tightened, but she said nothing.

"You don't have to decide today, or tomorrow, or even next year," Rostam said, his voice steady, patient, "but eventually, you'll have to figure out whether you want to be found if you do want that back, if you've put yourself through whatever penance you think you deserve to be loved like that. Damned gharib is going to come back to you eventually, and you have to weather your own guilt to own up to whether you deserve to be loved like that again."

He tapped a finger lightly against his temple, then moved it down to his chest. "Both here," he said softly, "and here."

She inhaled, slow and deep, but the breath felt tight in her chest.

She wanted to argue. To tell Rostam that it wasn't the same. That Yasher had walked away first, that he had left because of her, because of what she had done, because of what she had become. That she had only given him the space he had already taken.

But she wasn't sure that was true.

Yasher loved her. She knew that with a certainty that ached, that had always been there between them, in the brush of his fingers, in the way he whispered her name like a prayer, in the intensity of his touch, as if he was trying to hold on, trying to carve her into him, to make sure she was part of him. She had felt it. And yet—she had let him go.

Rostam's words lingered, unshaken by the wind, settling deep into the hollow spaces inside her. *You'll have to figure out whether you want to be found.*

But she did. Of course she did. She had never wanted anything more.

That wasn't the question. The question was whether she she would ever deserve it again.

She only knew that she still loved him.

He let the silence settle before speaking again, his tone even, careful.

"I know the weight of a choice made in the moment. I know how it lingers, how it twists itself into your chest and refuses to let go. I don't need to hear every detail to understand that what happened back in Sakasan, you're carrying it like a wound you won't let close. Don't keep re-opening it because you think you deserve the pain."

Her throat tightened, but still, she didn't look at him.

Rostam sighed, not in frustration, not in impatience. Just the slow, steady breath of someone who had seen this kind of pain before. "When you're ready to talk, I'll be here."

She wanted to believe him. Wanted to believe that time, distance, and all the things that had broken between her and Yasher did not make them irreparable. Rostam had found his way back to Enayat after years apart. Their love had been shaped by duty, by sacrifice, by the space between them, but in the end, they had returned to each other.

She wasn't sure she and Yasher had that same kind of tether. Not any longer.

She turned her head slightly, just enough to see Rostam's steady presence beside her, the quiet understanding in his gaze. He had never asked for more than she could give, not when she was a child, not when she was grown. He didn't ask for more now. But that was what made it worse.

Because she didn't have an answer for him.

***

THE SUN BEGAN to dip below the horizon as they rode into Rumatin after so many days on the road, casting long shadows across the familiar streets.

She slowed her horse as they passed through the narrow streets, the familiar scent of spice and brine curling thick in the cooling air, slipping beneath her collar, sticking to her skin. It should have felt like home.

The streets she had walked without thought now felt like the spaces between the past she had lost and maybe, the future she had yet to claim. A future standing on her own, that she had expected until a little girl with ribbons in her hair brought her together with a charming gambler.

And across the water—the Citadel.

Farah pulled her horse to a stop.

The Veil of Takhsha was secured in a strongbox as it should have been when they left this city at first, but she could still feel the restored relic's pull like an unspoken reminder of everything that had been lost. She had thought she would feel relief knowing that the corruption had been burned away, that it was no longer Mazdavir's twisted tool. That Pari had saved it, saved all of them.

Pari had saved them. But no one had saved Pari.

Farah's fingers tightened around the reins. Actions always have consequences. Her actions, her consequences.

She clenched her jaw, steadying herself, forcing her focus back on the water before her.

The relic, now bound and secured, would soon be locked away in the Citadel's vaults, hidden among the others, a final reminder of what had been lost—and what had been saved. The Shard of Ameretat, the relic Yasher and she had fought for together, would rest beside it, along with so many others they'd found in Behnaz's gallery. It seemed like a lifetime ago. She no longer knew if they were worth what had been lost.

Behind her, the others dismounted, their presence

steady, silent. Mehran and Younis moved efficiently, securing the horses, making arrangements for the final leg of their journey. Rostam lingered, his sharp gaze pressing into her back, but he said nothing.

Taj, for all his usual energy, only watched her, his brow furrowed, as if trying to find the right words.

There were no right words.

She could feel them all behind her—waiting, watching.

The barge that would carry them across the straits would leave in the morning.

Tonight, she would sleep in a real bed, as real of a bed that would be found in the garrison.

Tomorrow, she would step back onto the streets of the Citadel.

Tomorrow, she would deliver the Veil to the vault, to be locked away with the other relics, to be protected, to be hidden away.

Tomorrow, she would have to tell Shirin that Pari would not be coming back.

As Farah stared across the straits, the wind curling around her, she reached into the folds of her coat and withdrew the small letter that had been waiting for her upon their arrival in Rumatin. The wax seal was already broken; she had read it once, briefly, before tucking it away, unwilling to let the words settle.

She let her eyes skim over the ink once more.

FARAHNAZ,

The court waits for no one, but that does not mean it does not observe. There are those eager for your return and those who would see you falter. The Citadel is not what it once was, and you will not return to the same place you left a few weeks ago.

The atmosphere within the Citadel has shifted. Unseen forces moving quietly, pulling at the fabric of the familiar. While it is not for me to say more in this letter, know that there are changes unfolding beneath the surface, some of which will be impossible to ignore when you return.

I remain here, as ever. An ally, should you choose to have one. The path ahead is uncertain, but we can walk it together if you so choose.

We have much to discuss.

Siavash

Farah exhaled slowly, rolling the letter between her fingers before tucking it away once more.

Siavash was clever. Strategic. He had never promised unwavering loyalty, never pretended to be a man without ambition. He had his own goals, his own path to carve, just as she did.

The wind carried the scent of salt and distant fires. She let herself breathe it in, tasting the night air as she turned her horse toward the barracks.

She would step into the world she had once belonged to tomorrow, but she was not the same woman who had left it.

She had broken things she could never fix, lost people she could never replace. The girl who had once believed she could be enough, who had clung to duty like it might save her, was gone. In her place was someone else.

And she did not know yet if her conviction alone was enough.

But she had work to do, to recover what was left of who she had been, and then to become someone better.

Not for redemption. Not for forgiveness.

But because she had to be.

With a final glance at the dark water stretching toward the horizon, Farah pressed her heels into the horse's sides, guiding it forward. The road was waiting.

And she was still here to walk it.

EPILOGUE

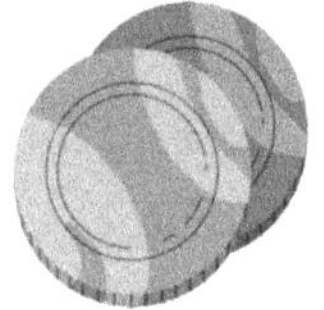

THE REBEL CAMP outside Tamidh was nothing like Yasher had anticipated. It wasn't the desperate cluster of exiles his informants had described. Instead, it was an organized, purposeful settlement, a place that had settled into the land as though it had always been here, as though it had a claim to this piece of earth. Thin smoke rose from chimneys, mixing with the rich scent of roasting grains and spiced stew from mud brick, squat buildings. Riders moved in and out, carrying messages between distant outposts. Even as evening shadows stretched across the camp, it never slowed—every movement deliberate, every action with intent.

It reminded him of another camp. Another time.

The last rebel camp he had been in had been different —smaller, rougher, held together by little more than desperation and borrowed time. And yet, he had belonged in his own way. He had chosen to stay. Not because of the rebellion, not because of their cause, but because of *her*.

He could still see her face in the firelight, the way she had looked at him—like he was something real, something solid. The way the world seemed to pause between tasks and duty, and he had found her in that fleeting moment, fragile yet burning bright. She had let him close. And for that brief instant, everything felt possible.

That camp had been temporary, but it had offered him something alive—a reason to stay, to fight. This one? This one had been built for more than survival. Built for the long haul.

Had Rostam done this? Had he shaped these people into something greater, even in the short time he had spent among them before returning to Enayat's side? Yasher wouldn't have been surprised. The man left everything sharper than he found it. A soldier first, a leader second, and a force that could turn people into something unbreakable if he believed in them enough. He'd never believed in Yasher, but he had believed in *her*.

He swallowed hard, his fingers tightening around the coin in his palm. Every flicker of it made him think of her, of the way she had once stood beside him, of the trust she had placed in him. Until that trust was broken, surrounded in vines and shadows.

Rostam's disapproval was always easy to carry. It was always there—silent, heavy, a reminder of everything Yasher was not. He had never been enough for *her*. Not in Rostam's eyes, and certainly not in his own.

And he had left, proving the commander true yet again. Walked away when she needed him most. He hadn't stayed, hadn't fought for her, hadn't even allowed himself to truly believe they could find their way back.

And now? Now the only thing left was the distance between them.

He tried desperately to erase her from his thoughts, but failed over and over again. The ache twisted deep, not just because he had failed to protect Pari, but because in his weakness, he had walked away from her too.

His head shook, forcing his thoughts back to the camp, back to the movement of the rebels, the weight of the air thick with plans and purpose. Whatever Rostam had left behind here, it had taken root. These weren't just desperate fighters anymore. They were something else. Something stronger. Something ready.

Jeta had talked their way into the camp within an hour of arrival.

She had led them through the canyons and past the rebel scouts with the ease of a woman who had walked the world long enough to belong anywhere she pleased. When the first sentries had stopped them, wary and armed, he had braced himself for a fight. But Jeta had stepped forward, casual, unbothered, wearing that new face but with the weight of her older one, and spoken in that same unshakable tone she always used when she knew exactly what she was doing.

She hadn't claimed to be anyone of importance, hadn't flaunted knowledge of the rebellion or its leaders.

"Two travelers looking for shelter," she'd said easily, hands loose at her sides, posture nonthreatening but assured. "We heard whispers of Tamidh. Thought we'd see if the wind carried anything real."

When the guards remained hesitant, she had tipped her head, eyes gleaming with something sharp.

"You need people," she had continued, voice smooth as still water. "The right kind. I'm the right kind. I know things. I can help. And as for him" she gestured at Yasher with a flick of her wrist, "he's got his own uses."

He had bristled at that, but Jeta had shot him a look that silenced him before he could argue.

The rebels hadn't let them in immediately. They had been questioned, scrutinized. But she never faltered. She answered in half-truths and small insights, gave away just enough knowledge to make them believe she had more—more than they could afford to turn away.

And just like that, they were in.

Now, weeks later, they had settled into the edges of the camp, neither fully trusted nor dismissed. Yasher wasn't sure which suited him better. He wasn't here for their cause. The rebels treated him like he was another disillusioned fighter looking for a new war, or another rogue with nowhere left to go, no one waiting on him elsewhere. Maybe they weren't wrong. He wasn't sure either.

Jeta, with her effortless ability to weave into any group, had already found her place among the strategists, trading whispers and insights with the people who planned the war from within their canvas-walled halls. She had a way of slipping into spaces as if she had always belonged there, a talent as much as a skill, worn so naturally it was hard to say where practice ended and instinct began. It was the same trick, over and over. The art of becoming indispensable.

He'd seen it before. In a girl with charcoal-stained fingers and a too-knowing gaze, a child who had never asked permission to belong because she simply did, wherever she was. Pari had carried herself the same way, stepping into lives with quiet certainty, making space for herself in ways no one ever thought to question. But she was gone now. And he was still here.

Jeta had always worn her years well—like armor, like something earned. He had known her first by the silver that streaked through her braid she constantly wore, the lines at the corners of her eyes that deepened when she smiled that sharp, knowing smile. The weight of time had always sat comfortably on her shoulders, something she carried with pride, with purpose.

That weight had disappeared in the cavern. Her hair was dark again, black as ink, her skin smooth, untouched by the years that had once defined her. She moved like a woman as old as time in one moment, and then someone not far past her majority in another.

Her eyes were the one thing that had not changed. Those still held the weight of centuries, deep and endless, the same green as the old-growth forests where he had been raised. Watching him. Knowing too much.

He spent his time pushing through whatever this block remained from Sakasan—not training. Training implied structure, rules, understanding. This was none of those things. Just long hours in the outskirts of the camp, where the wind howled through the canyons and the sun left his skin raw. Just him and Jeta, testing his Luck, stretching it, pulling at its seams like a gambler trying to rig a game that had changed around him. One he no longer knew.

It wasn't the same anymore. He wasn't sure what it was. The Luck he had once worn so easily, the thing that had always felt like an extension of himself, was shifting, unpredictable, and at times, untouchable. It would surge when he didn't call it, vanish when he did. He would flip a coin, willing it to land on its edge, and instead, the wind would change, sending dust spiraling into his eyes, and the coin falling from his hand. He would step into a fight expecting a dodge to go his way, only for his opponent's strike to slip past his guard and bruise his ribs. Even the smallest attempts to guide it felt... wrong. Too much force, too little, an echo of something else guiding his hand instead of his own will.

It pulled at him now, like a storm waiting beyond the horizon. Stirring restlessly, just out of reach. He wondered if it was even his at all anymore.

Jeta watched him, silent as ever. Not indifferent, but patient, like someone waiting for the inevitable. She never offered false promises, never claimed it would settle. She only observed, measured, and waited.

Like she was taking note of the way his Luck twisted, like she had seen it before—like she had already guessed where it was leading. Maybe she had.

He should have asked. Should have demanded answers, should have pushed her the way she pushed him. But every time he met her gaze, the words dried up in his throat, his instincts pulling back before he could get too close to whatever truth lay behind her silence.

So, he didn't ask.

Because deep down, he already knew he wouldn't like the answer.

Every time he tried to focus, tried to *force* his Talent into something he could control, he felt them. The ghost of a small hand tugging at his sleeve, asking for a story. A laugh, bright and sharp, echoing through a cavern as if the darkness had no right to exist where she stood.

Pari.

His chest ached. His Luck twisted.

Beneath it all, something deeper. Something heavier. A presence that had shaped him just as much as that little girl, if not more. He could still feel *her,* the woman he loved more than anything in this gods-infested world even now. Her body pressing against his, the curve of her spine beneath his palm, the way her breath had hitched when he pulled her close. The memory of her fingers tracing slow, reverent lines down his back, her lips against his throat, the way she had whispered his name.

He still didn't say her name. Couldn't.

But she was there, all the same. Beneath his skin, in the spaces between his ribs, in the hollow ache where something had been carved out of him and never quite healed. She was in every breath that stilled in his chest, in every flicker of his Luck when it twisted against him, unruly and restless, like it had lost its center—like it had lost her.

STANDING at the edge of the clearing where they had been sparring, Yasher exhaled sharply, rubbing his wrist where a thin scrape still burned from where his Luck had backfired earlier. Jeta watched him, arms crossed, a bemused smirk curving her lips.

She sighed, rolling her shoulders, and stretched out one arm. "You're getting better," she said, flexing her fingers, as if testing the movement in her joints. "Not good, mind you, but better."

"You still hesitate," she said. "You think too much. Or not enough. I haven't decided yet."

He rolled his eyes, shifting his weight onto one arm. "Real helpful, old woman."

She waved a hand in the air, dismissive. "It's not a matter of skill. Not entirely. Your instincts are good, your reaction time is decent. But you're still fighting your own Talent like it's something to be tamed, like it's something outside of you."

She chuckled, shaking her head. "You're not exactly easy to teach, you know."

He huffed a breath, dragging a hand through his sweat-dampened hair. The warm air of Tamidh pressed against his skin, thick with the scent of sand and distant rain. "Yeah, well, forgive me if I don't have centuries to figure it out like you."

Something flickered in Jeta's expression, brief but knowing. "Mm," she hummed. "A shame. I quite like having centuries."

He hesitated, watching her carefully.

She never spoke about it outright—not about what she was. He had seen impossible things in his life, but that had been something else. Something older.

And he wanted to know.

"How?" The question left him before he could stop it. "How does it work? You being the Voice of Ameretat. The whole... not staying dead thing."

Jeta raised a brow, tilting her head. "Curious, are we?"

Yasher rolled his eyes. "I've been curious, Jeta. You just talk in circles."

She grinned, sharp and teasing. "It's more fun that way."

He exhaled, exasperated. "Jeta."

She lifted a hand in surrender, but her eyes gleamed with amusement. "Fine, fine. The short version? I am a tool. A vessel. Ameretat's Hands in the world, for as long as she deems me useful, which has so far been... let's see... around 460 years, give or take." She stretched her arms, her hands clasped above her head. "It has... benefits. And a rather irritating lack of permanence when it comes to dying."

He frowned. "You don't want to come back?"

Her smirk faltered, just slightly. "Sometimes, *saqalu*. Sometimes not." She glanced at him, something unreadable in her gaze. "Immortality is a long damn time. But I have work left to do, otherwise I'd already be arguing with that pompous bird about the House of Song and his need to *weigh* everything."

He couldn't pretend to understand the weight of centuries. But something about her words settled uneasily in his chest.

She sighed, dusting her hands off on her coat, her voice losing the edge it normally carried.

"Of course, it's different from our little herald. Not

only was she so young, but Rashnu never did have much patience for the gray in things, or in people. To take the time to understand that people are different. No, instead it's all black and white. Right and wrong. Life and death. Order and chaos." A ghost of a smirk crossed her lips, though there was no real humor in it. "He is always such an absolute ass about it. A bird should follow the wind, not attempt to dictate where it should go."

He let out a slow breath, willing himself to keep still.

She glanced at him then, her gaze too knowing, too careful. "Pari did what she thought was right," she continued. "Maybe Rashnu gave her the strength to do it and not the stamina, but the choice? That was hers."

His breath hitched before he caught it, pressing his teeth together so hard his jaw ached. The coin in his fingers slipped, nearly tumbling to the ground before he caught it again—too fast, too sharp. His palm burned where it had landed, the metal warm like it had been left in the sun.

He wasn't ready for this conversation. Not now. Maybe not ever.

She sighed, rubbing a hand over her face, then tilted her head at him, too sharp, too assessing. "You can barely say her name."

His jaw locked, his muscles tightening, breath drawn sharp between his teeth.

Jeta lifted a brow. "And yet, she's not the only name you won't say. At least you don't flinch like I've slapped you when I say the little herald's name."

His fingers twitched. He turned his coin over across his fingers, faster now, like it could keep his thoughts from spiraling, from catching on the things he didn't want to think about. She was giving him an opening. A space to speak, to let out the weight that hammered against his ribs.

He said nothing.

She didn't sigh, didn't push. But when she turned back to him, she studied him closely.

"Fine," she said lightly, but there was something sharp beneath it. "You don't want to talk about them yet. That's your choice." She huffed, stepping past him, brushing dust from her coat. "Keep running all you want. Doesn't change where you'll end up."

Yasher didn't answer. Because he *was* running.

From Pari, gone to that fucking bridge. And from *her*, more than likely arguing with nobles in the Citadel right now, or on yet another task for the Mashya, forgetting him.

From the grief curling inside him like a wound that wouldn't close.

He sighed, rolling his wrist as if the movement might ease the weight pressing against his skin. The bracelet still sat against his skin, heavier than it should have been. The same one she had locked around his wrist when she hadn't trusted him, when she had seen him as nothing more than an inconvenience in her path. It had been a shackle. A warning.

But it had stopped been just that. She had stopped looking at him like a burden. Not when she had leaned into him on cold nights, her fingers curling in his coat as if she was the one trying to hold onto something solid. Not when she had whispered his name like it was a promise, like she was trying to carve it into the spaces between them. And not even now, when it sat against his skin like a weight he didn't know if he wanted to carry—or if he was terrified of losing.

Not that he could remove it even if he wanted to. It was sealed with her Talent, bound to him in a way no ordinary blacksmith could undo. He would need a metallurgist—a real one, not just a man with a hammer and anvil—to break it free.

He couldn't bring himself yet to seek one out.

Because some part of him already knew, if it were gone, if that last tangible thing of hers disappeared from him, it would truly be done between the two of them.

The coin spun, flashing gold as it caught the firelight, end over end, just as it always had. A simple trick. A comfort. A test. He had done this a thousand times before—called the flip, felt the way his Luck bent reality around him, watched it land exactly as he willed it to.

"Tails," he murmured, more to himself than to Jeta. A habit. A certainty.

Except this time, the coin never landed.

One second, it was there. The next, it was gone.

Not lost. Not misplaced. Just... gone.

He stilled, his fingers tightening around nothing, the absence of weight somehow heavier than the coin itself had ever been.

Jeta exhaled through her nose, tilting her head slightly as she watched him. Her eyes flickered with something unreadable, something sharp and assessing.

"Huh," she muttered, tapping a thoughtful finger against her arm. "That's... new."

Slowly, he flexed his fingers, as if the movement could bring the coin back, as if it had just slipped through the cracks of the world rather than disappearing entirely. But there was nothing. No flicker of Luck reaching back for him. No whisper of probability bending to his will. Just absence.

Jeta's gaze lingered on him, sharp and assessing, before she sighed, shaking her head. "I'd suggest you find that coin, *saqalu*. You might want to know where it went."

He exhaled sharply, rubbing his wrist, but didn't argue. He'd come to terms with his Talent, since he had accepted that his Luck was his and his alone, he wasn't so sure anymore who led who.

Above them, the sky had turned to deep indigo, the stars emerging one by one. In the distance, the rebel camp moved with quiet purpose, war brewing in the spaces between words. He'd spent his whole life moving from one gamble to the next, one step ahead of the game, never stopping long enough to feel the weight of the pieces he left behind.

But now? Now the game was changing.

He didn't know if he was the one holding the cards.

Author's Note
and Acknowledgements

Thank all of y'all that have come along for the ride on my second book in the Emari Chronicles, The Veil of Takhsha. I feel like the majority of authors out there will say that the second book can feel so much more difficult to write than the first, and this was so true for Veil.

The Veil of Takhsha wasn't some divine bolt of inspiration — more like a slow roll of thunder that wouldn't let up. I knew this story had to be told the second I finished *The Hand of Mashyana*, but getting there? Let's just say it wasn't pretty. It turns out, writing a second book while promoting your first, holding down a day job, and trying not to burn out completely is... a lot. Shocking, I know.

Veil is darker than Hand, not just because it's the second book, but because what do you do with two broken people who really do love each other but don't really know each other, when you have to pick up the pieces of a broken kingdom with no map, and when the gods walk away from their own Voices and leave them to try and navigate evil? When I began the first draft, I wasn't really sure exactly where to take the story. I knew that Farah and Yasher would have to break, because let's be honest, neither of them were really ready for one another, but they were never going to address it without something absolutely awful happening.

Enter the little girl who was left behind by a god, and another Voice for another god who lived far too long to help them navigate and mourn. Believe me, between my betas and I'm sure as this book is released, I can hear the wails of 'Dammit, Amber' all the way from Atlanta when y'all hit *that* scene. I did write a completely different scene in the first draft and well... it just didn't work. I tried, man, I tried, but it just wasn't hitting right for the story. There weren't any real consequences for making poor choices, and it was just not right for the characters, the story, and not right for the series. So throw it all at me, but it had to happen, y'all.

I can't be more thankful to my writing tribe. Brandy Gibson came back for another book as my editor, and I can't be more happy at the end result, even through my sometimes insane ramblings of 'I want to blow this up and start all over.' when I've just been stuck in my own head for too long. You are a rock star, working even through surgery recovery to help me out with getting this book released.

Along with Brandy, I really need to give huge thanks to my lovely beta reader team — Terri Boerwinkle, Tammy Bulson, Valerie Peek, Anna Perkins, and Alicia Ostrowski. Each of you made Veil even better with your feedback. Y'all are absolute joys to work with and I hope you'll be ready to come back to Emari with the next one.

Liz Bock really outdid themselves again with this cover, but I think they were really happy when I finally stopped saying, 'What about changing this?' when they were hand-drawing all of the ornaments on the cover. They'd sigh, mutter to themselves, and get back to it, even putting up with me taking up their time by working through different scenarios while I was writing.

And before I sign off on this second installment of the world of Emari, thank you, Dear Reader, for joining me to share what happens after Farah and Yasher saved things the first time. While I can't promise sunshine and rainbows, I hope that you come along for the next one.

Amber Hansford - August 2025

ABOUT THE AUTHOR

Amber Hansford grew up a Navy brat, moving up and down the East and West coasts for most of her youth, finally landing in Atlanta, Georgia and working in the tech industry for many, many years. She's been a front-end developer, designer, product manager, and UX Director, working on everything from major league sports sites to supply chain software.

Throughout it all, though, she was writing.

For most of the time, her writing was really just for her, whether it was fanfic or original work, she kept it to herself. Sometime around the early 2000s, she found fanfiction.net and decided to try and share some Highlander (the TV show, not the movie) fan fiction she'd written a few years prior at the urging of some IRC folks who were all enamored with Methos. The rest, as they say, is history.

When she's not writing, her Too-Much Gene takes over, and you can find her at Dragon Con as the track director for the Filk Music Track, working on her freelance design and development work, or trying her hand at a new hobby that's struck her fancy as a potential Apocalypse Skill™. Lately, that's been embroidery, which may not be Apocalypse-worthy, but she seems to enjoy it.

Find out more about Amber and her books at amberhansford.com

facebook.com/amberhansfordauthor

instagram.com/amberhansfordauthor

threads.com/@ahansford

tiktok.com/@amberwritesthings

bsky.app/profile/amberh.bsky.social

Thank you for buying this Polymath Publishing book.

To receive bonus content, information on new releases, and see what Amber's up to in general, sign up for her newsletter, Ink & Ash.

amberhansford.com/mailing-list

Or visit her online at

amberhansford.com